FEARLESS

FEARLESS

FEARLESS · SAM · RUN

FRANCINE PASCAL

SIMON PULSE

NEW YORK   LONDON   TORONTO   SYDNEY   NEW DELHI

alloy**entertainment**

Produced by Alloy Entertainment
151 West 26th Street, New York, NY 10001

SIMON PULSE

An imprint of Simon & Schuster Children's Publishing Division

1230 Avenue of the Americas, New York, NY 10020

This Simon Pulse paperback edition February 2012

Fearless copyright © 1999 by Francine Pascal

Sam copyright © 1999 by Francine Pascal

Run copyright © 1999 by Francine Pascal

All rights reserved, including the right of reproduction in whole or in part in any form.

SIMON PULSE and colophon are registered trademarks of Simon & Schuster, Inc.

For information about special discounts for bulk purchases, please contact Simon & Schuster Special Sales at 1-866-506-1949 or business@simonandschuster.com.

The Simon & Schuster Speakers Bureau can bring authors to your live event. For more information or to book an event contact the Simon & Schuster Speakers Bureau at 1-866-248-3049 or visit our website at www.simonspeakers.com.

Designed by Angela Goddard

The text of this book was set in Dante MT Std.

Manufactured in the United States of America

10 9 8 7 6 5 4 3 2

Library of Congress Control Number 2011935898

ISBN 978-1-4424-4631-1

ISBN 978-1-4424-4632-8 (eBook)

These books were originally published individually.

CONTENTS

FEARLESS

To my daughters,

Jamie Stewart, Laurie Wenk, Susan Johansson

GAIA

Losers with no imagination say that if you start a new school, there has to be a first day. How come they haven't figured out how to beat that? Just think existentially. All you do is take what's supposed to be the first day and bury it someplace in the next month. By the time you get around to it a month later, who cares?

When I first heard the word *existential*, I didn't know what it meant, so I never used it. But then I found out that no one knows what it means, so now I use it all the time.

Since I just moved to New York last week, tomorrow would have been my first day at the new school, but I existentialized it, and now I've got a good thirty days before I have to deal with it. So, like, it'll be just a regular day, and

I'll just grab my usual school stuff, jeans and a T-shirt, and throw them on. Then just like I always do, I'll take them off and throw on about eighteen different T-shirts and four different pairs of jeans before I find the right ones that hide my diesel arms and thunder thighs. Not good things on a girl, but no one else seems to see them like I do.

I won't bother to clean up when I'm done. I don't want to trick my new cohabitants, George and Ella, into thinking that I'm neat or considerate or anything. Why set them up for disappointment? I made that mistake with my old cohabitants and . . . well, I'm not living with them anymore, am I?

George Niven was my dad's mentor in the CIA. He's old. Like fifty or something. His wife, Ella is much younger. Maybe thirty. I don't know. And you certainly can't tell from the way she dresses. Middle of winter she finds a way to show her belly button. And she's got four hundred of these little elastic bands that can only pass for a skirt if you never move your legs. Top that with this unbelievable iridescent red hair and you've got one hot seventeen-year-old. At least that's what she thinks. We all live cozy together in Greenwich Village in a brownstone—that's what they call row houses in New York City. Don't ask me why, because it isn't brown, but we'll let that go for now.

I'm not sure how this transfer of me and my pathetic possessions was arranged. Not by my dad, He is Out of the Picture. No letters. No birthday cards. He didn't even contact me in the hospital last year when I almost fractured my skull. (And no, I didn't almost fracture my skull to test my dad, as a certain asshole suggested.) I haven't seen him since I was twelve, since . . . since—I guess it's time to back up a little. My name is Gaia. Guy. Uh. Yes, it's a weird name. No, I don't feel like explaining it right now.

I am seventeen. The good things about seventeen is that you're not sixteen. Sixteen goes with the word *sweet*, and I am so far from sweet. I've got a black belt-in kung fu and I've trained in karate, judo, jujitsu, and *muay thai*— which is basically kick boxing. I've got a reflex speed that's off the charts. I'm a near perfect shot. I can climb mountains, box, wrestle, break codes in four languages. I can throw a 175-pound man over my shoulders, which accounts for my disgusting shoulders. I can kick just about anybody's ass. I'm not bragging. I wish I were. I wish my dad hadn't made me into the . . . thing I am.

I have blond hair. Not yellow, fairy-tale blond. But blond enough to stick me in the category. You know, so guys expect you to expect them to hit on you. So teachers set your default grade at B-minus. C-plus if you happen to have big breasts, which I don't particularly. My friend from before, Ivy, had this equation between grades and cup size, but I'll spare you that.

Back in ninth grade I dyed my way right out of the

blond category, but after a while it got annoying. The dye stung and turned my hands orange. To be honest, though (and I am not a liar), there's another reason I let my hair grow back. Being blond makes people think they can pick on you, and I like when people think they can pick on me.

You see, I have this handicap. Uh, that's the wrong word. I am hormonally challenged. I am never afraid. I just don't have the gene or whatever it is that makes you scared.

It's not like I'll jump off a cliff or anything. I'm not an idiot. My rationality is not defective. In fact, it's extra good. They say nothing clouds your reason like fear. But then, I wouldn't know. I don't know what it feels like to be scared. It's like if you don't have hope, how can you imagine it? Or being born blind, how do you know what colors are?

I guess you'd say I'm fearless. Whatever fear is.

If I see some big guy beating up on a little guy. I just dive in and finish him off. And I can. Because that's the way I've been trained. I'm so strong, you wouldn't believe. But I hate it.

Since I'm never afraid of anything, my dad figured he'd better make sure I can hold my own when I rush into things. What he did really worked, too. Better than he expected. See, my dad didn't consider nature.

Nature compensates for its mistakes. If it forgot to give me a fear gene, it gave me some other fantastic abilities that definitely work in my favor. When I need it. I have this awesome speed, enormous energy, and amazing strength all quadrupled because there's no fear to hold me back.

It's even hard for me to figure out. People talk about danger and being careful. In my head I totally understand, but in my gut I just don't feel it. So if I see somebody in trouble, I just jump in and use everything I've got. And that's big stuff, and it's intense.

I mean, you ever hear that story about the mother who lifted the car off her little boy? That's like the kind of strength regular people can get from adrenaline. Except I don't need extra adrenaline because without fear, there's nothing to stop you from using every bit of power you have.

And a human body, especially a highly trained one like mine, has a lot of concentrated power.

But there's a price. I remember once reading about the Spartans. They were these fantastic Greek warriors about four hundred something B.C. They'd beat everybody. Nobody could touch them. But after a battle they'd get so drained they'd shake all over and practically slide to the ground. That's what happens to me. It's like I use up everything and my body gets really weak and I almost black out. But it only lasts a couple of minutes. Eventually I'm okay again.

And there is one other thing that works in my favor. I can do whatever I want 'cause I've got nothing to lose.

See, my mother is . . . not here anymore. I don't really

care that my dad is gone because I hate his guts. I don't have any brothers or sisters. I don't even have any grand-parents. Well, actually, I think I do have one, but she lives in some end-of-the-world place in Russia and I get the feeling she's a few beans short of a burrito. But this is a tangent.

Tangent is a heinous word for two reasons:

1. It appears in my trigonometry book.

2. Ella, the woman-with-whom-I-now-live-never-to-be-confused-with-a-mother, accuses me of "going off on them."

Where was I? Right. I was telling you my secrets. It probably all boils down to three magic words: I don't care. I have no family, pets, or friends. I don't even have a lamp or a pair of pants I give a shit about.

I Don't Care.

And nobody can make me.

Ella says I'm looking for trouble. For a dummy she hit it right this time.

I *am* looking for trouble.

A WALKING TRAP

HE LAY SPRAWLED IN A HALF-CONSCIOUS PILE,
AND SHE WAS TEMPTED TO DEMAND HIS WALLET
OR HIS WATCH OR SOMETHING.

THE POINT

Don't go into the park after sunset. The warning rolled around Gaia Moore's head as she crossed the street that bordered Washington Square Park to the east. She savored the words as she would a forkful of chocolate cheesecake.

There was a stand of trees directly in front of her and a park entrance a couple hundred feet to the left. She hooked through the trees, feeling the familiar fizz in her limbs. It wasn't fear, of course. It was energy, maybe even excitement—the things that came when fear should have. She passed slowly through a grassy stretch, staying off the lighted paths that snaked inefficiently through the park.

As the crow flies. That's how she liked to walk. So what if she had nowhere to go? So what if no one on earth knew or probably cared where she was or when she'd get home? That wasn't the point. It didn't mean she had to take the long way. She was starting a new school in the morning, and she meant to put as much distance between herself and tomorrow as she could. Walking fast didn't stop the earth's slow roll, but sometimes it felt like it could.

She'd passed the midway point, marked by the miniature Arc de Triomph, before she caught the flutter of a shadow out of the corner of her eye. She didn't turn her head. She hunched her shoulders so her tall frame looked smaller. The shadow froze. She could feel eyes on her back. Bingo.

The mayor liked to brag how far the New York City crime rate had fallen, but Washington Square at night didn't disappoint. In her short time here she'd learned it was full of junkies who couldn't resist a blond girl with a full wallet, especially under the cover of night.

Gaia didn't alter the rhythm of her steps. An attacker proceeded differently when he sensed your awareness. Any deception was her advantage.

The energy was building in her veins. Come on, she urged silently. Her mind was beautifully blank. Her concentration was perfect. Her ears were pricked to decipher the subtlest motion.

Yet she could have sensed the clumsy attacker thundering from the brush if she'd been deaf and blind. A heavy arm was thrown over her shoulders and tightened around her neck.

"Oh, please," she muttered, burying an elbow in his solar plexus.

As he staggered backward and sucked for air, she turned on him indignantly. Yes, it was a big, clumsy stupid him—a little taller than average and young, probably not even twenty years old. She felt a tiny spark of hope as she let her eyes wander through the bushes. Maybe there were more . . . ? The really incompetent dopes usually traveled in packs. But she heard nothing more than his noisy X-rated complaints.

She let him come at her again. Might as well get a shred of a workout. She even let him earn a little speed as he barreled toward her. She loved turning a man's own strength against him. That was the essence of it. She reversed his momentum with a fast knee strike and finished him off with a front kick.

He lay sprawled in a half-conscious pile, and she was tempted to demand his wallet or his watch or something. A smile flickered over her face. It would be amusing, but that wasn't the point, was it?

Just as she was turning away, she detected a faint glitter on the ground near his left arm. She came closer and leaned down. It was a razor blade, shiny but not perfectly clean. In the dark she couldn't tell if the crud on the blade was rust or blood. She glanced quickly at her hands. No, he'd done her no harm. But it lodged in her mind as a strange choice of weapon.

She walked away without bothering to look further. She knew he'd be fine. Her specialty was subduing without causing any real damage. He'd lie there for a few minutes. He'd be sore, maybe bruised tomorrow. He'd brush the cobwebs off his imagination to invent a story for his buddies about how three seven-foot, three-hundred-pound male karate black belts attacked him in the park.

But she would bet her life on the fact that he would never sneak up on another fragile-looking woman without remembering this night. And that was the point. That was what Gaia lived for.

"Who can come to the board and write out the quadratic formula?" Silence.

"A volunteer, please? I need a volunteer."

No. Gaia sent the teacher telepathic missiles. *Do not call on me.*

"Come on kids. This is basic stuff. You are supposed to be the advanced class. Am I in the wrong room?"

The teacher's voice—what was the woman's name again?—was reedy and awful sounding. Gaia really should have remembered the name, considering this *was not* the first day.

No. No. No. The teacher's eyes swept over the second-to-back row twice before they rested on Gaia. *Shit.*

"You, in the . . . brown, is it? What's your name?"

"Gaia."

"Gay what?"

Every member of the class snickered.

The beautiful thing about Gaia was that she didn't hate them for laughing. In fact, she loved them for being so predictable. It made them so manageable. There was nothing those buttheads could give that Gaia couldn't take.

"Guy. (Pause) Uh."

The teacher cocked her head as if the name were some kind of insult. "Right, then. Come on up to the board. Guy (pause) uh."

The class snickered again.

God, she hated school. Gaia dragged herself out of her chair. Why was she here, anyway? She didn't want to be a doctor or a lawyer. She didn't want to be a CIA agent or Green Beret or superoperative *X-Files* type, like her dad had obviously hoped.

What did she want to be when she grew up? (She loved that question.) A waitress. She wanted to serve food at some piece-of-crap greasy spoon and wait for a customer to bitch her out, or stiff her on the tip, or pinch her butt. She'd travel across the country from one bad restaurant to the next and scare people who thought it was okay to be mean to waitresses. And there were a lot of people like that. Nobody got more shit than a waitress did. (Well, maybe telemarketers, but they sort of deserved it.)

"Gaia? Any day now."

Snicker. Snicker. This was an easy crowd. Ms. What's-her-face must have been thrilled with her success.

Gaia hesitated at the board for a moment.

"You don't know it, do you?" The teacher's tone was possibly the most patronizing thing she had ever heard.

Gaia didn't answer. She just wrote the formula out very slowly, appreciating the horrible grinding screech of the chalk as she drew the equals sign. It sounded a lot like the teacher's voice, actually.

$$x = \frac{-b \pm \sqrt{b^2 - 4ac}}{2a}$$

At the last second she changed the final plus to a minus sign. Of course she knew the formula. What was she, stupid? Her dad had raced her through basic algebra by third grade. She'd (begrudgingly) mastered multivariable calculus and linear algebra before she started high school. She might hate math, but she was good at it.

"I'm sorry, Gaia. That's incorrect. You may sit down."

Gaia tried to look disappointed as she shuffled to her chair.

"Talk to me after class about placement, please." The teacher said that in a slightly lower voice, as if the rest of the students wouldn't hear she found Gaia unfit for the class. "Yes, ma'am," Gaia said brightly. It was the first ray of light all day. She'd demote herself to memorizing times tables if meant getting a different teacher.

Times tables actually came in pretty handy for a waitress. What with figuring out tips and all.

NOT CLOYING

He saw her right after the seventh-period bell rang. She seemed dressed for the sole purpose of blending in with the lockers, but she stood out, anyway. It didn't matter that her wide blue eyes were narrowed or that her pretty mouth was twisted into a near snarl—she was blatantly beautiful. It was kind of sick the way Ed was preoccupied with beautiful girls these days.

There weren't many people left in the hall at this point. He, of course, had permission to take his own sweet time getting to class. And she was probably lost. She cast him a quick glance as she strode down the hall. The kind of glance where she saw him without actually seeing him. He was used to that.

He felt a little sorry for her. (He was also preoccupied with finding ways of feeling sorry for people.) She was new and trying hard not to look it. She was confused and trying to look tough. It was endearing is what it was.

"Hey, can I help you find a classroom or anything?"

She swiveled around and glared at him like he made a lewd remark. (Was she some kind of mind reader?)

"Excuse me?" she demanded. She wasn't afraid to give him a good once-over.

"You look lost," he explained.

Now she was angry. "This is not what lost looks like.

This is what annoyed looks like. And no, I don't need any help. Thanks."

It was the spikiest, least gracious "thanks" he'd ever heard. "Anytime," he said, trying not to smile. "So what's your name?"

"Does it matter?" She couldn't believe he was prolonging the conversation.

"Mine's Ed, by the way."

"I'm so happy for you." She gave him an extra snarl before she bolted down the hall to the science wing.

He smiled all the way to physics class. He almost laughed out loud when he passed through the door and saw her shadowy, hunched-over form casting around for a seat in the back.

She was in his class; this was excellent. Maybe she'd call him a name if he struck up another conversation. Even curse him out. That might fun. God, he'd probably earn himself a restraining order if he tried to sit next to her.

He was so tired of saccharine smiles and cloying tones of voice. People always plastered their eyes to his face for fear of looking anywhere else. He was fed up with everybody being so goddamned nice.

That's why he'd already fallen in love with this weird, maladjusted, beautiful girl who carried a chip the size of Ohio on her shoulder. Because nobody was ever mean to the guy in the wheelchair.

September 23

My Dearest Gaia,

 I saw a mouse race across the floor of my apartment today and it made me think of you. (What doesn't make me think of you?) It reminded me of the winter of Jonathan and your secret efforts to save his little life. I never imagined I'd think longingly upon an oversized gray field mouse whose contribution to our lives was a thousand turds on the kitchen counter, but I grew to love him almost as much as you did.

 Oh, Gaia. It feels as if it's been so long. Do you still love rodents and other despised creatures? Do you still carry a pocket full of pennies for luck? Do you still eat your cereal without milk? Do you ever think about me anymore?

 I write it and think it so often, it's a mantra, but Gaia, how desperately I hope you'll forgive me someday. You'll understand why I did what I did, and you'll know it was because I love you. I have so many doubts and fears, my darling, and they seem to grow as the days between us pass. But I know I love you. I'd give my life for you. Again.

Tom Moore lifted his pen at the sound of the text. God, he hated that sound. He didn't need to look at his phone to know who was summoning him. It wasn't as if he had friends and family swarming about—it was his self-inflicted punishment that if he couldn't be with his daughter, he would be alone.

He snatched the wretched little device from his desk and threw it across the room, mildly amazed at his own rare show of temper as the text bounced off the windowsill and skittered across the wood floor. It was always the same people. It was always an emergency. By tomorrow he'd be in a different time zone.

Before he picked up the phone, he walked to the ancient aluminum filing cabinet and opened it. He thumbed through the files without needing to look. Locating the thick pile of papers, he placed the letter at the front, just as he always did with all the others, unsent and locked in the drawer.

A STUPID HOBBY

MACDOUGAL AND LAGUARDIA—*BZZZZT*—
SLASHING VICTIM, FEMALE, AFRICAN AMERICAN
IN HER THIRTIES—*BZZZZT*—
YOUNG MALE PERPETRATOR—*BZZZ* . . .

HER FAVORITE PLACE

"Hello, Ceeendy."

"Hi, Zolov. What's shaking?"

"Shakeeeng?"

Gaia laughed. "How are you playing?"

Zolov worked his mouth. He drew his wrinkly brown hand over his lips, thinking about the question seriously, "I beat everyone."

"Of course you did," Gaia said loudly. "You're the best."

He nodded absently. "Tank you. You are a good geerl."

In spite of the fact she was practically shouting at him, Gaia could tell he was reading her lips and that it was tiring for him. He sat back in the sunshine, ready for his next opponent, who would very likely not show. His favorite chessboard was set. As always, it was presided over by one of the Mighty Morphin Power Rangers, a red, helmeted action figure he'd probably picked up in somebody's garbage. He never played without him.

Gaia would have sat down across from him if she'd had more than twenty cents in her pocket. Instead she lay back on the bench and closed her eyes.

This park, these chess tables, was Gaia's favorite place. It was her home in New York more than George and Ella's house ever would be. Zolov was at least ninety years old and thought her name was Cindy, but even so, he was her favorite person.

Who says I have no life? she mused as she stretched her arms behind her head, feeling the fabric of her gray T-shirt creeping over her belly button. She inhaled the scent of sugary nuts roasting in a pushcart nearby. This was her favorite place, and that was her favorite smell. It was so sweet and strong, she could practically taste it. One of these days she was going to buy a big bag of those nuts and scarf them down without even pausing to breathe.

She felt a shadow come over her face and squinted one eye open. "Hey, Renny," she said. "You ready for 'dimes of demonstration'?"

Renny was a thirteen-year-old Puerto-Rican boy— Gaia's second-favorite person. He was a self-proclaimed poet and such a whiz at chess he hustled great sums of money out of almost anybody who was dumb enough to sit down across from him. Today his face didn't light up with its usual bravado.

Gaia sat up and put a hand over her eyes to block the sun. "You're scared I'm going to steal your money and make you cry?" she taunted. She scanned the tables for a free board.

As she did, her eye snagged on a new piece of graffiti splayed on the asphalt just to the left of Zolov's usual table. A swastika. It was at least a foot across, and the white paint was as fresh and bright as a new pair of sneakers. Gaia's stomach

was filled with lead. Could it be for her benefit? she wondered. Could somebody possibly know how the Holocaust
had decimated her mother's family and made her grand-
parents into heroes? No. Not likely, She was being paranoid.
How would anyone know about her Jewish background? In
fact, when she told some people, they acted all surprised—
like if you had fair hair and blue eyes, it wasn't possible. That
really annoyed her.

Her eyes flicked over the ugly shape again. Had Renny
seen it? Had Zolov? But did they think anything of it?

For some reason Renny wasn't jumping in with his usual
rhyming insults and eager put-downs.

"Gaia, you oughtta go home," Renny said almost
inaudibly in the direction of his sneakers.

This was odd. "What's up, Renny?"

"It's gonna get dark," he noted.

"Thanks, Ren. It usually does."

He was wearing a stiff new jacket that advertised its
brand name from three different spots. He licked his lips.
"You oughtta, you know, be watching out," he continued.

"For what?" she asked.

He considered this question a moment. "The park is real
dangerous after dark."

Gaia stood, impatient. She swept a strand of hair behind
her ear. "Renny, cut the bullshit. What's the matter? What
are you talking about?"

"Did you hear about Lacy's sister?" His face was slightly pink, and he wasn't meeting her gaze.

"No, why?"

"It was on the news and everything. All the kids are talking about it. She got slashed in the park last night," Renny explained. "She had to get sewn up from her eyebrow to her ear."

"God, that's awful," Gaia said. "What kind of blade?"

"What?"

"What kind of blade?"

Renny gave her a strange look.

"Was it a razor blade?" Gaia persisted.

"I guess. I don't know." He looked up at her a little defiantly. "How am I supposed to know?"

"Just asking, Renny." She softened her tone. "Thanks for warning me. I do appreciate it."

He nodded, his face growing pinker. "I was just . . . you know, concerned about you." He tried to look very tall as he shuffled away.

Gaia swung her beat-up messenger bag over her shoulder as she watched him. She had a bad feeling about this. She sensed that Renny was no longer satisfied with the insular world of chess misfits. He was starting to care what the big boys thought—those stupid boys who hung around the fountain, trying to look tough. Renny was smarter and funnier and more original than they'd ever be, but he was thirteen.

He was at that brutal age when many kids would sell all the uniqueness in their character for the right pair of shoes. She longed to tell him not to spend so much time in the park, to go home to his mother, but who was she to talk?

Yes, Renny might be concerned about her. But not as concerned as she was about him.

She herself loved this misfit world, Gaia mused as she surveyed the tables. Curtis, a fifteen-year-old black kid, was sitting across from Mr. Haq, a Pakistani taxi-cab driver who appeared to like nothing more than parking his yellow cab on Washington Square South and killing an afternoon over a chessboard.

She loved that people who couldn't begin to pronounce each other's names played and talked for hours. She loved that a forty-something-year-old cab-driver and a fifteen-year-old from the Manhattan Valley youth program had so much in common. She loved getting a break from the stupid hierarchy of high school.

She loved that there weren't people like . . . well, people like . . . him.

The him was walking by slowly, looking confidently over the boards in play. His hair was light in color—a tousled mixture of blond and brown and even a little red. His chinos were cuffed, and his preppy gray jacket flapped in the autumn breeze. Gaia felt her stomach do a quick pitch and roll. She felt queasy and strangely alert at the same time.

You didn't find people who looked like that . . . as in, stunningly, astonishingly good. People like him sipped coffee at Dean & Deluca or swing danced on Gap commercials or spouted Woody Allen-style dialogue on *Dawson's Creek*, where they belonged.

So what *the hell* was he doing lingering over chessboards with the freaks and geeks? She had half a mind to walk right over and tell him to get lost.

This was her favorite place, and he had no business here, reminding her of things she would never be.

DON'T BE AFRAID

"Thank you, Marco, you're a sweetheart."

Marco nodded at the woman, making sure to tilt his chin so she had a good look at his left side, the side where his broken nose hardly showed at all. "No problem." He kept his voice deep and smooth. She probably thought he was like twenty-five or something.

She took a long sip from the bottle of Coke he'd brought

her, exposing her pale neck. She lifted one leg to rest on the low wall of the fountain, revealing several more inches of thigh under her stretchy aqua miniskirt. He tried not to stare. Or did she want him to stare?

He stopped breathing completely as she slowly, slowly brushed her fingers over his upper arm. "What happened here?" she asked.

He glanced at the purplish bruise. He paused before answering and cleared his throat, trying to make certain his voice didn't come out squeaky. "Nothing much. I got jumped last night. These three big guys thought they were real tough. Probably black belts in karate or something."

Her eyes widened in just the way he'd hoped. "You're okay? Did you call the police?"

"Uh-uh. That's not how we—how I—do things." Marco ran a hand through his dark hair. It had come out perfectly today. "I've got some friends who will back me up if those guys ever come back here." Marco loved the way she watched him when he talked. So he kept talking. He wasn't even listening to what he was saying.

Man, she was gorgeous. She was older than he, twentysomething at least, but sexy as hell. Like some kind of goddess with her straight red hair and green eyes. And the legs on her. He couldn't look away.

He'd first noticed her at the beginning of the summer. All the guys noticed her—it was hard not to. She lived around here, he guessed, because she walked by this fountain almost every afternoon. He wasn't the only one who magically turned up each day around four o'clock to watch the show.

Lately he'd noticed she'd started returning his looks. Just a glance at first, but then her eyes stayed longer. Last week she'd said hello to him, and he'd practically peed in his pants. Today she'd been late, so most of the guys had wandered away, but some kind of crazy instinct made him stay.

He took his eyes off her breasts for a moment to see if he spotted anybody he knew. He would love for any one of his buddies to see him right now.

Just then she reached toward his collarbone and rested her index finger on the pendant that lay there. The electricity from her touch surged through his chest and seemed to throw his heart off rhythm. "What is this?" Her voice was almost a whisper. "I've seen this before."

He studied her face before he answered. He wasn't sure how much to tell—how much she really wanted to know. "It's, uh, it's called a hieroglyph—you know, like ancient Egyptian writing? It's the symbol for . . . uh, power."

"Where have I seen it before?" Her green eyes fixed on his.

His glance darted around the fountain. "I don't know. Maybe you saw one of the other guys wearing it. Maybe a tattoo on somebody's arm. It's kind of a . . . I don't know . . . kind of a . . ."

His voice trailed off awkwardly. He didn't want her thinking he was some kind of thug. He sure didn't want anybody to overhear him telling her secret stuff.

"A mark?" she supplied "Some sort of identification?" She didn't appear wary the way most girls he knew would. Her eyes were wide and intense, fascinated.

"Yeah. Like that."

"Ah. I see. Are you part of—"

Marco sucked in his breath. Suddenly this didn't seem so cool. What if she was an undercover cop or some kind of informer? He'd heard of stuff like this. He backed up, putting a few feet between them. "I gotta be going. It's, like, after six, and I—"

With two steps she closed the distance. "Marco. Don't be afraid of me." Her fingers fluttered over his cheek. "Don't tell me anything you don't want to. I'm just . . . interested, that's all! I'm interested in everything about you."

All the blood in his body seemed to pool in his head. He felt dizzy, "You're not, like, a cop or anything?" He was pretty sure she'd have to say so if she were.

She laughed. "No. Most definitely not." She gave him a look. It was a mischievous, sexy kind of look. "*Definitely* not."

Gaia smacked the shortwave radio that sat on the table next to the bed. Her bed. She had trouble thinking of anything in this house as hers.

"Piece of crap," she murmured. She'd picked up the radio at a junk shop on Canal Street. She'd gotten it to tune in to the local police frequency, but the damn thing emitted almost nothing but static. She rearranged the antenna she'd rigged until she heard a break in the fuzz. She rolled off the bed and walked to the window. Ah, that was good. She could decipher various bleeps that sounded almost like words. She stood by the door. Oh, it liked that. Now she could actually understand the words.

Bzzzzt—MacDougal and LaGuardia—*bzzzzt*—slashing victim, female African American in her thirties—*bzzzzt*—young male perpetrator—*bzzzz* . . .

Dammit. She tried jumping up and down.

—lost him in the park—*bzzzzzzzzz* . . .

Shit. Gaia grabbed the radio and threw it off the table. What a stupid hobby. Why couldn't she just watch *Roswell* like a normal girl?

Well, for one thing, because the television was in the so-called family room. It would mean walking past, possibly even fraternizing with, George and his bimbo bride. It wasn't that she didn't like George. She did. He was trying really hard to make her feel comfortable. He tried so hard, in fact, that she found it awkward to be around him. He put on this peppy voice and asked her about her classes or her friends. What was she going to say, "I see my math teacher through crosshairs"? "My best friend has Alzheimer's"? George wanted something within the universe of normal, and she simply couldn't give him that.

Ella was another story. Stupid, vain Ella she genuinely disliked. There were Ella's fingernails, her passion for Victoria's Secret catalogs, her love of Mariah Carey. That was about it for Ella. How in the world had a sensible man like George fallen prey to a tarty thing like her? And God, he had fallen.

Gaia really needed some air. She strode to the door of the room and listened for signs of life. What sucked was that her room was on the fourth floor of a four story house because she hated walking past every other room on her way in and out. She was like a latter-day Rapunzel except her hair was only a few inches below her shoulders, slightly fried, not all that blond, and furthermore, who the hell was ever going to climb up to give her a hand? The guy in the wheelchair from school?

What she—and Rapunzel, frankly—needed was a decent ladder.

Gaia opened the door slowly. Hopefully George was still

at work and Ella was—who ever knew where Ella was? By profession Ella considered herself a photographer, but Gaia had a hard time taking her seriously. It gave Ella an excuse to saunter through hip downtown neighborhoods with a camera slung over her shoulder. Apparently she got the odd commission to photograph somebody's dog or living room or something. Her "work" as George called it in his pious way was displayed over most of the wall space in the house—mostly artsy black-and-white pictures of dolls' heads and high-heeled shoes.

Thank God for the automatic camera that makes it all possible, Gaia thought sarcastically as she crept through the hallway and down the stairs.

At the second landing she was faced once again by "the photograph." Most days she averted her eyes. Although Ella hadn't taken it, it was by far the most upsetting in the house. It was a picture of a seven-year-old Gaia with her parents, snapped by George the week he visited them at their country house in the Berkshires. Once Gaia looked at the photo, she found it hard to look away and, after that, hard to get her mind to cooperate with her.

The Gaia in the picture made her think of a little monkey, clinging to her dad with long skinny arms, her wrists circled by several filthy friendship bracelets, her narrow shoulders lost in the beloved brown fisherman's sweater he'd bought for her on a trip to Ireland. Gaia's smile was big and exuberant, so pitifully unaware of what the next year would bring.

Now Gaia moved her gaze to her mother, even as she willed herself not to. If Gaia's face in the picture was all embarrassing openness, her mother's was pure mystery. No matter how many times Gaia searched it, no matter how clearly she saw those features, she felt she couldn't tell what her mother really looked like. She *needed* something from that face that it never gave. The same miserable questions started their spiraling march through Gaia's brain: *Why am I holding Daddy and not you? Why aren't I beautiful like you? Did you love me anyway? Did you ever know how much I loved you?*

And then, as always, the thoughts go so uncomfortably sad, they didn't even come in words. Her throat started to ache, and her vision swam. She couldn't pull enough air into her lungs. Without exactly realizing what she was doing, her hands shot out and yanked the framed photograph off the wall.

"What are you doing?"

Gaia spun around. Her heart was bouncing in her chest, and it took her a moment to focus her eyes on Ella. She cleared her throat. She took a deep breath. She tried to rearrange her posture into something less rigid.

"I am removing this picture from the wall."

"Can I ask why?"

"Sure."

Ella waited impatiently, "Okay, why?"

Gaia placed the picture facedown on the bookcase. She glanced at her watch. "I didn't say I'd answer."

Ella got that eye-rolling martyred look. "Gaia, you know George loves that picture. He put it up for you."

Gaia cleared her throat again. She tried shrugging, but it didn't come off with the indifference she was aiming for. "If George put it up for my benefit, he won't mind if I take it down."

Ella's hands found their way to her hips as they mostly did within a few minutes of starting a conversation with Gaia. "I swear, Gaia, George does so much for you. I would think you could at least—"

Gaia tuned out the shrill voice as she made her way down the rest of the steps and out the front door. She knew every word of the speech. There wouldn't be any vocabulary words or clever turns of phrase. Ella wasn't going to surprise her.

Gaia took the sidewalk at a near run. She felt like she might explode. The sky was darkening as she turned left on West 4th Street, leaving bustling outdoor cafes, overpriced little restaurants, all-night delis, her favorite subterranean record shop behind her in a blur.

She headed straight for the park. No one was going to scare her out of her shortcut. And certainly not tonight, not in the mood she was in. And in fact, she hoped they'd try. Let them find her instead of some kid or some old guy who wouldn't know how to handle it. Maybe if she did this enough, those creeps would learn that everyone who looked vulnerable wasn't necessarily so. What a gorgeous lesson to teach them. After all, wasn't that what her gifts were all about? Power to the little people!

MR. VALIANT

SHE SPUN AROUND, INSTANTLY ACCOSTED BY
STRANGE BLURRED IMAGES. A FLASH OF CHROME.
TWO LARGE WHEELS.

Three more steps. Okay, five more steps. Okay, ten more. Just to the maple tree. Okay, not that one, the one behind it.

She was a little nuts. She knew it. Skulking around Washington Square Park for three hours and twenty-three minutes, counting steps (and okay, seconds), looking for trouble. It could be called entrapment. That's exactly what she wanted to do, entrap those lowlifes.

Gaia lingered under the tree, feeling drops of sweat sliding down her spine. Wasn't New York City supposed to be getting cool in September? The smell of late season pollen was so thick, it felt like paste in her nostrils. Please, somebody. Anybody. She'd come here with the secret hope that one of the notorious slashers would have a go at her, but now she'd grown desperate. She would take absolutely any criminal, from petty shoplifter to ax murderer; she really wasn't choosy. Hey, who even needed a criminal? She was ready to pounce on the strength of a big mouth or a bad attitude.

But she wouldn't. Gaia would never attack anybody unprovoked. She would never do more harm than necessary. That was the code, and as much as she hated her father, she was still bound to honor it. It was bred into her, just like her blue eyes that seemed to change shade with her mood, the weather, the color of her shirt. Just like her love of sweets.

She had to use her Miraculous Gift (that's what her father always called it) as a force for good. Her mission was to draw out violent behavior and squash it, not to produce more violence.

But sometimes carrying out her mission felt more self-indulgent than honorable. Did it count as a good deed if you enjoyed yourself? She liked to think she thrived on self-defense. But there were times, really upsetting times, when she saw the line between defense and offense as clear as day and barreled toward it. Hey, she had an extraordinary talent, and she wanted to use it.

What if one day she crossed that line that separated good guys from bad guys? It would be easy. There was only a hair's width between them. Why hadn't anyone warned her that inside the crucible of real anger, good and bad were so nearly the same?

Worse yet, what if one day she'd stop being able to see the line at all? She wouldn't know anymore if she was good or bad or crazy or sane. Maybe Gaia didn't know the meaning of scary, but that sounded an awful lot like it.

Gaia made a slow loop around the maple tree. She had to get out of this park, but she really didn't feel like going back to George and Ella's. God forbid George would put on that earnest face and try to talk about "her loss" as he often did after Ella complained about her.

She didn't feel like walking on Broadway—the street

was mobbed with NYU students, tourists, and shoppers at every hour of the day. Instead she turned south on Mercer Street. She loved the deserted, canyonlike feel of the narrow street and the sound her steps made on the cobblestones. She'd walk straight down to Houston Street and see what was playing at the Angelika.

Suddenly, as if in answer to a prayer, Gaia heard voices behind her. She stopped and fumbled through her backpack as if she were looking for something. Jeez, what a girl had to do to get mugged in this city.

The voices turned into whispers, and then she heard footsteps, slow. Oh, *yes*. Finally. She turned toward the noise, pasting what she hoped looked like a terrified expression on her face. Inside, her heart was leaping with anticipation.

There were three of them, and they looked young— around sixteen or seventeen. Two of them had shaved heads. The smallest brandished a razor blade. Gaia detected more than a hint of nervousness under his swagger. She backed up (fearfully, she hoped), wanting the situation to escalate. She hated herself, but there it was.

The little thug was up front, covering the ground between them with a menacing lurch. The other two were hanging back, present to witness this feat of loyalty. It was becoming obvious to Gaia what was up here, and it pissed her off.

Come on, boys, she silently encouraged them. *Come and get me.* Her mind hovered on the swastika she'd seen painted on the ground in the park. That coupled with the shaved heads and the leather jackets gave her the strong suspicion that these assholes were some kind of neo-Nazi white supremacist outfit.

Her concentration was so keen, she had to remind herself to keep breathing. She couldn't let her anger get the best of her. She had to play this just right. If she struck back too quickly, she might scare them away. The kid was trying hard to look tough, but his toughness went about as deep as the sheen of sweat on his upper lip.

Now. He was right on her, razor blade lifted. She screamed helplessly as she drew back her arm for a sharp blow to his wrist. And just as she balanced her weight to deliver the strike she heard a thunderous shout and a commotion behind her.

Suddenly noise was coming from every direction. Her adrenaline was rising fast, but her focus was thrown. She spun around, instantly accosted by strange blurred images. A flash of chrome. Two large wheels. She jumped back to try to make sense of it.

"Get away from her!" a familiar voice shouted.

Gaia's razor-blade-wielding attacker fell back in confusion.

Equally confused, Gaia swiveled her head.

"It's okay, Gaia! Go! Run!"

She watched in perfect amazement as Ed, the guy in the wheelchair from school, rolled into the fray. Her very own knight in shining armor come to save the day.

"You've got to be joking," she muttered under her breath. But no, there he was. Mr. Valiant.

Now what was she supposed to do? She couldn't just burst into action with Ed sitting on the sidelines. He'd see everything. He'd know far more than he was allowed.

It was one thing showing an attacker her tricks. Every time she did this, she made a wager that her attacker wouldn't confess to being pounded by a girl, and she'd never been wrong. But Ed was a different story. Ed would tell the nifty adventure to everybody in school. They'd probably recruit her for the judo club or something.

The adrenaline was surging through her veins, and the primary person she wanted to strangle was Ed.

The three attackers had been as surprised as she by Ed's arrival, but they were now regrouping.

Okay, fine. She'd take a couple of hits. She wouldn't let the razor blade near her, but that would be easy enough to dispose of in a stealthy way. They'd hit her. She'd scream. Somebody would hear the noise and call the cops. The three losers would feel manly and dangerous and go away. The little one would earn his initiation on somebody else.

It was disappointing as hell, but she'd deal.

Ed Fargo pushed his wheels as fast as he could. He sailed over the curb and bumped along the cobblestones. He'd often dreamed of running over somebody with his wheelchair, but he'd never actually done it before. His lungs ached for air and his arms ached with exertion as he plowed through the low bushes and into the guy with the razor blade. Thank God he'd been coming along Mercer just then. Thank God he'd heard the scream.

He heard the powerful meeting of metal and shin bone. "Ahhhhhhh!" The attacker fell backward.

"Gaia, get out of here!" Ed shouted again. He'd never felt quite so important in his life.

She looked stunned. Why the hell wouldn't she get her ass out of there? Was she paralyzed with fear? So traumatized, she couldn't move a muscle? Thank God he'd arrived when he had. "Please go!" he commanded.

The guy with the razor blade fumbled back up to his feet, and his two accomplices came closer in for backup. Ed realized he didn't have much time. Panic was taking hold of his chest. He looked at Gaia's frozen form. He looked at the three hoods gathering for attack. Oh, man. This time their vicious eyes weren't focused on Gaia; they were aiming directly at him. Oh, oh, oh.

His brain was spinning. His heart was pounding at least five hundred times a minute. The obvious thing to do was get out of there as fast as his arms would carry him, but he couldn't. He couldn't just leave Gaia standing there. She'd be slaughtered.

"What is wrong with you?" Ed bellowed at her. "Get the hell out of here *now!*"

Three big angry thugs were closing in and that stupid girl wouldn't move. Panic was now weirdly tinged with resignation. He was dead. If they wanted to kill him, that is. Maybe they'd be satisfied just mangling him or slashing him to ribbons.

The biggest of the three took hold of the armrest of his wheelchair and gave it a powerful shove. Ed collided hard with the street and rolled from the toppled chair.

This was sad. It sure would have been handy if my legs worked right now. He looked up at the stripe of night sky between the old cast-iron buildings, waiting for the first blow. He put his arms over his face for protection.

Slam! He heard the sound of a foot connecting with hard flesh and then a deep moan. Was that him? Had he made that noise? He heard another searing blow. Jesus, was he so far gone, be couldn't even feel the pain?

He moved an arm away from his face and cracked open one eye. He heard a groan and then a barking shout. Strange. He was pretty sure his mouth was shut. He opened the other eye and sat up. Then he shut both eyes again. Had he gone into cardiac arrest and died already? God, that was quick. Weren't there supposed to be a lot of warm feelings and long tunnels and a bright light?

He simply could not have seen what he thought he saw. He was dead. Or hallucinating. Maybe that was it. His mind was dealing him some truly mind-bending hallucinations. Awesome ones, as it happened. He opened his eyes again. His mouth dropped open.

Gaia Moore, the lovely girl with the slim frame and sullen expression who haunted the back of his physics class, had suddenly transformed into Xena, Warrior Princess, only blond and even more beautiful. She crushed the jaw of Thug 1 with a roundhouse kick. She struck Thug 2 in the chest with such violence, he was left gasping for breath. Thug 3 came swinging at her from behind, and she spun around and neutralized him with a stunning kick-boxing move he'd only ever seen executed by Jean Claude Van Damme.

Holy shit. Could this actually be real? Gaia's dauntless, intense, angry face looked real. The thonk of her sneakered foot in Thug 1's belly sounded real.

Unbelievable. Gaia was a superhero. Hair flying, limbs whirling, she was the most graceful, powerful martial artist he had ever laid eyes on. Her every move was a mesmerizing combination of ballet and kung fu. And not only was she magical, she was lethal. Thug 1 was writhing on the ground,

Thug 2 was ready to flee. Although Thug 3 appeared to be rallying, Ed almost pitied him.

Suddenly Ed sucked in the moist night air. A chill began in his fingertips and crept up his wrists and arms. He saw only a flash at first, and then the image resolved itself. Thug 3 had a knife. Ed saw it clearly now glinting in the street-light, looking awfully real.

Oh, my God.

Did Gaia see the knife? Did she realize what was coming? He certainly couldn't tell by her expression. Her eyes revealed not even the tiniest hint of fear. Jesus, she was tough. That or paranormally stupid.

"Gaia!" he heard his own voice bellowing, "He's got a knife!"

Her gaze didn't flicker. She stood there motionless as Thug 3 went after her. She looked as if she were in some kind of deep meditation.

Ed was hyperventilating. He didn't care how tough Gaia was; she couldn't defend herself against an eight-inch blade. Presumably her skin was made of the same stuff his was. He had to do something.

He supplied his seizing brain with some oxygen, then dragged himself toward his wheelchair. He pulled it upright and set his sights on the slouching back of Thug 3. Ed's legs might be useless, but his arm strength was formidable. He launched the chair like a missile.

Strike! The chair hit its mark, and Thug 3 staggered forward. Ed briefly registered the look of surprise on Gaia's face as Thug 3 careened into her and sent her sprawling backward. His stomach clenched. Oh, God. That hadn't been his intention at all.

Now the guy retrieved his knife and leaped on top of Gaia. Worse yet, from Thug 2's cowardly hideout behind a parked car, he saw the tide turn and was racing back to join the fight. Ed dragged himself toward Gaia as fast as he could, his eyes fixed on her throat and the knife hovering over it. "Stop!" he roared. "You're going to kill her!" He felt tears stinging his eyes.

It happened so fast, Ed wasn't sure he'd actually seen it. Gaia delivered a powerful kick exactly to the groin of Thug 2 and almost simultaneously struck Thug 3 in the side of the neck with her hand. Thug 3 rolled over, unconscious. His knife skidded along the stones. Thug 2 pitched to the ground, screaming in pain.

Gaia was instantly on her feet. She scooped up the knife and stepped over the prone body of Thug 3. Suddenly Thug 1 and Thug 2 seemed to forget their pain and sprinted for safety like jackrabbits in traffic.

Ed was watching Gaia, his heart overflowing with relief and admiration, when she surprised him again.

She got to the sidewalk and collapsed. Her legs literally crumpled under her body, and without a noise she fell in a heap on the pavement.

Gaia breathed deeply and waited for it to pass. She wouldn't struggle to move or attempt to get to her feet. She knew by now it wouldn't work. The only thing to do was wait.

Pretty much right on schedule, she heard a noisy approach and felt a hand on her shoulder. Argh. She didn't need to open her eyes to see the worried, eager face.

Once he'd reached her, she heard him collapse beside her. Listening to his labored breathing, Gaia's heart was pulled forcefully by two equal and opposite desires:

1. Her desire to hug Ed for his valiant, misguided efforts on her behalf.
2. Her desire to murder him for being such an unbelievable pain in the ass.

"Are you okay?" He touched her shoulder again. She could hear the fear in his words.

She would have really liked to rouse herself right then. It was unthinkable that he should see her in this state of weakness—to see what happened to her after one of these episodes. And yet there was just no way around it short of killing him, which, though tempting, didn't seem all that sporting under the circumstances.

"Gaia? Gaia?" His voice was rising with panic.

"Mmmm," she mumbled.

"Oh, God, are you hurt? Did they hurt you?"

A yellow cab cruised past them, slowed for a stop sign then drove on. If anyone in the car saw them, they apparently hadn't felt the need to get involved. That was New York City for you. Its inhabitants set a high standard for unusual.

With great effort she fluttered open her eyes and very slowly, by inches, shook her head. The sidewalk made a really bad pillow.

"What's the matter? Should I call for an ambulance?"

She gritted her teeth. If she'd had any energy left, she would have rolled her eyes. "Mm. Mmm." After another pause she reinforced it with another slight shake of her head.

"No? Are you sure?"

She wasn't accustomed to anyone seeing her like this and it was irritating. She found the strength to open her eyes for real and concentrate on Ed's face. It had suddenly become a much more significant face—the face of the guy who knew her secrets.

Holy shit. How had she let this happen?

It was so ironic. So ironic and pitiful and stupid and weird, she wanted to laugh. For some reason this guy had become her self-appointed guardian angel and nearly gotten her killed in the process. How typical that her guardian angel would be a slightly scruffy ex-skate rat in a wheelchair who caused so much more trouble than good. How strange it was that he suddenly knew more about her than anyone else on planet Earth. (Except her father, of course.)

Gaia had been so careful over the years to keep everything secret. It was another of her father's curses: *I'll make you into a freak and not let you tell anyone.* Not like she was going to tell, anyway. She had no confidant and meant to keep it that way. Besides, the strange facts of her life were all connected. Telling a little would ultimately mean telling a lot.

"Gaia? Please tell me you're okay?"

It always seemed that when her body sank into this state of paralytic exhaustion, her mind zoomed into overdrive. She summoned the energy to move her lips. "I'm fine," she whispered.

"You don't look so fine."

Patience, Ed, she asked of him silently. She felt the energy returning to her muscles. It was tingly at first, as if her whole body had fallen asleep. She groaned a little as she sat up. She studied Ed. Worried, terrified, astonished, concerned Ed. She couldn't help but smile a little.

"I'm fine," she said. She paused for breath. "Except for the fact that I may have to kill you."

TO: L
FROM: ELJ
DATE: September 25
FILE: 776244
SUBJECT: Gaia Moore
LAST SEEN: Mercer Street, New York City 10:53 p.m.

UPDATE: Subject observed in fight with 3 suspected gang members, one armed with knife. Attack complicated by appearance of young man in wheelchair. Motive unclear. Confirmed subject's mastery of jujitsu. Subject displayed other martial skills previously documented. All 3 attackers subdued. Subject appeared injured but later observed to walk from incident unharmed.

TO: ELJ
FROM: L
DATE: September 26
FILE: 776244
SUBJECT: Gaia Moore

DIRECTIVES: Identify and create file on young man in wheelchair.

ISSUE IMMEDIATE INSTRUCTION: Subject not to be injured *under any circumstances*. Repercussions will be severe.

GAIA

There is this other really freakish thing about me. I've never told anyone. I'd be way too humiliated.

Humiliation, by the way, is a truly terrible emotion. It's at the bottom of the pile. Much worse than fear. I bet. Since I don't have to have fear, why do I have to have humiliation? If only I could toss it wherever fear went. And while I was at it, I'd get rid of anger, hurt, compassion, betrayal. And selfishness. Oh, and guilt. Definitely guilt. It's out of there. Without all of those things, I think I could imagine maybe being happy someday.

Hey, that's it. I, Gaia Moore, have discovered the secret to happiness. People have been searching for it since the beginning of time, but it took me, a seventeen-year-old with no philosophical, medical, or psychological training, to discover the truth:

Lobotomy. You don't have to feel anything at all.

You heard it here first, folks. And a full frontal lobotomy probably costs no more than the average nose job.

Okay, where was I? Oh, yeah. No wonder I'm digressing— I don't feel like putting this into words.

I'm a virgin.

No, no. It's way worse than that. I wish it were only that.

I've never had a boyfriend.

True, but nope. That doesn't convey the depth of this particular humiliation.

I've never kissed anybody.

Okay, there you have it. Can you say "loser"?

Let me try to soften this information with an excuse or two. When I was twelve, I had something approaching a boyfriend, in a preboyfriend kind of way. His name was Stephen, and he lived around the corner. He was the one with the right kind of hair (light brown, straight, no cowlicks), the right kind of bike (specialized, like you care), the right kind of jeans (Gap, at the time). His parents had the right kind of car (red Jeep, good stereo) and a very large pool. For these reasons the popular girls sought him out. I liked him because he was secretly just as weird as me. We both played chess and knee football. We concocted these elaborate fantasy games set in Camelot or a mile under the sea, long after imaginary games are socially acceptable (age four, roughly). We were nerdy enough to watch Bill Nye, the Science Guy, but cool enough not to admit that to anybody but each other.

Hold on. Wait just a second. Why am I telling you all this? Am I really so desperate that I'll try to pass off a neighbor without underarm hair as some kind of romantic conquest? This represents a new low.

But it points to something real, which is that I'm stunted. My love life got left behind with the rest of my life the autumn after my twelfth birthday. Eventually, when the moving van came, I told Stephen I hated him, just so as not to leave any threads dangling.

My life ended then, but I keep growing.

I usually pride myself on the fact that I don't care about being a freak or a misfit. I don't care what people think of me. But for some reason this kissing business, this lack of kissing business, bothers me, and I can't pretend it doesn't.

That's the very worst thing about it, really. How much it bothers me. How much I think about it.

I'm going to be brutally honest right now, and hopefully afterward I can snap back into some more comfortable state of denial.

Ready? Okay.

Of all the terrible things that have happened in my

life—my mom, my dad, the life I lost—I'm such a vain, petty, and selfish person that I am most ashamed of the fact that nobody has ever kissed me.

This thought drives me to more than the desire for a lobotomy. This drives me to something worse.

Yo, Rapunzel. Forget the ladder. There's a faster way down.

BITCH QUEEN

TEN YEARS FROM NOW HEATHER'S AWFULNESS
WOULD HAVE CAUGHT UP WITH HER, AND SHE'D
BE A DISGRUNTLED WRETCH PINING FOR THE
GLORY DAYS.

"I started thinking/not drinking was better for me/so it got me to thinking/about getting a lobotomy . . . "

"What did she just say?" Gaia was sitting behind a very large, very expensive mug of coffee across from Ed and squinting at the band that was playing in the far corner. Gaia was happy to ignore them. She'd seen plenty of unplugged garage bands in her day. But these weird snippets of songs kept floating into her consciousness and sticking there the way raspberry seeds stuck in her molars.

"Huh?" Ed asked.

"That singer. Did you hear the words?" Gaia asked.

Ed strained to listen over the clink of spoons and the hissing of the cappuccino machine. "Something about a lobotomy."

"You're joking," Gaia declared.

Ed gave her a puzzled look. "If so, it wasn't a very funny joke."

"No, I mean, she didn't actually say lobotomy."

"Okay, she didn't." Ed shrugged. "Why does it matter?"

Gaia stirred her coffee. "Never mind." She studied the singer. She looked a little like Ashley Judd before the makeup went on. An East Village version, anyway, with a wool stocking cap, hair so messy it was coagulating into dreads, and a tattoo of a spider that perched on her collarbone.

Gaia fidgeted in her chair. She didn't want to leave too much silence because Ed might bring up what happened last night and she really didn't want him to.

"You know what the problem is with these fancy brown sugar packets?" Gaia held one up. "The granules are too big. They don't dissolve. They just hang around in the bottom of your mug, so your coffee isn't as sweet as you want it to be until you get to the last sip, which is so sweet, you want to puke."

Ed looked both puzzled and slightly amused. "Huh. Hadn't thought of that." He gestured at the counter. "They have regular sugar up there."

Gaia nodded. Why had she gone for coffee after school with Ed?

Because he'd asked her, mainly. Because he'd tried to save her life, even though she'd ended up saving his. She should have remembered, before she'd accepted, that going for coffee with someone usually meant talking to them.

Ed was looking at her a little too meaningfully. He stretched his arms out in front of him. "Listen, Gaia, I just wanted to tell you that I—"

"I don't want to talk about it," Gaia jumped in quickly.

"Sorry?"

"I don't want to talk about it."

"What is *it*?"

Now he really was going to think she was a wacko. "It. Anything."

"You don't want to talk about anything?" Ed asked carefully.

Gaia tugged at her hair, awkwardly. "I don't want to talk about last night. I don't want you to ask me any questions."

Ed nodded and digested that for a minute. "Hey, Gaia?"

"Yeah?"

"I'll make you a promise."

"That sounds heavy."

Ed laughed. "Just listen, okay?"

"Okay?"

"I promise that I won't ever ask you any questions, all right?"

Gaia laughed, too. "I think that was a question."

"Fine, so it was the last one."

"Fine."

Gaia was starting to sense too much friendliness in the air, so she stood up. "I'm going to, um, get that regular sugar. I'll be right back."

"Good."

"Okay."

She walked to the counter with her mug. This was so cozy and normal seeming, she felt as if she were inhabiting somebody else's body. Absently she dumped two packets of white sugar into her coffee.

Oh, yes, she was just a happy girl in the West Village, having coffee with a friend.

A troop of familiar-looking people streamed in. They were from school, she realized. The self-designated "beautiful people." There were three girls and two guys, and they were laughing about something. Their manner, and wardrobe screamed, "Put me in a Banana Republic ad right now!" One girl in particular was quite beautiful, with long, shiny dark hair, dark jeans, and a collared shirt that was whiter and crisper than anything Gaia had ever owned.

Much as she wanted to dismiss them as they swarmed around her at the counter, ordering various combinations of lattes, au laits, con leches, and mochas in pretentious Italian sizes, Gaia couldn't help imagining some alternate universe where she was one of them.

What if she were witty and well dressed and carefree? What if her biggest dilemma in life were whether to order a grande latte or a magnifico mocha? What if that fairly cute one, the boy in the beat-up suede jacket, called her all the time? She studied his dark hair, so pleasantly dilapidated, and his hazel eyes. She allowed herself a look at his lips. What if he'd kissed her? Not just once but hundreds of times?

She felt a weird tingling in her lower extremities as the fantasy evolved in her mind. He'd be standing next to her, studying the coffee board, as familiar to her as a brother, and he'd reach for her without really thinking about it. She'd be wearing a cute little lavender sweater set and crisp khakis instead of these oversized drawstring army pants and her faded blue football tee. He'd loop an arm around her hips and draw her a little closer and order something she knew he'd order because he always ordered it. Then he'd order for her, too. Not because he was an asinine pig, but because he knew she loved hazelnut mochaccino even though it did cost six dollars. Then he'd pay, even though she'd tell him not to. And she'd say something so funny and adorable that he'd look at her, really look at her, and remember how beautiful she was and how much he loved her. Then he'd lean toward her and kiss her on the mouth. No tongue or anything. That would be tacky in the middle of a cafe. His kiss wouldn't be long or filled with questions or expectations because he could kiss her anytime he wanted and he didn't have anything to prove. It would be soft and real and simple, yet mean a thousand loving things. She would kiss him back, but not in a way that was desperate or inexperienced. And then—

Gaia suddenly realized that the boy she was kissing in her mind's eye had transformed. Gone were the dark hair and the suede jacket, replaced by ginger-colored hair that curled around his temples and a preppy gray twill jacket with a corduroy collar. And then she realized that this person who'd barged right into her fantasy was none other than him, the guy from the park—the guy who'd wandered by the chess tables. How did he get here? she demanded of herself stridently. Who invited *him*?

"Gaia?"

She was so startled and unnerved that she forgot she

even had hands, let alone a steaming mug of coffee in one of them. In horror she watched the mug sail from her grasp and the brown sugary stuff leap out of it and land all over the front of that very white, very crisp shirt of her alternate-universe best girlfriend.

The girl screamed.

"Oh, shit," Gaia muttered.

Suddenly everybody burst into motion: The fairly cute boy was grabbing up napkins, the girls were buzzing all over their friend, the other boy was plucking pieces of mug from the mess on the floor.

Of course, Gaia knew that the right thing to do was apologize a lot, hand the girl a few napkins, make a self-deprecating remark, and offer to get her shirt dry cleaned. But for some reason Gaia did none of those things. She just stood there, gaping like a complete moron.

The offended girl turned on her with narrowed eyes. "*Excuse* me, but you just poured boiling coffee down my shirt."

"I—," Gaia began.

"What the hell is your problem? Are you some kind of idiot? Could you at least apologize?" The girl didn't look so pretty anymore.

"I just—I—I'm really—"

"Hel-*lo*?" the girl demanded. "English? Do you speak English? *Habla español?*" This was apparently humorous to herself and to her friends.

Gaia really had been working up to a sincere and heart-felt apology, but this girl no longer deserved it. "Bitch," Gaia said under her breath. It was completely the wrong thing to do. The worst thing to do, but Gaia had a talent for that.

The ex-pretty girl stiffened. "*What?* Did you just say what I think you said? Who the hell do you think you are?"

Gaia turned away at this point. It was the only thing to do. Gaia heard the girl railing and threatening as she returned to the table and a shell-shocked-looking Ed.

"Gaia, can I ask you one question, just one, and this is really the last?" Ed didn't wait for her to respond.

"Do you get in fights *everywhere* you go?"

THERE'S THIS GIRL

"Marco! Over here."

Marco glanced around the restaurant casually, as if he hadn't noticed her the instant he'd walked through the door. Man, she was hot. She was wearing dark denim jeans today and a formfitting pink sweater.

"Hey, how's it going?" he said, treating her to his most charming smile and sitting down across from her.

She returned his smile and for a moment laid her hand on top of his. She was making him dizzy again.

A waiter hustled by and dropped two menus. The place was still noisy, but the after-school crowds were clearing out. Marco checked his hair quickly in the mirror that coated the restaurant's side wall. He was glad he'd refused to shave his head like the other guys. He consulted the filthy laminated menu. Was he supposed to order something? He suspected she hadn't asked him to meet her here because she was hungry.

"So, Marco, tell me how you've been." She was studying him intently and ignoring her menu. She leaned close. He felt a gentle foot on his.

Yes, dizzy. Really dizzy. "I've been, uh, pretty cool." He swallowed.

"What's been going on in the park?"

Shit. Was he supposed to be able to think when she was doing that with her foot?

"Not much," he said. "Couple of my buddies got beat up last night."

She looked more interested than concerned. "Who did it?"

"I'm not sure. Some real tough guys, I guess. Some guys who know how to fight." Now her foot was gone, and he really wanted it back.

"You'll get them," she said confidently.

He liked the way she said it and the way she looked at him. He nodded real slow, the way his buddy Martin's older brother did. "Bet your ass," he said.

"I need to ask you something," she said.

Where was her foot? Had he done something wrong? "Yeah?"

"There's this girl, a friend of mine. She likes to hang out in the park. I know there's a lot of stuff going on. You know, slashing and whatever."

"I heard about that," he said, his look just as knowing as hers.

"I want to make sure nobody touches her, okay? She's a real sweetheart, and I don't want her getting hurt."

The foot was back. Marco felt a dull buzz in his ears. "Right. Okay. You point her out to me in the park, and I'll take care of it."

The restaurant was nearly empty now. The waiters were sitting at a round table at the very back, eating their own snack. Marco felt a hand on his knee under the table. He had to stifle a groan. He leaned toward her and snaked his hand around the back of her neck. He kissed her hard, and she kissed him back. Her sweet smell combined with the heavy scents of fried wontons and cabbage. Her soft, blissful tongue explored his while the brown Formica table jammed into his stomach. God, he wanted to do it right here.

Suddenly her tongue and her hands were gone and she was standing. "Come on." She gestured at the door. "I know a place we can go."

WHO'S HEATHER?

Ed saw her the following afternoon, sitting at a chess table near the southwestern corner of the park, and his heart sped up a little. The late September breeze was blowing her blond hair out of its messy ponytail and around her face. She'd shed her rumpled jacket to reveal a sleeveless white T-shirt and lithe, sculpted shoulders. Her muscles were defined, but long and graceful. In the sunshine he noticed a few freckles along the bridge of her nose. Her eyes looked less stormy gray and more Caribbean turquoise in this light.

Her opponent at the chessboard was a man in his thirties wearing a baseball cap and a pair of expensive sneakers and appearing to concentrate about ten times harder than she was.

She was wearing an expression he hadn't seen on her before—sort of wide-eyed and distracted. She gazed around. She examined her fingernails. She even appeared to giggle while losing a pawn. Was this actually Gaia?

Ed's legs were for crap, but his eyes were excellent. It was definitely Gaia. Either that or her ditzy twin sister.

He watched in surprise as she lost two more pawns and a knight. Her opponent was looking pretty pleased with himself. He was also allowing his eyes a few breaks from the board to gawk at Gaia. *Pervert,* Ed thought irritably.

Gaia lost another pawn. She might be able to take Bruce Lee in a fight, but she sure sucked at chess. She giggled again. It was a weird sound. Like a parakeet mooing or something. What was up with her?

Gaia's opponent snatched up her rook, and suddenly her manner changed. She focused with a slight frown on the board and started making moves rapidly. The man was smiling at her when she looked up from the board again. He looked so patronizing and full of himself that Ed suspected he was about to ask her out. He hoped Gaia would break his jaw.

Instead she said, "Checkmate," in a matter-of-fact way. Ed read her lips more than he actually heard her say it.

Ed watched with blossoming pleasure as the man's face fell and his mouth snapped shut. He looked confused, then a bit suspicious, and then downright sour as he pulled out his wallet and handed over a twenty. As he walked away with his *New York Times* tucked under his arm, his overly youthful baseball cap looked even more absurd. Maybe he was in his forties.

"Go, Gaia," Ed said, wheeling over.

She turned toward his voice, her eyebrows connecting over angry eyes. "What, are you spying on me?"

"No, I'm strolling through the park and stopping to say hi to a friend," he countered. "A paranoid friend." He *was* basically spying, but she didn't need to know that.

Her fierce eyes relented a bit "Oh."

"I see you discovered how to play chess right there in the middle of the game. Wow."

She cocked her head and almost smiled. "Gee, yeah. Lucky timing, huh?"

"And you made twenty dollars to boot," Ed added. "Poor bastard didn't know what hit him."

"So you were spying," Gaia accused, but she didn't look mad anymore.

"Maybe a little," he admitted.

She sighed. "You know, Ed, if you learn any more of my secrets, I really will have to kill you." She stood and slung her weather-beaten messenger bag over her shoulder.

He shrugged. "Okay. I guess."

She started walking toward Washington Place, and he followed her.

"But before you do," he continued, "I was wondering, will you go to a party with me tonight?"

She stopped and turned on him, her eyebrows drawing together again. "Are you joking? Of course not."

Since his accident Ed had become a near professional button pusher, but nobody's buttons gave him quite the thrill that Gaia's did. Most people pretended to be civil for too long. Gaia got spitting mad right away.

"Come on, it's a school party. Allison Rovitz is having it—you know, Heather's friend?"

"Who's Heather?" She was walking again.

"The girl you, uh, met over coffee yesterday," Ed said, quickly catching up with her.

Gaia shook her head in disbelief. "Boy, you sure do make it sound tempting."

Ed nodded. "It might be fun. Besides, it would be good for you to meet some people," he suggested brightly.

Gaia stopped short and glanced around her. "What is going on here? Are the cameras rolling? Are we secretly starring in an after-school special? *Wheelchair Boy Befriends Angry Orphan Girl?*"

Ed laughed genuinely. "So I'll meet you there at nine? I'll leave the address on your answering machine."

"No!" Gaia almost shouted.

"Why not?" Ed persisted. "You don't have anything else to do."

"Yes, I do," she shot back.

"Like what?" Ed demanded.

She was silent for a few seconds. "Okay, I don't." Gaia glared at him. "Rub it in."

Ed loved the way she pressed her lips together. He loved the way she stood with one hip stuck out. He tried not to be obvious when he admired the way her hair fell perfectly, framing her face and stunning eyes, no matter how hard the wind tore at it. He had heard of this mythic species, beautiful girls who were not conscious of the fact that they were beautiful. He'd seen them represented in movies and on TV—unconvincingly for the most part. He'd read about them in books. But he'd never actually met one in person until Gaia.

"I know why you won't go," Ed said suddenly.

Gaia's patience was waning. "Why?"

"Because Heather's going to be there. You're scared of Heather." Ed stated confidently.

Gaia put her hands on her hips. She looked like she really did want to kill him. "Ed. I am not *scared* of Heather. Trust me."

KLUTZ GIRL STRIKES AGAIN

What in the world was she doing? Gaia walked extra fast along Seventh Avenue, past Bleecker, past the duplex psychic shop blazing with neon, past the shop (one of many) that pierced you anyplace you could think of, past the bustling gay bars on Christopher Street.

As much as she despised getting railroaded into a stupid party full of people she was sure to hate, there was a small but unsquashable part of her that was happy to be out on a Saturday night with someplace to go.

She was going because she wasn't afraid of Heather and because she really didn't have anything else to do. But she was mostly going because Ed had asked her. He was the first person in her entire high school career who'd cut through her defenses long enough to ask her to a party. He was the first person she hadn't succeeded in scaring off, in spite of her usual efforts.

The party was at 25 West Fifteenth Street. West meant west of Fifth Avenue, but not by much, so she hung a right at Fifteenth. Weeks ago, before she'd even moved here, she had committed a map of lower Manhattan to her near perfect visual memory.

She glanced down at her dark jeans and trashed sneakers.

It would be impossible to tell from looking at her that she had spent over an hour getting dressed. She'd put on some mascara, then washed it off. She'd tried on three pairs of nearly identical jeans before finally closing her eyes and grabbing a pair randomly. She'd even changed her socks. Her one lasting concession to beauty was buried under shoes and (carefully chosen) socks—toenail polish in a hue called Cockroach.

As the address grew near, she spied one of the things she most disliked about New York residential life: a doorman. How much did you have to pay a guy to dress up in a butt-ugly polyester suit and embarrassing hat and open your damn door? And where were the door*women*, anyway? She hadn't seen a single one since she'd been here. Maybe she'd change her life's ambition from waitress to doorwoman. "Doorwoman." It sounded like some postmodern urban superhero.

Of course, this particular doorman wanted to know her name and whose apartment she felt privileged enough to visit. "Ed Fargo," she told him. "Visiting Allison Rovitz in apartment 12C."

The doorfellow gave her a once-over. "You don't look like an Ed."

"Tell my parents that. It's a real burden," she told him.

He shook his head, as though wishing he never had to speak to another scruffy, attitude-wielding seventeen-year-old as long as he lived.

He consulted his list, then waved a hand toward the inner lobby. "Go ahead."

"Why aren't there any doorwomen?" she nearly shouted after him as the elevator door closed.

The party in 12C could be heard throughout 12, from what Gaia could tell. She felt her muscles tense at the shrieks of laughter and loud buzz of conversation spilling into the hallway. This was kind of a momentous event. Although her capacity for nervousness was nil, her capacity for insecurity was all there. She tucked some hair behind her ear. She took a deep breath and pushed open the unlocked door.

What was she expecting exactly? Some deeply narcissistic part of her thought everybody in the place would know that even though she was a junior, she had never been to a real high school party before. They would fall silent and turn to stare at her.

In fact, the only difference between before she had come and after was that there was one more beating heart in a very crowded apartment.

Okeydoke. Yes, here she was. Suddenly she was sure she'd been born with an extra gene for social awkwardness. Time to find the real Ed Fargo and hope he still thought she was entertaining.

She squeezed past a knot of people in the foyer who didn't care about her at all. In the living room she recognized a girl from her history class, a couple of guys who had lockers near hers. Every flat surface was covered with soda cans and beer cans in about equal number. A lot of people were smoking—mostly girls. On a table in the corner were raw carrots and dip and some unappealing chips and salsa. The meager food table was quickly being taken over by cans and cans and cans and makeshift ashtrays. Were anybody's parents here? She'd heard that New York City parents let their kids drink at parties because nobody drove anywhere afterward.

The sweet, suffocating smell of marijuana made its way over. She zeroed in on the little clutch of people passing around the joint before she turned and walked in the opposite direction. She had less than no time for that. Were those kids really so confident in their sanity, they could tempt fate?

When she finally caught sight of Ed's wheelchair in the dining room, she stifled the strong urge to sprint over to him and give him a hug. She walked toward him as slowly as she could manage, as though expecting to encounter hordes of friends and acquaintances along the way.

Gaia was shy. She'd forgotten that about herself, but she was. She was more comfortable beating the crap out of somebody than chatting about the weather. She could be sullen and obnoxious and irritable all day long, but she couldn't think of a single way to start a friendly conversation.

"Hi, Ed," she said lamely, once she was near.

"Gaia! Holy shit!" He smiled big. "You actually came."

"I never miss a party," she said wryly.

"Wow. You look great," he said.

"No, I don't."

"Okay, you don't. Hey, this is Claire." He pointed at a long-haired Asian girl he'd been talking to. "Claire, this is Gaia."

Claire waved and smiled. She was smoking a cigarette.

"And this is Mary. Mary, Gaia, et cetera."

Mary was tall, with wavy red hair. She waved in a perfunctory way and took a swig of beer.

"You're new, right?" Claire asked.

"Yes." Gaia answered.

"Where are you from?" Claire wanted to know.

Ed shifted in his chair.

Gaia cleared her throat. "Uh. Memphis" It was a lie. She didn't want to play the "oh, really, do you know . . . ?" game about anyplace she had actually lived.

"Really? I have a cousin in Tennessee," Claire responded predictably. "In Johnson City?"

"Oh?" Gaia nodded blankly.

Suddenly there was a swell of noise from the direction of the front door. All eyes turned.

"Hey, Gaia, check it out," Ed said. "It's your best friend."

Gaia gave him a mean look. It was Heather and friends—the same group from the cafe plus a couple of Hollywood extras. Heather really was beautiful when she wasn't snarling. Judging from the energy she and her crowd brought into the apartment with them, the party had only started at that moment.

Claire studied the group carefully. "I guess Heather didn't bring her boyfriend. Too bad. That guy is altogether hot."

Mary looked unimpressed. "He's a big college man. He goes to NYU. What's his name again? Carrie says he doesn't like coming to high school parties."

Of course Heather would have a gorgeous, snotty boyfriend who was in college. Of course. Gaia could only imagine what kind of asshole the guy must be to choose Heather as a girlfriend.

"I guess we're blessed even to have Heather," Gaia mumbled, instantly cursing herself for being snide.

Mary glanced at Gaia appreciatively. "Yes. I mean, who better to make the rest of us feel fat and friendless?"

Gaia laughed and felt a surge of . . . something. Optimism, was it? Hope? Social acceptance? She wasn't sure exactly—it was so unfamiliar. But here she was, maladjusted freak-thing Gaia Moore, gabbing with people who could very easily have been her friends. It was utterly alien, but not in a bad way. Only now she had to try to think of something else to say.

Heather led the wave of party energy through the living room toward the dining room and, no doubt, the kitchen, where the beers were waiting. Gaia wondered a bit warily if Heather would recognize her.

As it turned out, she did.

"Oh, my God!" Heather shrieked, wheeling around to face Gaia straight on. "It's Klutz Girl! What are you doing here?"

Suddenly all eyes really were on Gaia. Her social success was evaporating quickly.

"I would watch out for this girl," Heather warned loudly. "Don't give her anything to eat or drink or you'll end up with it on your shirt."

Heather's friends tittered loyally.

"Who let you in here?" Heather demanded.

Gaia studied the small place on the girl's neck just below her chin. She could deliver one swift blow to that spot and put her out.

"I invited her," Ed said, filling the awkward silence at least momentarily.

"Excuse me, *Ed*," Heather said nastily. "I didn't realize it was your party."

"I didn't realize it was yours," Ed responded.

Allison, the actual party giver, was watching the scene unfold with the rest of them. Heather turned to her.

"Al, did you realize this bitch was coming to your party?"

Poor Allison looked frightened.

"Don't worry about it, Allison. I'm going," Gaia said. She strode through the apartment without looking back.

It didn't matter so much that she was back on the outside, Gaia consoled herself as she opened the front door and passed through it. This was Heather's time. Let her have it. Ten years from now Heather's awfulness would have caught up with her, and she'd be a disgruntled wretch pining for the glory days. Let her have high school. Gaia was holding out for something better.

Gaia stood sullenly at the elevator bank and punched the down arrow. Mercifully the elevator doors opened right away.

At least she was back in her comfort zone.

GAIA

Some things I like:

- Chess
- Slurpees
- Road Runner cartoons
- Eye boogers
- W. B. Yeats
- Ed

Some things I don't like:

- Heather
- Ella
- Skim milk
- Butterflies
- Baking soda toothpaste
- Myself

A thing I hate:

- My dad

MEETING
SAM MOON

RAIN PLASTERED THICK DARK CORDS OF HAIR
TO HIS FOREHEAD. NOW THAT IT WAS NO LONGER
PERFECT, SHE COULD SEE IT WAS BEAUTIFUL.

"Hi, Zolov."

The old man squinted at Gaia for a few seconds before he recognized her, then he smiled.

"Hey, Curtis," she said to Zolov's opponent. "Where's Renny?"

The fifteen-year-old chess fixture shrugged. "He hasn't been coming around anymore."

Gaia nodded and looked for a free table. She was happy to be there, even without Renny. She was glad that the bleak sky threatened rain and that the air was finally turning cold. All that warm sunshine seemed to demand perkiness and pastel-colored clothing.

She watched Curtis leaning far over the board, studying Zolov's sequence. She almost laughed to herself. She couldn't believe she was watching an ancient Jewish man in a threadbare wool overcoat teaching the Ruy Lopez opening to a black kid dressed head to toe in Tommy.

She turned her affectionate gaze to the right, and suddenly her mood went into free fall.

Him.

What the hell was *he* doing here?

God, he was good-looking. He was wearing that same gray jacket, this time with a pair of jeans and just the right shade of dark, perfectly scuffed leather shoes. Go away, she ordered him silently. Go back to where you belong.

He didn't go away. Instead he came very close, and her mouth felt dry. Why did she all of a sudden care that she hadn't run a brush through her hair that morning? So she looked like a homeless person. What was it to him?

Oh, shit. He was looking at the board set in front of her. His eyes glanced over the empty chair across from her.

He was stopping!

He was sitting down!

He was staring right at her!

Then she felt mad. What, was he on some kind of field trip from normal-people land? Was he the Jane Goodall of the popular set, here to take notes?

It didn't help that just a few days before he'd appeared *uninvited* in her romantic fantasy and *kissed* her, for God's sake. "Do you want to play?" he asked, just like that.

He wanted to play her! What! Didn't he know that it was illegal in a cosmic sense for a guy who looked like him even to get near a board? The gods of social stratification would zap him but good.

Fine. If he insisted on turning the world upside down, what could she do? She'd play him. She'd point out to him which pieces moved which way as though she'd only recently learned herself, and then she'd hustle as much money out of him as possible. She could probably get two or three fast games out of him before the rain began to fall.

"Hello?" He scrunched down a little in his chair to try to gain eye contact.

"What?" she blurted out irritably.

"Do you want to play?"

She was so flustered, she couldn't pluck one arrow from her quiver of hustling tricks. "Fine."

"Don't feel like you have to."

Oh, wasn't he just honorable.

"No, it's fine. I only just started playing myself." God, she sounded wooden. Her acting really needed some work.

"Okay. You start, right?"

"No, I mean, I think. Well, we usually—" Dammit. She took a black pawn and a white one and mixed them up behind her back. She enclosed each in a fist and stuck them out toward him. "You pick."

He pointed to her left hand, and she produced a white pawn.

"You go first," she said.

He looked tentative. "It's kind of a custom to play for money here, isn't it?"

Custom? Yes, it is, O Great Doctor of Losers.

"Usually," was what she said.

"How much?"

"I dunno. Twenty?"

He blew out his breath. "Wow. Okay."

"Okay."

What was it about him that bothered her so? That he was the kind of guy who'd never look twice at a girl like her? Okay, well, there was that.

She couldn't find major fault with his wardrobe. It wasn't like he was wearing a Rolex or anything.

She didn't hate him just because he looked like . . . that. Even she wasn't quite that shallow or rabidly judgmental.

What was it, then?

He was so . . . confident. That was the big problem. Here, in her place, where he had no right to be, he was so goddamned sure of himself. He probably had no sense of humor, least of all about himself.

She couldn't wait to kick his ass.

THE FIRE HOSE TEST

Sam Moon wasn't sure what to make of this girl. He'd sat down at her board because she was new, and that always represented an opportunity.

Well, okay. That wasn't the only reason. Another reason was that in spite of her somewhat disastrous personal hygiene, she was pretty. A pretty girl at a chessboard wasn't your everyday sight. He hadn't even realized just how pretty until he was within a couple of feet and had a chance to really look.

Some friends of his from high school used to rate a girl's attractiveness by what was known as the fire hose test. If the girl's looks were all about makeup and hair and clothes, she'd look like crap if you shot a fire hose directly in her face from point-blank range. A genuinely pretty girl would still look good. Now, this girl here looked as though a hose actually had blasted her, so there was no leap of imagination necessary to know that she passed the test. Passed it with an A, he decided as she bit her lip and tapped impatiently on the queen's pawn.

"Okay, here goes," he said, thumping to E4.

She predictably took E5.

Pretty as she was, though, she was annoying. She obviously thought she knew what she was doing—under her truly flimsy pretense that she didn't. Maybe she'd won some high school tournament or something. Whoop-de-do. She had no business taking over a table here.

And why was she glaring at him like that? What had he done to piss her off?

He'd give her hope for a few minutes and then shut her down. He could really use the twenty bucks.

He flinched a little as a clap of thunder roared overhead. The air felt heavy with coming rain. He'd give her a very few minutes.

THE RAIN STARTS

She was surprised. Not alarmed or anything. Just a little surprised.

She hadn't expected him to respond so adroitly to her opening. They'd progressed quickly to the midgame, and she'd achieved almost no advantage. Now the wind was blowing in soot-colored clouds and thunder rolled through the sky and she was looking at the possibility of a complicated endgame.

He wasn't the doofus she'd imagined. That much she had to admit. She hadn't thought it possible to have perfect orthodonture and a good haircut and also be great at chess, but then, she was only seventeen. There had to be a few things left to learn.

She wasn't pretending anything anymore. She was too focused on the board. All attempts at inane, gee-whiz posturing had fallen away.

His manner had changed, too. His concentration on the game was so full, he let out these tiny, almost inaudible grunts every so often. He had this funny tick of drumming his fingers against his bottom lip before he made each move. She couldn't exactly remember what about him had seemed so self-satisfied.

She unintentionally knocked her knee against his under the table. He glanced up.

"Sorry," she mumbled. Her face felt warm. She prayed it wasn't actually turning pink.

His hair had fallen over his forehead. She couldn't read the expression in his eyes.

She commanded her own eyeballs back to the board.

A fat, cold raindrop landed on her scalp. Damn. Why couldn't she just finish this up?

MORE RAIN

Tiny drops of sweat were collecting in his hairline, bleeding into the raindrops slapping on his head. Drops dribbled down his neck, and his sweater was starting to smell funky. He was concentrating too hard to care.

The girl moved her king's bishop.

Ugh. He closed his eyes briefly in disgust at himself. Why hadn't he seen the pin? What was wrong with him?

He was forced to defend with a knight. That was a tempo lost.

The main thing wrong was that this girl was totally

shocking. She was not good. She was very, very, very good. Where had she come from? She couldn't be from around here because he felt sure he would have met her in tournaments before. She had to be an internationally ranked player. Either that or he suddenly stunk.

He'd sacrificed material to no avail. She'd dismantled one of his most trusted combinations. But even so, it was a really exciting game. Her play was not only smart and challenging, but unorthodox. Who had taught her? Who was she?

He glanced up at her. Her light hair was soaked flat with rain. Her blue eyes darkened to mirror the sky, and they were steady with concentration. She was somewhere around sixteen or seventeen years old. He hadn't detected any accent, which would have at least helped to explain how she was so good. It seemed like foreign players always dominated in competition.

The harsh, defiant set of her face had dissolved now. Self-consciousness had fallen away as her focus intensified. Her eyes were lovely, rimmed with long, dark (wet) lashes. Her cheekbones were exceptionally prominent for a person her age. Her face was open now and almost sweet. Raindrops stood on her bare arms, and her T-shirt was . . .

She snapped her rook into the center of the action.

Okay, better not to look anymore. He was screwing up here. Lucky for him there weren't many beautiful girls who played chess, or he'd probably be bowling right now.

His heart was speeding with nervousness and excitement. He could feel warmth radiating from her legs, so close to his. His palms felt tingly.

Think about chess, you idiot, he ordered himself.

A FLOOD

Yes, alarming. It was now officially alarming. He was up a knight and coming on strong. How had she misjudged him so badly?

He was probably the best person she had ever played except for her father, maybe, and Zolov, who was nuts.

She studied his face. He was older than she, but not by much. Maybe twenty. He had to be an international master at least. She wasn't on the chess circuit, but she knew an extraordinary player from a good one.

And as he played he was becoming real to her. His little ticks were so peculiar. The skin around his fingernails was ragged from being picked at too much. Tiny blue veins zigzagged under the surface of the transparent skin beneath his eyes. Rain plastered thick dark cords of hair to his fore-head. Now that it was no longer perfect, she could see it was beautiful.

Suddenly she had this powerful urge to touch the pale skin above his wrist, where she could see his pulse thump-ing. She stared transfixed at that spot, feeling that her own heart was beating out the same rhythm.

Oh, Gaia. She almost groaned out loud. Get a hold of yourself, girl.

This was an inexplicable reaction she was having to him. Was she profoundly low on sleep, maybe? When had she last eaten?

Another bolt of lightning blazed through the sky. Maybe it was the plunging barometer? The electricity in the air?

When she looked back at the board, she felt dizzy and disoriented. A chess game like this one meant holding a million teetering moves and possibilities in your mind, and here all at once she'd dropped them. The crowd of pieces left on the board had gone from a thrillingly complex and significant battle in one second to a meaningless jumble the next.

Blood rushed to her face. She tried to kick-start her memory, to patch together her lost strategy. But it was as though the whole thing had existed in someone else's mind.

Rain blanketed them. Steam rose from the surround-ing pavement. Goose bumps pricked up and down her arms.

Why had neither of them suggested giving up this ridiculous contest and going inside?

He was looking at her. Not silently, impatiently demanding her next move, as she would expect. Just looking. Looking for something. Rain dotted his eyelashes with diamonds, formed rivers down his cheeks.

His eyes had taken hers, and she couldn't look away.

Then she felt something grab hold of her chest. It wasn't fear. It couldn't be. But what was it? She had to get out of there.

With a flick of her index finger she felled her precious king. "I'm sorry," she murmured. "I have to go." She got to her feet, reaching into her bag for her wallet. He stood, too. She fumbled the wet leather and pulled out a twenty-dollar bill, then jammed it in his palm.

"No. No," he told her. The bill fluttered to the ground, but neither of them stooped to get it. She was already walking, and he was hurrying alongside her, confused, surprised, stammering for a word.

"W-Wait. Please," he whispered.

She was almost running. In her sneakers the water squished around her toes. The rain was so loud, it filled up all of her senses.

She hurried from him and from the strange perception that a million frozen feelings were about to thaw and the flood would certainly drown her.

BOTTOMLESS

He watched her go, feeling a terrible tightness in his throat. What had she done to him?

It had all happened in that moment, when he'd met her eyes and, like a mystic, seemed to see her past and future. Her past was haunting, marked by bottomless wounds, and the future was terrifying because it included him.

NO BAD DOGS

FOR THE LAST TWENTY-FOUR HOURS HIS MIND
HAD BEHAVED MORE LIKE A BADLY TRAINED DOG
ON A TOO LONG LEASH.

"I wish my name were Fargo."

Gaia was walking so fast, Ed Fargo was having a hard time keeping up with her. Her movements were strangely jerky, and her mouth was going a mile a minute.

"Why is that?" he had to practically shout at her because she kept getting ahead.

"It's cool name," she said.

"You could marry me if you asked really nicely," he proposed.

"Yeah, right."

"What's the matter with Moore?" he asked as they rounded the corner of Charles Street and Hudson.

"I don't know." Gaia's eyes weren't quite focused. She wasn't completely paying attention to what she was saying or where her feet were going. "Moore . . . Less," she mused absently. "Hey, Gaia Less. Guileless. I like that."

He was getting annoyed. "Gaia, would you please slow down? I'm kind of in a wheelchair here."

She glanced back at him. "Oh. Sorry," she mumbled.

In her expression Ed saw traces of impatience but no embarrassment, no pity. He loved her.

"Guileless," he continued. "What does it mean?"

"You know, without guile."

"What does guile mean?"

"Deceit, duplicity, dishonesty."

He slowed down a bit more. "Gaia, how do you know these things?"

She shrugged. "I'm smart."

"And modest, too."

"Modesty is a waste of time," she pronounced.

"I'll keep that in mind."

They passed Zuli's bakery and the tiny store that sold homemade ravioli. A woman passed them, pushing a toy poodle perched in a baby carriage. Gaia didn't even seem to notice.

"For somebody so smart, you sure bombed the physics quiz today," Ed pointed out.

"Yeah, well. Parabolas are so simple, they're boring."

Ed laughed. "I'll have to remember that excuse to tell my parents the next time I get a D."

Suddenly Gaia stopped and grabbed his shoulder. "What's that?"

"Ouch," he said, and she lessened her grip on his clavicle. "What?"

"That music." She yanked him around the corner. "Do you hear it? Where's it coming from?"

He pointed across the street "That band we heard at Ozzie's. They practice in the basement of that building."

"How do you know?"

"Because I'm smart."

Gaia rolled her eyes. "What's the name of the band?"

"Huh?"

"The name of the band?"

"Fearless. They're always playing around the neighborhood. Ozzie's on Friday afternoons, Dock's on Wednesday evenings, and fully amplified at The Flood most Saturday nights. Our local OTB takes bets on when they'll actually get signed."

Gaia had completely tuned out.

"Ha-ha. That was a funny joke," Ed pointed out.

Gaia nodded dumbly. "Fearless?" she asked "No way."

Ed shrugged. "No reason to lie." He was bored with this conversation.

Gaia paused for another moment as slow lyrics drifted up to the street.

". . . And I'm a stone/falling deeper/into your black, black ocean/let me drown . . . "

Gaia was off again like a shot.

"Where are we going now?" he asked, almost breathless in his effort to catch up.

"I don't know. We're strolling."

"Oh."

They strolled for a while in silence.

"Hey, wait a minute," he said, slowing down warily as they sailed past Sixth Avenue without a pause.

"What?"

"I have a feeling we're strolling to the park."

"So?"

"I don't want to go to the park."

Gaia looked annoyed. "Why not?"

"Because innocent people are getting slashed there practically every day. Because there are evil bald guys carving swastikas into trees. Do you watch the news?"

"Ed, it's broad daylight."

"That doesn't stop you."

"Stop *me*? Stop me from what?" she asked.

"From finding people to get into fights with," he responded.

She looked slightly abashed.

"Let's walk down Broadway toward Soho," he suggested.

Gaia was quiet, fidgeting with the threads hanging off the bottom of her jacket, but she did follow him at least.

"What's the matter?" he asked.

"I'm trying to think of a way to apologize for the other night," she explained.

"What do you mean?" he asked.

"For ruining that party you invited me to."

"You didn't ruin it," he said comfortingly. "We all had a perfectly good time after you left."

She kicked his wheel.

"Gaia, Jesus!" He regained control of his chair. "I was

just kidding. I left right away. I tried to catch you, but you were too fast for me."

She slowed down a little. "Really?"

"Yeah. Anyway, it wasn't you. It was Heather who was out of control."

"You think so?"

He laughed. "For once, yeah."

"She's such a raving bitch," Gaia declared.

Ed shook his head thoughtfully. "There's actually more to her than that."

"You know her well?" Gaia asked, clearly surprised.

"Sure. I went out with her for a few months."

Gaia stopped cold in the middle of Bleecker Street. A truck honked loudly.

"Gaia, go!" Ed commanded, and she did.

"No way," she stated when they were safely on the other side of the street.

Ed looked at her peevishly. "You say that too much."

"Sorry. But I mean it. No way."

Ed held up his hands. "It's true. Heather and I went out for a while before my accident."

"Wow." Gaia was obviously struggling to absorb this. They walked for three blocks in silence.

"Hey, Gaia?" he asked finally.

"Yeah?"

"Are you ever going to ask me why I'm in a wheelchair?"

"No," she said.

"Why not?"

"Because if I do, you would have the right to ask where I lived before, or why I'm a black belt in karate, or what happened to my parents."

"Oh." he said. "Okay."

And they kept walking.

THAT GIRL

Sam wasn't walking through the park because he wanted to see that girl. He didn't want to see that girl. She was trouble.

And he had a girlfriend. That was the more important point. He had a girlfriend, and he was late to meet her, and even though it was almost dark and he knew he shouldn't be cutting through the park with all of the crap that was going on, he was doing it anyway.

But not because he wanted to see that girl.

Although he was running late, he could count on the fact that Heather would be at least twenty minutes later and that she would show up with a noisy entourage. She would be all out of breath and apologize fervently for being late, as though her lateness depended on such a rare and extenuating matrix of once-in-a-lifetime circumstances that it could never possibly happen again. And the next time she would be just as late.

He should just tell her it bugged him. He was basically a punctual person, and he didn't appreciate all the dramatic entrances. He didn't love the entourage, either.

But if he did tell her, she would probably listen and stop, at least for a while. And then where would he be? What could he complain about? What reason would he have for breaking up with her?

Ooh. That last bit just slipped out. He hadn't totally meant to have that thought.

Heather was gorgeous. Heather was smart. Heather was confident and funny. Heather, though only a senior in high school, was the envy of all his college friends. Heather was even capable, when she let go of her own mythology for a few minutes, of being a decent person.

But these were not good reasons for going out with a person, and he knew that in his heart. So why did he stay with her?

That was complicated. It hinged on a lot of stuff about his old life and his old self, and he didn't feel like thinking about it just now.

His thoughts wandered back to the girl. *The girl.* He'd certainly never thought so much about a person whose name he didn't know. His mind slipped back to her every time he gave it a moment's freedom. He kept picturing her eyes, infinite as the sky. His mind used to be so obedient, so precise. For the last twenty-four hours it had behaved more like a badly trained dog on a too long leash.

Did she live in the neighborhood? Where did she go to school? Would she come back to the chess tables in the park? If she did, would he try to talk to her? Would he ask her to play again?

His heart rate was rising at the very thought.

Okay, enough.

He was so distracted, he veered off the path and nearly crashed into a sign. He looked up at it.

Curb Your Dog, it said.

A MISTAKE

If she saw him, she would just change course. Gaia's eyesight was good. She would spot him before he spotted her, before any interaction needed to take place.

Strictly speaking, walking through the park wasn't the smartest way to avoid him. But it was the fastest way to get home after she dropped Ed off at his house. And now that it was dark, it was by far her best chance for getting jumped or slashed by one of those neo-Nazi bastards.

She wasn't going to go out of her way for this guy.

Usually the park was still busy at this hour when the weather was good, but tonight it was nearly deserted. People were spooked by the reports of slashing. Lots of kids had been talking about it in school that day.

Gaia paused to take off her jacket and tie it around her waist. Slashing was such a random, mean-spirited brand of violence and the whole Nazi mythology so profoundly hateful, she was particularly eager to draw it out. She liked to think of herself as a trap. A walking trap.

As she dawdled in the wooded area near the dog run, she heard whispers. Oh, man. Could it be this easy? She strained her ears to hear and ambled a tiny bit closer. She couldn't really make out the conversation, but she did see the flash of a knife. Not a blade this time, a real knife. Four guys were huddled together, probably plotting their next attack.

Me! Me! Choose me! she thought. Jeez, what a wacko she'd become. She made as much noise as possible while still appearing naive and oblivious. She really hoped none of them would recognize her from a previous run-in.

She walked as slowly as she could without actually stop-ping and yet within moments found herself on the open, brightly lit sidewalk of Washington Square West untouched. So it wasn't her lucky night. Maybe tomorrow.

She felt sulky and suddenly quite alone. It was weird, this business of having a friend, she decided, thinking of her long, aimless walk with Ed. It made being alone less fun.

Gaia looked up and saw a figure crossing the street toward her. It was a girl, and she appeared to be heading straight into the park. Gaia's mind flashed to the knife she'd just seen, and she bent her steps toward the girl. She didn't realize until she was a few feet away exactly which girl it was.

"Is that Gaia?" a not-friendly voice demanded.

It was Heather. This really wasn't Gaia's lucky night. Gaia was immediately struck by the fact that Heather was alone. Where was the famed boyfriend? Where were the adoring, fashionably dressed friends?

"Listen, Heather," she began matter-of-factly, "you prob-ably shouldn't—"

Heather bristled and walked on. "Leave me alone, bitch."

Gaia wasn't sure what to do. Follow her? "Heather, I really don't think—"

"Get away from me," Heather snapped. "I don't care what you think."

Gaia had intended to be helpful, but now she was angry.

Let the stupid girl get slashed. It wasn't Gaia's responsibility. If anybody deserved it, Heather did.

Gaia's temper smoldered as she continued across the street. She was just about to turn onto Waverly when she spotted more familiar faces. They were all three Heather acolytes. One was named Tina, she believed. The other was a girl whose name she didn't know, and the third was the good-looking guy from the cafe.

This time she was just going to keep walking, but one of them stopped her.

"You're Gaia, right?" the non-Tina girl asked.

"Yeah."

"Have you seen Heather, by any chance?"

Gaia looked from one to the next. This didn't seem like a trick or anything. "Yeah, I just saw her about a minute ago. She was cutting through the park." Gaia gestured in the general direction.

"Thanks," they all said. They weren't oozing warmth, but they seemed perfectly friendly.

"Hey, uh . . . Tina," Gaia called over her shoulder.

They all stopped and turned.

"You really shouldn't go through the park. There's a bunch of whacked-out guys in there, and at least one of them has a knife."

Tina and her friends looked surprised and alarmed in varying degrees. "Shit. Okay. Right."

"Thanks," the guy said again.

Gaia watched with satisfaction as they skirted the park, staying on the lighted sidewalk.

See? She'd done her good deed. She wasn't a bad person. She could go home in peace.

E D

Sometimes I dream I'm skating. Not a ramp or half pipe like one of those Mountain Dew commercials. My feet are planted on a board, and I'm steaming along straight and steady. First it's maybe a sidewalk and then a street and then it becomes a highway of at least four lanes. Then the board transforms into an airplane, and I'm in the cockpit. It's a passenger plane, I guess, but I'm not aware of having responsibility for any passengers. I have this sense of excitement and anticipation as I accelerate, gaining intense, powerful speed. Fast, fast, faster. I feel sure I've passed that speed you need to leave the ground. But I'm still on the highway. I'm still zooming past houses and fields and forests.

The highway bends slowly into a curve. It curves again. I become conscious of road signs—Deer Crossing, Boulders Falling, you know those. And I begin to pay attention to them. I realize I've adjusted my speed from about a million miles an hour to just a few above the speed limit. I peer into the side mirror of my airplane to check for cops.

After a while it's a forgone conclusion that I won't be taking off. Just a plain fact, like any of the others we learn to live with. I'll be following signs on the highway in my jumbo jet, built to fly thirty-five-thousand feet above our blue Earth.

NO PEACE

AND SHE FOLLOWED THEM THROUGH THE EXIT,
DISTINCTLY AWARE OF THE HUGE CLOUD OF HATE
BEHIND HER.

Before he passed through the school entrance the next morning, Ed knew there was something wrong. The halls were extra crowded, but not loud enough. Kids were gathered in little dots held together by hushed voices. A lot of eyes were darting around. The air had that heightened energy, that guilty pleasure of tragedy.

"What's going on?" he asked the first person he came to, a vaguely familiar girl with a magenta crew cut.

"God, it's so scary," she said. He could tell she was trying to rein herself in to project the right amount of sobriety. "Heather Gannis got shot in Washington Square last night She's in the ICU at St Vincent's."

"Jesus," Ed muttered. That sick zingy feeling, as if his blood were suddenly carbonated, started under his stomach and spread through his limbs. "Do they know who did it?"

The girl was already gone, so he wheeled up to the nearest group. "What happened? Who did it? Is she going to be okay?" he burst in loudly. He didn't feel like being measured and coy.

The five faces above him were practically caricatures of gravity. "The police claim they have suspects, but there hasn't been an arrest," a black-haired girl answered. "Nobody knows exactly what happened. They think it was some kind of gang activity—this white supremacist group—connected to the slashings."

"But it was a shooting," he argued.

"No, it wasn't. It was a stabbing," a guy said.

"A stabbing?" Ed asked.

At least two of them nodded.

"She's in ICU?" Ed continued, feeling impatient. He needed this information to slow his speeding heart. He actually cared about the facts and their implications, unlike most of the rumormongers.

"In a coma," another girl added.

He sighed in frustration. "We're talking about Heather?"

Black-Haired Girl's face closed in annoyance. "Obviously" she snapped.

Ed wheeled away, shaking his head. He had a feeling that if he talked to every one of the groups in the hallway, he would get a slightly different story from each.

This was surreal and terrifying. Heather wasn't the kind of girl who got shot or stabbed or stepped into a hospital for any reason but to visit her grandmother after elective surgery. He couldn't help but think of Heather's parents and sisters.

His experience on Mercer Street with Gaia came back to him in full detail—the knife, the fear, the chaos. How had the world become so malignant? New York City was transforming from the eccentric but comfortable place where he'd grown up into the dangerous, angry place he'd always heard about.

"Attention, students." Principal Hickey's voice came blasting through the loudspeaker. "There will be an all-school assembly this morning directly after homeroom. Attendance is mandatory." Even the principal's solemnity sounded phony and exaggerated.

Ed wheeled slowly to homeroom, his mind ricocheting from big, appropriate thoughts about crime and death and police investigations to weird little inappropriate thoughts like whether Heather was wearing one of those hospital gowns that tied in the back, and, if so, who had undressed her. Then he felt guilty about having that second category of thoughts and tried not to have them, which took up a certain amount of mental energy in itself.

He was sitting in homeroom, trying not to have any thoughts at all, when he overheard Gaia's name mentioned. He didn't turn because he didn't want to disrupt the conversation.

"Gaia Moore saw what?" asked Becca Miller, a girl with long, supercurly hair who always sat behind him.

"She saw the guy with the knife in the park," responded Samantha something, a friend of Becca's, in a voice hushed but intoxicated with the thrill of conveying important information.

"What are you talking about?" Becca asked.

"Gaia was in the park just a few minutes before Heather got slashed, and she saw the guys who did it."

"Tell me you're kidding. How do you know this?" Becca demanded.

"Tina Lynch told Carrie she was with Brian and Melanie last night and they saw Gaia, right outside the park. Gaia told Tina she'd just seen Heather going into the park. But Gaia warned Tina and those other guys not to go into the park—that she'd just seen a guy with a knife."

Ed's mind was spinning with the number of names and personal pronouns, but also with the ramifications of what he was hearing. Gaia was involved. Of course she was. If trouble was magnetic north, then Gaia's head was a huge chunk of iron. In the short time Ed had known her, he'd almost gotten killed, watched three thugs get demolished, witnessed two catfights, seen one slashing victim's family crying on the news, and now learned his ex-girlfriend was in a coma.

Of course Gaia was there. How could it be otherwise?

But what had she done, exactly?

He couldn't trust these girls or really anybody but Gaia to tell him what had happened. And Gaia would give him the unvarnished truth. He and Gaia were alike in that way. They both took special satisfaction in telling you the one true thing you really, really didn't want to hear.

A SMELLY MONSTER

Gaia hadn't paid much attention to all the whispering at first. She had learned to be good at ignoring it. In her experience whispering either:

1. Didn't include her
   or
2. Was about her.

And in neither case could she take part.

So it wasn't until the assembly that she heard the news.

"As many of you know, a tragedy befell our school community last night," Principal Hickey intoned to the enormous, totally silent all-school assembly. Gaia should have known right then that something was seriously wrong by the simple fact that people were actually listening to the guy. "Heather Gannis was slashed in Washington Square Park last night. She lost a great deal of blood before she was discovered by friends and fellow students. She is in critical condition at St. Vincent's Hospital. I know you all join me in sending Heather and her family our . . ."

He kept talking, of course, but Gaia didn't hear. An ugly, evil creature with smelly fur and sharp fangs was gnawing on her intestines, and that was hard to ignore.

Her thoughts from the previous night returned to her word for word.

Let the stupid girl get slashed. If anybody deserved it, Heather did.

But I didn't mean that, a small, panicky voice inside Gaia claimed pitifully. I meant to warn her. I was going to, but—

Shut up! Gaia screamed at her own mind. If she'd had a tire iron, she would have clubbed herself with it. She'd heard too many excuses in her life. She couldn't stomach them, especially not from herself.

The principal was droning on about safety precautions now, and the attention he'd commanded was lost. Kids were talking, whispering.

Gaia realized when she looked up that hundreds of eyes were bouncing around and landing on her again and again. What could she expect? She had known exactly what Heather was walking into, and at least three other people in this very auditorium knew that she knew. She could have saved Heather, and she didn't. She let a petty, stupid conflict, probably based more on her own jealousy than anything else, destroy another person's life.

The fanged creature devoured several more feet of intestine and moved on to the lining of her stomach.

Everybody was standing up and milling around. Gaia guessed that the assembly was over. Numbly she got to her feet and let herself be moved along by the crowd. Just beyond the doors, in the lobby of the auditorium, the puffy, tear-stained face of Tina what's-her-name bobbed into view.

Gaia stopped.

If only shame were part of fear. If only self-loathing were part of fear.

If Gaia were a better person, she would have offered some comforting words. She didn't. She remained the person she was.

"What *happened* last night?" Tina asked her in a voice tinged with hysteria. "What was Heather *thinking* going in there alone? Did you talk to her? Did you tell her what you'd seen in the park?"

Gaia realized Tina wasn't judging her. Not yet. She was inviting Gaia to commiserate, to take part in the why-oh-why-oh-why that churned her restless mind. She wanted to think the best of Gaia.

Other people had gathered. Some were comforting, others being comforted. Several friends clutched Tina supportively.

"I—I didn't," Gaia said stiffly. "I didn't warn her."

Tina's face took a few moments to register this. "What do you mean?"

Gaia had to remind herself to breathe. "I mean I didn't tell Heather about the guy with the knife."

"Why not? Why didn't you?" Tina's shiny doe eyes turned into slitted bat eyes.

The crowd of people readied their looks of horror but held off, waiting for an explanation.

A part of Gaia wanted to describe to all these eager

sets of ears how Heather told her off, called her names, but she knew it would sound just like the lame excuse it was. She deserved the blame for this. She would take it without flinching. "I just didn't."

Tina was crying now. "God, what's the matter with you? You warned us but not her? Do you hate Heather so much that you wanted her to get killed?"

Amid the loathing, judging faces, Gaia suddenly spied blue. Dark blue uniforms, dark blue hats. The fragments resolved into two policemen.

Could you actually get arrested for failing to warn someone? Gaia wondered irrationally. The faces parted to let the police come through. The hum of voices in the lobby grew to a roar.

"Are you Gaia Moore?" one of them, a tall black man, asked.

"Yes," she answered. Were they going to handcuff her right here, in front of the entire student body?

"Would you please come with us to the precinct? We have some questions to ask you."

The man asked it like a real question, not a rhetorical one. He waited for her answer; he didn't slap on any handcuffs.

"Yes," she said. "Of course." And she followed them through the exit, distinctly aware of the huge cloud of hate behind her.

That was one plus about profound self-loathing. Nobody could hate you worse than you hated yourself.

DIFFERENT BUT THE SAME

"And at approximately what hour did you see Heather Gannis approaching the park from the west side?"

Gaia couldn't quite pull her eyes from that vague middle distance to focus them on the detective sitting across from her.

"About seven forty-five, I guess."

"You guess?"

"I wasn't wearing a watch at the time. I'd dropped off a friend at First Avenue and Fourth Street at seven-thirty and then walked directly to the park on my way home. I figure it would take roughly fifteen minutes to walk from First and Fourth to Washington Square West," Gaia replied. She was on autoanswer. It felt to her that she'd already fielded at least a hundred thousand questions, and they hadn't even gotten to the meaty part.

"Fine. And what exactly happened when you saw Heather?" the detective asked. Detective Anderson was his name. He was in his forties probably, with thinning medium-brown hair, slightly pocked skin, and pale eyes. He looked just as tired and harassed as detectives always looked on those realistic cop shows.

Gaia let out her breath slowly. Did he really want the catty details? "I—um—sort of stopped her, and she—uh—"

Gaia broke off and glanced at the detective. "See, Heather and I weren't exactly on friendly terms. A few days ago I spilled hot coffee on her, and since then—"

"Since then?" he prompted.

"We've had, uh, words, you could say," Gaia explained.

"I see." The detective nodded. "So you disliked Heather, did you?"

"I was told she is still alive."

"Excuse me. I'm sorry. Yes." Detective Anderson looked genuinely awkward. "You dislike Heather," he amended.

"That's a tough thing to say about a girl in a coma, sir," Gaia pointed out.

"Right. Yes. Okay." He sighed and shifted in his chair. "But as of yesterday evening, you and Heather were enemies?"

"Am I a suspect in this case?" Gaia asked, staring him dead in the eye.

He cleared his throat and shifted again. He moved his mouth a few times before any sounds came out. "Uh, no. You're not."

"Okay." She settled back in her chair. She knew she wasn't a suspect, because she knew they'd assembled a police lineup, because she'd overheard it being discussed when Detective Anderson was hunting around for cream for his coffee. She knew he was trying to pretend like she was so he could manipulate and intimidate her more easily.

"So, back to the story," she said, chilly but helpful.

"Heather told me to leave her alone, and I did. Less than a minute after walking past her, I ran into her friends—Tina and two other people whose names I don't know. I think you know the story from there. After that I walked home. You have all that information already."

Detective Anderson looked even more harassed and tired. "Right. Now am I to understand that you did not warn Heather as to what you'd just seen moments before in the park?"

"No, sir."

"But you did warn the three people you saw subsequently?"

"Yes, sir."

He waited for an explanation that didn't come. After a while he stood up. "All right, Gaia, that's it for the moment. Would you come with me? I'd like you to look at a lineup."

She followed him through the precinct to the viewing room, listening to directions, warnings, assurances associated with a lineup. She felt floaty and distant as she took in the hodgepodge of beat-up office furniture, papers, files, boards, maps, clippings, notices, charts, the pathetic set of twigs on a windowsill that had probably been a live plant a decade or two ago.

It was so different in particulars, but so generally the same as the precinct where she'd spent the night as a twelve-year-old in San Rafael, California, after her mother was murdered, when they couldn't figure out anyplace else to put her.

HER FAULT

"Gaia! Gaia! Are you okay?"

It was Ed, waiting outside the police station for her, and she wasn't happy to see him. Who ever said misery loved company? Her misery did not love company. Her misery loved to be alone. Her misery threatened to bludgeon company.

"I'm fine." She hardly stopped. Another funny thing about having friends was that they expected things of you. They made you want to not be a terrible, awful, execrable person. They made you feel even worse when you were one. It was a lot easier not to have any friends.

"Gaia, wait. What's going on?" He rolled along after her.

She was tempted to find a quick set of stairs to ascend. Jesus, she really was an awful person.

"Haven't you heard from the angry hordes at school? I put Heather in the hospital. Didn't they tell you?"

"They—I—I mean—," Ed stammered.

"Come on, Ed. They did, didn't they?"

"But Gaia, you know it's not true," Ed argued, breathless from rushing to keep up with her. "You are not responsible for Heather. Even if you had warned her to stay away from the park, she would have cut through, anyway. She wouldn't have listened to you. There's nothing you could have done."

Gaia made a sharp turn onto West Fourth. Ed's tires practically left skid marks.

"Gaia, are you even listening?" Ed demanded.

She didn't bother to stop at the light on Seventh Avenue.

"Gaia! Come on!"

She practically sprinted all the way down Perry Street and pulled up short in front of George and Ella's house.

"Listen to me. What happened to Heather was scary and horrible, but it was not your fault."

Gaia walked up all fifteen steps of the front stoop before she turned around to look at him. "Ed Fargo. Thank you for trying beyond all possible reason to be my friend," she said quietly. "But it was my fault."

She turned her key in the door, went inside the house, and shut the door firmly behind her. She went up three flights of stairs with the grace of a robot. Once in her room she walked straight to the vintage turntable she'd recently hauled from the garbage and set up on the mantel. She reached behind the pile of records she kept in the nonfunctional fireplace to the LP in the very back.

She'd long ago memorized every centimeter of the faded, brittle record cover, memorized every word. She took out the record gingerly and set it on the player. She didn't need to study the grooves to know exactly where to set the needle.

The music filled the room, loud enough to destroy the

speakers, to infuriate Ella, to explode her own head.

It was the second movement of the Sibelius violin concerto, the darkest, saddest piece of music on the planet. It was her mother's favorite—her weird, beautiful Eastern European mother with the embarrassing accent. Her mother knew all of Tchaikovsky, Rachmaninoff, Sibelius, and Prokofiev, and nothing of Nirvana or any music Gaia held to be important at the time. She'd been so annoyed at her mother for that.

But now the soaring, wailing violin touched Gaia's cracked heart, and she did something she only allowed herself once or twice a year.

She lay down on the floor and cried.

THE
OPPOSITE
OF LOVE

HE NEEDED TO PULL HIMSELF OUT OF THIS
TRANCE, TO GET A LITTLE DISTANCE.

NOT THINKING OF AN
ELEPHANT

Sam sat in the waiting room of the intensive care unit, rhythmically whacking his heel against the foot of the couch. It was just like hospital waiting rooms were supposed to be: genuine Naugahyde couch and chairs, plastic side tables displaying magazines you wouldn't have wanted to read in the late nineties when they came out. A mounted television showed some wretched soap opera that might as well have been filmed and closed-captioned in that very hospital.

He hadn't seen Heather since last night, and he felt nervous. Finding her in the park eighteen hours before, white as the moon in a dark puddle of blood, was such a potent jolt to his system, he was still breathing, moving, thinking too fast.

God, she'd looked so fragile and broken. He'd thought she was dead until he detected the faintest, slowest flutter of a pulse in her wrist. After that everything exploded into sound and motion. Screaming ambulance sirens, police sirens, people hurrying every which way.

He hadn't slept since, of course, so his senses were oddly distorted—colors were too bright, noises too shrill, smells too acrid. Time was disjointed. For example, hadn't it been at least two hours since Heather's parents had disappeared with a doctor into Heather's room, telling him they would be out in ten minutes?

What little peace he had would be shattered when Heather's sisters arrived from their colleges and Heather's friends stormed the place the moment school let out. A bunch of those friends had already camped out in the waiting room through their lunch period, spewing millions and trillions of words.

But Sam would suffer them. He would deprive himself of food and drink and sleep and continue to torture himself with this ridiculous soap opera as punishment, laughably slight though it was.

What was the punishment for? For contemplating a breakup with Heather not half an hour before she nearly bled to death. For sitting here, his skin intact as a newborn's, while Heather lay slashed in a coma. For thinking nonstop of *that girl*.

Mistake. Big mistake. Better not to think of thinking about her because then suddenly he was thinking of her. No. Stop. Heel. New thought.

New thought . . . He dragged his mind back to an absorbing topic, one he could worry and fiddle with obsessively, like a bloody hangnail. What was that girl's name? The one Tina and Co. had blathered on about for a solid hour? Maia. No. What was it? Gaia? Something like that. How he hated her. Loathed and despised her. What kind of person would

let an innocent girl walk straight into a situation they knew
was deadly? How petty and small and cowardly this girl
Gaia must be.

Of course, the knife-wielding devil who attacked
Heather deserved the real blame. But he was beyond hating.
He was beyond imagining. Gaia, on the other hand, was a
classmate. She was one of them.

Ah. This was good. Righteous indignation got him back
on course every time. If he could just keep this focus, keep
railing loyally against Gaia, he wouldn't have to think for
minutes at a stretch of *that girl*.

THE BOYFRIEND

Gaia dreaded this worse than she would dread a group hug
with Ella and George or thirty-three simultaneous root
canals or even trying out for the cheerleading squad. But she
would make herself do it. She would drag herself right up to
the eighth floor of this hospital, past the bevy of Heather's
friends who detested her, the desperate parents who were

too broken up to care about her, the steadfast, adoring boy-friend who'd maybe take a nanosecond from his grieving to curse her name. It was the right thing for Gaia to do. The fact that she dreaded it so much only made it seem more necessary.

Gaia emerged from the elevator and hesitated in front of the nurses' station.

"You're a friend of Heather Gannis?" the orange-haired nurse asked without even looking up from her computer.

"I—"

"Waiting room on your left," the nurse said, still not looking up.

Gaia loitered another moment, feeling wrong about going to the waiting room under false pretenses. But what was she going to do, pour out her heart to the overburdened nurse? Like she'd care that Gaia dumped coffee on Heather or that Heather bitched her out at a party?

"Okay," Gaia said, as meekly as she'd ever said anything. "Thanks."

Walk. Walk. Walk, she ordered herself.

Okay, there they were, spilling out into the hallway. The Friends. When they saw her, would they make a scene right there in the waiting room? Throw stones? Burn her at the stake?

The first murderous glance came from Tina herself. Many others followed as Gaia attempted to slip past the too full room. The murmur of hushed conversation stopped.

Tina gaped at her but was apparently so appalled, she couldn't speak. Instead the good-looking boy who'd been with Tina last night, the old suede-jacketed star of Gaia's cafe fantasy, stepped in.

"Why are you here?" he demanded.

Why was she here? That was a good question.

Because it was the last place on earth she wanted to be?

Because self-flagellation was the only thing that felt right?

Gaia's real answer made her sound like a kiss-ass, so she didn't want to say it out loud: She was here because she wanted and needed to apologize to Heather, even if Heather couldn't hear. Gaia didn't want to pander to the crowd, and she wasn't looking for social resurrection. She was perfectly happy being a pariah. That was as comfortable to her as a pair of old shoes.

So, as often happened, she said nothing. She continued on her way down the hall without a particular plan in mind.

The second room on the right, through a wide-open doorway, was Heather's. Gaia drew in a sharp breath and quickly averted her eyes. She hadn't meant to go right there exactly. She hadn't imagined how Heather would look, frail as a bird, hooked up by scores of tubes to machines that dripped and machines that bleeped, shorn of the self-consciously cool clothing and the beauty that made it so much easier for Gaia to ridicule her. Gaia suddenly felt like throwing up.

There was something much, much worse than your enemy receiving praise, fame, and riches and living happily ever after with an exceptionally handsome guy: your enemy getting slashed in the park after you hoped it would happen.

Her eyes swept into the room again. There, as expected, she saw the dark head of The Boyfriend, bowed over Heather's prone, still body. Maybe he was crying.

Oh, shit. Shit. Shit. Gaia had no right to be there. What had she been thinking?

It was some selfish hope for exoneration that brought her, nothing nobler than that. Now what? She'd walk herself to the end of the hall. She'd wait a minute or two. She'd walk herself back out to the reception area, maybe find a waiting room on another floor, keep her own private vigil for a few hours—or days, if necessary—until things settled down. And then, as politely as possible, she'd apologize to Heather's parents and ask if she might have permission to apologize to Heather. They'd think she was a complete freak, but that hardly mattered, did it?

Gaia trudged to the end of the hall. On her way back she cast one last look in Heather's room. Quiet though she was, The Boyfriend chose that very moment to look up.

Gaia's eyes stuck to his, and she couldn't move them.

Her body reacted before her mind. Her head swam. The Coke she'd had for lunch climbed up her esophagus. All oxygen departed her lungs.

It was him. He was it.

It, him, he was Heather's boyfriend.

The evil, ugly monster with the matted, stinking hair and the razor-blade fangs moved up from her stomach and took a chomp at her heart.

Gaia staggered toward the elevator so he wouldn't see her when her knees gave out.

A SALTED SLUG

In retrospect, it would have been so much better if Sam had stayed where he was.

Instead, for no good reason, he allowed his unfaithful legs to carry him from Heather's side, where he belonged, down the hall and after *the girl*.

It was impossible for him to explain why. He didn't decide to do it. His body was just suddenly up and moving. It was like when the doctor thwacked your knee. You didn't *decide* to kick your foot.

"Wait," he said as she fled from him just as she had a few days before.

Heather's sisters and a crowd of friends blocked the

hallway, impeding the girl's progress. She dodged and wove like a running back facing a defensive line.

"Leaving already, Gaia?" he overheard Carrie Longman say in an unmistakably hostile voice.

The girl broke through the line and made for the elevator bank. Sam followed her there along with a lot of whispers and nasty looks. It honestly did not occur to him that *the girl* was the girl Carrie had been addressing until he was facing her, just two feet away from her, in front of the elevators.

His thoughts were covered in molasses. They moved achingly slowly with big gaps between them.

The girl Carrie had been addressing was called Gaia. . . .

This girl he was now gaping at was called Gaia. . . .

This girl was *the girl* . . .

The girl was Gaia . . .

Gaia was the one who had . . .

"Y-You're Gaia," he said to her.

She was silent for a long time, just staring. Her eyes were too much for him.

"You're The Boyfriend," she said slowly.

It sounded like a felony, like an atrocity, the way she said it.

"Sam. My name is Sam."

"Oh." Her face was strangely open, her eyes a whirlpool.

He was scared to let himself read them this time. He was scared of getting sucked in.

"I—you—w-w-we—," he stammered. What exactly did he want to say?

He could see from the panel above the nearest elevator that it was climbing toward them. 3 . . . 4 . . . 5 . . .

"You're the Gaia who saw the guy with the knife in the park last night," he blurted out in a disorganized rush. "You're the one who didn't warn her."

The girl's face was a little too white for a person with a beating heart. Her hands trembled at her sides. She nodded.

"W-Why? I don't understand. Do you dislike her that much?"

"I—I guess I do."

Silence. 6 . . . 7 . . .

He needed to pull himself out of this trance, to get a little distance. He needed to remember who needed defending here. He looked away from her, summoning his shield of righteous indignation. "What is wrong with you? Are you some kind of monster?" He hated the way his voice sounded.

She took so long to respond, it was punishing. Those wide, boundless eyes pinned him to his spot with a look that made him feel horrible, like a salted slug.

"You're not what I thought," she said finally.

Why should *he* feel horrible? *He* hadn't done anything wrong.

The elevator arrived on eight. The doors opened with glacial slowness.

Suddenly he hated her. It was only partly rational, partly fair. She was the source of all the problems, of Heather's condition, of the shameful, disloyal thoughts that had invaded his brain. Now in her face, in her eyes, he saw none of the tenderness or the possibilities he saw before.

"I hate you," he said, amazed as the babyish words emerged from his own mouth.

She stepped into the elevator. "I hate you, too."

He watched her face until the doors closed.

Unbidden, that stupid saying entered his mind: that one about hate not being the opposite of love.

COLD COFFEE

"Who picked CJ out of the lineup?" the older woman asked, leaning over the table that divided them, resting her chin in her palm.

Marco could see down her lavender blouse to the tops of her breasts spilling out of a white bra with lace edges. He wanted to kiss her and touch her so bad. She always wanted to talk first. That was the way most girls were, in his experience. So his mouth went one way and his mind another.

"Nobody knows for sure. Some guys think it was that blond girl—that, uh, friend of yours. A couple of them saw

her in the park last night before that other girl . . . you know."
He didn't feel like going any deeper into this particular subject. He wanted to talk about how good her shiny red hair
looked all loose like that and the dream of his she'd starred
in last night.

She crossed her legs under the table, and her knee
brushed his. "I heard on the news that the girl who was
slashed—they didn't release her name—is out of a coma and
expected to make a full recovery," she said.

"Yeah? That's good news for CJ. They'll stick him with
assault instead of murder. He never meant to hurt her so bad."

"CJ's in custody? Nobody came up with bail?" she asked.

He pressed his shin against hers. "Nah. It was like a hundred grand or something. His mother lives in Miami. She
doesn't even know about it."

"So maybe you'll need to take over in his absence?"

Marco lifted his shoulders so they looked extra big.
"Yeah, that's the plan. Tarick, you know, Marty's older
brother, wants me to, uh, take care of this old Jew foreigner
in the park, this crazy guy who sits over by the chess tables."

She nodded and sipped her coffee.

Marco looked down at his own coffee. He'd hardly
touched it. He'd only ordered it because it seemed more
mature than a Coke. The coffee was cold now, and an iridescent grease slick quivered on the top. Everything in this
diner was greasy, but the tables in back were private.

Why was she so fascinated by this stuff? Nothing seemed

to shock her or upset her. Was she a writer for a magazine or something? Even though she was older, she was so freakin' sexy, he didn't care much as long as she changed the names and all that.

"Why the old guy?" she asked.

Marco shrugged. "'Cause he's there. He's kind of a joke in the park. This loser kid who wants to be part of things—Renny is his name—he loves this old guy. Marty and them think it would be funny."

"Are you going to do it?"

Marco smiled in a way he thought was both tough and mysterious. "I'll see."

She didn't smile back. "Do you want something else?" she asked. "A Coke?"

He couldn't wait anymore. He stood and grabbed her hand. "I want to get out of here."

She remained seated. "I want to finish my coffee."

GAIA

1 poppy-seed bagel with cream cheese
1 large coffee with milk and 2 sugars
3 Wint-O-Green Life Savers

When I was twelve, my mind's eye would sometimes flash on excruciating images from the night I lost my mother. They destroyed me, but I couldn't stop. The worst thing you can do in that situation is order your mind *not* to think of something. You know, the old "don't think of an elephant" problem. So I invented these tactics for distraction.

The first line of defense was to think about kids at school. Not my friends, exactly, because I didn't have many of those, but the people I fantasized about being friends with. I'd weave these scenes filled with cute dia-logue about the fun we'd all have palling around together.

The second line of defense was imagining a boy to fall in love with. What would he look like? What kinds of things would he say to me? Would it be love at first sight, or would it take me a few minutes to overwhelm him with my charm?

If those two didn't work, I exiled my mind to listing European capitals, which my dad made me memorize when I was three.

And finally, if my mind offered absolutely no place to hide, if thinking at all was sheer torment, I would distract it by cataloging what I'd eaten the day before.

Tonight, lying on the floor of my room, the first three attempts led to:

1. Heather
2. Sam
3. Belgrade

I skipped directly to yesterday's breakfast.

THE PRETTY
ONE

SAM WAS WATCHING THE PLACE ACROSS THE PARK
WHERE GAIA'S BACK HAD BEEN MINUTES BEFORE.
"I DON'T KNOW," HE SAID ABSENTLY. "I GOT
DISTRACTED, I GUESS."

NUTS

Heather was going to be okay.

Heather was expected to make a full recovery.

Gaia was so happy, she felt like telling the man behind the sandwich counter at Balducci's.

"Roast beef?" he asked her.

"Yes," she said. "On that." She pointed to an extravagant-looking roll.

It was all over school today, all anybody was talking about. That and the part Gaia played in the catastrophe. The way the rumor mill was spinning, Gaia expected she would be charged with the slashing herself before the end of the day.

And that was, admittedly, part of the reason why it was 11:45 a.m. and Gaia was buying a sandwich rather than listening to her imbecilic math so-called teacher botch an elementary explanation of sine and cosine.

She paid for the nine-dollar sandwich and headed down Sixth Avenue, swinging the green-and-white bag. Zolov would eat like a king today. She imagined his face when she surprised him at the unusual hour.

Cutting was a serious offense, as she'd been told a few thousand times. Ooooh. She pictured the vice principal calling George at work. Or, God forbid, Ella.

She almost skidded to a stop at a pay phone at the corner of

West Eighth. She plunked in her quarter and dialed George's work number. "George Niven, please."

George's voice came on a few seconds later. "This is George Niven."

"Hi, George. it's Gaia. How's it going?"

"Just fine, Gaia. Just fine." He sounded surprised and pleased. "You sound like you're . . . uh. . . ."

"I'm actually calling from a pay phone, because I left school early, because I wasn't feeling well."

"I'm sorry to hear that." His voice was filled with such genuine concern, she felt a little bad. "Did you speak to—"

"It's nothing serious. It's . . . well, you know, it's *that* time of the month, and I get these really bad cramps sometimes." Gaia knew there was no faster way to get a man off the phone than to bring up her period.

"Right, right. Of course. Understood." She'd never heard him talk so fast.

Poor George. It was hard enough having a girl in your house, let alone one who arrived fully formed at the age of seventeen.

"So, would you just give them a call and let them know what's up?" she asked.

George was clearly so traumatized, he didn't argue. "Yes. I'll give them a call at the . . . uh, office there. You, uh, just let Ella know. She'll take care of you. There's, uh, there's no better sick nurse than Ella."

Gaia almost laughed at that one. Ella's skirts were too tight to sit at a bedside, and she probably couldn't distinguish aspirin from arsenic. God help George. Love was more than blind. It was deaf and dumb, too. It was catatonic. It was vegetative.

Sixth Avenue passed her by in a stimulating buzz. The buses, the baby strollers, the three-man Peruvian band that played on the corner, the delis overflowing with fruit and flowers, the guy selling dirt-cheap tube socks, underpants, and secondhand books from a card table set up by the curb.

The world was fresher and a lot more spacious when you were supposed to be in school. Kind of like a public pool during adult swim.

She rounded the corner of West Fourth in eager anticipation. Maybe today she would buy a bag of those sugary roasted nuts. The exquisite smell was already reaching her nostrils. Yes, today would be the day.

She breezed into the park, actually appreciating the sunshine for once. It made the place seem so different from the malicious gang nest where Heather had been slashed. She saw Zolov's hunched, familiar back and almost ran for him.

Then she stopped short. She dropped the bag and watched the silver-foil-covered sandwich roll over hexagonal gray stones. She put her hand to her heart.

He was there. The Boyfriend. Sam. Whatever.

He was sitting directly across from *her* friend, concentrating on the chessboard. How dare he? Was he trying to hustle poor old Zolov? Couldn't he see the old man had nothing to lose besides his terrible coat and his Power Ranger? Shouldn't he be in school or something?

She hoped the old man would summon up all his skill and beat the crap out of him.

The Boyfriend, Sam, whatever, looked scruffier today. The cuffs of his flannel shirt weren't buttoned, nor were they rolled up. His hair was sticking up a little in back, and his eyes looked tired. Probably from staying up all those hours worrying about Heather.

Blah. *Blah*. The thought made her sick.

Gaia grabbed the sandwich and stuffed it back in the bag. Now what? She didn't want to see him or talk to him, but she didn't want to flee like a little mouse, either.

Of course he had to look up right then. Right then, as she clutched her pathetic green-and-white bag, paralyzed with uncertainty, eyes round and startled.

Why did he have this effect on her? Why? Had she some intuitive knowledge, the day they played chess, that he was Heather's boyfriend? Did she recognize he represented the best possible way to torment herself?

She couldn't be having these alien feelings about Heather's boyfriend. It was too cruel a coincidence. Was somebody up there having a belly laugh at her expense?

Her mind flashed back to their last encounter in the hospital, and she wanted to groan out loud. She felt her cheeks turning warm.

No doubt about it. She was a femme fatale. A romantic

heroine for the ages. A heartbreaker. A female James Bond. A role model for girls everywhere.

Of the two boys Gaia had ever met in her *entire life* who could have possibly ever maybe meant something important to her (and coincidentally, the only two who had ever beaten her in chess—Stephen from around the corner being the first), she'd told them both she hated them. She was two for two.

No wonder she'd never kissed anybody. "I hate you" wasn't exactly come-hither. It wasn't a big turn-on to most guys. Not ones who belonged on this side of prison, anyway.

Maybe she could sell a book touting her romantic advice. *Gaia's Rules.* Not only should you not call the sucker back; go ahead and tell him you hate him.

And as a follow-up she could publish her popularity secrets. Okay, it was time to go somewhere else. Time to let up on the mean-yet-indifferent laser beams she was directing from her eyes.

She wheeled around, sandwich bag in hand, and walked toward the fountain. It was a beautiful, warm day. Why didn't she just go to the fountain? That was a normal thing to do.

The benches were filled with mothers of babies, nannies, college students, people who didn't have jobs. There, directly in front of her, bathed in the buttery shade of a yellow umbrella, stood the pushcart filled with nuts so sugary and delicious, the smell alone could make you hallucinate.

And she was going to buy a bag. So what if her stomach felt like it had been stapled shut?

"One bag, please," she said to the cart's proprietor as he stirred the caramelized mass. She thrust two dollars in his hand, and he gave her the warm, paper pouch filled with sticky nuts. The smell was a living thing. She put one in her mouth. She chewed. She tried another.

She kept chewing as she walked herself from the fountain to the dog run near the perimeter of the park, feeling her hopes deflate as the grease from the nuts soaked through the paper to her fingers.

Sugar-roasted nuts, as it turned out, could be added to the list that included vanilla extract and bread and meeting a guy you could fall in love with—things that smelled a lot better than they tasted.

SIX MINUTES AND A PAWN

"Checkmate."

Sam glanced up in surprise. Zolov wasn't looking at him with his usual winking smile of triumph. He was looking at him with pity.

He had lost? Already? How could that be?

Of course, he always lost to Zolov. In spite of his insanity, Zolov was a truly great player. In his day the old guy had beaten or drawn many of the greatest chess players in the world. But usually Sam and Zolov fought their way through long, dramatic battles, masterful exchanges of material. Today it was six minutes and a pawn.

"Vhat happened to you?" Zolov asked.

Sam was watching the place across the park where Gaia's back had been minutes before. "I don't know," he said absently. "I got distracted, I guess."

"By zat geerl?"

Sam couldn't breathe. He was choking. Was it possible to choke to death on your own saliva? "W-Who?"

"Za preetty vun. She's smart, too, you know."

"I—uh—I don't know who you mean."

Zolov was now smiling. "I teenk you do."

Sam almost bit his tongue in annoyance. After two years of listening to Zolov theorize about the young man who sold sodas by the fountain (World War I Polish spy called Tuber), the social worker from the homeless coalition (malevolent alien from a whole other solar system), the old man picked quite a moment to be perceptive.

"I gotta go," Sam said, standing. "Good game," he lied, handing Zolov a five. "I'll see you Thursday."

"Sam?"

Sam turned around in amazement. Zolov called him "boy" and "keed" and "you," but he never called him "Sam."

"Yeah?"

"You go get zat geerl and tell heer I vant my sand-veech."

"No way," Sam muttered to himself. No way was he ever going anyplace near that kind of trouble again.

SAM

As a child, I was a disaster. I had a terrible stammer, which made me shy and pitifully awkward. My teeth pointed in every direction, and my hair was so thick, it lay in a stack on my head.

It started early. I was a maladjusted baby. You may think all babies are at least a little bit cute, but I wasn't. I didn't walk till after I was two. I don't think I learned to talk at all until I was four years old.

My stammer was triggered by everything but by nervousness most of all, and I was always nervous. It was your classic catch-22: My nervousness made me stammer, and the more I stammered, the more nervous I got. I even stammered in my thoughts.

I was badly isolated. I spent all my time either on the computer or playing chess. Or playing chess on the computer. I started playing in chess tournaments when I was about six. Even among chess geeks I was considered untouchable. Stop by a chess tournament sometime, and you will see how truly scary that is.

I have an older brother to remind me of all this, in case I ever forget.

When I was twelve, my parents started to worry about me in earnest. I suspect they were embarrassed to take me anyplace. I had a crash course in speech therapy. Several, to be honest. A vengeful orthodontist installed an aircraft carrier worth of metal in my mouth. My mom dragged me to a haircutter who cost about a thousand dollars. She outfitted me at the Gap.

By the time I returned to school for seventh grade, I was unrecognizable. I actually considered changing my name and just starting from scratch.

So I guess you could say life as I know it began when I was twelve. I was born that first day of junior high.

I'm fine now. Even good, according to a lot of people. I know how to dress. I know how to speak. And even so, I'm still good at chess.

I masquerade as one of the blessed. One of the normal, effortless joiners who believe, without thinking about it too deeply, that the world exists for people like us. It's a lie, of course. I come, from the other side. I know what it's like over there.

There are still vestiges of dorkdom in me, (See my use of the word *vestiges*, for example.) They pop up all the time. They remind me that if I were born in another age, say, prehistory—before braces and speech therapy—I would be the dorkiest caveman who ever lived. And the person I was probably meant to be.

MELTING AWAY

HER GAZE SWEPT OVER SAM'S STILL BODY, AND
SHE HAD AN ALMOST OVERWHELMING NEED TO
GO TO HIM, TO KNEEL OVER HIM AND MAKE SURE
HE WAS BREATHING.

FIRST AND SECOND
PUNCHES

She wasn't *that* pretty. Okay, she was that pretty. But not pretty like Heather—the kind of pretty that everybody noticed right away. Gaia's face, devoid of makeup or any expression meant to please, was unfortunately more mesmerizing to Sam every time he saw it. God, and those eyes. They haunted him. He couldn't get a fix on them—one time they were the endless azure of a summer sky, another time the blue-violet of early evening, and still another the indescribable color of a typhoon.

He turned up LaGuardia. It was almost eight-thirty in the evening, and he wanted to get to the hospital to see Heather before visiting hours were up. He'd cut through the park. Just a corner of it.

But it wasn't just the way Gaia looked. Was it because she was so unbelievably good at chess? Granted, that had really thrown him. But that couldn't explain it fully, either.

He had every reason to dislike her. He *did* dislike her. No decent person would have treated Heather the way Gaia had. For a while he'd tried convincing himself that he was thinking about her so much because he disliked her, but it wasn't working anymore.

Sam was a rational person. Overly rational, if you listened to

Heather or his mother, or most of his friends. He wasn't romantic. He wasn't poetic. He wasn't nostalgic. He wasn't obsessive—until this week, anyway. What was wrong with him? What were the chances that she, Gaia, had thought about him even a minute for each hour he'd thought of her?

He was a rational person. He would figure this out, and maybe then he could make it go away, he assured himself as he glanced toward the chess tables, squinting through the darkness to see that none of the few shadowy figures was hers.

He didn't see her, but he did see something strange. He moved closer.

He first recognized the hunched shape of Zolov swaying to get to his feet. Another figure was hovering, bearing down on the old man. He heard a groan, first quiet, then it grew loud and terrifying. Sam was running before he was able to process what was happening.

"Zolov!" he shouted.

The old man was waving his arms, trying to defend himself from the attack. He shouted hoarsely in a language Sam didn't understand.

It was a young man, Sam realized as he raced toward them, and he had a razor blade.

"Get away from him!" Sam shouted.

The young man turned his head and locked eyes with Sam for a millionth of a second. He was young, dark haired, intense, pumped up on adrenaline or something else. Sam hated him. What kind of monster would attack a fragile, crazy old man? Sam watched in horror as he threw Zolov to the ground.

Zolov cried out. Sam saw blood on the old man's face, flooding the crags and wrinkles. His heart was seized with panic. He threw himself at the attacker and shoved him as hard as he could. Thoughts were only fragments moving through his mind at uneven speeds. The attacker lost his balance, but only for a moment. He steadied himself and came at Sam.

There was a fist, really big. Sam heard an awful-sounding crack, then saw the orange insides of his eyelids. He blinked his eyes open. He was still on his feet. His cheekbone was blazing with pain. One eye was pounding, already swelling with blood.

The fist was coming again, but time was slow now. Slow enough for Sam to dodge the fist and to remember that he had never been in a fight before, that he was out of his league. He willed his hand to clench. He trained his good eye on the guy's mouth. He swung as hard as he could.

His knuckles connected to soft flesh. The guy grunted. Sam felt a surge of energy so strong, it seemed to erase his memory, to blow out his consciousness. He swung again without thinking. He caught an ear this time, hard. The guy staggered to one side, caught his balance. He didn't come back at Sam, as Sam was expecting. Instead he stepped backward, putting several more feet between them.

"You're dead," he hissed at Sam through blubbery, swollen lips. "I'm going to kill you." And then he ran off.

Sam was almost instantly kneeling at Zolov's side. The old man was groaning softly. Sam took his shirt and gently wiped away blood so he could determine the seriousness of the wound. It appeared to be shallow and less than two inches in length but bleeding heavily. Zolov's eyes fluttered open, then shut again. His breath was short and raspy. Sam was suddenly terrified the old man's heart was going to stop. He hated to leave him, but he needed to get help.

"Zolov," he whispered, cradling his head. "You're gonna be okay, but I need to call an ambulance. I'll be back as fast as I can." He laid the gray, frizzled head on the soft ground. He stood looking at him for another moment before he took off at a sprint for the public pay phone.

ANOTHER MISTAKE

As soon as Gaia heard the noise the fine, light hair on her arms prickled and her skin was covered with bumps. She had the feeling sometimes that when she sensed danger, her vision and her hearing became almost supernaturally acute. She could almost feel her muscles feasting on oxygen, preparing for action. She knew the muffled cries and moans were Zolov's well before she actually saw him.

Zolov's attacker broke away as Gaia flew to the old man's side. She put her arms around the frail shoulders, examining the wound on his face. There was a certain amount of blood, but it was already thickening around the slash. That was a good sign. She clutched him gently. "You're going to be fine," she promised him, not wanting to leave him in his disoriented state.

But she had to because, amazingly, the demon who had attacked the old man was still within sight. Gaia ran like hell. In the darkness she saw nothing more than his silhouette.

The attacker sprinted toward the south edge of the park. Gaia flew after him, her rage undergoing nuclear fission as her feet pounded the pavement. What kind of monster would attack a helpless old man?

He was fast, but she was faster. She literally launched herself from the ground and tackled him from behind. He shouted in surprise. They rolled together across a grassy patch, limbs tangling. Strong arms circled her hips, pulling her down. They tumbled again before she managed to pin him under her. She secured his torso between her knees and shoved his head to the ground. Her hands were tightening around his neck before she looked him in the face.

She closed her eyes in disbelief. When she opened them again, her heart changed places with her stomach.

It was Sam.

She was so astounded, she let go of him, and in an instant he'd flipped her over. Now he was kneeling over her, pressing her shoulders into the ground with his hands.

"*Gaia*, what do you think you're *doing*?" he bellowed at her.

She saw clearly now that one of his eyes was purple and almost swollen shut. Her mind was whizzing, trying to make sense of it.

"Zolov is hurt," Sam yelled only inches from her ear. "He was slashed. I need to call for help!"

Her ears rang painfully. "Y-You," she choked out. "I thought you—"

"You thought I what? I slashed him? Are you insane?" Sam's eyes—or the one that was still open, anyway—were wild with adrenaline. Her waist was gripped too tightly between his knees. He was digging the heels of his hands into her chest.

In a lightning-quick move she managed to get one hand around each of his arms and pulled them out from under him. His weight collapsed on top of her, and she quickly flipped him over again. She drove her knee into his abdomen and held him steady with her forearms. "Then who did it?" she demanded.

He stared at her with a mixture of anger and disbelief. "Some asshole who's going to get away if you don't *get the hell off me!*" He wrapped his arms around her back in a bear hug and tried to roll her again, but this time she wasn't budging.

He was holding her so tight, her face was buried in his neck. "Fine," she said as well as she could, considering her lips were pressed against his skin. "Let me go, and I'll let you go." But neither of them moved.

"Fine. You let go first," he demanded in her hair. His voice was strained by the presence of her knee in his stomach.

Gingerly, slowly, she let up the pressure from her knee.

"Whoa!" she called out as he threw her off him, fast and surprisingly hard. Her butt landed on the pavement "Ouch," she complained.

She was mad. She couldn't help herself. As soon as he was on his feet she sprang to hers and shoved him. He reeled backward a couple of steps, then leaped at her and shoved her right back.

Her eyes widened in disbelief. As soon as she caught her balance, she stormed at him. He was a lot taller than she, so she had to jump to jab her shoulder into his solar plexus.

"Uff!" he grunted. She was satisfied to see she'd nearly knocked the wind out of him. She put two hands on his stomach and pushed him to the ground.

With admirable speed he rolled toward her and hugged

her ankles, "Oh!" she shouted in surprise as he pulled her legs out from under her. She fell directly on top of him.

In anger and confusion she grabbed the first thing she could—his hair, as it turned out. He grabbed hers right back. She was lying on top of him, one arm around his neck. His legs were clasped around hers, his arm circling her waist.

Where had her great fighting prowess gone? She'd been baffled, confused, angered by this guy who wasn't extraordinarily skilled or trained. And now she'd been reduced to pulling hair?

"There he is!" a voice shouted.

From their tangle on the grass they both looked up, mute.

SHARP EDGES

"Oh, shit," Sam mumbled, still clutching Gaia as the guy who had attacked Zolov came near, flanked by two guys on each side. The guy's lips were grossly misshapen, and he looked mad enough to dismember, if not kill.

Suddenly Sam found himself holding Gaia even tighter,

but strangely, his motive had transformed. He no longer wanted to pull her limb from limb; now he felt an urgent need to protect her.

There were five of them. Count them, five. Three of them were big. Two of them looked young—in their middle teens, maybe, and not totally filled out. For a moment he buried his eyes in Gaia's soft, pale hair.

If it weren't so surreal and horrendous, he would have laughed. In the last five minutes he'd thrown the first and second punches of his life, found himself wrestling on the ground with the object of his infatuation—not only brilliant at chess but a match for Hulk Hogan. Now he was holding her in his arms and smelling her hair as he faced imminent death at the hands of five angry gang members while his ancient friend and mentor was possibly bleeding to death.

"Get off your girlfriend and stand up," the slasher demanded roughly.

Somehow it didn't seem necessary to point out that Gaia was not his girlfriend. They sorted out their limbs and both stood up. They exchanged a look, filled with things he couldn't decipher. Amazing how quickly your enemy seemed like your friend when faced with a worse enemy.

"Jesus, it's *her*," one of the guys said.

Sam looked at Gaia again. He couldn't guess what that meant. "Leave her alone," he barked at them, stepping forward. He suddenly felt like he was playing a role in a movie, portraying a character who said and did things he never would. Best to keep pretending because reality—namely five guys (and possibly one girl) who wanted to kill him—was hard to take.

"Gaia, go," he said in a low voice. "I'll be okay." Ha! Had his character really just said that? She was standing so close, he could still feel the warmth of her body. It was intoxicating—really not what he needed at the moment.

The guy, the swollen-lipped slasher, was only a few feet away now, bouncing a little on the balls of his feet. His friends had circled Sam and Gaia. Two of them wore floppy hoods, covering their shaved heads and keeping their faces in shadow. Another had a do-rag pulled low over his forehead. As he looked at them Sam was weirdly calm and disconnected. He was resigned to getting beat up. He felt more scared about what they might do to Gaia.

"Let her go," Sam said.

The guy's smile was grotesque with the swollen lip pulling in odd directions. "My bud CJ thinks she did him wrong."

One of the hooded guys came forward and grabbed Gaia by the shoulders. He dragged her several yards from Sam, pinning her arms to her sides in a bear hug.

The horror was now dawning on Sam. He felt bile rising in his throat. Anger mixed with fear to make desperation. Gaia's eyes were huge and luminous.

He went after the guy who held her. Fast, without letting himself think too much, he hauled off and punched the guy, catching his jawbone so hard, his knuckles blazed. Gaia slipped quickly out of the guy's grip.

Get away, he urged her silently. Run away and get—

He'd grabbed her waist and was about to physically shove her when a slamming blow to the back of his head shattered his mind. He spun around and got a sharp kick in the stomach. He was lying on the ground now, disoriented by the number of arms and feet and faces spinning against a sapphire sky. A kick landed on his chest and took his breath away.

He saw Gaia's face over him, glowing white like an angel's. Broken thoughts and feelings lay in pieces, with edges sharp enough to cut. He reached for her. He wanted to tell her something, but he couldn't fit the aching, full-hearted feelings into words. The last thing he saw from the corner of his eye was a Timberland coming at the side of his head. After that, thankfully, he saw and felt nothing.

SLEEPING BEAUTY

Gaia wasn't afraid. She was never afraid. But she felt the abstract terror of a world without Sam, without the idea or the possibility of Sam, and she didn't want to live there. It felt so dark and arid that it would surely dry up all of her senses and parch her last blossom of hope.

Her rage exploded, less controlled, more intense than ever before. The five of them became an indistinguishable mass to her, without human features. She took them on as one multilimbed creature. Her adrenaline carried her, so she didn't have to think or count or predict.

She took one of them out with her fist. Clean, just like that. Another one required a combination of kicks to finish him off. In the process she took a sharp jab in the ribs and another guy's fist caught her in the forehead as she tried to duck. She could feel the blood gathering at the wound. The red drips were a nuisance in her eyes, but she was too far gone to feel pain.

Two of the guys bobbed in her peripheral vision. The third she had head-on in her sights. She planted a kick in that vulnerable place in his neck just as another one slammed her from the side. Another down, she registered as she tried to find her balance. Then came another slam from the side. The blood stung her eyes and tinctured her mouth with its coppery flavor. Head wounds bled too much. It was a shame. She might not have enough time.

Two weaving heads, eight thrashing limbs. It was an ugly but simpler creature that remained.

Her gaze swept over Sam's still body, and she had an almost overwhelming need to go to him, to kneel over him and make sure he was breathing.

Bam! A blow to her stomach sent her sprawling on the ground. *Focus, Gaia,* she urged herself. She had to focus as hard as she possibly could to get them through this. Loss of blood made her hazy and faint.

Another guy came rushing toward her at an angle she could use. She caught his momentum and threw him over her head. He rolled twice. It gave her enough time to get back to her feet. But just as she did the other one smashed her from behind and sent her back to the pavement. As she raised her head, she saw a pale, scared face peering from a stand of trees. She knew the face. He took a few steps forward.

"Renny, you little shit, get over here!" the bigger of the guys bellowed.

Renny was frozen, except for his face, which quivered like a squirrel's.

Suddenly Gaia felt her arms wrenched roughly behind her back. The two of them were holding her. She tried to jab her way free with her elbow, but she couldn't move it.

"Come on, little boy, here's your big chance!" the other guy called.

Gaia didn't feel like writhing to get out of their grip. It was a waste of time. The blood was leaving her head and making her feel tired. She wished she could just pass out and be done with it.

"Renny! Step up, man. You in or out?"

Renny took another step forward. He looked terrified at the sight of Gaia, no doubt something right out of a horror movie with all that blood on her face and shirt.

Suddenly Gaia saw the dull glint of steel. She thought she was imagining it at first. But even the idea was enough to clear her foggy head.

Yes, it was real. She could see it clearly now. The fat-lipped guy was pushing a gun, a .38-caliber pistol, into Renny's hand. Where had it come from? Why hadn't she been paying better attention? "Finish her off, Renny, Do it now!"

Gaia's adrenaline level notched up. Her body was on full alert, but her mind had entered that dreamlike state, wondering numbly, philosophically, whether this was the end of her life. There were few physical brawls she couldn't find her way out of, but a gun changed everything. It empowered the cowardly and rendered skill, bravery, and character useless. That was why Gaia, though she was trained to be an exceptional markswoman, never used one. She'd rather lose on her terms than win on those. Now the gun was in Renny's hand. Shaky, but pointing directly at her. He wasn't looking anywhere near her eyes.

Oh, this was hard to take. Was little Renny, her favorite chess whiz, really going to sink a bullet into her? It seemed like a very bad life where that would happen. If he was going to, she hoped he would get on with it because she didn't feel like sticking around much longer to watch.

Renny looked like he was going to puke. His eyes were glazing over, and his skin was the color of iceberg lettuce. He came up so close, she could hear his breath. She was staring down the barrel of the gun. She pulled her eyes back to Renny's.

Look at me, she demanded of him silently. Look at me! *Look at me!* If he was going to do this, let him do it for real. Let him know the full meaning of popping that trigger.

Don't be a coward, Renny. Look at me!

At last he did. His eyes lighted on hers. He hesitated only a moment. Then he turned and ran like hell. Gaia heard the gun clattering on the pavement.

Good boy, Renny, she told him silently as he sprinted for the streetlights.

"Freakin' coward," one of the guys muttered.

It gave Gaia the burst she needed. She slammed her heel as hard as she could into one guy's shin. When he let her go to clutch his leg, she wrenched herself free from the other guy and followed up with a searing blow to the side of the injured guy's head. Then another rapid jab to his abdomen. He crumpled, gasping for breath.

She lunged for the gun, grabbing it from the ground.

Without a pause she hauled off and threw it. It traced a high arc through the sky. She didn't have time to watch where it landed.

She faced the last one now. He was familiar to her from another time, but her head was too blurry to cobble together a memory. His lips were swollen, and his jacket was speckled with blood, probably hers. Gray spots grew and multiplied, clouding her vision. She heard the punch to her shoulder before she felt it. She stepped back and shook her head in the hope of clearing it. She came forward and cracked her fist across his nose. His fist landed hard on her cheekbone. She reeled back, losing her footing, almost falling directly onto Sam.

On your feet, girl, she begged herself. But then she heard something. It was faint but approaching fast and sounded to her more beautiful than a Mozart symphony. The guy heard it, too. He stopped. Listened. He gave her a last look before he ran.

Bless you, Renny, she thought as she fell back against Sam, listening to the siren coming near.

She turned as gingerly as she could. She put her hand on Sam's chest. He was breathing. He definitely was. She put her hand gently on his cheek, then skimmed her fingers over his battered eye. She smoothed his hair back from his beautiful forehead. She hadn't touched another human being like this in almost five years. Transfixed, she ran her trembling hand from the cool softness of his upper cheek to the masculine stubble of his chin. His perfect skin was broken in several places. What had she done to him?

And almost more disturbing, what had he done to her?

Tears spilled from her eyes and mixed with the blood drying on her face. A drop of the pink moisture landed on his forehead. And another. It blended with the beads of sweat on his brow.

She felt like she was entering a trance as she lowered her face toward his. She touched her lips against his with exquisite gentleness, slowly deepening the kiss as she surrendered her heart.

She heard voices coming near. She lifted her head. Sam's eyes fluttered open and then closed again.

She could die now. She laid her head on his chest and melted away.

TO: L

FROM: ELJ

DATE: October 2

FILE: 776244

SUBJECT: Gaia Moore

LAST SEEN: Washington Square Park, New York City, 8:37 p.m.

UPDATE: Subject hospitalized after prolonged fight with several gang members and a man identified as Sam Moon, age 20, sophomore at NYU. Three gang members arrested at the scene, two others fled. Old man known as Zolov was taken to the hospital and treated for a surface wound to the face. Subject received surface wound to the head, resulting in considerable loss of blood. Multiple contusions. Expected discharge 10/3.

TO: ELJ
FROM: L
DATE: October 2
FILE: 776244
SUBJECT: Gaia Moore

Unacceptable. Subject was not to be injured *under any circumstances*. Contact me immediately for new placement.

DANGEROUS HOPE

WHEN HE WAS NEAR HER, HIS OWN MIND
BETRAYED HIM. THE SMARTEST THING HE COULD
DO WAS STAY AWAY FROM HER PERMANENTLY.

BOY FLOWERS

"It's so trendy, almost bleeding to death. All the cool girls are doing it."

Gaia didn't open her eyes. Instead she considered the voice, felt the calloused hand wrapped around hers. She meant to smile, but it came out wobbly. "Hi, Ed," she said.

When she opened her eyes she saw a small bundle of orange carnations perched in a Snapple bottle on the bedside table. "Those are such boy flowers," she noted in a weak, slightlty raspy voice.

"What do you mean?"

"Only a boy would buy dyed carnations," she explained. "Girls buy less obvious stuff, like tulips and irises."

"Are you saying you don't like them?"

"No, I do like them. I accept that you are a boy. I'm happy that you are a boy."

Ed looked happy that he was a boy, too.

"So who did you beat up this time?" he asked.

"That sounded like a question," she said.

"Oh, yeah. This is like reverse *Jeopardy*. Um . . . let's see . . . You beat up ten guys, each four times your size, and one poor bastard got in a lucky punch."

She nodded. "Pretty much. Only multiply the equation by one-half."

171

"Only five guys." He shook his head. "You're losing your edge."

Gaia studied his face thoughtfully. "I guess you could say it was six guys—only one was kind of a mistake."

"A mistake."

"I got in a fight by accident with Sam—Heather's boyfriend."

"Wow, you really do get around."

"I didn't mean to. I thought he'd slashed Zolov, the old guy who plays chess in the park. But it turned out Sam was only trying to help."

"I see. But you discovered that *after* you knocked his head off." He made an obvious effort not to let the end of his sentence bend into a question.

"Sort of," she admitted.

"Mmmm. Maybe you'll find an excuse to beat up Heather's parents next."

"Ha-ha-ha."

Gaia closed her eyes. Her right cheekbone was throbbing, the cut on her forehead stung, and her stomach muscles ached. She was suddenly too tired to think.

"Hey, Ed," she finally said.

"Yup."

"Thank you for trying to be my friend."

"Am I succeeding? Uh . . . I mean . . . " He cleared his throat. "I am succeeding." He said it in a deep, smooth voice, like a news anchor.

She laughed. "Annoyingly well."

He squeezed her hand. "I'm glad."

She moved her toes under the stiff sheets. "Is Heather still in the hospital?" she asked.

Ed nodded. "Two doors down."

"You're joking."

"No, they moved her out of the ICU. She's going home tomorrow, just like you. Maybe you two can have a joint party."

Gaia sighed. "I still need to apologize to her."

"I don't see why."

"For almost getting her killed," Gaia said.

"But that wasn't your fault."

"Yes, it was."

"It wasn't."

"Was."

"Wasn't."

"Was."

"Wasn't."

"Was."

Ed let out his breath in frustration. "Gaia."

"What?"

"You have got to get over yourself."

"What do you mean?"

"Not everything bad that happens has to be about you."

For no reason that she could understand, tears flooded Gaia's eyes. Something big grew in her throat that prevented her from swallowing. Ed was getting close to a place that hurt, and she wanted him to go away. She tipped back her head so the tears wouldn't spill over her bottom lids. Thank the Lord for water cohesion.

Ed watched her carefully. His expression was gentle but serious. "You're tough as hell, Gaia, but you're not a god. You're made of the same stuff as the rest of us."

"Ed?" she asked in a thick voice. "Would you leave now? I think I can only handle having a friend in five-minute bursts."

REMEMBER HEATHER

Zolov was in room 502. Heather was now in room 724, and Gaia was in room 728. Sam had been released from the emergency room last night He had slept—or at least lain—in his own bed most of last night. Today he made his rotations like a physician. Like a disoriented, exhausted, overwrought, inept physician who hadn't actually gone to medical school.

He had no idea what happened last night. It was a complete mystery why he wasn't dead and who'd fought off the gang. One of the policemen thought it was Renny, the kid who'd called 911, but that didn't make much sense. One of the paramedics jokingly suggested it was Superman.

Sam had this strange, hazy memory of Gaia . . . but no. That was obviously a fitful hallucination—a product of his own deranged fantasy life.

Zolov's slashing wound was minor, but he was so old, the doctor on call wanted to observe him for another twenty-four hours. Zolov seemed to Sam in happy spirits and was very fond of the hospital food. He'd already discovered an orderly who loved to play chess.

Heather lay in the bed only a foot away from him, almost good as new and being released the following afternoon.

Gaia, he hadn't actually spoken to. He'd only prowled around the door to her room like a cat burglar, wanting to catch a glimpse of her but feeling too weird to actually enter.

"So Carrie told me that Miles and them are all coming over tomorrow night. It was supposed to be a surprise, but . . . you know."

Sam didn't know, but he nodded, anyway. Heather had been chatting gaily at him for almost an hour. She was propped up in her bed, surrounded by at least a billion flowers, wearing her own pink linen robe. The bouquet he'd carefully chosen was hidden behind two veritable towers of greenery and a gargantuan basket of fruit. Nurses and doctors and scores and scores of visitors slipped in and out, attending to her as if she were a reigning queen. Her face was flushed and lovely.

"And you'll be there, right?"

Sam glanced up. He'd forgotten to listen to the first part of the question. He nodded again.

"Great. I mean, my mom is going to, like, shit if I'm not in bed by ten. But it will be fun, anyway."

Heather didn't know Gaia was just down the hall. She'd accepted his explanation for his swollen purple eye with a minimum of questions. She'd cooed about how brave he was and how he'd avenged her, which wasn't true, of course, but whatever.

". . . Don't you think?" She was looking at him expectantly after a long soliloquy on something or other.

Sam nodded, grateful Heather only asked yes or no questions and rhetorical ones at that.

"I figure we can just order more if we run out," Heather continued.

How had Heather managed to turn a hospital stay into such a social whirlwind? he wondered as two more random friends waved at her from the doorway. "We'll come back," one of them whispered loudly in a we're-cool-to-the-fact-that-your-boyfriend-is-here kind of way.

"Right," he said absently.

He was thinking about whether or not the door to room 728 would be fully open and what he might say if he did venture into room 728. And then he felt ashamed. What kind of asshole obsessed about a troubling near stranger when his girlfriend was in the hospital?

He was considering this when Heather's face changed distinctly. He turned to see why. He clamped his jaw down so hard, he nearly crushed his back teeth.

"Um, hello?" It was Gaia hovering at the door. Her face was tentative. He'd never seen her hair down before. It was a pale, beautiful yellow, and there was lots of it—it fell below her shoulders. Her few freckles stood out in the fluorescent light.

Heather's expression turned from surprised to pinched and angry. "What are you doing here?"

"I—I—um, actually spent the night down the hall because—"

Heather shook her head in disbelief. "I swear to God, it's like you're stalking me."

Gaia looked desperately uncomfortable as her gaze shifted from Heather to Sam and then back again. Her skin looked so pale, it was almost translucent. She tugged and fidgeted with her grayish purple hospital gown. "I don't know if you heard, but I . . . there was . . . this fight last night and . . ."

"Do I care?" Heather's voice was so harsh, Sam winced inwardly.

"No, it's just . . ." Gaia sighed and started over. "It doesn't matter. I just wanted to tell you that I'm very sorry for not warning you about the guy with the knife in the park. It was a bad and dishonorable thing to do, and I don't need you to say it's okay or anything. I'm not looking to be friends. But what I did was wrong, and I'm very sorry for it."

Sam's heart moved up through his chest and into his throat as he watched Gaia. He saw something in her eyes (when he let himself) that was so profoundly vulnerable and scarred that her defiance only made it more moving and distressing to him. Was he the only one who saw it? Was he imagining it? He found himself hoping with unfamiliar passion that Heather would be kind to her. Gaia's speech was met with at least a minute of silence.

"Are you done?" Heather finally asked.

Sam's heart dislocated his tonsils. He couldn't swallow. He was supposed to be on Heather's side. She was his girlfriend, and furthermore, she was the one who'd been wronged. But he struggled against the impulse to put his arms around Gaia and tell Heather to go to hell.

Gaia nodded.

"Then please go away," Heather said. She was capable of causing hypothermia when she felt like it.

Gaia left just as Heather's mom arrived in the doorway Sam practically leaped to his feet. "Heather, your mom probably wants some time with you," he mumbled, needing to get out of that room if he was ever going to breathe again.

"Hey, Mrs. Gannis," he said politely, bolting past her.

He paused for a moment or two before following Gaia into her room. Although it was only a matter of thirty feet from Heather's, it belonged to a different universe. Aside from a pitiful clump of bright orange flowers in a sticky-looking glass bottle, it was colorless, empty, quiet. Gaia was sitting with her arms around her knees on the radiator under the window, staring out at the rain.

"Gaia?" he said.

She turned around. She had those eyes again. "Hi."

She looked like a waif in her hospital gown. Her feet were bare, her ankles surprisingly delicate. Her toenails were mostly covered in chipped brown polish. She had such a big presence, he'd never realized how slight she could appear.

It was too quiet. He needed to say something to her, but the feelings stirring in his core weren't getting anywhere near his mouth. He found his legs taking steps that brought him close to her.

"How are you doing?" she asked softly, filling a tiny part of the silence.

"Oh, fine," he said, as if that were a surprising question. "What about you?"

"Fine. I'm going home tomorrow."

"I'm glad."

He shifted his weight from one foot to the other. "So, where are your folks?"

Her pupils seemed to dilate, but she didn't look away. "I don't have any."

Sam wanted to slit his throat. And yet somehow the information didn't completely surprise him. "I'm so sorry. I didn't mean—"

"That's okay," she said quickly. "How could you have known?"

"I—I didn't . . . I—I just . . ." His voice petered out. So much for the speech therapist.

"Sam," she said.

His name sounded different than it ever had before. "Yes?"

"I am very, very sorry for attacking you last night. I wish I had it to do over."

For some odd reason, he found himself smiling a little. That was the one thing in his life he would have left just the same. "No, no. It wasn't your fault. I'm the one who's sorry . . . for . . . for everything."

"I seem to have a lot to apologize for," she said quietly, studying her fingernails. Her hands were exceptionally graceful, although her nails were bitten down to the quick.

"Some people do, and they say nothing," he murmured. He hoped she would know what he meant.

She nodded.

"Gaia, do you have any idea what happened last night?"

She tilted her head. "What do you mean?"

"I mean, somebody beat up those guys and . . . saved my skin. Maybe yours, too. Do you have any idea who it was or how it happened?"

Her eyes didn't move from his. She was looking for something from him as intently as he was from her. "Probably no more than you," she said equivocally.

He took a deep breath. "I have these strange fragments of memories, but . . . well . . ." He found his cheeks warming at the images in his mind. "But they don't make sense."

Gaia shrugged. "Oh."

"I mean, you didn't . . ." His voice was obviously beseeching, but he couldn't supply the rest of the question.

She wasn't going to help him.

"Maybe it will come back to one of us," he said lamely.

"Maybe."

He stuck his hands in his pants pockets. "Did you see Zolov today?"

Gaia smiled. "Yeah. He's happy. He keeps asking for more pudding."

Sam smiled, too. Suddenly he wanted to stay here and smile at her for the rest of his life.

"Yeah," he repeated stupidly.

She lifted up her arm to brush a strand of hair from her face and as she did revealed a deep, prune-colored bruise on the tender underside of her arm. "Oh," he said out loud, his breath catching. Suddenly he wasn't just close to her but nearly touching her. Two of his fingers hovered around her elbow.

She lifted her arm again and glanced at the bruise, wondering at his reaction. "This?" She turned out her arm and offered it to him.

For some reason the dark, angry bruise on her soft, sweet skin pained him beyond words. It was a helpless spot, even on Gaia's body. She has no parents, he found himself thinking disconnectedly. She has a terrible bruise on that hidden, sad part of her arm and she has no parents.

Without thinking properly, he let his fingertips land on her skin just above the inside of her elbow. Gaia looked down at them, but she didn't flinch. Together they watched his fingers slowly graze the damaged spot so gently, he wasn't sure whether he felt her skin or simply her warmth.

The warmth radiated up into his face, now bent over her. He was hypnotized by that passage of skin. He inhaled her subtle fragrance—a faint but tantalizing mixture of chamomile and Chap Stick and caramel and faded laundry detergent.

Was he breathing? Was his heart still beating?

"It's nothing much," she said in something just above a whisper. "You should see the ones on my stomach."

Oh, God. The mere thought of her stomach was a mistake.

"And this," she said. She lifted a curtain of gold hair to show a nasty bruise on her hairline just above her ear.

Now his hand was on her hair. He'd first realized it last night, that her hair was magical stuff. It was weightless and sparkled with strangely mutable color—as if it were shot through with sunlight.

His eyes were on her wound, then suddenly his lips. It had nothing to do with thinking. If it had anything to do with thinking, he never would have done it. Because he was a cautious, rational person. Everyone said so.

His lips touched her hairline so tenderly. She breathed into him, letting her head, her body relax against him. She let out a tiny sound. A hum, not a word.

He'd found his purpose with her, in that touch of his lips, in those few seconds. Without caution or anything related to reason, he knew (he didn't know how he knew) that he had a unique power. He alone had it. Did she know? Did she care? Would she hate him for it? Or would she, could she, love him?

As his lips moved with exquisite gentleness from the bruise in her hairline to the bandaged cut over her left eyebrow, he knew that he somehow possessed the power to kiss her and make her better. It was a puzzling, inexplicable kind of certainty that came only in dreams. It was an idea so complex and fragile that if he even blinked, he feared he would lose it.

Let me show you, he thought as his lips moved toward hers. Let me show you what I can do.

She was staring up at him in wonder. Her fingers had wrapped around his. Her breath was slow and just barely audible. Her lips were parted in a question. Her blue-violet eyes opened into a billion possible worlds.

"There you are!" The booming words cut through the spell with the force of an ax.

The pretty, plump nurse who'd spoken to them was carrying only a paper cup and some pills. "There you are!" she said again, this time clearly to him. Her voice was so loud, it was disorienting. Sam wished he had a remote control to pause her or at the very least turn down the volume.

"You're *Heather's boyfriend, right?*"

Could they hear her all the way uptown? he wondered absently.

"*She's looking for you—asking everybody where you went.*"

Could they hear her in Harlem? In Connecticut? At the North Pole?

Sam had traveled deep into a netherworld, and it was hard coming back. He looked at Gaia, but her face was turned to the window.

"Gaia?"

When she turned back to him, her face was different.

"Yeah?"

"I'll see you later?"

"Sure, maybe," she said.

Her eyes were no longer the color of the clear night sky

soaring up into a universe of stars and moons and planets and galaxies. They were iced over. Shut.

"Hey, Sam," she called as he walked toward the door.

He felt something dangerous as he turned to her.

"You and Heather make a great couple," she said. Her voice was as frigid as her expression.

All hope and warmth drained away. He blinked.

"I'm not sure how to take that," he said.

She shook her head. "It doesn't matter."

Sam's sore muscles tightened. He pulled his eyes from her face and forced the fuzzy clouds in his mind apart, letting in the cold light of reason.

He was awake. He was fully awake, and the dream was gone. Now he could remember that he disliked Gaia. Even hated her. She was trouble. Within a week of meeting her he'd been beaten to a pulp and two people he really cared about were in the hospital. Gaia was angry and dangerous. When he was near her, his own mind betrayed him. The smartest thing he could do was stay away from her permanently.

The smartest and most rational thing he could do was to get himself back to Heather's room and remember why he loved her.

DISTRACTION À LA GAIA

2 Krispy Kreme doughnuts
1 Granny Smith apple
1 large coffee with milk and 3 sugars
5 roasted nuts

AND
FINALLY . . .

HE REFUSED TO LOOK UP AND PAY HER FACE ANY
ATTENTION AT ALL UNTIL HE FELT THE METAL
BARREL AGAINST HIS TEMPLE.

She was so angry, she'd picked a fight with George. She was so angry, she was wearing her highest heels. Even her aqua miniskirt wasn't helping her mood.

Marco put his hands on her hips and pushed her against the wall.

The only thing the stupid, vain kid had going for him was his looks, and now he was monstrous with his swollen nose and misshapen lips.

"Come on darling," she whispered to him. "We need some privacy." She removed his hands and used them to lead him down the narrow hall of the Gramercy Inn to room 402, their very own love nest.

Once he was in the room, she plucked the Do Not Disturb sign off the inside doorknob and hung it on the outside. She closed the door hard and locked it. She clattered the key down on the glass-topped bureau.

He was already pulling his cotton T-shirt over his head. She saw deep bruises on his ribs and shoulder. Slob that he was, he threw the shirt on the ground and came toward her with those inexhaustible hands.

"Darling," she cooed, "you know I need to talk to you. I asked you not to hurt my friend, and now I've learned she's in the hospital."

Marco, as usual, was in no mood for talking. "Mmmm," he said, burying his face in her neck.

This had been fun two days ago. Today it wasn't.

"Marco, did you hear me?"

He had the unbelievable gall to throw her on the bed. She took her handbag with her. As he kissed her, she fumbled with the latch and opened it

"Marco, I asked you a question."

His hands were gliding under her shirt. They were cold today.

He refused to look up and pay her face any attention at all until he felt the metal barrel against his temple. His eyes grew round; his lips opened. He spluttered but couldn't find words.

Ella gave him another few seconds to fully appreciate her change of mood before she pulled the trigger and sent a silent bullet deep into his head.

She untangled herself from him and deposited the gun into her slim, square bag. She straightened her clothes and glanced in the mirror. Her lipstick was still perfect. She smiled wide. None on her teeth.

This interlude had done nothing to quell her anger. But now it was three o'clock, and Gaia, the true source of her temper, would be home from the hospital. Ella slung her bag over her shoulder, enjoying the weight of the gun, and strode to the door without a backward glance.

She was so tired of that girl.

SAM

To Molly Jessica W. Wenk

TWO THINGS

. . . WITH HER BACK TO HIM AND HIS GUN DUG
INTO HER HEAD, SHE WAS ALMOST DEFENSELESS.

It really wasn't *that* far. Gaia Moore studied the small garden four stories below her window. Well, it wasn't *her* window, exactly. It was one of three back windows that belonged to the top floor of the New York City brownstone of George and Ella Niven, her so-called guardians. George was a CIA friend of her dad's from way back when. "Way back when" was typical of the vagueness you got when living with spies and antiterrorist types. They didn't say, "You know, George, the underground assassin I met in Damascus?"

"Gaia?"

Gaia flinched at the voice materializing in her ear. Ella Niven's voice didn't seem to react to air molecules in the normal way. It was breathy and fake intimate, yet carried to the far reaches of the house without losing any of its volume.

"Guy-uhhhhhhh!" Ella bleated impatiently from her dressing room one floor below.

Gaia inched open the window. The window frame was oak, old and creaky with its lead chain and counterweight.

"Gaia? The Beckwiths will be here any minute! Come down now! George asked you to set the table twenty minutes ago!" Now Ella sounded downright whiny.

Gaia could smell bland, watery casserole-like odors

climbing up the stairs and mixing with Ella's strong, spicy perfume. George was a sweetheart and a terrible cook but probably a better cook than potato-brained Ella, who wasn't a sweetheart and never set foot in the kitchen except to whir up a fad-diet shake. The unspoken rule when they had company was that George prepared the food and Ella prepared herself.

Gaia grabbed a five-dollar bill from the top of the bureau and stuffed it in the pocket of her pants. Keys or no keys? That was the question. Mmmm, No keys, Gaia decided.

When the window was open just enough, she climbed out.

Although Ella might think otherwise, Gaia wasn't having dinner with the Beckwiths. They were old State Department people, certain to ask questions about her parents, her past, and her future, her parents, her parents. Gaia could not deal. Why was it that people over the age of thirty felt the need, when confronted with a "young person," to ask so freaking many questions?

Gaia had never agreed to make an appearance tonight. In fact, when Ella had demanded her presence a few hours earlier, Gaia had told Ella she would jump out the window before she'd have dinner with the Beckwiths, and she wasn't kidding.

The autumn air was scented with dry leaves and frying garlic from the Italian restaurant on West Fourth Street. Distantly Gaia smelled chimney smoke and felt a moment's longing for a different life, when she'd had parents and a pretty house in the Berkshires with a fire in the fireplace every autumn and winter night. That life felt like it belonged to a different person.

She knelt on the narrow windowsill and gripped it with both hands before she lowered herself down. Errg. Her feet tapped blindly for her next toehold while her fingers began to tremble with the exertion of holding up the full weight of her body. Wasn't there a window top or trellis around here somewhere?

At last the toe of her sneaker found purchase in a deeply pitted slab of brownstone. She sank her weight into it, releasing her cramping fingers. And just then, the brownstone cracked under the weight and she fell.

She winced in surprise and annoyance, but she didn't scream. Her mind didn't abandon its rational sequence.

She fell several feet before her hands jammed against the windowsill of a third-floor window, and she miraculously arrested her fall, saving her skull from the slate patio below.

God, that hurt. Angry nerve endings throbbed in her palms, but her heart beat out its same steady rhythm. Air entered her lungs in the same measured breaths as always.

That's why Gaia Moore was different. A freak of nature. Gaia knew that any normal person would have been afraid just then. But she wasn't. She wasn't afraid now, and she wouldn't be ever. She wasn't born with whatever gene it was that made ordinary people feel fear.

It was like something was missing from her genetic tool kit. But doctors weren't sure exactly what it was. They only knew it seemed to affect her reaction to fear. Scientists know the basic setup—there's a master gene that triggers a series of minor genes that in turn control fear reactions. After extensive testing they came up with the theory that one or more of Gaia's genes in that cascade might be inactive or just plain missing.

Something moved on the other side of the window and Gaia squinted to get a better look.

Oh, crap. It was Ella.

Obviously hearing a noise, Ella swiveled her head from the mirror where she was gunking up her eyelashes with mascara and stared into the darkness outside. Ella was both dumb and otherworldly alert. She was self-obsessed but controlling at the same time. Gaia felt her blood start to boil at the mere sight of George's young, plastic wife. Whenever Ella was around, Gaia began to wonder if Mother Nature had given her extra capacity for anger and frustration when she'd left out the capacity for fear.

Gaia's fingers were straining so hard on the windowsill, she felt her muscles seizing up. *Go away, Ella. Go away now!*

A less annoying version of Ella would have figured the noise was just a pigeon or something and gotten on with her elaborate primping ritual. But this being the actual Ella, she came right over to the window and started to open it.

Gaia glanced back over her shoulder, eyeballing the distance between her dangling feet and the patio. It had been reduced to twelve or fifteen feet.

Ella succeeded in throwing open the sash, narrowing her suspicious eyes. "What in the . . . ? Oh, Christ. Is that Gaia? Gaia!"

Gaia raised her head from her painful perch, and their eyes met for a fraction of a second.

It was weird. Ella was vapid and worthless at least nine-tenths of the time, but when she got really mad, her face became sharp and purposeful. Almost vicious. Like if Barbie were suddenly possessed by Atilla the Hun.

Ella's fingers were only inches from Gaia's. "Oh, hell," Gaia murmured, and let go.

Wump. Her feet took the brunt of the impact, then her knees, then her hands slapped down to steady her. Her knees stung, and she rubbed her hands together, doubting whether she'd ever have feeling in her palms again.

"Gaia! Get back here now!" Ella shrieked.

Gaia peered up momentarily at Ella's white face leaning out of the window. Gaia really hadn't wanted to make a scene. Poor George was never going to hear the end of it.

"Guy-uhhhhhhhhhhhhhhhh!"

Without another look behind her, Gaia ran for the back of the garden. Briefly she paused to glance at the seven fat goldfish swimming in the tiny pond before she leaped over it.

She scaled the five-foot garden fence with exceptional grace.

Ella's supersonic voice followed her all the way to Bleecker Street and then dissolved amid the noisy profusion of shops, cafes, and restaurants and the crush of people that made the West Village of Manhattan unique in the world. In a single block you could buy fertility statues from Tanzania, rare Amazonian orchids, a pawned brass tuba, Krispy Kreme doughnuts, or the best, most expensive cup of coffee you ever tasted. It was the doughnuts, incidentally, that attracted Gaia.

She walked past the plastic-wrapped fruit laid out on beds of melting ice and into the deli, where the extravagant salad bar at its center emitted a strong, oily aroma. It was called a salad bar, but it was filled with the least healthful stuff Gaia could imagine (apart from doughnuts, anyway). A trough of deep-fried egg rolls, chicken blobs floating in a sea of pink grease, and some slop vaguely resembling potato salad if you quintupled the mayonnaise. Who ever ate that stuff? Gaia didn't know for sure, but she would have bet her favorite Saucony sneakers that the smelly egg rolls she saw now were exactly the same smelly egg rolls she'd been seeing for the last month.

She made a beeline for the doughnut shelf. Crullers? Cinnamon cakey ones? Powdered sugar? Glazed? Chocolate?

Oh, who was she kidding? She'd been jonesing for a sticky chocolate doughnut all evening. Why pretend any other kind came close? Her mouth was watering as she laid the crumpled five on the counter. The pretty young Korean woman took the bill and gave Gaia her change without really looking up. Somehow, in spite of the fact that they saw each other nearly every day, Gaia and this woman never made any sign of recognition. That was a New York thing—pretend anonymity—and frankly, Gaia liked it. It was perfect, what with Gaia being a not-very-friendly person with a lot of secrets and an embarrassingly large appetite for doughnuts.

Gaia said no thank you to the plastic bag and carried her box of doughnuts in her still-numb hands out of the store, along Bleecker Street toward Seventh Avenue. She figured if you weren't woman enough to carry your doughnuts with pride, you shouldn't be eating them.

Her feet went into auto-walk. They knew their way to Washington Square Park by now. That was her favorite place to eat doughnuts or do just about anything. She chose the perfect park bench, clean and quiet, and sat under a canopy of red-turning leaves that carved the glowing night sky into lace. Hungrily she tore open the box.

Yum.

This moment suddenly contained the entire universe. Hell was eating George's food, watching Ella flirt shamelessly with Mr. Beckwith, and fielding questions about her parents she couldn't imagine answering. This doughnut, this bench, and this sky, on the other hand, were heaven.

NO BULLET

"Don't move."

Okay. Gaia's pupils sped to the corners of her eyes, but she didn't turn her head. Okay, it felt very much like the cold barrel of a gun pressed against her neck. Okay, if Gaia were to feel fear, now would be an obvious time.

The drying leaves were rustling sweetly overhead, the picturesque little puddles cast the glow of the streetlamps back up into the sky, but there wasn't a soul in sight besides the heavy-breathing, perspiring young man crushing the gun into her trapezius muscle.

He was standing behind the bench, but she could make out enough of him through her straining peripheral vision to recognize the nasty little hoodlum she'd seen in the park many times. His name was CJ Somethingorother. She'd not only beaten up his friends but identified him in a police lineup two weeks before as the gang member who'd stabbed Heather Gannis in the park. It didn't tax her imagination to think of why he wanted to scare her. Even hurt her. But kill her?

"Don't freakin' move an inch, bitch."

She sighed. She glanced longingly at her box of doughnuts.

"I *mean* it!"

Ouch. Jesus, he was going to puncture her flesh with the goddamned thing.

He was breathing heavily. He smelled like he'd been drinking. "I know you killed Marco, you sick bitch. And you're gonna pay."

Gaia swallowed hard. Suddenly the doughnut was a bitter clump in her mouth that she couldn't choke down. This guy's voice didn't carry the usual stupid bravado. He wasn't just trying to feel like a man.

Sweat trickled from his hand down the barrel of the gun.

He was dead serious, partly scared, maybe crazy.

Gaia had wondered what had become of Marco. He was a vain, annoying loudmouth, the most conspicuous of the thuggy neo-Nazi guys who contaminated the park. She could tell from the new graffiti she'd seen around the fountain that one of their number was dead.

Now it made sense. Marco was gone, and his boys believed Gaia killed him. That wasn't good news for her. Gaia felt sure there was any number of people who would have wanted to kill Marco.

"I didn't kill Marco," she said in a low, steady voice.

"Bullshit." CJ dragged the gun roughly from her neck to her temple. "Don't mess with me. I know what you did. That's how come you're gonna die."

She could feel her pulse beating against the dead, blunt metal.

CJ steadied the gun with both hands, breathing in deeply.

Oh, God. This was bad. Gaia eased her left hand along the thickly painted wooden slats of the bench.

"Don't move!" he bellowed.

Gaia froze, cringing with pain at the pressure of the gun against her head. A surge of anger ripped through her veins, but as badly as she wanted to break his neck, she recognized that in this position, with her back to him and his gun dug into her head, she was almost defenseless.

She tried to subdue her anger before she opened her mouth.

"CJ, don't do it," she said tightly. "It's a mistake. You're wasting your time here—"

"Shut *up!*" he screamed. "Don't say *anything!*"

His hand was poised on the trigger. He was going to do it. He was going to kill her right here, right now. If she moved, he would just kill her sooner.

She prayed for an intervention of some kind. A noise, a voice, even a car horn. She could turn the tiniest distraction into an opportunity. If he even flinched, she could wrench away the gun and demolish CJ with a couple of quick jabs. But the park and its surrounding streets were eerily calm.

Her mind entered into that dream state, in which you process things without quite believing them. This was it? This was the end? This was what it felt like to die?

The barrel shook as he tightened his grip on the trigger.

She could see the taut, quivering muscles in his forearm.

The wind had ceased. It seemed there was no one alive on the planet. The night was so silent, she could hear the grinding of his teeth. Or was it her teeth?

His muscles strained, her heart stopped, her eyes squeezed shut. He pulled the trigger.

Her mind was in free fall. Perfectly blank. Then, like the burst of a firecracker, came a searing moment of under-standing and regret, so complete and profound it shouldn't have been able to fit into a small fraction of a second—

Click.

What was that?

She turned her head. She realized her whole body was shaking. CJ looked just as shocked as he stared at the gun.

It hadn't fired. There was no bullet lodged in her head.

Not yet, anyway. Thank God CJ was an incompetent cave boy. Now, if she didn't get off her butt quick, she'd lose the only chance she had to save it. She shot up to her feet, grabbed CJ by the arm that held the gun, and used it to flip the bastard right over her shoulder. His body smacked hard against the pavement. The gun skidded off the path and into the brush.

She stared at his seizing body for a second. Under normal circumstances she would have stayed to pummel him like he deserved, but tonight she was too genuinely freaked out. She needed to get out of there. Her brains, thankfully, were still safely in her skull, but her emotions were splattered on the pavement.

Gaia ran. She ran as fast and gracefully as a doe. But not so fast that she didn't hear the tortured voice screaming behind her.

"I will kill you! I swear to *God* I will kill you!"

GAIA

Tonight, as I sat on the park bench waiting for my head to explode, I had one moment of clarity in which I learned two things.

1. I have to find my dad.

I just have to. As angry as I am, as much as I hate him for abandoning me on the most awful, vulnerable day of my life, I don't want to die without seeing him one more time. I don't know what I'll say to him. But there's something I want to know, and I feel like if I can look in his eyes—just for a moment—I'll know what his betrayal meant and whether there's any love or trust, even the possibility of it, between us.

2. I have to have sex.

Oh, come on. Don't act so shocked. I'm seventeen years old. I know the rules about being safe. If my life weren't in very immediate jeopardy, maybe I would let it wait for the exact right time. But let's face it—I may not be around next week, forget about happily ever after. Besides, I've been through a lot of truly awful things in my life, so why should I die without getting to experience one of the few great ones?

Who am I going to have sex with?

Do you have to ask?

All right, I have an answer. In that moment, when my fragile mindset was shattered, the face I saw belonged to Sam Moon. Granted, he hates me. Granted, he has a girl-friend. Granted, his girlfriend hates me even more. But I'll find a way. 'Cause he's the one. I can't say why; he just is.

I wish I could convince myself that CJ wouldn't make good on his threat. But I heard his voice. I saw his face. I know he'll do any crazy thing it takes.

I won't go down easy. But I'd be stupid not to prepare for the worst.

Am I afraid? No. I'm never afraid. But the way I see it, dying without knowing love would be a tragedy.

DESPERATE

SHE HATED THAT PALE BLOND HAIR,
A COLOR YOU RARELY SAW ON A PERSON
OVER THE AGE OF THREE.

A BOMB

"You sound weird."

"How do you mean?" Gaia asked.

"I don't know. You just do. You're talking fast or something," Ed said as he clenched the portable phone between his shoulder and his ear and eased himself from his desk chair to his wheelchair.

Ed Fargo was honest with Gaia, and Gaia was honest with Ed. He appreciated that about their relationship. With most girls he knew, girls like Heather, there were many mystifying levels of bullshit. With Gaia he could just tell her exactly what he was thinking.

Ed's mind briefly flashed on the hip-hugging green corduroys Gaia was wearing in Mr. McAuliff's class today.

Well, actually, not *everything* he was thinking. There was a certain category of thing he couldn't tell her about. That's why it was often easier talking with her on the phone, because then he couldn't see her, which meant he had fewer of those thoughts he couldn't tell her about.

"I had a bad night. That's probably why," Gaia said.

Ed wheeled himself down the shabbily carpeted hallway of his family's small apartment. Family photographs lined the walls on both sides, but Ed didn't seem to see them anymore. "A bad night how?" he asked.

"I almost got shot in the head."

Ed made a sound somewhere between laughter and choking on a chicken bone. "You w-what?"

That was another thing about Gaia. She was always surprising. Though too often in an upsetting way.

Gaia let out her breath. "Oh, God. Where to start. You know that guy CJ?"

Ed slowed his chair to a stop and clenched the armrests with his hands. "The one who slashed Heather? Isn't he in jail?" he asked with a sick feeling in his stomach.

"I guess he got out on bail or something," Gaia said matter-of-factly. "Anyway, CJ's friend Marco is dead, and he thinks I killed him."

Ed groaned out loud. How had his life taken such a turn? Before he'd first laid love-struck eyes on Gaia in the hallway outside physics class, he wouldn't have believed he would ever have a conversation like this.

"Marco is dead? Are you sure?"

"Only from what CJ told me."

Ed sighed. The really crazy thing was, in the brief time he'd known Gaia, so many violent and alarming things had happened, this wasn't so staggeringly out of the ordinary.

"Hey, Gaia? If trouble is a hungry great white shark, then you're a liquid cloud of chum."

Gaia's laugh was easy and comforting. "That's a beautiful image. I love it when you get poetic."

Ed resumed his roll down the hallway and into the galley kitchen. His late evening phone reports from Gaia, distressing as they sometimes were, had become as precious a ritual as his eleven o'clock milk shake.

"So tell me," Ed prodded, hoisting himself up a few inches with one arm to reach the ice cream in the freezer. "Tell me how it happened."

"Okay. I was sitting in the park, minding my own business—"

"Eating doughnuts," Ed supplied.

"Yes, Ed, eating doughnuts, when that loser came up from behind and shoved a gun into my neck."

"Jesus."

"I didn't take it seriously at first. But it turns out this guy is half crazed and deadly serious."

"So what happened?" Ed asked, milk shake momentarily forgotten.

Gaia sighed. "He actually pulled the trigger. I thought I was dead—a wild experience, by the way. It turned out he must have loaded the gun in a hurry because there was no bullet in at least one of the chambers. I took that opportunity to throw him."

Ed's mind was spinning. "Throw him?"

"You know, like flip him."

"Oh, right," he said.

"You're making fun of me again," Gaia said patiently.

Ed shook his head in disbelief. "I'm not, Gaia. It's just . . . you blow my mind."

"Well, speaking of, I think this guy CJ is dead set on killing me. I'm scared he's really going to do it," Gaia said.

"You're scared?" Ed asked a little nervously. Having seen Gaia in action, he would have imagined it would take more than a pimply white supremacist with a borrowed gun to hurt Gaia. It would take something more on the order of a hydrogen bomb. But if Gaia was scared, well, he had to take that seriously.

"Figure of speech. I'm scared *abstractly*," Gaia explained.

Ed rocked a tall glass on the counter. "Gaia, you worry me here."

"Don't worry," Gaia reassured him. "I mean, think about it. CJ is kind of a moron, and I happen to be okay at self-defense."

Ed felt reassured. That last part was an understatement to rival "Marilyn Manson is an unusual guy." He could hear Gaia thumping her heel against her metal desk. He realized the ice cream was melting and spreading along the countertop. He absently scooped some of it into the blender.

Prrrrrrrrrrrrr.

"Ed! I hate when you run the blender when we're talking," Gaia complained loudly.

"Sorry," he said. By the time she finished complaining, the milk shake was frothy and smooth. That was part of the ritual.

"I don't want to die," she said resolutely. "You know why?"

"Why?" he asked absently, sucking down a huge mouthful of vanilla shake.

"I haven't had sex yet."

Ed spluttered the mouthful all over his dark blue T-shirt. Cough, cough, cough. "What?"

"I don't want to die before I've had sex."

Cough, cough.

"Right," he said.

"So I need to have sex in the next couple of days, just in case," Gaia added.

Cough, cough, cough, cough, cough, cough, cough, cough, cough, cough—

"Ed? Are you okay? Ed? Is somebody around to give you the Heimlich?"

"N-No," Ed choked out. "I'm (cough, cough) fine."

In fact, he had about four ounces of milk shake puddled in his lung. Could you die of that? Could you drown by breathing in a milk shake? And shit, he'd like to have sex in the next couple of days, too. (Cough, cough, cough.)

"Ed, are you sure you're okay?"

"Yesss," he answered in a weak and gravelly voice.

"So anyway, I was thinking I better do it soon."

"It?"

"Yeah, it. You know, *it*."

"Right. It." Ed felt faint. Milk shake, as it turned out, was much less handy in your veins than, say, oxygen. "So, who . . . uh . . . are you going to do *it* with? Or are you just going to walk the streets, soliciting people randomly?"

"Ed!" Gaia sounded genuinely insulted.

"Kidding," he said feebly, wishing his palms weren't suddenly sweating.

"You don't think anybody's going to want to have sex with me, do you?" Gaia sounded hurt and petulant at the same time.

"Mmrnpha." The noise Ed made didn't resemble an English word. It sounded like it had come from the mouth of a nine-month-old baby.

"Huh?"

"I . . . um . . . " Ed couldn't answer. The truth was, although she made every effort to hide it, Gaia was possibly the most beautiful girl he had ever seen in his life—and that was including the women in the Victoria's Secret catalog, the *SI* swimsuit issue, and that show about witches on the WB. Any straight guy with a live pulse and a thimble full of testosterone would want to have sex with Gaia. But what was Ed going to say? This was *exactly* the category of conversation he couldn't have honestly with her.

"Anyway, I do know who I'm going to do it with," Gaia said confidently.

"Who?" Ed felt his vision blurring.

"I can't say."

Ed definitely wasn't taking in enough oxygen. Good

thing he was in a chair because otherwise he'd be lying on the linoleum.

"Why can't you say?" he asked, trying to sound calm.

"Because it's way too awkward," Gaia said.

Awkward? Awkward. What did that imply? Could it mean . . . ? Ed's thoughts were racing. Would it be too crude to point out at this juncture that although his legs were paralyzed, his nether regions were in excellent working condition?

He felt a tiny tendril of hope winding its way into his heart. He beat it back. "Gaia, don't you think you'll need to get past *awkwardness* if you really plan to be doing *it* with this person in the next forty-eight hours?"

"Yeah, I guess." He heard her slam her heel against the desk. "But I still can't tell you."

"Oh, come on, Gaia. You have to."

"I gotta go."

"Gaia!"

"I really do. Cru-Ella needs to use the phone."

"Gaia! Please? Come on! Tell."

"See ya tomorrow."

"Gaia, who? Who, who, who?" Ed demanded.

"You," he heard her say in a soft voice before she hung up the phone.

But as he laid the phone on the counter he knew who'd said the word, and it wasn't Gaia. It was that misguiding, leechlike parasite called hope.

ONE SMALL COMMENT

The time had come. Heather Gannis felt certain of that as she slammed her locker door shut and tucked the red envelope into her book bag. She waited for the deafening late afternoon crowd to clear before striking out toward the bathroom. She didn't feel like picking up the usual half-dozen hangers-on, desperate to know what she was doing after soccer practice.

Okay, time to make her move. She caught sight of Melanie Young in her peripheral vision but pretended she hadn't. She acted like she didn't hear Tannie Deegan calling after her. Once in the bathroom she hid in the stall for a couple of minutes to be sure she wasn't being followed.

Heather usually liked her high visibility and enormous number of friends, but some of those girls were so freakishly *needy* some of the time. It was like if they missed one group trip to the Antique Boutique, they would never recover. Their clinginess made it almost impossible for Heather to spend one private afternoon with her boyfriend.

Heather dumped her bag in the mostly dry sink and stared at her reflection. She wanted to look her best when she saw Sam. She bent her head so close to the mirror that her nose left a tiny grease mark on the glass. This close, she could see the light freckles splattered across the bridge of her nose and the amber streaks in her light eyes that kept them from being the bona fide true blue of her mother and sisters.

Her pores looked big and ugly from this vantage point. Did Sam see them this way when he kissed her? She pulled away. She got busy rooting through her bag for powder to tame the oil on her forehead and nose and hopefully cover those gaping, yawning pores. She applied another coat of clear lip gloss. For somebody who was supposed to be so beautiful, she sure felt pretty plain sometimes.

She wished she hadn't eaten those potato chips at lunch. She couldn't help worrying that the difference between beauty and hideousness would come down to one bag of salt-and-vinegar chips.

As she swung her bag over her shoulder and smacked open the swinging door, she caught sight of the dingy olive-colored pants and faded black hooded sweatshirt of Gaia Moore. Heather's heart picked up pace, and she felt blood pulsing in her temples.

God, she hated that girl. She hated the way she walked, the way she dressed, the way she talked. She hated that pale blond hair, a color you rarely saw on a person over the age of three. Heather wished the color was fake, but she knew it wasn't.

Heather hated Gaia for dumping scorching-hot coffee all over her shirt a couple of weeks ago and not bothering to apologize. Heather hated Gaia for being friends with Ed Fargo, her ex-boyfriend, and turning him against Heather at that awful party. Heather *really* hated Gaia for failing to warn Heather that there was a guy with a knife in the park, when Heather was obviously headed there.

All of those things were unforgivable. But none of them kept Heather up at night. The thing that kept her up at night was one small, nothing comment made by her boyfriend, Sam Moon.

It happened the day Heather got out of the hospital. Sam was there visiting, as he was throughout those five days. He had disappeared for a few minutes, and when he got back to her room, Heather asked him where he'd been. He said, "I ran into Gaia in the hallway." That was all. Afterward, when Heather quizzed him, Sam instantly claimed to dislike Gaia. Like everybody else, he said it was partly Gaia's fault that Heather got slashed in the first place.

But there was something about Sam's face when he said Gaia's name that stuck in Heather's mind and wouldn't go away.

Heather's mind returned again to the card floating in her bag. She sorted through the bag and pulled it out. She needed to check again that the words seemed right. That the handwriting didn't look too girly and stupid. That the phrasing didn't seem too . . . desperate.

She'd find Sam in the park playing chess with that crazy old man, as he often did on Wednesday afternoons. And if not, she'd go on to his dorm and wait for him there. She'd hand him the card, watch his face while he read it, and kiss him so he'd know she meant it.

She was in love with Sam. This Saturday marked their six-month anniversary. He was the best-looking, most intelligent guy she knew. She loved the fact that he was in college.

She had made this decision with her heart. Sam was sexy. Sam was even romantic sometimes. He wasn't a guy you let get away.

So why, then, as she wrote the card, was she thinking not of Sam, but of Gaia?

Dear Sam,

These last six months have been the best of my life. Sorry to be corny, but it's true. So I wanted to celebrate the occasion with a very special night. I'll meet you at your room at eight on Saturday night and we'll finally do something we've been talking about doing for a long time. I know I said I wanted to wait, but I changed my mind.

You are the one, and now is the time.

Love and kisses (all over),

Heather

LONELY
HEARTS

HE SMILED AT HER. THIS TIME IT WAS SWEET,
OPEN, REAL.

"That stupid punk will not kill Gaia!" he thundered. "Do you understand?"

He strode to the far end of the loft apartment and kicked over a side table laden with coffee mugs. Most rolled; one shattered. One of the two bodyguards who hovered in the background came forward to clean them up.

He spun on Ella. He hated her face at moments like this. *"Do you understand?"*

"Of course I understand," she said sullenly. "I wasn't expecting her to climb out the window," she added in a scornful mumble.

"Learn to *expect* it!" he bellowed, "Gaia is *not* an ordinary girl! Haven't you figured that *out?"*

Ella's eyes darted with reptilian alertness, but she wisely kept her mouth shut.

"Gaia is no use to me dead. I will not let it happen. I don't care how crazy the girl is. I don't care if she throws herself in the path of a bus. I will *not* let it happen!" He was ranting now. He couldn't stop now if he wanted to. He'd always had a bad temper.

"Show me the pictures," he demanded of Ella.

Reluctantly Ella came near and put the pile in his hands.

He studied the first one for a long time. It was Gaia sitting alone on a park bench. Her face was tipped down, partly obscured by long, pale hair. Her gray sweatshirt was sagging off one shoulder. Her long legs were crossed, and a little burst of light erupted from the reflective patch on her running shoe. A box of doughnuts sat open on the bench next to her.

Her gesture and manner were so familiar to him, he felt an odd stirring in his chest. Though Gaia was undeniably beautiful with her graceful, angular face, she didn't resemble Katia. Katia had dark glossy hair, brown eyes flecked with orange, and a smaller, more voluptuous build.

In the next picture Gaia's head was raised, and in the shadow behind her was the boy pointing the gun at her head. The boy looked agitated, his eyes wild. Yet Gaia's face was impossibly calm. He brought the picture close. Remarkable. Utterly fascinating. There was no fear in those wide-set blue eyes. He would know. He had a great gift for detecting fear.

Gaia was indeed everything he had heard about her. All the more reason why he could not accept another ridiculous close call like this one.

He glanced at the next picture. The boy was leaning in closer, his face clenched as he prepared to pull the trigger.

"Keep that boy and his stupid friends away from her," he barked at Ella.

"Yes," she mumbled.

"He will not get that gun anywhere near Gaia!"

"Yes, sir."

He glared at Ella with withering eyes. "Hear me now, Ella. If *anyone* kills Gaia Moore, it will be me."

Ella's gaze was cast to the ground.

He studied the next picture in the pile. This one showed Gaia standing in all her ferocious glory, flipping that pitiful boy over her shoulder. Her face was wonderfully alert, intense. She was magnificent. More than he could have hoped for.

No, Gaia didn't resemble Katia, he decided as he studied the lovely face in the picture. Gaia resembled him.

LIKE A DRUG

She probably wouldn't even be there. Why would she? She'd be avoiding him if she had any sense.

Sam Moon hurried into Washington Square Park with his physics textbook tucked under his arm. Then again, if *he* had any sense, he'd be avoiding *her*. Instead he was darting around the park at all hours like some kind of timid stalker, hoping to catch a glimpse of her.

He approached the shaded area where the chess tables sat, surveying them almost hungrily. No. She wasn't there. It verged on ridiculous, the physical feeling of disappointment that radiated through his abdomen.

He kept his distance, reviewing his options. He didn't want to plunge right into chess world because then all his cohorts would see him and he'd be stuck for at least a game or two. And he'd found out the hard way that when Gaia was on his mind (and when wasn't she?) he was a lot worse at chess.

Maybe she had come and gone already. Maybe she'd caught sight of him from a distance and taken off. Maybe she really did hate him—

"Moon?"

Sam practically leaped right out of his clothes. He spun around. "Jesus, Renny, you scared the crap out of me."

Renny smiled in his open, friendly way. He was a wiry-looking, barely adolescent Puerto Rican kid who was quickly becoming a lethal chess player. "You looking for Gaia?"

Sam's face fell. Was his head made of glass? Was his romantic torment, which he believed to be totally private and unique, available for public display? Was everybody who knew him talking and snickering about it? Even the chess nerds, who wouldn't ordinarily notice if you'd had one of your legs amputated?

"No," Sam lied defensively. "Why?"

"I figure you're getting tired of whipping the rest of us.

Gaia could probably get a game off you, huh?"

Sam studied Renny's face for signs of cleverness or mockery. No. Renny wasn't being a wise guy. He wasn't suddenly Miss Lonely Hearts. Renny was thinking the same way he always thought, like a chess player.

Sam let out a breath. He tried to relax the crackling nerve synapses in his neck and shoulders. There was a word for this: *paranoia.*

"Yeah," Sam said in a way he hoped was nonchalant. "Maybe one or two. If she was on her game."

"Yeah," Renny said, "she's unbelievable." Renny's eyes got a little glassy, but Sam could tell he was fantasizing about Gaia's stunning end play, not about her lips or her eyes.

Unlike Sam.

"Yeah," Sam repeated awkwardly.

"See you." Renny clapped him on the back agreeably and waded into chess world. Sam watched Renny take the first open seat across from Mr. Haq, whose taxicab was predictably parked (illegally) at the nearest curb. That was the downside of playing Mr. Haq. If the cops came, he abandoned the game and put his cab back into action. And no matter how badly you were creaming him, Mr. Haq would always refer to it afterward as "an undecided match."

Sam found his way to a nearby bench with a good view of the chess area. He opened his physics book, lame prop that it was.

What had happened to his resolution to forget about Gaia? He'd decided to put her out of his mind for good and focus all of his romantic energy on Heather, but Gaia was like a drug. She was in his blood, and he couldn't get her out. He was a junkie, an addict. He knew Gaia was bad for him. He knew she'd undermine his commitments and basically ruin his life. But he obsessed about her, anyway. Was there a twelve-step program for an addiction like this? Gaia Worshipers Anonymous?

He remembered that antidrug slogan that had scared him as a kid. *This is your brain.* He pictured the sizzling egg. *This is your brain thinking of Gaia.*

Clearly his decisions, vows, determinations, and oaths to forget Gaia weren't enough. Maybe it was time to try a different tack.

What if he attempted to relate to her as a normal person? Just talk to her about everyday things like school and extracurricular activities and stuff like that? Maybe he could demystify the whole relationship.

Maybe he and Gaia could even have a meal together. You couldn't easily idolize a girl while she was stuffing her face. She would probably order something he hated like lox or coleslaw. She would chew too loudly or maybe wear a bit of red cabbage on her front tooth for a while. Maybe she would spit a little when she talked. Afterward she would have bad breath or maybe a grease spot on her pants, and voilà. Obsession over.

Yes. This was a practical idea. Demystification.

Because after all, although Gaia came off as a pretty extraordinary person on the outside, on the inside she was just the same as anybody else.

. . . right?

A LAME COME-ON

She was a mess.

She was a nightmare.

She should have her license to be female revoked.

Gaia turned around to look at her backside in the slightly warped mirror that hung on the back of the door to her room. Earlier that day she'd picked up a pair of capri pants off the sale rack at the Gap in an effort to look cute and feminine. Instead she looked like the Incredible Hulk right after he turns green and bursts out of his clothing.

What kind of shoes were you supposed to wear with these things? Definitely not boots, as she could plainly see in the mirror. Was it too late in the year to wear flip-flops?

Sam was not going to fall in love with her. He was going to take one look and run screaming in the opposite direction. Either that or laugh uncontrollably.

Why was she torturing herself this way? In her ordinary life she managed to pull off the functional style of a person who didn't care. She had no money, which occasionally resulted in the coincidental coolness of thrift shop dressing.

But now that Gaia actually cared, she had turned herself into a neurotic, insecure freak show.

Caring was to be deplored and avoided. Hadn't she learned that by now?

She stripped off the pants and pulled on her least-descript pair of jeans. She pulled a nubbly sweater the color of oatmeal over her head.

Better ugly than a laughingstock. That was Gaia's new fashion motto.

She had to get out of the house before Ella sauntered in and recognized the beaded necklace Gaia had "borrowed." Ella was a whiny, dumb bimbo, but she had a nose for fashion trends. Gaia had every intention of returning the necklace before it was missed, so why cause a big fuss by asking?

Gaia thundered down the three flights of stairs, slammed the painted oak-and-glass door behind her, turned her key in the lock, and struck out for the park.

And to think she'd come home after school to work on her appearance.

She hurried past the picture-perfect row houses. Lurid red geraniums still exploded in the window boxes. Decorative little front fences cast long shadows in the late day sun, putting Gaia's shadow in an attenuated, demented-looking prison.

After a few blocks, Gaia suddenly paused as the sound of heavy guitar music blared through an open basement window, followed by a raspy tenor voice. "framed/you set me up, set me out and/blamed/you tore me up, tore me down and/chained/you tied me up, tied me down and . . . " It was that band again—Fearless. For a fleeting moment Gaia wanted to shout through the window and ask them where they got their bizarrely Gaia-centric name, but she had to keep moving.

She didn't have much time. CJ probably wasn't crazy enough to open fire on her in daylight, but once the sun got really low, she had to be ready for it, especially hanging around the park. How typical of her new life in the biggest city in the United States that the guy she wanted to seduce and the guy who wanted to shoot her hung out in exactly the same space.

Her stomach started to churn as she got close. What was she going to say to Sam?

"Hi, I know you have a girlfriend and don't like me at all, but do you want to have sex?"

On the one-in-ten-billion chance that he agreed to her

insane scheme, what then? They couldn't just do it on a park bench.

Suddenly the actual, three-dimensional Sam, sitting on a bench with a clunky-looking textbook open on his lap, replaced the Sam in her mind.

Oh, crap. Was it too late? Had he seen her?

"Gaia?"

That would mean yes.

Swallow. "Hi." She tried out a friendly smile that came off more like the expression a person might make when burning a finger on the top of the toaster.

He stood up, his smile looking equally pained. "How's it going?"

She hooked her thumbs in the front pockets of her pants. "Oh, fine. Fine." What was she? A farmer?

"Yeah?"

"Yeah."

"Great."

Oh, this was awful. This come-hither Gaia was a complete disaster. Why couldn't she be cute and flirty *and* have a personality?

He was clearly at a loss. "Do you, uh . . . want to play a game of chess?"

She would have agreed to pull out her toenails to escape this awkward situation.

"Yeah, sure, whatever," she said lightly. God, what a wordsmith she was.

"Or we could just, like, take a walk. Or something."

"Great. Sure," she said. Had her vocabulary shrunk to four words?

"Or we could even sit here for a couple of minutes."

"Yeah," she proclaimed.

"Fine," he countered.

"Great," she said.

They both stayed standing.

This was pathetic. How was she possibly going to have sex with him when simply sitting on the same bench involved a whole choreography of commitment?

She sat. There.

He sat, too.

Well, this was progress.

She crossed her legs and inadvertently brushed the heel of his shoe. With lightning-fast-reflex speed they both swung their respective feet to opposite sides of the bench.

Or not.

Gaia studied Sam's face in profile. It made her a little giddy to realize what a hunk he was. A classic knee weakener. He belonged on television or in a magazine ad for cologne. What was he doing sitting near *her*?

He looked up and caught her staring (slack jawed) at him. She quickly looked away. She pressed her hand, palm down, on the bench and realized her pinky was touching the outer edge of his thigh. *Uh-oh.*

Should she move it? Had he noticed? Did he think she

had done it on purpose? Suddenly she had more feeling, more nerve endings (billions and billions at least) in her pinky than she ever thought possible. All of the awareness in her body was crammed into that pinky.

Now it felt clammy and weirdly twitchy. A pinky wasn't accustomed to all this attention. Did Sam feel it twitching? That would be awful. He'd think it was some kind of lame come-on. Either that or she'd lost muscle control.

Well, actually this *was* some kind of lame come-on and she *had* lost control.

The problem was, if she took away her pinky, he would know she noticed that she was touching him, and that would be embarrassing, too.

He moved his leg. Suddenly Gaia's pinky was touching cold, lonely, uncharged air. She felt the piercing sting of rejection. Jerk. Loser. She was ready to give up on the whole project.

Then he moved it back and practically covered her entire pinky. Oh, faith! Love! Destiny! Could she propose to him right there?

He smiled at her. This time it was sweet, open, real.

Her stomach rolled. She smiled back, fervently hoping it didn't look like a grimace and that her teeth didn't look yellow.

She heard a noise behind her. She jerked up her head.

She realized that the sun had dipped below the Hudson

River and the streetlamps were illuminated. Oh, no. Could it be? Already?

She had to go. Fast. She wasn't going to turn into a pumpkin, but she was very likely going to get shot in the head. That could easily put a damper on this fragile, blossoming moment.

The sound resolved itself into a footstep, and a person appeared. It wasn't CJ, but just the same, it put an end to the encounter as powerfully as a bullet.

It was Heather. The girlfriend.

COLD BLOOD

HER ADRENALINE WAS PUMPING NOW.
HER MUSCLES WERE BUZZING WITH INTENSITY.
SHE WAS AN EASY TARGET THIS CLOSE.

There were moments in life when words failed to convey your thoughts. There were moments when your thoughts failed to convey your feelings. Then there were moments when even your feelings failed to convey your feelings.

This was one of those, Heather realized as she gaped at Sam and Gaia Moore sitting on the park bench together.

They weren't kissing. They weren't touching. They weren't even talking. But Sam and Gaia could have been doing the nasty right there on the spot, and it wouldn't have carried the intimacy of this erotic union she now witnessed between them.

Maybe she was imagining it, Heather considered. Maybe it was a figment of her own obsessive, jealous mind.

She'd almost rather believe she was crazy than that Sam, *her Sam*, was falling in love with Gaia. It was too coincidental, just too cruel to be real. Like one of those Greek tragedies she read for Mr. Hirschberg's class. Gaia was the person she most despised. Sam was the person she loved.

Had she done something to bring this on herself? What was it the Greek guys always got smacked for? *Hubris*, that was the word—believing you were too good, too strong, invulnerable. The world had a way of teaching you that you weren't invulnerable.

Heather was paralyzed. Anger told her to get between them and make trouble, Pride told her to run away. Hurt told her to cry. Cunning told her to make Sam feel as guilty and small as possible. She waited to hear what Intelligence had to say. It never spoke first, but its advice was usually worth waiting for.

Her mind raced and sorted. Considered and rejected. Then finally, Intelligence piped up with a strategy.

"Sam," Heather stated. Good, firm, steady voice. She stepped around to the front of the bench and faced them straight on.

Sam looked up. Shock, fear, guilt, uncertainty, and regret waged war over his features.

Staring at them, Heather made no secret of her surprise and distress, but she overlaid a brave, tentative, give-them-the-benefit-of-the-doubt smile.

The effect was just as she'd intended. Sam looked like he wished to pluck out both of his eyeballs on the spot.

"Hey, Gaia," Heather said. Her expression remained one of naive, martyrlike confusion.

Gaia looked less sure of herself than Heather had ever seen her before. Gaia cleared her throat, uncrossed her legs, straightened her posture, said nothing. Heather detected a faint blush on her cheeks.

Now Heather looked back at Sam. She applied no obvious pressure, just silence, which always proved the fiercest pressure of all.

"Heather, I—we—you—" Sam looked around, desperate for her to interrupt.

She didn't.

"I was just . . . and Gaia, here . . ."

Heather wasn't going to help him out of this. Let him suffer.

"We were just . . . talking about chess." With that word, Sam regained his footing. He took a big breath. "Gaia is a big chess player, too."

Heather nodded trustingly. "Oh."

Sam looked at his watch. There wasn't a watch. A moment's discomfort. He regrouped again. "I gotta go, though." He stood up. "Physics study group." He offered his textbook as evidence.

"Right," Heather said. "Wait, I have something for you." She fished around in her bag and brought out the red sealed envelope. "Here. I was looking for you because I wanted to give you this." She smiled shyly. She shrugged. "It's kind of stupid, but . . . whatever." Her voice was soft enough to be intimate and directed solely at him.

He had to come two steps closer to take the card from her hand. This required him to turn his back on Gaia.

Sam glanced at his name, written in flowery cursive, and the heart she'd drawn next to it. When he looked at Heather again, his eyes were pained, uncertain.

He cleared his throat "Why don't you walk with me, and I'll open it when I get to my dorm?"

Heather nodded brightly. "Okay."

He pressed the card carefully between the pages of his

physics book and anchored the book under his arm. Heather took his free hand and laced her fingers through his as she often did, and they started across the park.

Sam said nothing to Gaia. He didn't even cast a backward glance.

But Heather couldn't help herself. She threw a tiny look over her shoulder. Then, without breaking her stride, she planted one fleeting kiss on Sam's upper arm; just the place where her mouth naturally landed on his tall frame. It was a casual kiss, light, one of millions, but undoubtedly a kiss of ownership.

"See ya," Heather said to Gaia, silently thanking Intelligence for dealing her yet another effective strategy.

It was funny, thought Heather. Intelligence and Cunning so often ended up in the same place.

NOT YET

What good was it being a trained fighting machine when you couldn't beat the hell out of a loathsome creature like Heather Gannis? Gaia wondered bitterly as she stomped along the overcrowded sidewalks of SoHo.

What a catty piece of crap Heather was. No, that was too

kind. Cats were fuzzy, warm-blooded, and somewhat loyal. Heather was more reptile than mammal—cold-blooded and remote with dead, hooded eyes.

Gaia was supposed to be smart. When she was six years old, her IQ tested so high, she'd been sent to the National Institutes of Health to spend a week with electrodes stuck to her forehead. And yet in Heather's presence Gaia felt like a slobbering idiot. She'd probably misspell her name if put on the spot.

"Oops. Sorry," Gaia mumbled to a man in a beige suit whose shoulder she caught as she crossed Spring Street.

Trendy stores were ablaze along the narrow cobblestoned streets. Well-dressed crowds flowed into the buzzing, overpriced restaurants that Ella always wanted to go to. Gaia strode past a cluster of depressingly hip girls who probably never considered wearing boots with capri pants.

Gaia caught her reflection in the darkened window of a florist shop. Ick. Blah. Blech. Who let her out on the streets of New York in that sweater? Exactly how fat could her legs look? High time to get rid of the—

Suddenly she caught sight of another familiar reflection. He was behind her, weaving and dodging through the throng, staying close but trying to avoid her notice. His face was beaded with sweat. One of his hands was tucked in his jacket.

Oh, shit. Well, at least you couldn't commit fashion blunders from the grave, could you?

She walked faster. She jaywalked across the street and

ducked into a boutique. She wanted to see whether CJ was just keeping tabs on her or whether he intended to kill her immediately.

Gaia blinked in the laboratory-bright shop. The decor was spare, and the clothing was inscrutable. In the midst of all the chrome shelving and halogen lighting there seemed to be about three items for sale, all of them black. It made for poor browsing.

CJ stopped outside. He knew she knew he was there.

"Excuse me, miss." An impatient voice echoed through the stark, high-ceilinged room.

Gaia spun around to see a severe-looking saleslady pinning her to the floor with a suspicious look. Salesladies in SoHo had a sixth sense for whether you could afford anything in their store. It was a superhuman power. It deserved to be investigated on *The X-Files*. This particular woman obviously knew that Gaia couldn't afford even a zipper or sleeve from the place.

"We're closed," the saleslady snapped. Her outfit was constructed of incredibly stiff-looking black material that covered her from her pointy chin to the very pointy tips of her shoes. Gaia couldn't help wondering if she ate breakfast or watched TV in that getup.

"The door was open," Gaia pointed out.

The woman cocked her head and made a sour face. "Apparently so. But we're closed."

"Fine." Gaia glanced through the glass door. CJ was pacing in an area of about two square feet. He was ready to pounce. She was pretty sure that the hand concealed in his roomy jacket held a gun.

"In the future, when you're closed," Gaia offered, trying to bide a little time, "you should consider *locking your door*. It's a common business practice. It not only alerts your customers to the fact that your store is closed but can help reduce crime as well."

"Are you done?" the woman asked, rolling her eyeballs skyward.

"Um, yeah." Gaia glanced out the door reluctantly. It opened outward. The glass was thick and well reinforced.

"Please leave."

Gaia backed up a few feet. "Okay," she said.

One . . . two . . . three . . .

Gaia slammed into the door at full strength.

Just as she'd hoped, the door flew open and caught CJ hard in the face, knocking him backward. She heard his groan of surprise and pain. It gave her the moment she needed to run.

SoHo, with its single-file sidewalks and indignant pedestrians, was not a good place for sprinting.

"Ex*cuse* me!"

"Yo, watch it!"

"What's your problem?"

Gaia left a stream of angry New Yorkers in her wake.

"Sorry!" she called out in a blanket apology. It was the best she could do at the moment.

She heard CJ shouting behind her. Then pounding footsteps and the protests of more unhappy pedestrians.

Gaia hung a quick left on Greene Street. She navigated the sidewalk with the deftness of a running back.

She heard screams as CJ (presumably) crashed into a woman with a screechy voice. He was gaining on Gaia. He cared less than she did about thrashing innocent bystanders.

Gaia hooked onto Broome Street and ran west. CJ was just a few yards behind. The street was clotted with traffic, and she needed to cross to the south side, where the sidewalk was clear. The crosswalk was too far. She heard more screams and then a man's voice.

"That kid's got a gun! A *gun*! Everybody down!"

"Damn it!" Gaia muttered. Her adrenaline was pumping now. Her muscles were buzzing with intensity. She was an easy target this close. Now what?

Parked cars were nose to tail at the curb without a break. Gaia pounced on the first parked car she came upon, putting both hands above the driver's side window and vaulting herself onto the roof. She was in full flee mode now, and she didn't have the luxury to care about making a spectacle. Thin metal thundered and buckled under her feet. She surveyed the traffic piled up behind the light. She jumped to the roof of the next-nearest car and picked her way across the street from car to car the way she'd use stones to traverse a river. Cars honked. Cabbies shouted. A shot rang out to her left. Oh, man.

CJ had beaten her to the other side of Broome Street. The idiot was shooting at her in front of hundreds of witnesses. God, she wanted to wring his crazy neck! It was no fair going up against someone with a gun and no sense.

The traffic light was about to change. Any second, the stones under her feet were going to start moving downstream. She hopped her way back to the north side of the street in half the time and sprinted along Broome Street to the east now. A fast left took her zigging up Mercer. Her breath was coming fast now. The muscles in her legs were starting to ache.

This lower stretch of Mercer was nearly deserted. If she just ran north, she could cut over a couple of blocks and get to the park. She could run her way out of this. She had her Saucony sneakers on her feet. Footsteps sounded behind her, and she accelerated her pace. She knew that if CJ paused to take aim, he'd lose her. *Faster, faster,* she urged her protesting leg muscles.

"You're dead!" he shouted after her.

Not yet, she promised herself. She could see the lights of Houston Street. She was getting close.

Suddenly her escape route was obscured by a large, silhouetted figure. As she got closer she realized his presence wasn't coincidental. In the side wash of a streetlight she recognized the face. She didn't know his name, but she'd often seen him with CJ and Marco and the other thugs in the park. A blade winked in his hand.

Ka-ping! CJ fired a shot, which bounced off the cobblestones several feet away.

Oh, this sucked. This really sucked. Another wave of adrenaline flowed through her limbs and sizzled in her chest. She dragged in as much air as her lungs could take.

She juked, but he wouldn't let her pass. CJ was hard on her heels, so she couldn't think of stopping. CJ would succeed in shooting her in the back if she gave him any time at all. The space between CJ and his accomplice was closing fast.

Come on. Come on. Come on.

The guy in front of her raised the blade. Gaia didn't stop running. She lifted her arm, drew it back, and without losing a step punched him as hard as she could in the middle of his face. "Sorry," she murmured to him. Judging from the sting in her fist, she'd broken a tooth or two.

A bullet seared past her right shoulder. Another past her knee. The toe of her trusty sneaker caught in a deep groove between the cobblestones and she went down hard, scraping the skin of her forearms and shins.

Shit. Oh, shit.

Her mind was dreamlike again. She didn't feel any pain from her ragged, bleeding skin or from the impact to her wrist and knees. There wasn't anything wrong with her nervous system. It was that every cell of her body was fiercely anticipating the dreaded shot. Some atavistic impulse caused her to bring her hands over her head and curl her knees up in the fetal position.

Time slowed to an eerie, inexplicable stop. Although CJ had been within a few yards of her, the shot didn't come. She took big gulps of air. There were no footsteps. No bullets. She heard nothing.

Slowly, slowly, in disbelief she lifted her head from the street. She turned around cautiously. Her legs shook as she straightened them under the weight of her body.

She peered into the dark, desolate street.

He wasn't there. He really wasn't. CJ had disappeared, just when his duck had finally sat.

It was impossible. It made no sense to Gaia. Something told her there was no reasonable explanation for this. But she also knew it would be a mistake to hang around and try to figure out why.

SAM

Sometimes I worry there's something wrong with me. Sometimes I worry I don't actually feel things like regular people do. Often I'm watching the world rather than actually living in it. It's not just that I feel distant from the world. The thing that worries me is that a lot of times, I feel distant from myself. I watch myself like I'd watch an actor in a movie. I think, I observe, I process, but I don't *feel* anything.

Have you ever felt that way? Have you ever sat at the funeral of your great-aunt, for example, and worn a solemn expression on your face and tried to tell yourself all the ways in which it was sad, without actually feeling sad at all?

Have you ever met somebody who said, "Oh my God, that's so funny!" all the time, but never actually laughed? I'm worried that's me.

When my parents split up when I was in fifth grade, I said all of the things a sad kid says in that circumstance. I even wrung out a few tears. When they got back together ten months later, I shared in the happiness. But for me it was abstract. I could sort of talk myself into feeling something— or at least into believing I felt something—but it didn't come naturally. The emotions certainly didn't rush over me like a wave. I was their eager host, never their victim.

Maybe that's really lucky; I don't know.

But the flip side of experiencing pain abstractly is that you experience pleasure that way, too. Sometimes Heather and I will be eating a romantic dinner together or making out in the park, and it feels really good and everything, but I find myself wondering if I'm missing out on something.

I think this is the reason I can't get over Gaia Moore. I think it's the reason why I'm intensely attracted to her and repelled by her at the same time. When I'm with her— when I even think of her—I feel things. I feel a wave brewing just out of reach, building and swelling into a breaker of dangerous proportions.

So maybe you can see why I have mixed feelings about getting close to Gaia. I'm not sure I want to lose control. I mean, who would willingly turn himself into a victim?

Maybe that's what love is—I don't know.

HAZARDS

SAM COULDN'T HELP SMILING.

"YEAH, I'M GETTING LUCKY. VERY LUCKY."

Gaia is in danger.

Tom Moore looked up from his laptop computer. He'd been thinking vaguely of Gaia all evening—there was nothing unusual in that—but this was the first time a specific thought coalesced in his mind.

For most of his life he'd discounted notions of telepathy with a certain scorn, but his last five years in the CIA had opened him up to almost any possibility. Was Gaia truly in danger? He felt the familiar worry roiling his stomach.

He looked out the window of the airplane. The plane was either crossing desert or ocean because the sky was almost clear of cloud cover and beneath him was blackness. There wasn't a single light or other sign of human life. He felt terribly lonely.

He wasn't worried about danger in any ordinary sense. Gaia could get herself out of most situations. Tom, of all people, would know. He was the one who'd taught her. In the case of a mugger or purse snatcher going up against Gaia, Tom would frankly fear more for the criminal than her. Gaia was intensely strong, a master of martial arts and most commonly used weapons, and moreover she was free of the fear that compromised ordinary people. Or at least she *was*—

Was.

What did he know of her now?

He knew where she lived and where she went to school. Twice a year he received a heavily encrypted notice of her safety and general progress from the agency. He looked forward to those updates with the fervor of a man grasping for a lifeline, even though they were absurdly short, stiff, and uninformative.

That was it. He knew nothing of her friends, her habits, her pleasures, her emotional state. He had no idea how she was coping with her losses or how close the danger was.

"Sir?" An attendant offered him dinner on a tray. The smell further distressed his stomach. The food on U.S. military planes was even worse than on commercial flights.

"No. Thanks. Maybe later."

"We should be landing in Tel Aviv in approximately seventeen minutes, sir."

"Very well."

Tom looked back at his computer screen. His current briefing involved hundreds and hundreds of pages that had been downloaded via satellite during the course of the flight. One couldn't escape even for a matter of minutes anymore.

He couldn't give his mind to the intricacies of desert diplomacy right now.

There were other dangers to Gaia. More insidious ones that struck close to home. And how could he possibly protect her? Apart from his memories, that was the worst pain he faced.

In the old days, when Gaia was still a child, he'd been purely blown away by her abilities. She was a miracle. His greatest gift. Her brilliance, her beauty, her athleticism, and most of all her God-given sense of honor astonished him every single hour he spent with her. He couldn't imagine what he had done in this life to deserve such a child.

But in these strange days he found himself wishing and praying that his darling, magnificent Gaia were a meek, ordinary creature, likely to catch the attention of no one. A daughter he could trust, above all, to stay out of trouble.

A THREAT

"Man, what happened to your teeth?" Tarick asked. His eyes were bugged out the way they got when he was excited about something.

Marty put his hand over his mouth. He was embarrassed. One front tooth was gone, and the smaller one to the side of it was cracked down the middle. "The girl got in a lucky punch."

CJ snorted and leaned back against the fountain in Washington Square. "The girl laid him out for like five minutes," he explained. "The girl kicked his ass." He was relieved that Gaia had busted somebody else for once.

Tarick turned cold eyes on him. He got up off the fountain wall and paced. "And you, my man. Not having a lot of luck, either?"

CJ could feel his face fall. He'd been dreading this little talk with Tarick for a good reason. "She's tough, man. She's, like, supernatural. And now she's got somebody watching her back. I had a bead on her down on Mercer Street. I had her, I'm telling you, and somebody wearing a parka and a ski mask bagged me from behind and ran off."

"Who was it?" Tarick asked. He looked doubtful.

"Somebody. I don't know. I told you—I couldn't see a face," CJ said.

"You're getting real creative about coming up with excuses," Tarick said.

CJ glared at him. It was unfair. "I am totally serious, man. Marty woulda seen 'em, too, but he was out cold."

Marty looked hurt, but he didn't say anything.

Tarick shook his head. He looked at his watch. He sighed, like he was holding back his temper.

CJ was starting to feel really uneasy. The midday sun had disappeared, and clouds were rolling in from the west. The October air was suddenly cold against CJ's bare head.

He felt goose bumps rising all along his back, coursing up his neck and scalp.

"CJ, my man," Tarick started slowly. "This is not hard. You got a powerful weapon. You know where this girl lives. You gotta do what you said you were gonna do."

CJ nodded.

"And you gotta do it, like I said, by midnight Saturday. We're not fooling around here, are we?"

CJ shook his head.

Tarick sat back on the fountain wall just inches away. He put a hand on CJ's bald scalp. "I need to be able to tell the boys we avenged Marco, you know what I mean?"

CJ wished Tarick would remove his hand. It wasn't supposed to be comforting. It was a threat.

"Yeah," CJ mumbled.

"So let's make it crystal clear here, okay?" Tarick increased the pressure of his palm against CJ's shrinking scalp. "Saturday at midnight. If Gaia's not dead . . ."

Tarick paused, and CJ stared at him expectantly.

"Then you are."

SEARCH

SEARCH: Thomas Moore
No Match Found

SEARCH: Special Agent Moore
Arlington, Virginia
No Match Found

SEARCH: Federal Agent #4466
No Match Found

SEARCH: Michael Sage
No Match Found

SEARCH: Robert W. Connelly
No Match Found

SEARCH: Enigma
No Match Found

SEARCH: My goddamned father, you stupid morons.
No Match Found

SEARCH:

Gaia threw the mouse at the monitor. She was getting frustrated. She'd hacked her way into the files of the appropriate federal agency, but the search engine refused to recognize her father's name, his old badge number, or any of his old aliases.

Was he with the agency anymore? Was he even still alive?

She'd always told herself the government would notify her if he were dead. The agency was the only place that knew her whereabouts. She'd also told herself that her dad had to have been up to some pretty covert and important stuff—like single-handedly saving the planet, for instance—to have abandoned her this way.

She told herself these things, but that didn't make them true.

Gaia heard a noise. Oh, no. If Ella was home, she'd have to jump out the window again. A moment spent with that woman was like chewing tinfoil. And this was not Gaia's computer to be performing illegal operations—or actually any operations—on.

She crept to the door of George's office on silent feet. The house was still. She crept back to the computer. According to the time in the right corner of the screen, she had seven minutes before Ella was due home. George wouldn't be home till after seven.

Okay. Now what? She drummed her fingers on the

mouse pad. She didn't know the name her father used. She didn't know where he lived. She didn't know where he was working. He'd never, in almost five years, made any attempt to contact her. Not quite your doting father.

She felt the old anger building. Time for a little distraction. As far as Gaia was concerned, a little distraction was worth a lot of solution.

Okay. Plan 2. Sam. She had been less successful with plan 2 than plan 1, if that was possible. Could you get lower than zero? Was it appropriate to bring in negative numbers for the sake of comparison?

She aimed her fingers back at the keyboard. She called up an address-locator website and typed in Sam's basic information.

Aha! All was not lost! Within seconds she had a definitive answer:

SamMoon3@culdesac.com

She was just one (borrowed) computer away from direct and private conversation with Sam.

Ha!

And she'd done it while leaving one full minute to hide before Ella got home.

Sam lay in his lumpy, steelframe twin bed, considering Heather's note. He didn't need to look at the note to consider it because he had stared at it so long, he'd committed it to memory.

Heather was ready. How long had he wanted to hear those words? How long had he fantasized about this very thing?

God, and after seeing him with Gaia, he'd expected her to be pissed or at least suspicious. But she wasn't. She was angelic and totally trusting. And he was an undeserving bastard who was about to get unbelievably lucky. Almost too lucky to be true.

So what was the problem?

Forget it. There wasn't a problem. He wasn't going to get derailed by thinking about the problem.

If there was a problem, that is. Which there wasn't.

He was really, really happy as hell, even if he didn't realize it one hundred percent yet.

Time to think about Saturday night. That was only two days away. Heather was coming here, to his dorm room, and they were going to . . .

Oh, man. He was starting to feel tingly. He stared up at the stained acoustical tile on the ceiling. It wasn't the most romantic sight. He glanced at the piles of clothes around his room. He looked at the mound of chess books, magazines, and clippings blanketing his desk. He eyed the new box of syringes he'd just bought for his diabetes treatments. He propped himself up on his elbow and studied the grayish sheet covering his mattress. Exactly when was the last time he'd washed that sheet? Had it been gray to start out with, or was it born white? The feet that he couldn't remember the answer to either question wasn't a good sign.

Wait a minute. Heather. Gorgeous, perfectly dressed, sweet-smelling Heather was going to come into this room? This pigpen? This landfill? Was he seriously thinking of lying her down on this filthy bed? It wasn't only unromantic; it was probably a health hazard.

He sat up with a jolt and swung his legs off the bed. He swept up a pile of clothes and threw them on the bed beside him. Lurking under the pile were dust creatures that belonged in a horror movie. Thank God his mother couldn't see this.

In his freshman year he'd kept up some semblance of hygiene (if you defined the term very loosely) because he had a roommate. But this year he had his own minuscule room, attached to a common room shared by three other guys. He pretended to get indignant when the other guys left spilled beer on the vomit-colored carpet in the common room or ground Cheetos into microscopic orange dust underfoot.

But that didn't mean he'd spent even one second looking after his own room. Usually if Heather came around, they hung out in the common room and watched TV or raided the minifridge. She hadn't inspected the frightening cave where he slept.

It was high time to reacquaint himself with the laundry room in the basement. He'd sweep out whatever flora and fauna were growing under his bed. He'd get rid of the altar to Gary Kasparov—no need to subject Heather to a full-on dork fest. Besides, the knitted brow of Kasparov didn't exactly put you in the mood.

He was just consolidating his massive clothes pile when the door swung open.

"Hey, Moon."

It was Mike Suarez, one of his suite mates.

"Does the word *knock* mean anything to you, Suarez?" Sam asked.

"Does the phrase 'lock your friggin' door if you don't want company' mean anything to you?"

Sam laughed. "The lock is busted. Half the time you turn the knob, it falls off into your hand." He made a mental note to get that fixed before Saturday.

Suarez watched him clean for a minute.

"You planning on getting lucky?"

Sam paused and rubbed his nose. Dust bits were flying in his nostrils, making them itch. "What do you mean?"

"I can think of only one reason why a guy cleans his room." Suarez said suggestively.

Sam's energy sagged at the thought of being such a cliché. He tossed the ball of laundry on the ground.

"So?"

Sam couldn't help smiling. "Yeah, I'm getting lucky. Very lucky."

CAN HE RESIST?

"She found nothing, of course," Ella stated, her voice ringing shrilly through the wide-open loft space, bouncing around its few polished surfaces.

"I see. And you were there watching her for the duration of her search?"

Ella's face showed impatience. "Certainly."

He pressed his lips together to signal his own waning patience. Ella, with her sleek body, her colorfully revealing clothing, and her poorly concealed moodiness acted as much the angry teenager as his bewitching Gaia. But as potently as Ella annoyed him, she had a value far beyond the dog-loyal bodyguards who remained within fifteen feet of him at all times. "Did she display any knowledge of her father's whereabouts?"

"No. Nothing current."

He flicked a tiny piece of lint from his dark blue slacks. "I see." He sipped coffee. "And he has made no attempt to contact her?" The question was rhetorical. He didn't even know why he'd asked it.

"No," Ella confirmed.

"How can he resist?" he mused in a quiet voice, mostly to himself.

"Sir?"

"How can he resist making contact with Gaia? She's all he has in the world after what happened to Katia. He adores her. He needs her. He knows she's bound to get into trouble." He was really talking only to himself.

"Yes, sir. Would you like me to continue to keep a record of her computer activity in case she makes any strides toward finding him?" Ella asked. Even when her words were perfectly dutiful, her tone was petulant.

He made a sharp exhale through his nose, which was the closest he came to amusement. "She won't find him. Although I despise Tom, I can't pretend he's an idiot, can I? She'll never find him, although you're welcome to leave a few red herrings that will keep her busy trying. I'm banking on the belief—no, the knowledge—that Tom will find *her*."

He picked up the impossibly slender computer from the table beside him. He'd just had a very simple and appealing idea. He sat back and crossed his legs, the computer perched on his knee. "Tom will come for her, and when he does, he's mine."

GAIA

There's one thing I want more than anything else, and I know I can never have it. I don't mean Sam or finding my dad. I'm talking about something inside myself.

I want to be brave.

And I'm not brave, in case you're wondering. Maybe I could have been brave, but I guess I'll never know.

The reason is that you can't separate bravery from fear. This is something I've thought about a lot. The people with the most fear have the greatest opportunity to be brave. A woman who is terrified of the water would be braver sticking her big toe in the swimming pool than I would be surfing a thirty-foot breaker in the Pacific Ocean. She would be overcoming something. She would be challenging herself. She would experience the pleasure of expanding her world, the freedom of exercising her will. I would be surfing a wave.

My mom used to say that a poor person who gave a dime to charity was more generous than a rich one who gave hundreds of dollars. In this example, I would be Bill Gates. Only richer.

I know for a fact that my mother was claustrophobic. And most especially, she was afraid of tunnels. Deeply, seriously afraid. I think it had something to do with her childhood in Russia, which was pretty tough. Anyway, the reason I know is because when I was seven, all my friends were taking gymnastics class a few miles away and I was desperate to go. My mom didn't want to take me at first, but I begged and pleaded. I wouldn't shut up about it. Finally my mom agreed. It turned out you had to go through a tunnel to get there. So even though I wasn't a very sensitive or nice kid, I realized my mom was basically flipping out in that tunnel. Her hands were dripping wet on the steering wheel, and her skin was whitish gray. She made these weird little moaning sounds. When we finally got out of the tunnel, she pulled over on the shoulder, rested her head on the steering wheel, and just stayed like that. I was upset, but she held me and promised me everything was fine.

Every Saturday for almost two years after that, my

mother drove me to gymnastics and picked me up.

When I think of that, I'm filled with horrible, wrenching, miserable guilt. I wish so much I would have dropped that stupid gymnastics class and never gone back. But I didn't. And I can't change the past.

So instead of that, I wish that for one single moment in my life, I could be brave like my mom.

FRAGILE
UNDERSTANDING

SAM'S LONG, BEAUTIFUL BODY CLAIMED
ALL OF HER SENSES.

SENT MAIL

Dear Sam,

    I have a very strange favor to ask you. I know you don't know me that well, and what you know of me you probably don't like. I am really, truly, sincerely sorry for what happened to Heather in the park and for the part I played in it. I know she's your girlfriend, so what I'm about to ask will sound particularly insane, but

Dear Sam,

    There's this guy named CJ, a friend and fellow neo-Nazi of Marco's, the guy who tried to kill us after slashing Zolov in the park. Well, would you believe Marcos is dead and CJ thinks I did it? CJ has completely lost his mind and is now hell-bent on killing me. And I came to this realization that before I die, I really want to

Dear Sam,

    I know I must seem like trouble to you. I know it must seem like bad luck follows me around. I know you probably wish you'd never seen my face, which I can totally understand. And lucky for you, after this coming weekend you'll most likely never have to see me again. But before then, I was wondering if you wouldn't mind

Dear Sam,

I am confessing to you in total confidence that in my seventeen years, I've had very little romantic experience. Okay, none. Well, actually there was this kid in seventh grade who kind of liked me but—

Anyway, I've been thinking about you a lot recently, and I was wondering whether—

Dear Sam,

Will you have sex with me? Saturday night, no questions, no commitment.

Oh, shit. Ella was home. Gaia had to get out of George's office right away. Ella would lose it if she found Gaia in here and there was no way Gaia wanted to deal with the witch in her present state of mind.

Oh. Oh. Gaia's eyes flew over the computer monitor. What should she do? Should she save one of these horrible letters to finish later? She had so many windows open on the screen, she couldn't keep track of them. She heard Ella's heels clicking down the hallway. Oh, no. Um. Um.

In desperation she clicked on the Send Later icon. She clicked the X in the top-right corner to exit the online service. Ella was slowing down. She was right outside!

Gaia threw herself under George's desk and held her breath. Ella paused in the open office doorway.

Don't come in here! Gaia commanded silently. *Go away now!*

Ella paid no heed to the telepathic messages. She walked right up to the computer and stared, squinting, at the screen.

Gaia knew for a fact that Ella was seriously nearsighted. But the woman was too vain to wear glasses and too stupid to put in contacts.

Ella placed her hand on the mouse.

What could she possibly want with the computer? Gaia wondered. No interface was user-friendly enough for Ella. Gaia had often snickered at the full library of "Such and Such for Dummies" titles on Ella's bookshelf.

Ella continued to stare dumbly at the screen. Her feet were a matter of inches from Gaia's shins. *Don't look down,* Gaia ordered in her head. *Do* not! Gaia tried to make her body as absolutely small as possible.

Ella clicked the mouse. Gaia heard the modem dialing up the online service and, within a few seconds, connecting. "Hello," the synthesized computer voice chirped.

What was going on? Gaia had never seen Ella in the same room with a computer before. Had she suddenly discovered the joy of online sex? Had somebody told her about the Victoria's Secret website?

Ella squinted at the screen for another moment and clicked the mouse again.

Please don't be long, Gaia begged silently. Her knees hurt, and her back was cramping. It was so dusty under George's

272

desk, she felt a sneeze threatening. If Ella was going shopping, it could take hours.

Then, as though obeying silent orders, Ella stood up, turned around and walked away. She walked right back down the hallway and up the creaky stairs.

Gaia's heart soared with relief. She uncrumpled her limbs and climbed out from under the desk. She was so busy congratulating herself, she didn't bother to look at the screen at first. Then the blinking box caught the corner of her eye. She came closer to read it.

"Your mail was sent."

A shiver crept down Gaia's spine. What? What mail had been sent? Probably just something of Ella's, Gaia tried to comfort herself.

She clicked on the file icon to investigate. Then she clicked the Mail Sent icon. She was starting to get a very bad feeling in her stomach.

It was one of Gaia's files. Somehow, by going online, Ella had sent a Send Later file. But which one? Gaia clicked twice on the file.

It came up instantly, the letters twice as big and black as any others on the screen. She felt like someone had kicked her brutally hard in the middle of her chest.

Dear Sam,

    Will you have sex with me? Saturday night, no questions, no commitment.

GAIA SIGHTING

Tom Moore was crossing another endless desert. For a man who traveled tens of thousands of miles every week of his life, he certainly spent a great deal of time in the same chair, studying the same screen. For a man who hadn't seen his daughter in five years, he certainly spent a great deal of time thinking about her.

Hundreds, thousands of pages of briefings swam before his eyes. He closed the document and looked around him. He was so accustomed to the hum of jet engines, he could hardly sleep without it. The only other passenger, his personal assistant, was asleep.

The ever present satellite connection allowed him to get online. He'd promised himself he wouldn't do this, but tonight, well, tonight his mind was once again burning with worry for Gaia, and he couldn't ignore it any longer.

His first search for her name called up nothing. That was as it should be if the U.S. government was doing what they'd promised. Then he reduced the search to just her first name and conducted it globally, typing in a series of passwords that allowed him a degree of access allowed to only a handful of people—access to virtually all e-mail posted on the web, for example. This turned up an enormous list. He allowed himself a look into one file. Just one. He'd pick it wisely, then he'd stop this nonsense and get back to his work.

He scrolled through the upper part of the list. He stopped on a note tagged by the re: field. It read:

re: supergaia

He opened the file:

TO: jackboot
FROM: stika

Gaia sighting at WSW. Call set for 2100 Sat. 2 guys and metal.

It was an unfortunately good guess. Tom's worry intensified as he read easily between the lines. He felt distressingly sure this Gaia was his Gaia. He could see that the posting had come from the New York City area and could easily assume that WSW meant Washington Square West, a very short distance from George's home and the school Gaia attended.

Now that he'd opened Pandora's box, the ghosts were all around him. He'd known this could happen. Now it didn't matter how critically his presence was needed in Beirut. He pressed the button for the intercom that connected his voice to the cockpit.

"Gentlemen," he said calmly, "I'm afraid I need to order a change in destination. Let's touch down for refueling. We'll be crossing the Atlantic tonight."

URGENT LONGING

Gaia padded quietly down the darkened hallway. She'd never been in a college dormitory before. When she reached the room number she'd gotten from the student directory, she paused. She combed her fingers through her hair, pushing long strands back from her face. She pulled self-consciously at the hem of her exquisitely soft red velvet tank dress. Taking a breath, she turned the heavy brass knob and swung open the door.

Her breath caught. He was there. He lay on his bed, his strong arms folded behind his head, propping his upper body against the bed frame. The rest of the room was oddly indistinct, shadowy and blurred. Sam's long, beautiful body claimed all of her senses.

He looked at her. He wasn't surprised. He wasn't upset. He wasn't happy, exactly, either. He looked . . . serious. Had he known she would come now? Had he wanted it?

His feet were bare and crossed at the ankles. His loose gray sweatpants were turned up a few times at the bottom. Keeping his eyes on her face, he swung his knees over the side of the small bed and stood. He started toward her, then stopped, leaving two feet between them. Slowly he reached his arm, making a bridge across the air, and placed two fingers on the inside of her elbow, that vulnerable place where oxygen-thirsty blood coursed closest to her surface. A chill stole up her neck and dispersed over her scalp.

She'd come prepared with a storm of explanations in her head: 1. Why. 2. Why now. 3. Why him. But in this moment, stating them felt like it would break the tentative, fragile understanding, nurtured and protected by silence.

She took a step closer. This was hard for her. She bent her elbow and wrapped her fingers around his wrist. Was he pulling her, or was she pulling him? She wasn't sure. All she knew was that she was now close enough to feel the warmth radiating from his skin. He put his arms around her. She felt his fingers on the nape of her neck. Suddenly her arms were circling his taut waist, pressing him against her, crushing her breasts against his broad chest.

God, she was dizzy. She was light-headed, giddy, tingling with excitement and disbelief. Her heart was too full to stay in her rib cage. Tears gathered under her lashes.

He bent his head down so close to hers, she could feel his soft breath on her cheek. Oh God, how she wanted this kiss. She'd waited a lifetime for it. She breathed in his subtle, masculine smell and faint mixture of clean sweat and eucalyptus-scented shaving cream. She lifted her mouth to his.

Her mind was a tumultuous sea, with thoughts listing and bobbing there. And all at once an image arrived. It was an image of her body, scarred and wounded, becoming whole and perfect under his healing lips. The picture was beautiful, and she wished she could keep it, but a wave crashed through, sending thoughts spinning and surfing in the chop.

Please, kiss me, she found herself wishing. *Please. I need you.*

And then, in a cruel trick played by fate, Sam not only failed to kiss her; he dissolved completely. He vanished into air. He was replaced by dim, grayish sunlight, a tangle of mismatched covers. The magical night in his bed was replaced by a harsh, wrenching morning in hers. No, not even in hers. In one that belonged to George and Ella. Her velvet dress was replaced by a worn-out T-shirt from Jerry's Crab House.

She turned over and buried her head in her pillow. Tears stung in her eyes. The loneliness was almost unbearable. As reality spread out before her, its stark contrast to the dream made it that much harder to take.

She wanted so much to retrieve the feelings . . . and that image.

What was that image again?

In that first moment of waking, it teased her with its closeness. It danced and sparkled on a wavelet at her feet. But then the vast ocean pulled back the tide into its dark, infinite belly, and now Gaia was faced with the terror of never finding it again. If she could only find it, she felt sure it would give her strength and maybe hope.

But she was left with nothing but the taste of Sam—her fantasy of Sam—on her lips and an urgent, painful longing in her heart.

(SIR) THOMAS MOORE

You may have noticed my name sounds familiar. I share it with a number of people, but most importantly the great scholar, statesman, and saint Sir Thomas More, born in England in 1478.

My mother was a devout Roman Catholic, and I assumed she picked the name to remind me of piety above all else. To remind me to choose God-given principles over king or scholarship or art . . . or even family.

Since I was a child, I felt the pressure of this name. I took it seriously. That's the kind of person I am, I suppose. I wanted to serve my country. I wanted to serve God. And if sacrifices were called for, I wanted to possess the courage to make them with honor.

My namesake set forth an almost impossible record of bravery. He watched his father imprisoned by King Henry VII because of his own deeds. He wrote a brilliant critique of English society in his work *Utopia*. Ultimately he was canonized for putting his head on the chopping block rather than compromising his basic beliefs for the benefit of King Henry VIII.

I never questioned the rightness of More's example until after I lost Katia and then Gaia. Now the question haunts me every day of my life.

In an ironic and unfortunate twist of fate, not long after my mother's death, I read a letter she'd written to her father around the time I was born. In it I discovered she didn't name me after Thomas More, honored saint and statesman. She named me after Thomas Moore, the Irish romantic poet.

ABOUT SEX

BUT MAYBE HE WOULD BE CURIOUS. AND MAYBE
A TINY BIT INTERESTED? WAS IT POSSIBLE?

A CREEPY PERVERT

"Gaia Moore? Are you with us?"

Gaia snapped her head up. She glanced around at the unsympathetic faces of her classmates. Which class was this? What were they talking about? She gave her head a shake to dislodge her heavy, demanding preoccupations.

Let's see. Ummmm. Ms. Rupert. That would be history. European history. Which century were they in now? Which country? She hadn't looked at her textbook in a while.

"No, ma'am, I'm not," Gaia replied truthfully.

Ms. Rupert's eyes bulged with annoyance. "You're not, are you? Then would you be so kind as to share with me and the rest of the class what you find so much more captivating than the court of King Henry VIII?"

Gaia drummed her fingers on her desk. Did Ms. Rupert *really* want to know the answer to that question?

"Yes, Gaia? I'm waiting." Her hands were on her hips in a caricature of impatience.

Apparently she did. "I was thinking about sex, ma'am. I was thinking about having sex," Gaia stated.

The class disintegrated into laughter and whispering. Everybody was staring at Gaia. It wasn't nice laughter. Since the incident with Heather getting slashed in the park, Gaia wasn't exactly Miss Popularity. She shrugged.

Ms. Rupert looked like she'd swallowed her tongue. She spluttered and turned deep crimson before she could get a word out. "G-Gaia Moore, get out of my class! Go to the principal's office *now!*"

"Yes, ma'am," Gaia said agreeably, striding to the door.

This was a lucky break, she thought, walking down the deserted hall with lightness in her step. The vice principal would keep her waiting outside his office for ages as a phony display of his importance and full-to-bursting schedule, and it was much easier to obsess about Sam without Ms. Rupert droning on about Henry VIII and all the various people's heads he'd chopped off.

What was Sam thinking? That was the central question nagging her. Assuming he'd received her psychotic e-mail and could tell it was from her, what must he be thinking?

That she was a nympho, for one thing. That she gave new meaning to the word *desperate*, for another. That she was an opportunistic couple wrecker, for a third.

But maybe he would be curious. And maybe a tiny bit interested? Was it possible?

She hardly dared hope.

In some ways she was happy she'd gotten the ball rolling, even if the note did make her seem like someone who deserved to be arrested and put under a restraining order. At least she'd opened up the conversation. At least it would give her the opportunity to say, Hey, Sam, I know this is weird, I know I seem like a complete sex-starved lunatic, but can I just explain?

She ascended a flight of stairs and was just passing the computer lab when she stopped. Hmmm. The room was dark, empty, and filled, not surprisingly, with computers. She needed only one, and she needed it only for a minute or two. Ms. Rupert would eat her own arm if she knew Gaia was making a detour, but so what?

Gaia crept to the back corner of the room and revived the sleeping monitor. Quickly she located the Internet server and signed on. She went to the site where she kept a mailbox and typed in her password.

Oh, God. There was mail! She held her breath and clicked on the envelope symbol. Her heart leaped. It was from Sam Moon! He had replied!

Was this good? Was this bad? At least it was something.

Now, calm down, she commanded herself. Okay. She clicked on the letter to open it.

Dear Gaia13,

Your letter was an unbelievable turn-on. I've been hard since I read it. You name the time and place and I am there, honey. I am all over you. I will make you scream, baby. I will make you beg for more. Once you feel my—

Gaia swallowed. She couldn't read any more. Her stomach felt queasy. This wasn't what she . . . she couldn't quite believe he . . .

Her eye caught on something in the routing information at the bottom of the letter. A phrase of coded gobbledygook in which she picked out the word *Canada*. She clicked on another series of boxes to get Sam Moon's personal profile.

NAME: Sam Moon
HOME: Victoria, BC
AGE: 62

Gaia's body was flooded with relief. She almost had to laugh. She had blatantly propositioned a sixty-two-year-old Canadian man. She exited the program and turned off the computer.

On the bright side, her beloved Sam Moon wasn't a creepy pervert, although he shared his name with one. On the less bright side, she was back to square one.

HOW HE FEELS

"So *what* is the problem?" Danny Bell wanted to know. He said it so loudly, Sam had to hold the phone a few inches from his ear.

"Well, I guess . . . I don't know." Sam scratched the back of his scalp absently. "I'm not really sure how I feel about her."

Sam watched colorful pipes weaving three-dimensionally through the computer screen that sat on his crowded dorm-room desk. He'd set the screen saver to come on after ten minutes of idleness, but when he was talking on the phone or procrastinating, the damn pipes seemed to take over his screen every thirty seconds.

"You're not sure how you *feel* about her?" Danny didn't go far out of his way to hide the incredulity in his voice. "Let me get this straight. You have a stupendously gorgeous girl-friend who you've been with for six months. She wants to have sex, and you're suddenly not sure how you *feel*?"

Sam could picture exactly the look on Danny's face, even though he was three thousand miles away. Danny was his oldest and closest friend from the neighborhood in Maryland where he grew up. In fact, Danny was the only friend he had from the old days, before Sam had remade himself from a stammering, buck-toothed chess nerd into a

287

decently dressed mainstream guy who went out with beautiful girls and cared what other people thought.

It was funny. Sam had changed, but Danny hadn't. Danny was still an unapologetic lover of chess and Myst and Star Wars. He was an engineering student at Stanford University, which was probably what Sam would have been had he stayed the course.

"Okay, there's a little more to it than that," Sam confessed. "See, I met this other girl."

"Aha," Danny said in a know-it-all way. "I had a feeling there was something more here. So what happened? Did you go out with her behind Heather's back?"

The pipes were hypnotic. "No, not exactly."

"But you're attracted to her."

Sam let out a groan. "Yeah, you could say that."

"What's she like?"

"Well . . . she's different from any girl I've ever met," Sam began slowly. "She's an uncanny chess player, for one thing. She's probably at my level or close to it."

Danny was silent for at least thirty seconds. "No way," he said at last.

"I'm serious."

"Jesus. What's her name? Have I heard of her or read about her?"

"No. She's mysterious like that," Sam explained. "She hasn't come up through the normal chess ranks. I don't know anybody who's played her in competition. I don't know how she learned. She's just . . . brilliant."

"Are you sure you're not just stupid when you're around her?" Danny asked.

Sam laughed. "I *am* stupid when I'm around her. But she really is good. The other guys who play chess in the park worship her—and not for her body, either. I wouldn't even play her again 'cause she'd probably beat me in a matter of seconds."

Danny was struck to the point of speechlessness. "So, what else do you know about her?" he asked finally.

"Well, I guess her parents aren't around anymore, and from what I can tell, she has very few if any friends. She just moved to New York, but I don't know from where."

"That's awful. Did you ask her where she came from?" Danny asked.

"No." The pipes were now making Sam nauseous. He moved from his desk chair and paced the three available feet of space in the room. One of the few benefits of a minuscule room was that the ancient phone cord reached every corner of it. "I can't explain why, exactly. It's like . . . I don't know. She doesn't give you the feeling that she really welcomes questions. She seems kind of . . . haunted in a way. I guess she's been through a lot in her life. I had this weird reaction to her the first time I saw her, like I knew everything about her even though I didn't know anything. I was intensely attracted to her and sort of scared off at the same time."

Sam heard Mike Suarez and one of his other suite mates,

Brendon Moss, firing up the TV for a baseball game. He moved to close the door to his room.

One of the great things about Danny was that he wasn't cool. He wasn't jaded or sarcastic. He wasn't embarrassed about having a real conversation. Sam could tell Danny things he wouldn't consider telling his other friends.

"Does that make any sense?" Sam finished.

"Um. Not really," Danny answered.

Sam sat down on his bed. (Now covered with a clean, nearly white sheet.) "Yeah, I know," he said. "I guess I'm hesitant to ask her anything because I'm not all that sure I want to hear the answers."

"Huh," Danny said. "Maybe she's a spy. Or an alien. Did you ever see that movie *Species*?"

Sam laughed again.

"So what does this girl look like?" Danny asked. "She can't be as pretty as Heather."

Sam thought that one over for a minute. "In a way she's not, and in a way she's much much more beautiful. She doesn't dress like Heather, or wear jewelry, or keep her hair nice. You don't get the feeling she's trying to be pretty. And she's got this kind of hard, angry expression on her face a lot of the time. But if you can get past that and really see her face and her eyes . . . she's by far the most amazing-looking girl I've ever met. I can't explain it."

"Wow," Danny said. "So why don't you try it out with this girl?" he suggested after considering it for a few moments. "It sounds like she's gotten under your skin."

"She has. That's exactly what it is," Sam said, rearranging his long legs as the weary dorm-room bed groaned under his weight. "But first of all, there's Heather to think of. And also, this girl is all about trouble. I can't even begin to explain to you the kind of trouble she causes. Heather is safe, and she's great And she's . . . ready."

Danny laughed. "Yeah. God, I wish I had your problems."

Sam walked over to the window and looked out at the courtyard. In New York City they called it a courtyard even if it was ten square feet of poured concrete, overfilled with plastic garbage cans and piles of recycling. "It's not as fun as it sounds," Sam said.

"Well, there's one obvious thing to do," Danny pointed out.

"Yeah, what's that?"

"Take out a piece of paper. At the top put Heather's name on one side and the other girl's name on the other, and make a list."

Heather	Gaia
My girlfriend	Not my girlfriend
My parents love her	Would frighten my parents
Not good at chess	Great at chess
Belongs in a magazine	Doesn't
Safe	Trouble
Loves me	Probably doesn't give a shit
Ready	?

Sam studied his list for a moment, crumpled it in a tight ball, and tossed it in the garbage. What was he, some kind of idiot?

GHOSTS

HIS HEART, HIS LIFE, HIS SENSE
OF LIFE'S POSSIBILITIES WERE SHAKEN.

REMEMBERING KATIA

Tom Moore knew he was crazy to be doing this. He walked down Waverly Place in the West Village with his head throbbing and his heart full. Just two blocks from here, in a tiny bookshop, he'd first laid eyes on Katia. It was probably the most important moment of his entire life, and yet he hadn't been back here in twenty years.

It was, without question, love at first sight. It was a freezing cold day in February, and the city was bleak and dismal. The previous night's snow was no more than a brown, muddy obstacle between sidewalk and street. He'd been looking for a rare translation of Thucydides for his graduate thesis. He was stewing about something—that his adviser hadn't credited him in a recent publication. He'd seen her as soon as he'd opened the door. The shop was a tiny square, for one thing. But Katia seemed to draw every atom in the place to her. In that moment Tom's entire life evaporated and a new one started.

She was sitting cross-legged in the corner, bent forward with a book on her lap. He remembered she wore gray woolen tights, under battered rubber boots and a red knit dress. Her hair was long, dark, and straight, falling in a shiny column on either side of her face. She was devouring a stack of books the way a starving person would devour a plate of food. He would never forget that image of her.

Up until that point, he'd had many relationships with women. Fellow college and grad students, pretty ones he'd met through friends. He'd traveled with girlfriends, even lived with one for a few months. And yet his heart had never been stirred until the time he saw Katia, a naive nineteen-year-old with cheap, old-fashioned Eastern Bloc clothing and a thick Russian accent. And then it was shaken.

His heart, his life, his sense of life's possibilities was shaken. In her eyes he became somebody he could believe in.

He paused after crossing Seventh Avenue. He shouldn't be here at all. He'd learned in the hardest possible way that a man who'd made enemies like his could not afford to have a family. His disguise was minimal. His presence was needed in Beirut. He could walk straight into Gaia if he wasn't careful. He was drowning his usually sane mind in a riptide of memories.

Still he continued on. And then stopped dead in his tracks. Of course. Of course. Virtually every single thing in New York City had changed in the last twenty years, and that bookstore remained. Katia was gone. The person he'd been with Katia was gone. Their beautiful daughter, the greatest pleasure in their lives, was alone. And the damn bookstore winked at him smugly. The riptide threatened. It dragged on his feet. Tom walked faster.

If he had any sense, he'd get back on that plane, his home away from work, and resume his mission. It was all he could show for the terrible sacrifices he'd made.

But he couldn't. He needed to see Gaia just once. From afar, of course. He'd drink her in with his thirsty eyes, make sure she was safe, and get back to his work.

Although Thomas, sainted statesman, had boarded the plane back in Tel Aviv, it appeared that the romantic poet had disembarked here in New York.

DARTS

"Wait, so you're not going to Robbie's tomorrow night?" Melanie asked Heather, scrambling to keep up with her friend's long, efficient strides. "According to Shauna, it's a two kegger with zero parents."

Heather shook her head. "Nope. Other plans." She smiled in a way that was mysterious and maybe a tiny bit smug. She glanced up the crowded block of Eighth Street. There were two good shoe stores before they even got to Patricia Field, and Melanie and Cory Parkes were already loaded down with shopping bags and struggling to keep up. Heather was famous among her friends for being a very fast walker and an intensely picky shopper, but the truth was, she no longer had a duplicate of her parents' credit card, the way many of her friends did.

"Other plans?" Cory demanded, gulping up the bait as always.

"Sam and I are . . . getting together," Heather offered.

"So bring him to the party," Melanie said, falling back for a moment as she rearranged her bags between her tired hands.

"I promised him we'd be alone for once," Heather explained.

"Oooh. Does this mean you're taking things to the next level?" Cory asked.

Heather smiled ambiguously. "It's a thought."

Melanie was getting that look. Her face crumpled a little when conversation turned to Sam, partly because she was envious that Heather had a mythically desirable boyfriend but also because it got in the way of Melanie's supercontrolling go-girl solidarity. Heather had a pessimistic feeling that Melanie's allegiances would change once she found a guy she thought was worthy.

"Besides," Heather said. "You know I can't drag him to high school parties anymore." She pulled up short at Broadway Shoes, one of their regular destinations. "Do you want to go here?" she asked.

"Let's go straight to Patricia Field," Melanie said. "They have these really cute mod dresses."

Cory strode alongside Heather eagerly. "Are you going to get the orange skirt with the thingies along the bottom you tried on last time? It looked so, so cool on you."

Heather shrugged. "Maybe. The lining was kind of itchy." The lining was only mildly itchy; the skirt cost ninety-five dollars.

They were a few yards down the block from Ozzie's Cafe when Heather's stomach dropped. It was funny. She saw Ed Fargo most days of her life. It had been over two years since they'd broken up. Yet still her physical reaction on seeing him was always the same—sometimes stronger, sometimes weaker, but always present.

He was sitting in his wheelchair at a front table by the window, seeming to scan every person who passed. His dark hair was crying out to be combed, and his awful mid-nineties cargo pants belonged in a Dumpster. But Ed managed to be powerfully attractive nonetheless. His jaw was a little sharp and his straight nose was a little long, but he had possibly the most beautiful mouth that had ever graced the face of a man. The parts of his face, though not flawless the way Sam's were, came together in a striking and disarming way.

As often happened, Heather had that strange, sad feeling of disconnect, knowing the ghost of the person she'd loved desperately, the one with legs that worked, was lurking within the person in the ghastly wheelchair, who needed special ramp entrances and kneeling buses.

She was shallow. She knew that. Ed was still the same person inside. He was still the same person inside. No matter how many times she said it and thought it, she couldn't make herself believe it.

She stopped abruptly and rapped on the glass. Ed looked up and smiled. It was a guarded smile. She was in a position to know the difference.

Her friends were already several steps ahead, but they had stopped now and were waiting for her. "Go ahead," she called, waving them on. "I'll meet you there in, like, five minutes." When they paused, she gestured again, less patiently. "Go. I swear I'll be there in a couple of minutes."

Once her friends started walking again, Heather stepped into Ozzie's and was embraced by the thick smell of coffee. "Hey, Ed," she said, sitting down in the empty chair across from him.

"Hey," he said back. "What's going on?"

"Nothing. Just, you know, shopping with the girlfriends."

Ed nodded.

"You're waiting for someone?" Heather asked. Before he had a chance to answer, she said, "Let me guess. Gaia Moore, right?"

He looked uncomfortable. "No, not really."

"Oh, come on."

"What?" Ed said defensively. "Sometimes she comes by

here after school and we have coffee. Sometimes I have coffee by myself."

Heather put her index finger on a drop of coffee that had spilled on the table. She spread the liquid in a widening circle. "You guys have gotten to be good friends, it seems like."

"Yeah."

Heather laughed at a memory, pretending it was repulsive. "Did you hear about her classic line in Rupert's class today?"

Though still guarded, Ed now looked interested in spite of himself. "No. What?"

"Rupert asked her why she wasn't paying attention, and Gaia said, and this is an exact quote, 'I was thinking about sex. I was thinking about having sex.'" Heather laughed again. "What a freak. People were mimicking her all afternoon. I'm surprised you missed it."

Ed waited for her to finish without even a smile. What had happened to the guy's sense of humor?

Heather needed a way in. She needed to make Ed talk to her. She sat back in her chair and rolled a piece of her hair between her finger and thumb.

"I've heard Gaia's stoking a major crush," she said, tossing a dart into the winds.

Ed remained wary. "Oh, yeah?"

"So says the rumor mill," Heather said provocatively. She took a calculated risk with a second dart. "Word is, the crush is on you. Tannie got a look at her notebook in precal. . . ."

Bull's-eye. Ed's cheeks flushed. He met her eyes with poorly masked excitement and curiosity.

On the one hand, Heather was pleased that her instincts served her so well. On the other hand, it pissed her off that Ed was obviously falling victim to Gaia, too. Had Gaia Moore been put on earth to punish her?

Ed crumpled an empty sugar packet tighly between his fingers. "I don't know about that," he mumbled. Guarded as he was, he did want to talk. "I think it's more about sex."

Heather yawned. Once she got started, it was genuine. "What do you mean?"

"Oh, I don't know." Ed seemed to wave a thought away. "She wants to lose her virginity. I guess if she's telling Ms. Rupert's class about it, it's not a big secret."

Heather looked in her purse, ostensibly for lip balm. "And who's the lucky guy?" she said suggestively.

"She hasn't said. It's a mystery."

"Aha." In near perfect detail, Heather's mind called up the image of Gaia and Sam sitting together on that bench in the park. Heather was starting to get an unpleasant feeling about this.

Heather located the tube of Chap Stick and ran it over her lips. "It's not a mystery to me," she said confidently.

"What do you mean?" Ed asked tentatively, crushing the bit of paper in his palm.

"It's obvious," Heather said, getting up from the table, "that the lucky guy is you."

It was a mean thing to say since Heather didn't believe it, but when she saw the naked hope and pleasure in Ed's eyes, her anger took over and she told herself he deserved it.

IMPOSSIBLE

STUPID, MORON, SHIT-HEAD CJ WAS STICKING HIS
STUPID GUN IN HER FACE AGAIN.

THE VIGILANTE

Ever since she'd woken from that dream, Gaia was so distracted, she could hardly remember to breathe regularly or feed herself or put one foot in front of the other when walking.

Ow. She kicked her big toe hard against a ledge in the cracked cement sidewalk and stumbled forward.

She certainly couldn't be bothered to come up with appropriate kiss-ass behavior for the vice principal, which was why she'd sat through detention, which was why she was walking home late.

She arrived at the corner of the park. Cut through or take the long way?

In her state, the right thing to do was go around. How was she going to make the dream happen if she got shot today?

She cut through, anyway. To do anything else was purely against her nature.

Would Sam be at the chess tables today, and if so, what should she say? It was time to get serious about her plan. No more being shy. No more being awkward. Her dream emboldened her.

Oh God, and there he was. She spotted him from the back, playing chess with Zolov. His elbow rested on the edge of the table, and he cradled his head in his hand. The last of the day's sun turned his tousled hair into gold. She could see a bit of his profile, the sensual curve of his mouth.

It was the perfect opportunity to proposition him, but she couldn't seem to make her feet go forward. She called up the dream again, but far from emboldening her, it turned her cheeks red and made her feel very shy. Those were the lips that had made her feel . . .

She heard scrambling behind her and spun around. *Oh, shit.* She took off at a run. CJ was lying in wait, of course, as she certainly knew he would be. Why was she so stupid? Couldn't she give up the death wish for even a day or two? At this rate she *deserved* to die a lonely, bitter, parentless virgin.

She cursed herself as she sprinted through the park and westward toward Sixth Avenue. It would be busy there this hour, hopefully busy enough to lose him.

Gaia raced onto the avenue. *Beeeep! Beeeeeeeeeeeeep!*

"Get the *hell* out of the *street!*" somebody screeched.

A maroon commercial van swerved to avoid her and plowed into the back of a taxicab. Gaia heard the crumpling of metal. The taxi rear-ended a black Mercedes-Benz convertible. The Mercedes drove up onto the sidewalk and crushed its headlight against a parking meter.

Oh, Jesus. Gaia ducked behind a stopped garbage truck as the air filled with shouting drivers slamming doors and the excited buzz of pedestrians crowding to watch the show. No one was hurt, Gaia was pretty sure of that, and the chaos gave her a second to collect herself. She spotted CJ on the curb, his eyes wildly scanning the street for her.

Don't move, she told him silently. *I'll be right there.*

This was all she needed—a chance to see him without being seen. She noticed with huge relief that he'd stuffed the gun back in his jacket. The sidewalk where he stood had largely emptied of people, who were drawn to the activity a little ways down the street.

Ducking as she crept along, she used the line of stopped cars to conceal herself. She had him directly in her sights, not ten feet away. *Now go!*

She pounced. In a single graceful move she captured both of his arms and wrenched them behind his back. She dragged him several yards off the busy avenue to the relative backwater of Minetta Lane. CJ growled and twisted his body to free his arms. He succeeded, or at least he thought so. The truth was, she was happy to let him come at her as long as the gun stayed out of his hands.

"Bitch," he hissed at her with a snarl. He took a step back to get some leverage, drew back his right arm, and launched his fist at her face. She dodged it easily. She felt relaxed, even—shamefully—a little excited. For Gaia a fistfight against one other person hardly drew a sweat. And CJ was just the kind of asshole she most enjoyed putting in his place.

He hauled off again, this time aiming the punch at her stomach. She caught it long before it landed. His exertion threw him so for off balance, she used the offending arm to lay him out on the pavement with the smallest effort.

He quickly found his feet and stood up, bellowing a long string of obscenities. He was squaring off, spitting mad, trying to find some way at her.

All right. It was tempting to linger but not a good idea. Time to close this thing out. He leaped at her sloppily, swinging both arms. She ducked and landed a swift, hard jab in his stomach. He doubled over, unable to breathe. She kicked him on the shoulder and sent him sprawling to the pavement. Now she knelt by his head, wrapped her forearm around his neck, and pulled him up onto her lap. She plunged her other hand roughly into his jacket, feeling around for the gun.

CJ gaped at her with surprise and fear, still unable to catch a breath. He probably thought she was going to kill him. And he did deserve it. What a joy it was to reverse their roles, to have him right where she wanted him. He should have known he didn't have a prayer against her one-on-one. Few people did. That wasn't bragging; it was just a fact. The gun was what threw everything.

"Don't you know better than to open fire in a crowded street, you stupid bastard?" she barked at him. Where was the damn gun? She tightened her grasp on his neck and made her way through his pockets. CJ's dark red wool cap got pushed to the side, revealing his stubbly bald head.

Unpleasant as it was, Gaia jammed her hand down his

shirt. She saw the ugly black hieroglyphs carved into the skin of his chest and made a mental note to never, ever consider getting a tattoo.

Okay. Now she was getting somewhere. She felt the cold butt of the gun with her fingertips. What a huge relief. In a rush of hopefulness she felt the possibility of this whole insane episode coming to an end and the world stretching out with her alive in it.

Maybe she could calm down about this sex thing and go about a relationship like a normal human being. Maybe she could take on the search for her dad in a thoughtful and intelligent way.

She gripped the gun, which CJ had secured in the tightly belted waistband of his pants.

Maybe she could—

Gaia shouted in surprise as an arm closed around her own neck. Her thoughts scattered, and she lost her hold on the gun as she was wrenched backward.

"Leave the kid alone!" a voice thundered much too close to her ear. She snapped her head around to look over her shoulder. Less than a foot away was the red face of a very large man in a disheveled suit jacket and tie.

What—?

The large man dragged her back another few feet. By now CJ had sprung to his feet and lightly patted the gun still tucked in his pants.

"Did she get your wallet off you?" the man asked CJ, concern clear in his voice. "You go tell the police all about it, son. There's a squad car around the corner."

Unbelievable. Gaia was speechless.

This guy wasn't a friend of CJ's, a fellow thug from the park, as she'd briefly imagined. This was a suit-wearing, forty-something-year-old, white-collar stranger on his way home from work. This was an angry citizen taking justice into his own hands. A vigilante. He believed she was mugging CJ. He was *protecting* CJ!

What an awful joke. CJ, out on bail, concealing an illegal weapon, had every reason not to seek the help of New York's finest. He only stayed long enough to sneer at Gaia, pull his hat back down over his ears, and smile.

"You're dead!" CJ shouted over his shoulder at Gaia as he took off at a run into the bedlam of the Village on a Friday night.

The big guy was practically strangling Gaia, but she was too miserable at the moment to do anything about it.

"I've heard about girl gangs," the man was saying, not to Gaia, but not to anyone else, exactly. "That kid may not want to turn her in, but you can be sure I'm not letting her go."

Obviously the man meant it because he started yanking Gaia toward Sixth Avenue. Was there any point in telling him the magnitude of his mistake?

"Um, sir?" She loosened his grip around her neck so she

could breathe and speak. "You have to let me go now." She locked her feet on the pavement and stood firm.

He stood up tall and puffed out his chest in indignation, even as he attempted to crush her trachea. He was at least six feet four and very powerfully built. His hair was dark and thinning on top. He looked like an ex-offensive lineman. Unless he was some kind of wretched, hypocritical wife beater, he probably wasn't used to fighting girls.

"Kids like you gotta be kept off the street," the man told her. "I don't want to hear any sob stories. You can save it for the cops."

Gaia sighed. Things were not going her way. "Look, sir," Gaia said reasonably. "I don't want any more violence tonight, but if you won't let me go, I'm going to have to force you, and it could hurt."

The man looked at her in disbelief. Then he laughed dryly. "You're going to hurt *me*?"

"I don't want to. I realize you're just trying to help out. I appreciate that."

He laughed again.

"I'm serious," Gaia said. "Let me go now."

He stared at her with undisguised amusement. "You're scaring me."

"Sorry, then," Gaia said flatly.

She gave him about ten more seconds to withdraw. She actually did feel bad, but what was she supposed to do? She wasn't getting booked and spending several more hours of her life in a police station. It brought back memories of the worst hours of her life. There was just no way.

She placed both of her hands on the man's arm that circled her neck. Without any more force than necessary, she took a deep breath and flipped him over her shoulder onto the ground.

He landed hard, what with being so huge and old. He let out a terrible squawk. As he lay there writhing in discomfort, staring at her as if she'd grown second and third heads, all traces of amusement disappeared from his face. She hoped very genuinely that he would feel better tomorrow.

"Sorry," she said again before she ran off.

NO MORE THINKING

"That's her! That blond girl!"

Gaia was rounding the corner of Bleecker Street less than sixty seconds later when she heard another commotion behind her. Gaia turned her head partway, and out of the corner of her eye she saw two policemen pointing after her. The big man in the suit had managed to sic the cops on her in record time.

She didn't turn her head any farther or slow her steps. The cops hadn't really seen her face yet and she meant to keep it that way.

It was wrong and bad to run away from cops, but Gaia was really tired now, and she hadn't done anything illegal, except maybe flip the balding guy, but he was strangling her, and he deserved it. Furthermore, she had given him ample warning.

She would just run away from them this one time, she promised herself. In the future she would be extra friendly and helpful to the police.

She was coming up on her favorite deli when she had a brainstorm. The hatch to the basement, a sprawling black hole in the sidewalk in front of the store, was open. She could disappear without having been seen, and the cops would probably be happy to forget about the whole thing. Were they really going to blame a high school kid for roughing up a guy three times her size? She practically dove into its darkness. She pulled the heavy metal doors shut behind her and clung to the top of the rickety conveyor belt used to stock the supply rooms. She heard footsteps banging along overhead. Hopefully they belonged to the cops.

Ugh. The place was pitch black and smelled awful. It was

unfortunate to be winded and gasping for breath in a place where the air was thick with dust and rotting food. There were certainly rats down below, but she didn't want to think about that too much.

Gaia glanced at the glowing hands of her watch. Five minutes took several hours to pass. At last she opened one of the doors a crack and peered out. Never had New York City air smelled so fresh. No sign of any police.

She opened it another few inches. She was either home free or a very easy target. Still no sign. Time to make her move. She threw open the hatch door and climbed out. Once on the sidewalk, she spun around.

What she saw made her freeze. Her blood seemed to stop in her veins. Black blotches clouded her vision. She put her head down to prevent herself from fainting, and when she looked up again, he was gone.

It wasn't a cop. It wasn't CJ. Who knew where he'd gone? The man she'd thought she'd seen in that split second looked uncannily familiar. He looked, although she was sure she'd imagined it, like her father. It couldn't have been. She was low on oxygen, overtired, overwrought. It couldn't have actually been him. But it shocked her to her core just the same.

On trembling legs she found her way home. She stopped at the bottom of the stoop, trying to regain her breath and her sense of balance. She prayed Ella wouldn't be home yet.

Deep cleansing breaths. In, one, two, three. Out, one,

two, three. She put her hands on her hips and bent her head low to keep the blood flowing into it. She wasn't going crazy. There could be people in the world who looked a little like her dad. Was that so impossible?

It was a crazy night. With all she'd been through, who could blame her for a minor hallucination?

"Say good-bye, bitch."

Gaia choked on her cleansing breath. Stupid, moron, shit head CJ was sticking his stupid gun in her face again. How much more could she take in one night? She was completely beyond reason. She was exhausted and mad and frustrated and totally freaked by the sight of that familiar man.

Without thinking, she shocked both herself and CJ by wrenching the gun right out of his hand and throwing it as hard as she could down Perry Street. She wanted him away from her. Now. That was it.

CJ ran after it.

"Can't you leave me *alone* for a couple of *hours*, you little *shit*?" she screamed after him.

Then she lumbered up the stairs to the front door, carrying with her the discomforting knowledge that in addition to losing her heart and her pride, she had also lost her mind.

The only thing she'd managed to keep was her virginity.

WEARING PATIENCE

"That stupid, stupid girl!" He paced the floor of the loft, pausing briefly to kick an ottoman out of his way. "Ella, did I not order you to kill that lowlife the same way you killed his friend? What is the problem here?"

Ella glared at the parquet floor. "I said I'm trying, sir."

"Clearly not very hard. You are a trained assassin, need I remind you, and he is a pathetic, imbecilic teenager. Do you honestly need backup?" He beckoned to his two omnipresent bodyguards, who stood at attention several yards away.

"No," Ella said firmly.

He glared irritably at Ella. Was she not adequately frightened of him anymore?

He methodically took a gun out of his drawer, walked over to her, and pressed the barrel to her forehead, "Ella, you know I would as easily kill you as ask you this a third time?"

She didn't meet his gaze. "Yes, sir."

"I've taken some pains placing you with that doormat George Niven, so I'm forced to be patient with you. But know this, Ella. My patience is wearing."

No, she wasn't frightened enough. He fired the gun so that the bullet nearly grazed her nose and ruptured a window-pane with a blast of noise. Ella jumped back in shock. Her eyes were momentarily filled with fear.

There. That was better.

"Trust me, Ella, if something happens to that girl, I will kill you and everyone you have ever cared about. I need Gaia, and I need her alive."

He walked to the wall of windows, watching the dying sun set flame to New Jersey's sky in a lurid show of color.

Perhaps it was time to move forward. Perhaps it was time to bring Gaia in.

CLINGING

How long had he been sitting here? Tom wondered, looking up at the ceiling of the diner absently. Cracks riddled the surface of the plaster, buried under multiple coats of high-gloss light orange paint. The color was the same as the bun sandwiching the burger that sat on his plate, which he hadn't found the appetite to eat.

He truly hadn't expected to see Gaia. He hadn't prepared himself for it. Now his fragile hold on life's priorities were shattered once more.

His baby. His child. His and Katia's. His throat ached at the memory of her face. He'd known she'd be grown-up now, much like a woman, but he didn't *know*. He hadn't been ready for it.

He'd always imagined she would grow up to be a beautiful woman, being Katia's daughter, but he was surprised by precisely how. She wasn't petite like her mother. She was tall and lanky, like him. Her hair had stayed that glorious pale yellow. He would have guessed it would fade and darken, as most child hair did, but hers hadn't. It had remained straight and soft looking. Her eyes were still deep, challenging blue. Some blue eyes looked pale and watery—more an absence of color than a color itself. But Gaia's were rich with pigment, a dense, tumultuous, changeable blue.

He'd desperately wanted to go to her. To hold her for just a few minutes. To tell her he loved her and thought of her every hour of every day. He needed her to know that she would never be alone; she would never be unloved as long as he was alive.

And if he had, what would she have said to him? Would she have glared at him in anger? In hurt? Could she ever forgive him for abandoning her?

Tom pulled his eyes back down from the ceiling, pinning them to the chipped Formica table on which his hands rested. What was the use of imagining it? He couldn't hold Gaia. He couldn't talk to her. To contact her would be selfish and put her in greater danger than she could ever know. His presence here at all was a terrible, senseless risk.

Five years ago he'd clung to Katia, and in doing so he'd as sure as killed her himself. He couldn't do that to Gaia. He'd already hurt her enough.

FROM THE
WAIST DOWN

HIS DESIRE ROSE TO AN UNQUENCHABLE THIRST

AS HE BURROWED HIS LIPS IN HER SOFT,

BUTTERY HAIR—

"Gaia, is that you?" Ed Fargo stared at the pretty brunette in the wide-brimmed straw hat, sunglasses, and flowery dress standing in the doorway of his family's apartment.

"Yes. Duh," she replied somewhat impatiently.

Ed studied her for another moment in confusion. "Why are you wearing a wig?"

"What wig?" Gaia asked.

"Have you been a brunette all this time and I just didn't notice?" Ed asked, feigning innocent surprise.

Gaia rolled her eyes. "I'm not wearing a wig, smarty-pants. I colored my hair with washable dye," she explained reasonably.

"Oh. Aha. Okay, then."

Ed shut the door behind him and locked it, and he wheeled along next to her down the hallway to the elevator. Gaia, typically, didn't offer any more information.

"Would you mind if I asked why?" Ed asked as the elevator arrived and Gaia pushed him in.

Gaia tapped her foot on the linoleum floor. "What happened to your promise not to ask questions?"

"I meant I wouldn't ask questions about big stuff," Ed said defensively. "Parents, past, unusual abilities. Not hair color. But fine. Don't tell me if you don't want."

Gaia sighed huffily. "Fine, I will tell you. But don't chicken out on me, okay?"

Ed put his head in his hand. "I have a feeling I'm not going to like the explanation very much."

"Okay?" Gaia pressed.

"Okay," Ed replied weakly.

The elevator arrived at the lobby, and the doors opened.

"Remember I told you CJ was out to get me?" Gaia asked, following him out of the elevator. "Well, he's still out to get me, and I'm sick of hiding out in my room. I wanted to go on this errand with you, but I don't want him to open fire again, particularly not at you. So that's why I look like this."

Ed swallowed. He let his wheelchair roll to a stop. "CJ is likely to open fire in the middle of the day?"

"Not if he doesn't recognize me," Gaia said breezily.

"But if he does?" Ed demanded.

"Yeah. Probably." Gaia took hold of the back of his chair and rolled him to the entrance of the building.

"Gaia! What do you think you're doing?"

"You said you wouldn't chicken out," Gaia reminded him, rolling contentedly along.

"I didn't realize my *life* would be in danger," Ed complained.

"It won't be," Gaia assured him without sounding at all convincing.

"Gaia! Stop pushing me! I'm being hijacked here!"

Gaia stopped. She took a breath. "Sorry," she said, like she meant it. She turned him around. "You're right. I'll take you back."

"No. I'm not saying . . . I'm just—" Ed sputtered. Why was Gaia so frustrating all the time? How did she always manage to stay in control of every situation? "Gaia, stop! Just stop."

Gaia stopped. She let go of the chair.

"Thank you," Ed said. He looked around the dull gray lobby with its drab fifties decor and hoped that no one he or his parents knew was within hearing distance of this conversation. "Now, don't roll me anymore."

"I'm sorry," Gaia said. "I really am. I won't do it again."

He glared at her in silence.

"Do you want to come or not come? It's totally up to you," Gaia said solicitously. "I promise I won't *touch* your chair."

She actually looked sweet as she waited for his response. Man, she made a fine brunette. Errrg. He knocked his knuckles against the armrest. Of course he would go with her, even if he *was* going to get shot at. That was the really pitiful thing.

"All right, Gaia," he said after he'd made her wait long enough. He wheeled into the bright sunshine of First Avenue, and she followed. "But slow down, okay? You're making me nervous."

"I'll try. It's just that I've had a rough couple of days, what with not getting killed and all."

"Right," Ed said, wondering how he'd ended up with such a friend.

They walked across the avenue and took East Sixth Street past all the Indian restaurants toward Second Avenue. Ed could smell the curry.

"So where are we going?" Ed asked.

"To buy condoms," Gaia replied.

(Cough.) "To buy"—Ed paused to clear his throat so his voice wouldn't come out squeaky—"condoms?"

"You gotta be safe," Gaia pointed out.

Ed scratched his head behind his ear. "Yes. Yes, you do," he said slowly. "Can I ask who they're for?"

"Me," Gaia said.

"Um . . . Gaia?"

"Yeah?"

"I don't know if you ever got to the unit in health class where they covered this stuff, but . . . uh, condoms are usually intended to be worn by the—"

Gaia punched him on the shoulder playfully but still too hard. "I don't mean I'm going to *wear* one, dummy."

He waited for her to offer some corrected version of her plan, but of course she didn't.

"So you're buying them for a guy?" he tried out.

"Yes," she said.

"And that guy would be . . . ?"

Gaia looked at him over her dark glasses. "Remember how I told you I wanted to have sex?"

"Yeah?" That was a hard conversation to forget.

"Well, obviously I'm going to need some condoms," Gaia explained as if she were speaking to a person with a very low IQ.

"Obviously," Ed said. His heart was racing, and he was feeling a bit queasy. He was miserably uncomfortable both with the remote hope that Gaia intended to have sex with him and the idea that she was planning to have sex with somebody else.

"Can you tell me who the lucky guy is?" His choice of words made him think of the conversation he'd had with Heather the day before. Had Gaia really written something about him in her notebook? As hard as Ed was trying to sound light and carefree, he felt his life's happiness was hanging on her answer.

"Nope," Gaia said.

Ed felt oddly relieved. "Okay. Let me ask you this. Have you told this person you're planning to have sex with him?" He hated himself for fishing, but he couldn't help it.

Gaia suddenly looked ill at ease. "No, not exactly."

"So you're just going to pounce on him in the dead of night?"

Gaia looked offended. "No. I'm not," she replied stiffly.

"Then what?"

"When I'm ready, I'm going to just go to where he lives and . . . ask him," Gaia explained a little defensively.

"Just ask him."

"Right."

"I see."

"Does that sound so bad?" she asked. Were her eyes searching, or was he imagining it?

She stopped in front of a discount pharmacy on Third Avenue and gallantly held open the door while he passed.

"Kind of unorthodox, I guess, but not . . . *bad*, exactly."

Gaia was already studying the selection hanging on the wall behind the counter. "So what do you think, Ed?" she asked him, squinting at the labels. "Lubricated? Ribbed? Ultrasensitive?"

Ed tried to breathe evenly. For a girl who'd been concerned about awkwardness a couple of days ago, she was really taking this in the teeth. "Jeez, I don't know," he said feebly. He scanned the back wall, which was jam packed with every brand of embarrassing merchandise—birth control, tampons, pregnancy tests, laxatives, hemorrhoid medicine. What sick mind decided that all that stuff went behind the counter where you had to ask for it by name? "You pick."

She pointed out the package she wanted to the cashier

man, who wore a sweater vest and a name tag that said, "Hi, my name is Omar." Omar, looking curious and somewhat amused, spent an extra-long time locating Gaia's choice. At last he slapped the bright red box on the counter, and Gaia paid up. Ed realized Omar was giving him approving, go-get-'em looks.

"Have fun," Omar said as they left the store.

Ed was certain his face was probably the shade of a ripe strawberry. He suddenly wished he weren't wearing a bright orange tie-dyed T-shirt.

"Do you think the guy is going to say no?" Gaia asked as they started back in the direction of his building.

"I'm not saying that."

"But you're thinking that," Gaia accused.

"No, it's just . . . I mean, look, Gaia, it's not your everyday thing to do to a guy."

Gaia nodded thoughtfully. "I realize that. I do. But I'm a little desperate here. I figure I can stay alive till tomorrow, but maybe not after that. If there's any chance of losing my virginity before then, I've just got to do it. Tonight."

"Tonight?" Ed couldn't hide his shock.

"Yeah."

"Tonight," Ed repeated numbly.

"Yes, Ed. Tonight. Saturday night."

Ed's brain felt like it was shutting down.

"So I'm just going to go right to his room and ask. Nicely,

of course. I won't insist or anything. And if he seems really reluctant or . . . "

"Freaked out," Ed supplied.

"Or freaked out," Gaia allowed, "I'll just tell him the truth."

Gaia paused to let him say something, but when he didn't, she surged ahead. When she was with Ed and her mouth got going, there was no stopping her.

"The truth is good. The truth is your friend. Seriously. I'll just say to him, Look, I'm probably going to get shot in the head tomorrow, and I really want to have sex before I go, so would you mind?"

Gaia looked at Ed again for some response. He couldn't even work his mouth anymore.

"And even if he thinks I'm completely repulsive and would rather have sex with his aunt, well, he probably still won't want to refuse a girl's dying request, will he? What do you say?" She turned to Ed with a genuinely hopeful look on her face.

Ed struggled for words. "I—I say. I say . . . have fun."

"Please tabulate your results according to the format Dr. Witchell presented in the lecture on Thursday."

The very droopy-looking kiss-ass teaching assistant droned on as Sam pictured the way Heather would look when she appeared in his room that night.

It was unfortunate that his lab section of biochemistry had to meet on Saturday. It was especially unfortunate on *this* Saturday, when his mind was impossible to contain.

Would she wear that short black skirt that made him drool? Maybe one of those miniature T-shirts she had that showed off her belly button? And what about under it? It probably wasn't a good idea for him to go there right now, but he couldn't help it. He pulled his chair up so his waist pressed against the table and further obscured his lap with his notebook. It was highly embarrassing to get excited in class—something he hadn't done since seventh grade.

He'd made his way into Heather's sexy satin bras before. That was a pleasure he was looking forward to. But it was the new frontier that piqued his interest. Would she wear satin panties to match, like the women in those lingerie ads?

Suddenly he wasn't picturing her clothes anymore; he was picturing himself taking off her clothes. He couldn't help that, either. And as the fantasy evolved he wasn't under the harsh fluorescent lights of a science lab anymore but in his (now almost clean) dorm room in low romantic light (he made a mental note to buy a candle). His body pressed against her soft skin, his hands exploring her luxurious curves. Her soft, dark hair tickled his chest. His lips trailed up her neck and under her chin.

He sighed (almost inaudibly) and kissed the lids of those mysterious eyes, the bridge of her thin, straight nose, the plains of her bewitching face. His desire rose to an unquenchable thirst as he burrowed his lips in her soft, buttery hair—

Sam looked up in alarm. His blissful fantasy screeched to a stop with jarring suddenness. It felt like somebody had ripped the needle off an old vinyl record spinning a Mozart symphony.

He wasn't kissing Heather. Where had this fantasy gone so far awry? Heather didn't have hair or eyes or legs like those. Somehow Gaia had arrived in his reverie uninvited. He should have been jolted, surprised, even repulsed by her sudden presence in his bed, but was he? No. The look and feel of her had sent his desire into some completely new stratosphere.

This was not good. This was very bad. What was he going to do?

"Sam . . . ? Sam, uh . . . Moon, is it?"

Sam blinked several times. It took him a moment to bring the TA's face into focus. When he looked around the lab, he realized that except for the TA, he was all by himself. The class was gone, over. The TA was gazing at him as if he were a particularly puzzling specimen in a Petri dish.

"I've kind of got to close up here, if you . . . uh . . . don't mind," the TA pointed out.

"Sure. Sorry," Sam said feebly, trying to coordinate his limbs to lift him out of his chair and walk him out of the classroom. "See you," he said over his shoulder.

Still in a fog, he walked down the corridor of the science building and out into the windy courtyard, where the bright, hopeful afternoon sun was threatened by blotchy gray clouds gathering on the horizon.

HEATHER

Little-Known Facts about me:

The summer before my sophomore year, I fell in love. It was the most idyllic summer you could possibly imagine. My family had rented a house in East Hampton that year. My mom and sisters and I stayed for the whole season, and my dad came out on weekends. Those were the days when my dad's business was doing really well.

Ed Fargo was spending the summer at his aunt and uncle's place just a few blocks away. Ed's folks are teachers, but his aunt is this big-time lawyer with a beautiful house right on the beach.

I was working at the farmers' market in Amagansett, and Ed was working at a surf shop on the Montauk Highway. Ed is a year older. You've met Ed, so you know he's seriously good-looking, funny, charming, self-deprecating, super-sharp, and generally a great guy. He was also an amazing surfer. This all took place before his accident, as I'm sure you've already guessed.

Anyway, our love story would take too long to describe here, but it was the most magical time of my life. Someday I'll turn that story into a romance novel, maybe somebody will even make a movie of it, and I'll earn millions of dollars.

The climax of that summer, so to speak, was a night in August, when Ed and I made love on the beach. The moon was full, and the surf was so gentle, we lay together in it. It was the first time for both of us. It was too perfect ever to be described in words, so I won't try.

One month later Ed was paralyzed from the waist down. He spent the next several months in the hospital and in physical therapy. He lost a year of school. Now he's sentenced to a wheelchair for the rest of his life.

Technically, I didn't break up with him. But I would have. Ed let me off the hook by doing it for me—that's the kind of guy he is. I was under a lot of pressure from my parents and everything. They didn't want me spending my youth taking care of a guy in a wheelchair—a guy they felt no longer had "possibilities."

Ed never acted like he hated me after that. In fact, we're still sort of friends. But in his eyes, when I have the courage to look, I see profound disappointment that can never be repaired or forgotten.

I don't need to tell you my parents love Sam. Gorgeous, brilliant, world-class-chess-playing, premed Sam. I'm only eighteen, but they'd be overjoyed if I married him tomorrow. It would relieve some of their financial pressure, I suppose.

You're probably wondering why I told Sam I'm a virgin. The reason is because Gaia is a virgin. I know it for a fact. I don't want Gaia to be able to give Sam something I can't.

Here's a little-known fact about Ed Fargo: He has a personal fortune of twenty-six million dollars. Probably more now because the settlement came over a year and a half ago, and money like that earns a lot of interest. His parents, acting on the advice (and guilt, I guess) of his aunt, sued over the accident, even though Ed begged them not to and he refused to testify.

Ed won't let anybody touch the money. He will never tell anyone he has it. I only know because I read about the windfall in the newspaper—no names, of course, but I'm one of the few people who know the strange circumstances of the accident. In fact, I first heard about the case because Ed's parents contacted me about testifying.

Here's another fact about Ed. His reproductive organs, to put it clinically, still work perfectly well. Not that it matters to me anymore.

READY.
OR NOT.

HEATHER PAUSED AT THE DOOR, HESITANT
FOR SOME REASON TO COMMIT HERSELF TO
THIS STRANGE NIGHT.

JUST GO

Gaia was as close to nervous as a girl who lacked the physical ability to feel nervous could be. She had taken a long bath and spent hours picking out a bra and underpants that wouldn't be completely embarrassing if revealed. She'd brushed her teeth twice.

She spent several minutes naked in front of the mirror, worrying that she was too fat. After she talked herself out of that, she worried she was too skinny—bony limbed, under-developed, and flat chested.

She couldn't stop herself from making comparisons to Heather. Her body wasn't as feminine as Heather's. Her breasts weren't as big as Heather's. Her feet were definitely much bigger. Her hair wasn't as thick as Heather's.

Gaia had even reverted to the tactics of a seventh grader by calling Sam to make sure he was in his room, then hanging up as soon as he'd answered.

Now, standing in the middle of the floor, wearing the slinky pink dress she'd "borrowed" from Ella and a pair of heels, she felt like a big, oafish fraud. Why was she even putting herself through this? Sam would take one look at her and tell her to get lost. Why did she think he would be attracted to her? Why in the world would he consider going behind Heather's back for *her*? Even if Gaia *was* going to be out of the picture by tomorrow.

She glanced at her watch. Arg. Urmph. It was almost eight o'clock. If she didn't leave now, Sam would probably head out for the evening, and she'd go to her grave a virgin.

She took one last look at herself. No, this wasn't going to work. She was no seductress. She wasn't going to fool anybody. She pulled the dress over her head and kicked off the heeled sandals. If she was going to go, she'd go as herself. She'd be honest. She pulled on jeans and a T-shirt and dug her bare feet into her running shoes. She thrust the package of condoms into her bag.

As a safety measure she tucked her hair into a wool cap which she pulled low over her eyes, wrapped a scarf over most of the bottom of her face, and slipped on a pair of glasses with heavy black frames. Not exactly sexy, but neither was a severe head wound.

Thankfully Ella was out, so Gaia could walk down the stairs like a sane human being. She locked the door behind her and struck out into the cool October night, knowing that this was going to be the greatest single night of her life or a complete and total nightmare.

"The green or the black?" Heather asked her sister Phoebe.

Phoebe leaned back on her elbows on Heather's unmade bed and sized her up. "The green is prettier; the black is sexier."

"Black it is," Heather said, pulling the close-fitting sweater over her head. "Can I borrow that gauzy dark red skirt?" she asked, scanning the many piles of clothing that covered her floor.

"Big night tonight?" Phoebe asked suggestively.

"I hope so," Heather answered in a way that was mysterious but didn't openly invite further questioning.

On the one hand, it was annoying that Phoebe came home from college almost every weekend. She was a sophomore at SUNY Binghamton and hated it there. She referred to it as Boonie U. and was constantly composing the personal essay for her transfer application. Heather reasoned that if Phoebe spent even half that time on her courses, she could actually make the grades to transfer. Heather didn't mention this to Phoebe, of course. Phoebe's old room had been partitioned off and rented out, so Phoebe stayed in Heather's room, and she was quite the slob. On the other hand, Phoebe had managed to accumulate lots of nice clothes—who even knew how—and usually let Heather borrow them.

"Sure," Phoebe said. She got up from the bed and planted

herself in a chair at Heather's vanity table. Phoebe leaned close to the mirror and pursed her lips. "Only it's dry-clean only, so don't mess it up."

"Yes, ma'am," Heather said, locating the skirt and pulling it over her hips. Phoebe was taller, but Heather was a little slimmer. "How does it look?"

"Fine," Phoebe said without even giving her a glance. She was rooting through her capacious makeup bag. "Have you seen my brandy wine lip liner? It's Lancôme, and it cost like twenty bucks. I'm sure I had it when I came last weekend."

Heather ignored her. Phoebe was always losing things and subtly blaming other people.

Heather slipped on her black nubuck loafers and checked her hair and makeup one last time. She felt keyed up and a little shaky. She wasn't sure where excitement ended and nervousness began. She checked her purse again to make sure she had the condoms.

"Okay, Phoebe, I'm taking off. See you later."

"See ya," Phoebe said absently, without taking her eyes from her reflection in the mirror.

Heather paused at the door, hesitant for some reason to commit herself to this strange night.

"Wish me luck," she added in a quiet voice, wishing in a way that this were a night from their innocent past in which the two sisters would practice gymnastics in the living room for hours and try to stay up late enough to watch *Saturday Night Live*.

But Phoebe was already too deeply involved in her cosmetics to respond.

SINCERE

"Ouch. Shit," Sam muttered, putting his index finger in his mouth. He'd tried lighting the candle, but the wick was buried in the wax, and when he'd dug for it in the hot wax, he'd burned himself.

He lit the wick again. It took this time, but the flame was sputtering and underconfident.

He sniffed at the air. Crap. The candle was advertised to smell like vanilla, which he'd hoped would cover any residue of dirty-room odor, but instead it smelled like floor cleaner.

He was nervous. He couldn't help himself. He glanced again in the mirror. It seemed stupid to take pains with his clothing when the whole point of this evening was to be taking them off as quickly as possible. He'd actually brought his khakis with him into the bathroom and taken an extra-steamy shower in the hope of getting out some of the wrinkles. He'd put on his softest oxford shirt and carefully rolled up the cuffs. It reminded him of Christmas Eve. All those hours he spent wrapping and tying up presents, when it was all torn up and discarded in a matter of moments.

It was already after eight. His suite mates had gone out. The place was eerily quiet.

He was ready for this. He wanted it. He wanted Heather. As he repeated those words in his head, he felt like a quarterback in the locker room, revving himself up for a big game.

He conjured up an image of Heather's lush body and felt his hormones starting to flow. And it wasn't just sex that he wanted, although face it, what guy could turn that down? He cared about Heather. He really did.

Sam found himself pacing the small (clean) room, reassuring himself. He wanted to do right by Heather. Her honesty and openness were genuinely touching to him. He wouldn't betray that or ever make light of it. Sure, he'd wrapped himself up nicely tonight, but she was the one giving the gift.

When the knock on the door came, the sound seemed to reverberate in his bones. He went to the door slowly, knowing who it was, of course, telling himself he wanted her fervently and yet wishing in a way it were somebody else.

A FAILED EXPERIMENT

Against his better judgment, Tom Moore saw Gaia rounding the corner of West Fourth Street and followed at a safe distance. As a father he needed to see her safely to her destination, wherever that was. Then he would get on a plane back to Lebanon and resume his mission, leaving romantic notions and painful memories behind.

Based on her strange outfit, Tom guessed Gaia knew she was in danger. With her remarkable hair stashed away under her hat and a scarf and glasses obscuring her face, she was almost unrecognizable. Gaia was well adapted to taking care of herself, he told himself as he followed her east toward Fifth Avenue. He'd taught her the skills she'd need, and her miraculous gifts more than outstripped his teaching and his own abilities, in truth.

Tom, too, had been a prodigy. He had an extraordinary IQ, almost perfect powers of reasoning, and an intuitive genius for understanding the motivations of the human mind—particularly the criminal mind. He had been virtually fearless until he lost Katia. After that he wore fear like a coat of chain mail every day of his life. Tom sometimes imagined that he represented nature's first—though failed—experiment at an invincible creature. Gaia represented its subsequent and much more perfect attempt.

Gaia paused for a traffic light, and Tom took the opportunity to pull out his cell phone. He pushed two buttons, connecting instantly with his assistant. "We'll fly from the base at nine-thirty," he told him.

It was with some sense of relief that he watched Gaia approach the door of a large building flanked by stone benches on either side. He could see from the awning that it was an NYU building, a dorm. It seemed a safe and relatively ordinary place for a girl to begin her Saturday night. He chuckled to himself at the pleasure it gave him to think that Gaia had friends and an active social life.

Maybe she would be okay. Maybe she could actually be . . . happy. The thought suffused him with unexpected joy.

Suddenly he was glad he had come. He was reassured. He could imagine his Gaia thriving here in New York. That knowledge would strengthen him for almost any trial.

He was just backing off when a glint of metal caught his eye from across the street. His thoughts and perceptions went into warp speed. It was a young man standing in the shadow of a tree, holding a .44-caliber pistol. The young man brought it up to eye level and trained it directly on Gaia.

Tom was across the street in a fraction of a second, never diverting his gaze from the gun. He was nearing his target, ready to throw his weight into the man, when suddenly the young man withdrew the gun. The young man's gaze was still trained on Gaia, but the hand with the gun hung at his side. Tom pulled up short, backing up against the side of a building to escape the young man's notice. When Tom looked back across the street, he realized that Gaia had already disappeared into the building.

Tom closed his eyes for a moment and caught his breath. Had that gun actually been trained on Gaia? Could he have been imagining the danger to her? With a sense of foreboding, Tom watched the young man conceal the gun under his shirt and stroll across the street, stopping under the well-lit awning. The young man glanced into the building and then took a seat on one of the stone benches. Tom knew he was settling in to wait.

Distress mixed with frustration as Tom took out his phone once again and pushed the same two buttons.

"Make it eleven," he told his assistant in an unhappy voice.

ED

My views on Luck:

Before my accident, I used to think I was the luckiest guy in the world. Then I had my accident, and I sort of believed I deserved it because nobody stays that lucky. I used to think that luck got around to each of us equally. When things went badly, you were sort of saving up for a stretch of good luck. When things went too well . . . You get the idea.

According to this theory, I would be in for some good luck, right? I mean, a guy who's in a wheelchair shouldn't have parents who bicker constantly, for example, or an older sister who's ashamed of him. He shouldn't be abandoned by the girl he believed to be his one true love.

But the theory is wrong. Luck doesn't shine her light on each of us equally. She is arbitrary, irrational, unfair, and sometimes downright cruel. There are people who spend their entire lives basking in her glow, and others never seem to get one goddamned break.

Luck is powerful. Don't mess with her. Accept her for what she is and make the best of it. I can't stand that people are constantly blaming other people when bad stuff happens to them. Somebody trips on a sidewalk, and they sue some innocent bastard for millions of dollars. It's *not* always somebody else's fault. Sometimes it's just luck. Bad luck.

Luck is unpredictable. She's not your friend. She won't stand by you.

Maybe in heaven it's different. I do hope so.

But here on earth, my friend, those are the breaks.

IT

HE COULDN'T HOLD BACK MUCH LONGER

WITHOUT A REALLY GOOD REASON.

THE BIG MOMENT

Sam had a new respect for biology. Although his mind floated somewhere near the acoustical tiles on the ceiling, his body did all the things a body needs to do in order to successfully propagate the species.

He gently, efficiently removed Heather's sweater and expertly navigated her tricky front-fastening bra. He gazed at her lovely breasts hungrily, feeling the blood flow to his nether regions quadruple in under two seconds. He pulled her skirt over her perfectly shaped hips, revealed dark purple satin panties equal to his daydreams, and forced himself not to go further yet.

Biology was exerting so much force, Sam had to battle himself not to remove that last bit of Heather's clothing or to pick her right up off the floor, put her on his bed, and hurtle forward into the main event. But he was a gentleman. He'd toughed it out before, and he could do it again. His older brother once told him that if you found you were undressing the girl *and* yourself, take a break and ask yourself whether you're pushing too hard.

Sam stuck to the advice, although it seemed like hours before Heather got around to removing his shirt. She seemed a bit tentative to him. Not scared, but not entirely sure of herself, either.

"We can stop anytime," he murmured against her ear, although biology was begging her not to take him up on the offer.

"No, I'm good," she whispered back.

She punctuated her point by sliding her hands under the waistband of his khakis. From his perch on the ceiling he heard a moan come from deep in his chest.

Now he saw his pants on the floor and only his blue-and-green-plaid boxers standing in the way of nudity. Soft, delicate lips poured kisses over his chest and stomach.

It was weird. His body was fully aroused and responsive, and his mind was remote. Was there a psychological term for this? Was there a treatment for it? Was this at all what death felt like?

He bitterly wished he could get his mind into the action. He'd picked a fine day for a complete out-of-body experience, he mused ironically.

"Ready?" he whispered, taking her hand and leading her to the bed.

Before taking a step, he studied her expression, waiting for her cue. Her face was flushed and intense, but not exactly the picture of lustful ecstasy. Was she holding back? Was she regretting this?

Or was he projecting *his* feelings onto her?

He took his eyes from her body so that biology would ease its choke hold for a moment. "Are you sure, Heather?

We don't have to do anything you don't want. We've got plenty of time."

In response she sat down on the bed, placed a hand on either side of his waist, and pulled him down on top of her. She commandeered his mouth with kisses so he couldn't ask any more questions.

"I'm sure. I'm sure I want to do it now," she said against his ear. Why did her tone suggest more grim determination than arousal? Suddenly he felt her hands on the elastic waist of his boxer shorts, pulling them down. Another moan escaped him. He couldn't hold back much longer without a really good reason.

"I love you," she whispered to his chest. He couldn't see her eyes to gauge the depth of her words.

"Mmmm," he said, knowing that wasn't the right answer.

Apparently she didn't need to hear more. She wriggled out of her own panties and pressed the full length of her naked body against his. His body was pounding with pleasure and anticipation. His mind was surprised by her assertiveness and her . . . hurry. It almost seemed like she was in a hurry.

The big moment was upon them, and biology was demanding they surge ahead. Sam felt for the condom on the table by his bed. With her help he put it on. With her guiding, demanding arms he entered her. Again he heard the deep groan thundering from his chest. He heard her breathy sigh. At last his mind was pulled down into the whirlpool. At last the sensations became so fierce and so pervasive, his body and mind joined together. At last he was consumed.

So much so that he didn't notice that a slight breeze from a crack in the door had snuffed the fragile flame of the floor-wax-scented candle.

CRUEL LUCK: 1

The hallway of Sam's dorm looked surprisingly like the one in her dream, but Gaia's feelings were different. She didn't feel sexy and bold. She felt insecure and deeply self-conscious.

First she knocked on the outer door that read B4–7. Sam's room was B5, so it had to be through there. While she waited for an answer, she pulled off her wool cap and shook out her hair. She unwound the scarf and stowed the ugly glasses in her bag. Her eyes caught the package of condoms floating at the surface of her bag, and the eager box threw her confidence even more.

Gaia knocked again. She waited for what felt like two weeks, but nobody came. Had Sam managed to slip out between the time she'd called and now? She thought she heard a noise inside. Was it okay to go in? Was it kind of a public room?

The thought of trudging back home to Ella and George's house in defeat, potentially only to be hunted down by CJ, was so unappealing, she turned the doorknob and walked inside.

It was a good-sized room, housing four desks, a mini-fridge, a hot plate, bookshelves, piles of sports equipment, notebooks, jackets, a couch that looked like it had been retrieved from a dump, and a very large television set. Gaia took a deep breath. No people, though.

Could Sam possibly be in his room? Maybe he was sleeping and he hadn't heard her knock. What if she were to creep in and climb into bed with him? Would he start screaming and call the police? Or would they have a beautiful, semi-conscious, dreamlike sexual encounter? Gaia's head began to pound at the thought.

She walked very quietly toward room B5. Her spirits lifted. It was just her luck. The door was open a crack, and she heard a sound from inside. It sounded almost like a sleep sound.

Gaia took another deep, steadying breath. *Do it,* she commanded herself. *You have to try.* She put out her hand and placed it lightly on the knob. The brass sphere was a little wobbly in her palm. She gave it the lightest push and let it swing open.

Physicists were always crowing about the speed of light, but in this case the light from the common room seemed to filter into the small chamber slowly, as though well aware it was not a welcome guest. In this case, light traveled at the speed of dawning horror, of rude awakening, of hopes being dashed—but no faster. Before Gaia's round, naked eyes, the form on the bed was illuminated.

Two forms.

2

Sam had believed his body and mind joined together as he made love to Heather. But in truth, they weren't actually joined until several seconds later, when his senses alerted him, in fast succession, to the subtle creaking of the door, the surprising influx of light, and most importantly, the stunned face of Gaia Moore. That was *actually* the moment when his body and mind snapped back into one piece.

2 ½

Gaia had never seen anybody having sex before, so the image was raw, crude, strange, terrible, and electrifying at the same time.

She should have dashed out of there instantly, but her astonishment seemed to lock her muscles, giving her eyes ample time to torture her with the sight of Sam's naked body, poetic even under these circumstances. His long, lean form was cupped against Heather's, their hips joined, dewy sweat shared between chests and arms, their legs a mutual tangle.

But by far the worst moment came when Sam turned and saw her. Her pain was too big to hide, she knew, and scrawled flagrantly on her face. Sam was baring his body, but she was caught exposing her soul. Her secret pain, her crushed hope, her sickly envy, and her queasy fascination were there for all to see. Worst of all, Sam saw her see him seeing all of this.

At last her muscles freed her, and she ran.

It wasn't until afterward that she realized she hadn't bothered to look at Heather. Heather didn't really matter much.

3

When Sam looked at Gaia's face, he thought his heart broke for her, but he realized later that it broke for himself.

JUST CRUEL

Heather watched Gaia's face with a disturbing sense of excitement. As full and complex as Gaia's expression was in that surreal moment, Heather knew she wouldn't forget it.

Heather realized later that she hadn't even looked at Sam's face. Somehow she knew his response without needing to look. At the time, it didn't really seem to matter much.

THE CHASE

JUST WHEN SHE'D SETTLED HERSELF ON THAT
BENCH AND HE'D GOTTEN HER TEMPLE BETWEEN
THE CROSSHAIRS, SHE'D TAKEN OFF AGAIN.

THE PARK . . .

Gaia strode down the sidewalk, tears dribbling over her cheeks, past her jawbone, and down her neck, hair streaming in the breeze. Her hat and scarf and whatever were someplace. What did it matter? If CJ wanted to shoot her right now, he could be her guest. In fact, she might ask him if she could borrow his gun.

At that moment she would have burned her eyes out rather than have to see that picture of Sam and bitch-girl ever again. But now the image was stored in her brain for good. Or at least until one of CJ's bullets came to her rescue. "CJ!" she called out semideliriously.

She walked blindly under the miniature Arc de Triomphe that marked the entrance to the park. She staggered to a bench and collapsed on it. She hid her face in her hands and cried. Her shoulders heaved and shook, but the sobs were noiseless. Why did her life always go this way? Why did it always seem to take the worst-possible turn?

Whenever she made the mistake of caring, of wanting something badly, life seemed to take that desire and smack her in the face with it.

What had she done to deserve this? Was it because she was strange? A scientific anomaly? Just plain made wrong? If she had fear, like a normal girl, would she also have been allowed to have a mother and a father and a boyfriend? And if so, was there any way she could go back and renegotiate the deal? Give me fear! she would say. Give me tons of it. Give me extra; I don't care.

No more caring, that was the golden rule. Forget about "do unto others" and all of that crap. Life's one great lesson was: Do not care. Not caring was a person's only real protection.

In the midst of sobs and tears and internal ranting, something made Gaia look up. Afterward, when she thought back, she couldn't say precisely what it was. But for whatever reason, she turned her tear-stained face up at that moment, and a terrible night became a perfectly mind-shattering one.

There, not fifteen feet away, standing against the trunk of a compact sycamore tree, was her father. In that split second she saw that he was thinner than he was five years before, that his face was more lined and angular, that his reddish blond hair was cut very short now, but he was unmistakably her father.

Gaia didn't jump to her feet as the result of any specific thoughts or decisions. One minute she was collapsed on the bench, and the next minute she was running toward him. He didn't run to her with open arms in slow motion the way long-lost relatives do in old movies. He gave her a look that was both surprised and pained, then he took off in the other direction.

Gaia followed him without thinking. She had to. She couldn't have stopped herself if she'd tried.

10TH ST. & 5TH AVE.

Exactly on schedule, Gaia had seen him standing under the tree. They had locked eyes and she had recognized him. As if on cue, she ran toward him, and he ran away from her. It's what her father would have done.

Now he would lead her to his loft on the Hudson River, just as he had planned. He was about to meet Gaia face-to-face. Excitement, true excitement, bred in his heart for the first time in many years.

For this great meeting the playing field wouldn't be even, of course. But when was it? He would go into it knowing everything about Gaia Moore, knowing her present, her past, her mother . . . intimately. She would go into it believing he was her father.

17TH ST. & 6TH AVE.

CJ cursed in frustration. He was so completely consumed by anger, he couldn't think straight anymore. Just when she'd settled herself on that bench and he'd gotten her temple between the crosshairs, she'd taken off again. He stowed his gun before anybody saw him and followed her.

Now he was badly winded, running, walking, dodging throngs of pedestrians, weaving through wide avenues dotted with traffic, staying with her each and every step. Not for a second would he lose sight of her blond hair, which luckily for him practically glowed in the dark.

Tonight was his night. He'd make sure of it. This couldn't go on another day. Tarick and his boys had made it clear. If he didn't kill Gaia tonight, he'd be dead by morning.

17TH ST. & 7TH AVE.

Tom kept the young man with the gun clearly in his sights as he ran. Here was an example of why agents were never allowed near the business of protecting their families. Tom had seen Gaia's face when she'd emerged from the dorm building, tear soaked and racked with misery, and he'd stopped thinking like an agent and started thinking like a father. He'd lost a step, screwed up.

Gaia had narrowly avoided a bullet, and now they were on the run.

BACK UP A MINUTE

Sam had never put on clothes faster. He felt disgusting about leaving Heather at such a moment, but his more urgent feeling was the need to catch up to Gaia and . . . what? He had no idea. Make her feel better? Make himself feel better? Tell her he wanted her desperately, body and soul, and the fact that he'd just been making love to Heather was an odd, irrelevant coincidence? That would be a complete lie, yet also true at the same time.

"Heather, I'm really, really sorry," he said to her numb-looking face as he raced for the door. He wasn't so sorry, however, that he waited for a response or even looked back at her once. He felt disgusting.

The elevator was many floors away. He ran for the stairs instead. He took them two and three at a time, stumbling at the bottom and practically crashing into the serene lobby like Frankenstein's monster. Gaia was gone, of course.

Sam ran to the door and scanned the sidewalk in either direction. No sign of her. Now what? If Sam hadn't felt the frantic pangs of a drowning man, he would never have involved the security guard in his predicament.

"Uh, Kevin, hey. Did you see a girl, a blond girl around eighteen, rush out of here?" Sam asked.

Kevin paused for an infuriating two and a half seconds to consider. "Tall, pretty, crying?" he asked.

Oh God, she was crying. "Y-Yeah that's probably her," Sam snapped, feeling an irrational desire to cram his hand down Kevin's throat and pull whatever informative words he had right out of there. And Sam *liked* Kevin. He and Kevin talked about the Knicks five out of seven nights a week.

Kevin paused again, savoring his important role in Sam's drama.

"Did you see which way she went?" Sam prodded, wild-eyed.

Kevin sighed thoughtfully. "Coulda been downtown," he said at last. "I'm pretty sure she walked downtown."

Sam was already at the door and out of it. "Thanks, Kevin. I really appreciate it." Most of his thanks were wasted on passersby on Fifth Avenue.

He ran toward the park. Of course she'd gone to the park. Every major event in his brief life with Gaia (with the notable exception of this evening) had taken place in the park.

Suddenly Sam had it in his mind that this was a good sign. If Gaia had gone to the park—their place, really—she would want him to find her there. If she was in the park, that would mean Sam could somehow repair this disaster.

When he caught a glimpse of yellow hair, sagging shoulders, and a face buried in familiar hands on a bench near the entrance, his heart soared irrationally. He would take her in his arms; he didn't care. He would tell her he loved her. How weird was that? But it was what his heart was telling him to do. He did love her. He loved her in a way he'd never come close to loving anything before. He'd known it for a while, even if he was too cowardly to say it or act on it. Now he would cut through all the chaos and defensiveness and confusion. He would take a risk for once in his life.

I love you. I love you, Gaia. The words were on his tongue, he could practically feel her in his arms, and suddenly, without warning, without even appearing to see him, Gaia leaped off the bench and started running.

Sam was destroyed. But he did find a reserve of insanity that pushed him to follow her.

A BRIEF VISIT WITH HEATHER

Heather sat very still on Sam's bed, half dressed, with her chin resting in her hands. The room was dark; the suite was perfectly quiet.

In her mind she knew she felt horribly wronged and betrayed and mistreated by Sam, but her insides felt strangely dry. She felt too dry for tears or any of the really muddy emotions. Why was that, exactly? Why did she feel so oddly calm and lucid?

When she thought of Gaia's ravaged face, she felt a burst of gratification and maybe even joy. They had a word for this in German, her mother's first language. *Schadenfreude.* It meant shameful joy—taking pleasure in somebody else's pain.

Heather knew she should have felt shamed by this, but she didn't. She should have felt shocked and furious at Sam, but she didn't quite. Maybe later.

Maybe she was just numb.

Or maybe in her heart she already knew that Sam had fallen in love with Gaia and that he had never truly been in love with her.

Or maybe it was really all because of Ed. Because of the awful things that happened with Ed, Heather's heart wasn't the soft, supple muscle it had once been.

Ed flicked off the light in the hallway. He wheeled back into his room and unbuttoned his shirt—his best, softest shirt. On the collar lingered a tiny whiff of the cologne he'd put on after his shower. It brought on a pang of wobbly self-pity, and the self-pity brought on anger and discontent. Self-pity was the single worst feeling there was, particularly if you happened to be in a wheelchair.

He hoisted himself into his bed and struggled to take his pants off his immobile legs. A close second, in the race of worst feelings, was helplessness.

Ed didn't need to brush his teeth. He'd brushed them twice two hours ago.

Why was he so sad? He didn't really think Gaia was going to come, did he? No, not really. Not rationally. But he'd made the mistake of listening, just a little, to the seductive whispers of that rotten, misleading bastard called Hope.

If there was some way Ed could have strangled Hope and put the world out of much of its misery, he would have.

Instead he laid his head down on his pillow and cast a glance at the glowing blue numbers of his clock radio. It was 10:02. Only 10:02. Not so late.

What if Gaia . . . it was still possible. . . . And maybe she . . .

Ed groaned out loud and put the pillow over his head. It did nothing to drown out the whispers.

HELL'S
KITCHEN

IF HER OWN FATHER WAS LEADING HER INTO AN
AMBUSH, WHAT WAS THERE TO LIVE FOR, ANYWAY?

39TH ST. & 11TH AVE.

Gaia's mind was blank. Her existence was all and only about keeping the tall man in the gray sweatshirt—her father, she reminded herself—in her vision. At this point Sam, Heather, and CJ were strangers to her, inhabitants of a different planet.

The fact that her father was running away from her was immaterial. The reasons for his presence here didn't cross her mind. She made no consideration of what she'd do or say when she caught him. Past and future no longer shaded her thoughts.

She wouldn't let him get away. She *would not* let him get away. Her consciousness was only as big as that thought.

Pedestrians, cyclists, cars, trucks, pets passed in an unobserved blur. She didn't pay attention to which streets she took and where they'd lead. Chasing was so much easier than being chased because it required no strategy.

The man—her father—was fast. He was clever. He almost lost her when she collided with the Chinese-food deliveryman someplace on the West Side. Her dad was still pretty nimble for an old guy. But Gaia was unstoppable. She was too focused to feel loss of breath or any ache in her muscles. Her father had trained her too well for him to have any hope of losing her.

Now they were in the West Forties, Hell's Kitchen, she believed it was called, and her father was showing signs of exhaustion. From Eleventh Avenue he peeled off sharply to the left onto a dark side street. Gaia pulled up short and turned to follow. In this creepy neighborhood the streets and sidewalks were virtually deserted. Streetlights were few and far between. She saw that the side street dead-ended into the West Side Highway. Her father had disappeared into a building. Which one, though? A second passed before her fine hearing picked up a thud. The inimitable sound of a closing door. Gaia traced the sound to the door belonging to the last building on the street, one overlooking the Hudson River. Quickly she raced around the corner to determine if the building had a second entrance on the river side. It didn't. She had him.

44TH ST.

Jesus, was she ever going to stop? CJ felt like his lungs were on the verge of collapse. He was in no shape to scramble thirty-some blocks uptown and all the way west to the river, much of it at a dead run.

Gaia was running away from him, but she never once looked over her shoulder to see him coming. Not even when he'd nearly picked her off on Hudson Street, after she'd collided with the Chinese guy on the bike. He'd locked on her head at point-blank range, and she'd stopped to help the Chinese guy up! The girl had ice in her veins. She wasn't a regular person.

When she turned off on the side street, CJ skidded to a hard stop, almost losing his balance. Gaia slowed down, then walked to the entrance to the building at the very end of the street and stopped. CJ didn't move from the corner. He felt his heart pounding like a jackhammer. But now it wasn't just exhaustion. It was excitement, too.

He secured the gun in both hands. He brought it up almost to eye level. Why wasn't Gaia moving—getting her ass out of there? Didn't she know he was there? She was crazy! She was a dead woman.

He tensed his right index finger on the trigger. "This is for Marco," he whispered. And with a huge, heady surge of accomplishment, he pulled the trigger and blew her away.

BANG

Tom Moore watched the young gunman from a distance. With deep concentration he observed the young man aim the pistol, aiming his own weapon almost simultaneously. He pulled the trigger and heard two explosions, a fraction of a second apart. With fear spreading through his heart he watched the young man go down. It was a good wound. Enough to scare a guy like that off. For now, he was out of the equation, and all that mattered was Gaia. Tom bolted around the corner in flat-out panic.

Gaia was alive. She was standing at the entrance to a building, looking around to see whence the shots had come. She was unharmed. She didn't even appear particularly concerned. Had she any idea how close that bullet had come to ending her life?

Tom ducked out of sight again. With relief flooding his body, he slid to the pavement and allowed himself a moment of rest to slow his speeding heart. Then he took out his phone and connected with his assistant. "There's a man down. I need you to report it to 911. Make the call untraceable."

GAIA'S BACK

Sam was weary and confused and fast losing his grip on reality. He'd chased Gaia for at least two miles of congested city streets up to this godforsaken neighborhood and onto a side street as dark and empty of people as a New York City street could be. What was she thinking? Did she have some plan in mind? And was he crazy, or was there more than one other guy following her?

What was Gaia into now? What had she really come to tell him when she'd barged into his room tonight? Nothing was clear to him anymore—except that Gaia was a source of astonishing complexity and trouble, and of course he knew that already.

Sam staggered along the street, catching a flitting glance of Gaia's back disappearing into an old loft building that faced the river. Now what the hell was he supposed to do?

He didn't pause to answer his own question. He just followed her, of course. He hoped she wasn't leading them both to their deaths. And at least if she was, he hoped he would get a chance to tell her that he loved her (in addition to finding her stupendously annoying) before he went.

HER FATHER

Gaia followed him up the stairs on silent feet. Did he know she was still behind him? Did he know she could hear his footsteps perfectly well in the darkness? She was certain her father could have evaded her more skillfully than this. Was it possible he wanted her to find him after all? What could it mean?

Complicated questions were filling up the purposeful blank that had been her mind. Eleven floors up, he exited the staircase. The heavy cast-iron door banged to a close behind him. She waited a second before following.

This had the feeling of an ambush. Gaia knew she should be cautious and prudent, but on the other hand, if her own father was leading her into an ambush, what was there to live for, anyway?

She walked through the door and found herself suddenly in a vast, well-lit loft. The ceiling soared twenty feet above her, and the floor under her feet was highly polished parquet. Enormous floor-to-ceiling windows spanned the entire wall facing the river. She could see the lights of New Jersey across the way and a garishly lit cruise boat churning up the Hudson.

She blinked in the light, regained her bearings, and turned around. There, standing before her, not ten feet away, was her father. He wasn't running from her any longer. He stood still, gazing into her face.

"Gaia," he said.

NOT
NOTHING

THE RAW PAIN THAT LIVED HIDDEN INSIDE HER
EVERY DAY OF HER LIFE HAD BROKEN FREE.

Gaia's heart was volcanic. Tears threatened to spill from her eyes.

It was really him. He was here with her. For the first time in almost five years she had before her the thing she'd yearned for most.

In those long, empty years she'd hardened her heart against him with anger and distrust, commanding herself not to care, not allowing herself the hope that he would ever come for her.

But now, in his presence, her heart's protective shell was cracking and threatening to fall away. She'd been so strong, so capable for all that time, and now she felt that the pressure of the misery and frailty and helplessness built up over those lonely years could flatten her in a torrent of sorrow and self-pity.

She was like the toddler who'd lost her mother in the grocery store, facing miles of grim, dizzying aisles and shelves with numb courage, not allowing herself the luxury of tears until she was back in her mother's arms.

Now Gaia's tears distorted her father's familiar features, the blue eyes so much like her own. It brought upon her wave after wave of memories that she hadn't allowed herself since he'd disappeared.

Her father scrupulously drawing castles when she loved castles, horses when she loved horses, boats when she loved boats. Making her waffles every Saturday morning through her entire childhood as she sat on the counter and told him stories. Teaching her algebra, basic chemistry, martial arts, gardening, marksmanship.

He was teaching, always teaching her, but he made it fun. On Mondays he would speak to her only in Russian, and she and her mother would make blintzes and potato latkes for dinner. On Tuesdays they'd speak only in Arabic and she and her mother would make kibbe and hummus and stuffed grape leaves. He and her mother took her on hikes in famously beautiful places all over the country to teach her about the natural world.

Most other fathers Gaia knew were good for one game of catch on Sunday after the NFL games had ended. Gaia's was different.

Now Gaia's father took a step closer. She didn't move.

That blissful childhood was what made it almost impossible to survive the night her mother was murdered and her father disappeared. She needed him and missed him so desperately, crying for him every single night, not understanding at first that he was really gone. And it wasn't beyond his control, the way it was for her mother. He was still alive. He chose something else in his life over her, and even when she became so severely depressed that she could barely eat or sleep or talk for weeks and then months at a time, still he stayed away. He never once called her or wrote. She wanted to die then just so her father would know that he had broken her heart.

Could she ever forgive him for that?

He took another step closer. And another.

His face was close and vivid now. A question hovered in his eyes.

Gaia's heart was a war zone. On the one side was the happiness and devotion her father gave her for her first twelve years. On the other was the brutal neglect for the past five. Which side was more powerful? Would Gaia's love or the anger win out?

She was watching his face very closely.

"Gaia," he said again, tentatively. He reached out to her.

Suddenly the battle shifted. Gaia wasn't sure exactly why. It was something in the way his mouth moved, something indescribably subtle, that made her know that this man was different than the one she'd adored above everything else for twelve years. Something fundamental had changed between the way he was then and now. She couldn't put her finger on it.

The anger surged forward in a fierce offensive, beating back the love with ruthless energy. The victory in battle was so quick and so decisive that when her father came another step closer and reached out his arms to embrace her, Gaia recoiled. Feeling the brief touch of his hands on her shoulders, she experienced no warmth, no affection. Nothing.

Well, not nothing. Anger.

She experienced such powerful anger that she shoved him away from her. "I don't want to see you," she told him.

The anger was building. It was terrifying. The raw pain that lived hidden inside her every day of her life had broken free, and she couldn't control it. She shoved him again, harder this time.

There was sadness and confusion in his face as he stumbled backward, or some semblance of it. She couldn't tell. She didn't know this man. His expressions weren't familiar to her.

She drew back her arm and connected her fist with his jaw. It made a satisfying crack. It was horrible, unspeakable of her to do this, to treat her own father this way.

And yet his expression conveyed no pain. He never took his eyes from her.

She was hauling off for another blow when her arm caught behind her. She spun around and realized for the first time that there was another person in the room. Over her shoulder she saw a tall, very broad man with dark clothing, short dark hair, and a completely blank expression.

Who was this? she wondered distantly, from beyond her rage.

The man held Gaia's arm tightly and twisted it behind her back.

What could her father have meant by this? Gaia wondered, staring at him in indignant disbelief. Was this some kind of ambush after all?

It didn't matter. The oversized man provided an opportune release for Gaia's exploding rage. With some zeal she broke his grasp. Instantly she grabbed a fistful of his hair in one hand and shoved her other hand under his armpit. She positioned her legs for the greatest leverage and swung the son of a bitch over her shoulder, laying him flat out on the wood floor.

She waited for him to scramble back up to his feet before she buried another jab in his stomach and kicked him brutally in the chest.

She was dangerous now. She wasn't in control. She had to put him away before she really did harm. She calculated the exact spot on his neck and struck fiercely with the heel of her hand. The man crumpled to the floor without a glimmer of consciousness, just as she'd expected. He'd wake up in a while. He'd be fine. It was her own wildfire temper that caused her concern.

Her father watched her intently. Beseeching her. She couldn't look at him anymore. If she didn't get out of there, she would do something she would truly regret.

"It's too late. You stayed away too long," she muttered to him as she turned and walked away. He was no longer her handsome, magical father; now only a pale reminder of sickening betrayal and loss, she needed him out of her sight.

She wished he were dead. That way she could treasure the time she had with him. She could carry on in life with the belief that love was real and happiness could be trusted. Now that cherished time, the foundation of her existence, was fatally poisoned by the knowledge that her beloved father had been a soulless viper all along.

THE DARK HALF

Tom Moore stood sweating in the dark stairwell on the eleventh floor of the largely abandoned loft building. He had a terrible feeling about this. Why had Gaia come to this place? He felt certain there was grave danger here. He sensed it so strongly, his brain clouded with dark, impenetrable fear. He hadn't had this feeling in a long time.

He was preparing to follow her when he heard the metal door creaking open just a few feet away. He hurled himself backward, concealing at least most of his body behind dusty boxes in the corner of the landing. He crouched there silently.

Gaia staggered through the door and into the stairwell. Her face displayed pure psychic pain. He stopped breathing as she walked within inches of him. Clearly she didn't see him because she continued down the stairs.

Tom felt as if his heart were being ripped from his chest. This was too hard, being near Gaia, seeing her pain, and not being able to help. But he was involved now, and how was he ever going to pull away again?

He knew he would follow her, but before he did, he needed to see what was beyond that stairwell door. Gaia had emerged physically unharmed, but nonetheless something had destroyed her in there.

He had a bad feeling about it. A black curiosity. Even as he crept to the door, he advised himself against it.

He opened the door with ultimate gentleness, wincing in anticipation of the slightest creak. He pulled it open about a foot and took a deep breath. Slowly silently he peered into the giant loft, his hand poised on the trigger of his gun.

Tom's glance lighted ever so briefly on a man of his own age and build sitting in the middle of the floor, elbows resting on knees, chin resting in hands, silently contemplating.

That man sitting on the floor was exactly Tom's build and exactly his age—to the hour. His face was more familiar to Tom's than any other, and yet Tom flew from the scene with the singular horror of a man who has seen the dead rise and walk.

Tom knew it was the man referred to, in his short, explosive life among the terrorist underground, as Loki, after the Norse god of the netherworld. But he also knew that the man's given name was Oliver Moore and that he was supposed to have died five years ago.

It was Tom's alter ego, his dark half, his brother.

IF YOU LOVE
SOMETHING . . .

"You let her go?" Ella asked in disbelief, returning to the loft from the floor below.

Loki said nothing. He sat there, meditative.

"After all that, you let her go?"

It was a great failing of Ella's that she couldn't keep her temper under control. She was self-destructively trying to get a rise out of him, and he wasn't in the mood to play. Ella made a grave error in allowing her dislike of Gaia to get the best of her.

For a man who had risen above (or perhaps fallen below?) his emotional impulses long ago, it was rather confounding to feel the sting of Gaia's rejection. He should have been delighted to see the rage and hatred she held for her father— or a man she believed to be her father, at any rate. Instead, in some primal way, he longed to see love in her eyes, no matter who she believed him to be. She was his daughter after all, genetically if not actually. She was the child of the woman he'd loved. In all of the sordid, black history between him and Katia and his brother, Gaia was the prize, and he meant to win her.

"You've lost her now," Ella prodded sullenly.

Loki stood and stretched. He walked toward the windows, admiring the sparkling panorama with fresh eyes. Suddenly he felt enormously hungry, like he'd woken from a very long sleep,

"Until Monday, perhaps," Loki informed her with a careless yawn.

"And why will she be back then?" Ella demanded snappishly.

Loki stood inches from the window, staring out, his hands pressed against the cold glass. He was in no particular hurry to answer Ella. He studied the dark precarious cliffs of New Jersey's Palisades for a long time.

"Because I've detained a certain friend of hers. We'll keep him. Weaken him for a day or so. On Monday morning Gaia will learn that if she doesn't come for him when I wish, I will murder him."

BAD CHOICE

Sam lay on the concrete floor, feeling the thumping ache in his shoulder and ribs, dully considering the pale shaft of light that crept into the far side of an otherwise black space. Where was he? Where was the light coming from? Why had he come here, and who wanted to imprison him?

He hadn't caught up to Gaia. He had no idea where she'd gone. But the insidious suspicion had taken root in his mind that she had led him here just to be beaten up and held captive by two large men in masks. Blind, lovesick moron that he was, he'd chased her right into a trap.

Why, though? What had he done? Who were these people, and what could they possibly want from him?

He heard the wail of sirens coming close and wished without much real hope that maybe they were coming for him.

This was a truly depressing twist. It was so awful that a part of Sam—not a part relating to his shoulder or ribs—almost wanted to laugh.

He'd had a choice between a safe, loving girlfriend and a seamy, mysterious troublemaker, and whom had he chosen? He had abandoned the culmination of a long-desired sexual encounter for a mad dash through city streets and the privilege of getting beaten up and locked up in a deserted building on the far West Side.

He had a choice, and he'd chosen wrong.

BEING BRAVE

Gaia's life felt bleaker and more desolate than the trash-strewn street where she walked. In one night the few joys she'd had or hoped for were obliterated. Her father—the idea of her father—was irretrievable. She had no choice but to accept now that Sam would never be hers. In her misery she allowed herself to imagine the scene between him and Heather after she'd run off. Sure, they were embarrassed, but once they got over it, they probably had a good laugh at her expense and got back to business—Sam more passionately than before in his joy and relief to have Heather in his bed and not a psychotic miscreant like Gaia.

She walked slowly down the forsaken street, wondering in the back of her mind where CJ was with his gun. She was ready for him now. Plans 1 and 2 had crashed and burned with equal horror. Not a single hope had survived the collisions. She officially had nothing to live for.

Chill winds blew off the Hudson. She was probably cold, she realized, but she was too numb to register it.

She looked around. Wasn't it just her luck that even CJ disappointed her when she wanted him?

Well, she reasoned, she could always load up her pockets with rocks and wade into the Hudson. She could always walk into the screaming traffic of the West Side Highway. She could find her way to the roof of any one of these buildings and leap off. It's not like her demise was dependent on CJ. *Suicide is the most cowardly act,* a voice inside Gaia's head reminded her. Where had she heard that?

For some reason, the smell in the air reminded her of the smell off the lake at her parents' old cabin in the Berkshires. Who knew why. This was gritty urban water, and that was pure mountain runoff.

For some reason, the smell reminded her of her mom, and the memory of her mom magically brought an image into her mind. It was her mom's face, clear and sharp— shaded by Gaia's raw feelings, maybe, but otherwise accurate. It was the way her mom looked dangling her bare feet off the dock, watching Gaia's attempts to fish for dinner, although she knew perfectly well that Gaia would end up throwing every single fish back into the lake.

It made Gaia's heart come back to life a little because

this was something approaching a miracle. Gaia could never remember her mother's face clearly. It drove her crazy that she couldn't. And yet here, in the midst of Hell's Kitchen, was Katia's beautiful and beloved face.

And for some reason, seeing her mother clearly right now reminded Gaia of something else.

Although she had lost the two things she longed for, it somehow opened up the opportunity for something she wanted even more. She had the chance to keep on living, even though she didn't think she could.

At the moment it felt to Gaia like a chance to be brave.

RUN

To Mia Pascal Johannson

GAIA

Do you know what hell is?

I do.

It's not fire and brimstone. Not for me, anyway.

It's watching your hopes die.

It's watching the guy you love—the guy who makes you understand why that poor sucker built the Taj Mahal, why Juliet buried a dagger in her chest, why that Trojan king destroyed his entire fleet—making love to another girl. A girl you despise.

It's seeing your father—a man you believed was a superhero—for the first time after five long years only to discover he was a dishonorable creep show all along.

Hell is experiencing both of those things in one night.

Hell is the way the ceiling looks above your bed when you open your eyes the next morning. Hell is the morning after that, when the ceiling looks just as hopeless, and you realize the pain hasn't begun to fade and that maybe it never will.

That is hell.

What is heaven?

I don't know.

I had an idea about it a couple of days ago, but that was before hope died.

If you happen to find out, will you let me know?

SAVE SAM

ONE OF HIS EYES WAS BLACK-AND-BLUE,
SWOLLEN SHUT, AND HE LOOKED FRIGHTENINGLY
PALE. WEAK.

"Hello? Anybody up there?"

Gaia had just stepped out of the shower when she heard the voice floating up the stairs to greet her. She wrapped a too-small towel around herself, went to the landing, and leaned into the stairwell. It was a familiar voice, but not one she expected to hear before eight o'clock in the morning.

"Ed?"

"Yeah."

"Um . . . what the hell are you doing here?"

She heard him laugh under his breath. "Just fine, thanks, and you?"

At the sound of his voice, a minute ray of happiness filtered down into the blackness of her mood. She hadn't spoken a word out loud since Saturday night, since everything . . . happened. Now it was Monday morning, and her words were so far back in her brain she had to hunt around for them. "N-Not that fine," she responded hoarsely. "I had . . ." How could she begin to convey the true horror that was her life? "Sort of a rough weekend."

"What else is new?"

She heard both affection and wariness in Ed's voice. He knew a "rough weekend" for Gaia meant more than teenage angst—that it would involve things like firearms and kickboxing.

"Tell me about it over breakfast," he called. "I brought bagels."

Her stomach grumbled loudly. One thing this city had going for it—authentic, fresh-out-of-the-oven bagels. They almost made up for the high price of Apple Jacks. She glanced down at herself and the small puddle forming under her feet. "I'm wearing a hand towel and a few cups of water," Gaia said, wishing Ella hadn't left early this morning, so that she could be disturbed by this exchange. At least Ella had taken George with her wherever she'd gone. Gaia disliked offending George as much as she enjoyed offending Ella.

"I repeat," said Ed, laughing again. "C'mon down!"

Gaia rolled her eyes, trying to ignore the undertones of the remark. Two minutes later, she'd slipped into her most-worn cargo pants and a gray T-shirt and was on her way downstairs, her hair dripping water over her shoulders. On the landing, she paused to study the familiar snapshot that hung in a frame there on the wall—the photograph George had taken so long ago of Gaia and her parents. Gaia had tried to get rid of it, but Ella insisted it remain. She squinted at it, looking hard at her father.

Her father. She'd seen him two nights ago. Actually seen him and spoken to him. *And decked him,* she reminded herself bitterly.

After that he'd disappeared—again.

Her stomach churned, both with confusion and with sadness. Why had he shown up here after all this time? What could it mean?

Was it some paternal sixth sense that had dragged him back into her life? Did he somehow know she'd been on the verge of ditching her virginity, and he'd crawled out from whatever rock he'd been hiding under all these years to give her an old-fashioned heart-to-heart talk on morality, safe sex, and self-control?

Or was it just one more whacked-out coincidence in her life?

She leaned closer to the photo and stared into his eyes.

They appeared to be soft, kind, intelligent eyes—and the smile looked genuine. The man she'd met on Saturday night had not seemed genuine at all. The warmth and gentleness she saw in the picture had been missing from that man. He was different somehow. Lesser.

Apparently abandoning your kid and living on the run could take a lot out of a person. In the kitchen, Gaia was met by the aroma of fresh bagels and hot coffee. Ed, who had positioned his chair close to the table, looked up from spreading cream cheese on a poppy seed bagel. "You didn't have to get dressed on my account."

She was annoyed at the blush his grin brought to her face. "Shut up." Her eyes narrowed. "How did you get in here, anyway?"

"Door was unlocked," Ed said. "You should really talk to your roomies about that. I mean this is a nice neighborhood, but why court robbery, or worse?"

Gaia collapsed into a chair. That was weird. George never left the door unlocked. Must've been another brilliant Ella maneuver.

"Do you think it's kismet that this place is handicap accessible?" Ed asked suddenly.

Gaia raised an eyebrow. "It's either kismet . . . or the building code."

"I'm serious," said Ed. "Do you have any idea how many places in this city aren't?"

She felt a pang of pity but squashed it fast. "So what's kismet got to do with it?"

"You happen to live in wheelchair-friendly digs. I happen to be in a wheelchair." Ed shrugged. "It's like the universe is arranging it so that we can hang out."

"The universe clearly has too much time on its hands." She sat down and pulled her knees up, leaning them against the edge of the table.

"Like lox?"

"Hate it."

"Then I'm glad I didn't buy any." Ed pushed a steaming cup of coffee across the table toward her. "Three sugars, no cream, right?"

Gaia nodded, refusing to be charmed by the fact that

he remembered, and took a careful sip. She could feel him staring at her.

"You look like hell," he said, shaking a lock of brown hair back off his forehead. Suddenly he appeared to realize this was not a smart thing to say to a girl—any girl. "I mean . . . in a good way," he added lamely.

Gaia gave him a sidelong glance. "That's funny. I feel like hell." She took another, bolder sip of the hot coffee, letting the steamy liquid warm her from the inside.

"Now we're getting to it," Ed said, clasping his hands together and then cracking his knuckles. "You were unsurprisingly unfindable yesterday, Gaia. So let's hear it." He broke off a piece of bagel and pointed it at her. "Who was the lucky guy and how did the ceremonial shedding of the chastity belt go?"

Gaia ignored the bile rising in her throat, picked up a marble bagel, and took a gigantic bite. There was a reason she'd avoided Ed all day yesterday—the need to avoid forced emotional spillage. "Subtlety isn't exactly a talent of yours, is it, Ed?" she said with her mouth full.

"Look who's talking."

He had a point there. She studied Ed for a moment—the just-this-side-of-scruffy hair, the eager yet wary brown eyes, the dot of dried blood on his chin where he'd cut himself shaving. Gaia hated that she had to talk about this, but she did. She'd sucked Ed into the whole sorry situation when she confessed her virginity. Like it or not, over the past few weeks she had made Ed a friend, or something very close. He might as well know the truth.

Gaia closed her eyes. Shook her head. Sighed.

"It didn't happen," she said. And her whole body felt empty.

Ed dropped the knife onto the floor with a clatter. "It didn't?"

"Ed!" She opened her eyes and glared at him. "Think you can sound just a little more amused by that?"

"Sorry it didn't work out for you." Ed cleared his throat, and she could swear he was hiding a grin behind his steaming coffee. Some friend. "So what happened?" he asked.

Gaia took another aggressive bite of bagel. She chewed and swallowed before answering. "Let's just say I was witness to somebody beating me to it."

"Shut up!" Ed's eyes opened wide. "Gaia, tell me who we're talking about here. You can't keep me in this kind of suspense."

Say it, she commanded herself. Just say it. "It was Sam Moon."

A sudden shower of chewed bagel bits pelted Gaia's arms. "God, Ed! Food is to go in the mouth. *In*," Gaia said, brushing off her arms irritably.

"Do you mean you walked in on Sam and . . . Heather?"

Ed choked out while simultaneously attempting to wipe his mouth.

Somehow, saying it out loud gave Gaia a bit of distance. The words were vibrating in the fragrant air of the kitchen. Outside of her instead of inside. "Ironic, isn't it?" Gaia asked, flicking one last bagel wad off her elbow.

Ed looked as if he were watching his life flash before his eyes—backward and in 3-D with surround sound. Gaia had never seen his skin so pale. She'd forgotten for the moment that Heather meant something to Ed as well. A big something.

"Man?" Ed let out a long rush of breath. His eyes were unfocused. "That had to suck."

It didn't suck. Sucking was getting busted for going seventy in a thirty-five-mile-an-hour zone. Sucking was losing a dollar in a Coke machine. Sucking didn't *hurt*.

"Could've been worse," she mumbled with a shrug. She wouldn't have believed it, except that it had actually gotten worse. The night had been full of mind-bending surprises. But she didn't need to share them now, if ever. They were highly dysfunctional family matters to be discussing over breakfast.

"What could be worse than walking in on the object of your seduction in bed with your mortal enemy?"

It was a decent question. Gaia was saved from needing to explain by the sound of the phone ringing.

Ed reached behind him, snatched the cordless from the counter, then slid it across the table to Gaia. She hit the button and held the receiver to her ear. "Hello?"

At first, nothing.

"Hello?"

"Gaia Moore?"

Her eyes narrowed. "Yeah? Who is this?"

The voice was distorted, like something from a horror movie. "Check your e-mail." It was a command. Maybe even a threat.

She felt as if ice were forming in her veins. "Who is this?"

"Check your e-mail," the voice growled.

The line went dead.

Gaia was on her feet, running for George's computer, which, luckily, he always left on. When she reached the den, she flung herself into the chair and punched at the keyboard. Ed, maneuvering his chair through the rooms, appeared soon after.

"What's going on?"

Gaia was too morbidly curious to answer. She clicked the mail icon and stared at the screen as it choked out the early, cryptic shadows of a video image, and she tapped her fingers impatiently on the mouse as the picture emerged slowly . . . slowly . . .

It was someone with his back to her, hunched forward.

His surroundings were vague, too much light. Gaia reached for the speaker, in case there was audio. There was. Staticky at first. Distant, fuzzy, then clearing.

"Maybe it's Heather, playing a joke," offered Ed. "To get even."

Gaia was so intent on the image she barely heard him. "I don't think so."

Over the computer speakers she heard his voice. . . .

"Gaia . . . ?"

Her heart seemed to freeze solid in her chest. No, no, no, no.

But the voice through the speaker repeated itself. "Gaia."

No! "Sam?"

As if he'd heard her, he turned to the camera, and suddenly there was Sam's face on the computer screen. One of his eyes was black-and-blue, swollen shut, and he looked frighteningly pale. Weak.

Ed angled his chair close to the desk. "Oh, shit."

Sam's face vanished, replaced by a blank screen, and then there was a blast of static from the speakers as the same distorted voice addressed her. "Gaia Moore. You can see from this footage that we have a mutual friend. Sadly, he's not feeling well at the moment. Did you know Sam is a diabetic? No, I would imagine you didn't . . ."

Ed stared at the blank screen. "Who the hell is it?"

Gaia shushed him with a sharp hiss as a graphic began to appear on the screen—a message snaking its way from the right side, one letter at a time:

C . . . A . . . N . . . Y . . . O . . . U . . .

The voice continued as the letters slid into view. "He's well enough for the moment, but around, oh, say, ten o'clock this evening he'll be needing his insulin, quite desperately. And that, my darling Gaia, is where you come in. You must pass a series of tests. You must pass these tests by ten o'clock tonight. If you do not, we will not wait for the diabetes to take over. If you do not pass these tests in the allotted time . . ."

The graphic slithered by: S . . . A . . . V . . . E . . .

". . . we will kill him."

S . . . A . . . M . . . ?

For a moment the question trembled there on the dark screen. CAN YOU SAVE SAM? Then the letters went spinning off into the infinite background, and another message appeared in an eye-searing flash of brightness. It read:

You will find on your front step a DVD. You will play it during your first-period class. DO NOT view the DVD prior to showing it in school.

Without warning, the e-mail broadcast returned, showing a close-up of Sam's beaten face, his frightened eyes, his mouth forming a word, and the word came screaming through the speaker in Sam's voice.

"Gaia!"

Then nothing. The image and the audio were gone, and the computer whirred softly until George's sickening screen saver—a scanned-in photo of Ella—returned to the screen.

Gaia sprang up from the chair and flew to the front door, which she flung open. The early October air sparkled, and the neighborhood was just coming alive with people on their way to work and school. Gaia paid no attention. Her eyes searched the front stoop until they found the package.

She lunged for it.

Gaia had no idea who had done this. She had no idea why. But she wasn't about to ask questions.

In that instant, it didn't matter that Sam had had sex with Heather or that he didn't return Gaia's overwhelming love for him and probably never would.

Sam life was in danger. For now, that was all that mattered.

THE KNIGHT

"What are you doing?" Ed demanded, wheeling himself out from the exit under the stoop, afraid for a moment that the package might explode in her hands.

But Gaia had grabbed her ever-present messenger bag and was down the steps. Ed aimed his chair to the left, toward the sidewalk. He could barely see Gaia over the row of potted shrubs as she sprinted away.

He caught up to her three corners later. One good thing about being in a wheelchair—even New York drivers slowed to let you cross the street.

She was bouncing on the balls of her feet, waiting for the light to change.

"Gaia, hold on. You can't just go to school and put that thing in the DVD player!"

She didn't turn to face him. "Watch me."

"What if it . . . I don't know . . . what if it starts spewing out poisonous gas or something?" Ed offered.

"This isn't a *Batman* episode, Ed!" Gaia spat out, glancing over her shoulder. "What do you think, the Penguin sent that e-mail?"

"No, but somebody just as wacko did!"

"Somebody who's got Sam." Her voice was grim. Determined.

"Yeah, I get that. But we need to think about this. You don't know what's on that DVD." He shook his head. "Okay, I admit, toxic vapor is a little extreme. But this whole thing is freaky, and I'm just saying we should be careful."

"You be careful," she snapped, "I'll be quick."

"Do you *never* think before you act?"

"Ed! Listen!" She grabbed the armrests of his wheelchair and leaned over to look him directly in the eyes. She was so close he could see the pores in the perfect skin around her nose. Her hair was still wet against her cheeks. "I don't know who is doing this or why," she said. "But I have to help Sam."

In the next second he watched, helpless, as she flung herself out into the middle of traffic. A cab swerved. A UPS truck hit the brakes. A bike messenger careened off a mailbox.

But she made it.

He expected her to go right on running, but when she hit the opposite sidewalk, she turned and looked at him.

It was probably the fastest look in the history of eye contact, but that look was loaded. It was part defiance, part desperation, and part apology.

"Go!" he shouted, his voice raw. "I'll see you there."

She nodded almost imperceptibly, then took off down the street.

He followed as fast as his confinement allowed. Thinking.

She wanted to sleep with Sam. Sam Moon. But she hadn't. It had taken complete self-control to keep from popping a wheelie in his chair when she'd confessed that Saturday night had been torture—the thought of her in someone else's arms, of someone else kissing her, had kept him awake all night. Awake and angry and sick to his stomach.

Because he loved her desperately. In mind, in spirit, in body. He wanted her.

So what if she wanted Sam? Seeing him with Heather must have cured that, right? The fact that she was rushing off to his rescue, no questions asked, just meant she was noble. One more thing to love about her.

Ed's remark about the universe setting them up came back to him, and he cringed. Stupid. Childish. Pathetic.

Yet on some level he'd meant it. He'd found her, that first day in the hall at school. She'd been so lost, and so not wanting to be lost. Ed knew how lost felt. He'd felt it every day since he'd first sat in this chair. Every day he was set apart.

He approached school and entered the crush of people. He imagined Gaia in her first-period classroom, slamming the mysterious DVD into the DVD player. What the hell is on the DVD? he wondered, feeling panic press into him.

And if he had to, could he rescue her from it?

He smiled bitterly at the ridiculous image. Sir Edward of

Useless Limbs, the knight in not-so-shining armor, rushing in to rescue the fair Gaia, Lady of Brutal Ass Kickings.

Remember that, pal? Three punks in one shot. And without even having to touch up her lip gloss afterward. His lady had no need for a knight. And, anyway, knights rode horses, not chairs.

He broke from the pack of students and rolled toward the handicapped entrance.

As he did on every other day of the school year, Ed entered the building alone.

TO: ELJ
FROM: L
DATE: October 11
FILE: 776244
SUBJECT: Gaia Moore

She is even more beautiful up close. And far more dangerous. For now, we proceed as planned. The trials have begun. We will test her limits. I want to see how far she will go for this boy. What she will risk. How much she is willing to lose.

The boy suffers, but it is all in the name of authenticity.

I have no doubt she will succeed on her own; however, if any complications should arise to impede her various quests, I will arrange for assistance. Her safety, as ever, is of utmost importance. She must not fail—for all roads lead to me. Tonight I will secure my position in her life. There is much to alter. Much to gain.

TO: L

FROM: ELJ

DATE: October 11

FILE: 776244

SUBJECT: Gaia Moore

I understand what is expected of me. The note is already written and waiting to be planted. Other objects with regard to this aspect of the plan are also in place.

GN and I will leave the city early. He will not be there to help her or to interfere in any way. He will not suspect a thing.

Tonight I will meet the pawn and see that he is where we need him to be, and when.

GAIA

Sam's face. Sam's bruised face. It came out of that computer at me like a kick to the teeth. And then he had to go and call my name like that.

I wonder if fear feels anything like desperation. Because that's what I felt when his voice came reverberating out of those speakers.

He called *my* name.

This probably sounds totally inappropriate, but there was a moment there . . . There was a moment there when I was glad he was calling *me*. And I can think of only two possible reasons why.

Reason #1. The kidnapper told Sam he was zapping his image to *my* computer, so who else's name *would* he say?

But I doubt the kidnapper is giving him any information pertaining to his rescue, so the chances of his knowing he was even being filmed are pretty slim. Besides, he doesn't know about my . . . talents, or my weird life, so why would he be calling out to me for help? It's not like he'd expect me to be able to come crashing in and kick his captor's ass—which I would do in a heartbeat, if only I knew where he was. So that brings me to:

Reason #2. He's thinking of me. (Could it be?)

Thinking of me insofar as a guy in hypoglycemic shock (or whatever it's called when diabetics need insulin) who may also be suffering a concussion can think.

Like maybe he screamed "Gaia" because Gaia was the first thing that came to his mind.

Gaia. *Me.* Gaia.

I don't know.

What I do know, though, is this: As long as there's an ounce of strength in my body, I am going to do everything I possibly can to do what that son-of-a-bitch kidnapper challenged me to do.

I'm going to save Sam.

And when I find out who did this to him, I'm going to take the guy down.

INDEPENDENT
FILM

SHE TOLD HERSELF THE ONLY THING THAT
MATTERED WAS THAT SHE'D PASSED
THE FIRST TEST.

WEIRD SHIT

"No, man! No, man, *please*! Don't!

CJ closed his eyes as Tarick lifted one rock-solid fist and slammed it against CJ's skull. His eye felt as if it had been dislodged from its socket, and his mouth instantly filled with blood.

"You let her go?" Tarick shouted, coming at CJ again. This time he wrenched CJ's arm—the one in the sling. The one with the bullet hole in it. The pain shot through his entire body like an explosion, and everything went blurry. CJ sank to the grimy concrete floor on his knees and then fell forward, savoring the feel of the cold, grainy surface against his cheek. It smelled like burnt cigarettes and blood. CJ knew it was the last smell he'd ever experience if he didn't do something.

"Kill him." Tarick's voice. "Now."

"No! No! Wait!"

He heard them loading the gun.

"I can still do it!" CJ shouted through the pain.

Suddenly he was being wrenched to his feet, and Tarick used one beefy hand to push CJ up against the wall by his neck. "We should have let you bleed to death in the first place, you useless piece of shit." Tarick spat in CJ's face, but CJ couldn't move a muscle. He just let the gob slide down the side of his nose and onto his chin.

"I can still do it," he repeated pathetically, choking on the words. Joey was hovering behind Tarick, gun clenched in his hand. He didn't even look sad or scared. He just looked ready.

Tarick released him and he fell to the ground, sputtering for breath. He bent over at the waist, thought better of taking his eyes off Joey, and forced himself to straighten up.

"Please. Tarick," CJ said, his eyes stinging. "Weird shit is always happening around this bitch. Guys with guns, like she's got a protector or something."

Tarick laughed, showing his yellowed teeth and flashing the stud that pierced his tongue. "This isn't a storybook, CJ," Tarick said. "She don't have a fairy godmother."

Joey cocked the gun.

"Please, man," CJ said, trying hard not to whimper. "Just give me one more chance. I won't let you down again."

Tarick's eyes roamed over CJ's broken and battered body. He sucked at his teeth, ran a hand over his shaved and tattooed head. He glanced at Joey, then looked back at CJ.

"All right, man," Tarick said with a quick nod. "You get one more chance."

CJ let out a sigh of relief and closed his eyes. Then Tarick's voice cut through the darkness, his breath impossibly close to CJ's ear.

"Screw it up again, and I kill you myself."

FLOATING

Heather Gannis did not walk so much as float. With her delicate chin tipped upward slightly, she moved purposefully but gracefully through the posthomeroom throng. The look of disdain on her pretty face was to remind the Gap-clad masses that she was, and would always be, their superior. Even if she didn't necessarily feel like it. They were the ones who'd elevated her to that status. She was the one who had to struggle daily to perpetuate the illusion.

She floated, seemingly high on her own significance, weightless in the knowledge that she, and she alone, had the best hair, the best blouse, the best ass.

She was Heather Gannis, too ethereal to simply walk.

That was how they saw her, anyway, and that was what they expected, maybe even needed. And she was the one they'd elected to provide it for them.

Sometimes she thought she'd be willing to chuck the whole popularity thing in a heartbeat. Other times, having swarms of admirers had its perks.

And so she'd float.

Today, though, she had to work harder than usual to pull it off. Today she was dealing with stuff. Big-time confusion. Insecurity—not about her beauty or her position at school, of course. Insecurity beyond the ordinary is-there-lipstick-on-my-teeth variety.

And Heather's self-doubt came in the form of the same pitiful little mutant who'd put her in the hospital. Gaia Moore.

What kind of name was that, anyway? Guy-uh. Sounded like a Cro-Magnon grunt rather than a name.

And Cro-Magnon girl had ruined everything. Shocker.

Saturday night had started out perfect. Then it had gotten even better.

She'd been in Sam's arms—securing what was hers, giving him what he wanted before Gaia had the chance to make an offer of her own.

Heather's motives for Saturday night had been part romance, part strategy. Sleeping with Sam would cement their relationship—take it to the next level. She was reasonably certain that Sam would forget Gaia completely if he believed Heather was committed enough to make him her first.

Sam wouldn't really be her first, of course—she'd lost her virginity to Ed long ago—but he'd *believe* that he was. She'd (briefly) considered telling him the truth, but decided "first" sounded so much more devoted than "next." Ed was her secret, and she was going to keep it that way.

But Gaia had her grubby little hooks in Ed, too. It made Heather's skin crawl to think about that. Ed followed Gaia around like a damn puppy dog.

She realized she was aching to see Gaia, maybe right now, in the hallway, where she could create some big, ugly scene that would make her look great and Gaia look even more pathetic than before.

She remembered with the small section of her brain in which she stored information about school that Gaia was in her first-period class. Fine. She could destroy her there just as easily. Smaller audience, but better acoustics.

Heather's mind spun (but she kept floating) and images of Sam, catapulting off the bed to chase after Gaia, burned in her mind. The Slim-Fast bar she'd eaten for breakfast threatened to come up. What had he been thinking? What was wrong with him, leaving her for Gaia, and just on the brink of . . . well, of everything?

But that bitch—that disgusting, creepy little bitch had shown up, and Sam had freaked.

On the upside, Gaia had looked absolutely miserable upon catching them in the act. Maybe now she'd get the message and back off. The girl had proof now, proof that Sam and Heather were the real deal. Of course, Sam's running after her might have given Gaia cause to wonder. . . .

Damn him! Why had he left? And why hadn't he called? That had been Saturday. This was Monday! No call, no personal appearance. She could have been home crying all weekend and he didn't even care.

A chill shot through her. What the hell had taken place when Sam caught up to Gaia Saturday? Had she said something, done something, to override Heather's sexual surrender?

Was there anything that *could* override sex for a guy? She doubted it, but still. Evidently Gaia had some weird power over Sam. Had she been able to use that power on Saturday, even as his hair was still tousled from Heather's own fingers?

Heather mentally checked her expression. No creases. No frowning. She had to look distant, aloof, as calm as always or else they might suspect. She lowered her eyelids slightly, pushed out her lower lip—sexy, sullen, unconcerned, and floating. Christ, this was getting old.

They called out to her and waved. Occasionally she'd reply, but not often enough to give them any substantial hope. And tomorrow she'd do it again.

And tomorrow. And tomorrow.

Shit! That reminded her. She had a Shakespeare quiz later this morning, and she hadn't even opened her notebook. What was it old Willie had said about the moon? The inconstant moon. Sam Moon. Inconstant, big time. Changeable. Fickle. And in love with Gaia Moore?

Maybe.

Heather entered her first-period class and immediately scanned the room to see if Gaia was there. To her amazement, the loser was actually present, actually had the nerve to show her face! Heather prepared herself to deploy her patented secret weapon—a look of death that could make even the thumb-heads on the wrestling team shiver in their sneakers—but Gaia seemed to be looking right through her.

Oh, this one was good. Most girls who found themselves on Heather's shit list would be groveling already. But this freak of nature had the audacity to diss her. On some level Heather was actually impressed. It was almost a relief to know there was someone who didn't shed all self-respect the minute Heather threw her a look.

Okay, so it was impressive. But it still pissed her off.

Heather slammed her books onto her desk, accepted some hellos from neighboring students, then noticed that the classroom television was on. The screen was blank—the same bright blue Michael Kors used last spring—and the DVD player light was blinking.

Thank God! Heather thought. A DVD was about all she could handle this morning. Probably something about the Civil War. Wait. This was economics, not history. Okay, something boring about supply and demand, then. Perfect.

She wouldn't even have to watch. She could study for Shakespeare and write vicious things about Gaia on the desktop. And wonder if Sam was out of her life for good now.

And if he was, was he in Gaia's life instead? Losing him would be bad. Losing him to her would be unbearable.

God, did that little witch actually believe she could do battle with her? Did she think she was better than Heather Gannis? And if she thought she was, how long would it be before the rest of the people in this school—flock of sheep that they were—began thinking it, too?

She didn't want to think about this. Not now. She wanted to get her mind off Gaia and Sam. She'd allow herself one nasty piece of desktop graffiti, then maybe she'd watch the stupid DVD after all.

AN ODD ANGLE

Sitting through homeroom was torture. What could the DVD possibly contain? Wicked neo-Nazi propaganda? Gang recruitment information? Or maybe something closer to home—a biographical account of her messed-up life, edited for the sole purpose of humiliating her in public? But since Gaia had no idea who'd kidnapped Sam, she couldn't even begin to pinpoint a motive, and therefore could not even venture a guess as to what purpose this DVD, this "test," might serve.

She was about to find out. First period. The moment of truth.

If anyone was surprised that the DVD was starting

before the teacher was present, they didn't mention it. Someone at the back of the room hit the lights. Gaia glanced over her shoulder and saw it was Ed, who'd just arrived. He was supposed to be in English now, wasn't he? But here he was, for moral support.

First bagels, now this. She felt a small cyclone of warmth in her stomach. So this was what friends did for you, huh? Gaia squelched the warmth. She couldn't risk getting used to it.

Ed shot her a look that was part encouragement, part panic. She turned away fast.

The blue screen gave way to a sudden blast of snowy static, then the scene focused.

It appeared to be a wide-angle shot of the upper half of a bedroom. The room was dimly lit, but Gaia could make out posters on the walls, an NYU pennant, a wide window with the blinds pulled.

And there were noises.

The usual New York background noises, of course—distant sirens, car horns, blaring radios. But over those came the more interesting noises.

Sounds like soft growling and deep sighs, sounds that seemed to caress each other.

Now where had she heard that before?

And then the camera panned down, pulling a form into focus.

It was an odd angle from which to film. Even Gaia, with her lack of experience in both filmmaking and lovemaking, knew that the subjects were unidentifiable. There was a broad back, encircled from below by svelte, ribbonlike arms that tapered into delicate hands and graceful fingers. But the camera angle was designed to provide no clear view of either face.

The noises deepened, grew urgent, began to resemble words.

"Oh. Oh my—"

All the air seemed to flee Gaia's lungs at once. She knew that voice. And now that she looked closer, the blanket covering the bottom half of the couple looked pretty familiar as well.

They, them, him, her.

Gaia gripped the edges of her desk. Shit! What should she do? Let it run? Or jump up (assuming she could actually get her body to jump, since she seemed to be paralyzed) and turn the thing off? After all, sooner or later she'd be making her own cameo in this film.

The class was catching on now, and the howling began. As far as Gaia could tell, they hadn't recognized the female lead just yet. The star herself, in response to the provocative remarks of her classmates, had only just looked up from something she was scribbling on her desktop.

The graceful fingers were now clawing at the broad back.

Out of the corner of her eye, Gaia could see Heather studying the screen. Heather's first instinct, it appeared, was to smile. Hell, it was funny! Funny, as long as it wasn't your inaugural sexual liaison being screened in first-period advanced-placement economics.

Gaia kept her eyes slanted in Heather's direction and watched as the perfect smile flickered once, then vanished. Realization flared in Heather's eyes just as her DVD incarnation was uttering her first line of dialogue.

"Oh my God . . . Sam!"

To which oh-my-God-Sam replied, *"Heather!"*

Busted!

Gaia snapped her attention back to the screen. Sundance, eat your heart out. Whoever this independent-film director was, he certainly had a flair for timing, because it was at this point that AP econ was allowed to enjoy the first close-up shot of the movie.

And it featured none other than Heather Gannis, perspiring elegantly, eyelids fluttering, flawless teeth clamped down on her lower lip.

The class exploded in reaction. Some of them shrieked in disbelief. Some laughed, some applauded wildly. Most just gasped. Heather, in a surprising gesture that made Gaia feel almost sorry for her, covered her face with one trembling hand and began to sob.

Gaia wondered absently if anyone had seen her stick the

DVD in the DVD player. If they had, this could get really ugly really fast. As if it weren't ugly enough already.

Two of Heather's girlfriends sprang to her side, ostensibly trying to comfort her.

"Somebody eject it!" one of them demanded.

"No pun intended!" replied someone on a choke of laughter.

Another of Heather's sidekicks—a girl named Megan— got up and moved toward the front of the room to turn off the television. Was it just Gaia's imagination, or did Megan seem to be taking her sweet time getting there?

AP econ was treated to a few additional renditions of "Oh my God, Sam!" before the electric-green-painted acrylic nail of Megan's index finger connected with the off button.

Instantly the class shut up, as if some cosmic off button had been punched as well.

The room went completely silent. Silent, except for the muffled gulping of Heather's crying.

Shame washed over Gaia.

Worse than fear, she guessed. It had to be.

Suddenly Gaia found herself silently pleading with Heather to go: Run. Get out. The silence pulsed as she kept her eyes glued to her desktop, willing her sworn enemy to escape. The girl was a bitch, sure, and a monster. But nobody, not even Heather, deserved this.

And then, as if she had sensed Gaia's unspoken plea, Heather catapulted out of her seat and stumbled toward the door. Megan and the other two handmaidens went running after Heather, looking appropriately concerned. But just before Megan disappeared through the door, she turned and fixed Gaia with a glare that Megan probably thought was menacing.

She knew. Which meant that in about 1.5 seconds Heather would know, too.

Ed made his exit as well, and the teacher picked that moment to arrive, stepping through the door but looking over her shoulder into the corridor.

"What's happened to Miss Gannis?" she asked.

"I think she lost something," one of the boys answered, biting back laughter. A giggle rippled through the room.

The shame swelled. Who was the monster now?

"Turn to page thirty-four," the teacher said.

In the wake of the X-rated DVD they'd just seen, the teacher's lecture on inflation and upward trends incited a few scattered chuckles and snorts. But Gaia was barely aware of them.

Numbly she wondered what Ed would say. He might be furious with her. After all, he and Heather had a history. Or maybe he'd just say, "I told you so," which, of course, would be even worse.

She told herself the only thing that mattered to her

was that she'd passed the first test, and that Sam was one step closer to safety.

She hoped.

HIGH SCHOOL DRAMA

Gaia hung back after the bell, until the classroom had emptied. Then she snatched the DVD and stuffed it into her beat-up messenger bag. She'd destroy it later. Crush it, or burn it, or something equally absolute. The last thing she needed was for it to wind up playing 24/7 on the Internet—the scene of her nightmares playing out for the global community's entertainment.

Ed was waiting for her in the hall.

So were Heather and a sea of salivating spectators.

Gaia took one look into Heather's very wet, very red, very livid eyes and considered walking right past her, rather than enduring the obligatory scene of high school drama that everyone was expecting. But Gaia stayed rooted in place. She'd done what she was about to be accused of. Some remote part of her was eager to clothe herself in blame. Maybe even needed to.

"Where did you get it?" Heather asked, her voice surprisingly even. "Where did you get that DVD?"

"I found it," Gaia answered. True. There was the requisite murmur from the crowd at this stunning tidbit of noninformation.

Heather's perfectly lined eyes narrowed. "You're not even going to deny it was you?"

"No."

Another murmur, this one louder.

"Are you going to explain?" Heather took a step closer. Megan and the other sidekicks exchanged a look that said things were about to get interesting.

"I didn't know what was on the DVD," Gaia said with a shrug. Also true.

Heather let out a noise that was somewhere between a shriek and asphyxiation. "Tell me where you got it," she said. She was right in Gaia's face. The tangy sweetness of her perfume made Gaia's nose itch. The girl was brave. But then, she did have the entire school behind her. And she didn't know what Gaia was capable of. Not that Gaia had any intention of letting Heather find out—let alone the ever-growing crowd.

"I already told you," Gaia said.

And then Heather pushed her. It was the kind of push

that normally wouldn't have affected Gaia in the slightest—
had she been expecting it. But Heather had caught her off
guard, and Gaia stumbled backward until her shoulders
pressed into the wall.

The crowd let out a little "ooh." Gaia righted herself,
standing up straight for the first time in recent memory.

Heather took the slightest step back, betrayed herself
with the smallest flinch. Gaia was sure she was the only one
who saw it.

"What kind of psychotic freak are you?" Heather said
loudly, shoving Gaia again.

This time Gaia didn't budge. "The kind of psychotic
freak you don't want to push again," she said under her
breath.

There were a few things Heather could do at this point,
and Gaia watched her face with interest as Heather ran
through the possibilities in a fraction of a second. Where
would the roulette ball land?

Would Heather:

A) call Gaia's bluff and push her again?

B) lose her shit and run?

Or

C) back off with some catty remark, thereby making
herself look like the bigger person and the victor?

"You're not worth it," Heather said.

So it was going to be C.

Good choice.

There was a disappointed muttering from the male contingent, a sigh of relief from the females. Heather backed up, fixing a wry smile on her face. "You do realize that your life at this school is beyond over," she said, then snorted a bitter laugh. "Not that it ever started."

The masses laughed and scoffed and made general noises of agreement.

Gaia said nothing. Moved not an inch.

Heather took this as cause to smile even wider, and turned to her friends. "Show's over."

And with that the crowd dispersed, punctuating Heather's threat with their own disgusted looks and comments.

Gaia didn't bother to look like she cared. She didn't care. Heather's idea of hell was social failure, but Gaia knew better. For Gaia, the ridicule of her fellow high school students was about as distressing as a hair in her spaghetti. Gaia took a deep breath. She'd let Heather have her moment. That was the best she could do in the way of an apology.

Now she could get back to what really mattered.

Sam.

Ed was the only one left. Ed and the few hallway stragglers who'd unluckily been too late to catch the action.

"You were right," Gaia said sharply before he could open his mouth. "I shouldn't have shown it without a preview."

Ed shrugged. "You didn't know. You couldn't have known."

Gaia's shoulders slumped. "Heather . . ."

"Good call not pummeling her, by the way," Ed said matter-of-factly.

"Yeah, well, she had enough for one morning."

Ed reached up, took Gaia's hand, and squeezed it. Gaia pulled away instantly, but Ed didn't even blink. "I wouldn't feel too bad about putting Heather in a compromising position if I were you," he said. "I think that was more Sam's responsibility, anyway, if you know what I mean."

"Ed!" Gaia said tersely.

"Sorry." He raised his hands in surrender.

Gaia adjusted her bag on her shoulder. "Forget Heather. Here's what I don't get—the e-mail said that showing the DVD was a test. So what did it prove? I mean, what could humiliating Heather have possibly gained for the kidnapper? If the DVD made some kind of demand or threat, that would make sense. But this was just . . . humiliating. And cruel."

Ed nodded. "I know what you mean. It was more like a practical joke. A demonic one."

"Maybe the kidnapper just wanted to see if I'd follow directions," Gaia said, glancing over her shoulder at the rapidly emptying hallway. "Which brings me to—"

"To how the kidnapper is going to know what you do and don't do," said Ed, finishing the thought for her.

Gaia sighed. "I guess we can safely figure that I am under constant surveillance."

"Guess so."

Gaia sighed again. "Creepy."

"Very."

"So where's the next test?" Gaia said, glaring at the grate-covered hallway clock. "If I have to jump through a bunch of hoops before ten o'clock tonight, why didn't they just give them all to me at once?" She was bouncing up and down again, raring to go. She didn't like this feeling of being watched, of being manipulated, of being out of control.

Sam was out there somewhere, suffering, and there was nothing she could do about it until these assholes decided to contact her. How was she supposed to handle this?

"I could be *done* by now," she said, watching the seconds tick by.

"You know what worries me?" Ed asked, his forehead creased. "Whoever this guy is, he seems to be striking very close to home."

"What do you mean?" Gaia wrapped her arms around herself. The anticipation was making her feel like she was going to explode through her skin.

"I mean you got lucky," Ed said, maneuvering his chair around a line of people waiting for the water fountain. "You went to Sam's room with a mission, remember? It could just as easily have been you on that DVD, Gaia."

Gaia tightened her grip on herself. She hadn't thought of that.

"Who knows? Maybe it was *supposed* to be you." Ed lowered his voice as a group of teachers passed. "And that would mean that whoever planted the camera in Sam's room has a serious inside line on you. I mean, even beyond constant surveillance. It's almost like he can read your mind. This can't be just about Sam."

Gaia checked the clock again. "It's not like I know anything about Sam." *Except that I love him . . . and I hate him,* she added silently as the contents of the DVD burned in her mind.

"But if the kidnapper wanted money or attention or something, why would they contact you?" Ed asked. "Wouldn't they send a ransom note to his parents or something? This whole thing is pretty random."

Gaia stopped walking and stared at a crack in the cinder block wall just above Ed's head. "So you think it's about me." Not a question.

"You're the one with all the secrets, Gaia," Ed said, lifting his chin in an obvious attempt to arrest her line of vision. "Whatever they are."

Gaia scanned the hallway again. No one suspicious. Nothing out of place. "Aren't you glad I won't let you ask questions? You're safer not knowing."

"Somehow I don't feel all that safe." Ed started moving again, narrowly missing the open-toed sandal of an oblivious freshman.

"God! Where are they?" Gaia blurted, covering her watch with her hand as if she could make time stop. "What if they sent another e-mail?" She started bouncing again, as if she were a boxer psyching herself up for a fight. "I can't just stand around like this, I have to find him."

They continued down the hall in silence, Gaia staring every passerby in the eye, glancing over her shoulder every third of a second. When she reached her second-period class, which she had no intention of sitting still through, the teacher met her in the doorway.

"Ms. Moore, I just received a note asking me to send you to the main office to pick up a package," Mrs. Reingold said with a vapid smile.

Gaia's heart gave a leap of actual joy. Good. Let's get on with it.

"Receiving gifts at school, are we?" Mrs. Reingold continued. "Do we find this appropriate?"

Gaia was about to tell the teacher exactly what we could

do with our idea of appropriate when Ed pinched her leg.

"You must have left your lunch at home this morning," Ed said.

"Yeah," Gaia snapped, glancing at the withered old teacher. "My parents don't like me to go through the day without three squares."

When Mrs. Reingold closed the classroom door, Gaia spun on her heel and practically flew to the main office. Ed was right behind her.

She burst into the office, told the principal's secretary who she was, and was handed a sealed envelope. Ed was waiting for her back in the hall. For a moment she just stared at the envelope.

"Please tell me you're about to read the nominees for Best Picture," said Ed, his face a little pale.

"I wish." Gaia leaned against the water fountain. She slid her finger beneath the flap and tugged, then pulled out a sheet of paper and began to read it aloud: "'Kudos on the successful completion of Test One.'" She looked up from the paper and frowned at Ed. "Kudos? Oh, great. So the guy's not only a maniac, he's a dork."

"A dangerous dork, Gaia. Keep reading."

SAM

Wrrrzzzzzzzz.

I am Sam Moon.

They said my name. I heard them. Good, because maybe I forgot it. Sam Moon, Sam Moon, Sam Moon.

Sam Moon.

Wrrrzzzzzzzz. Clank. Wrrrzzzzzzzz.

They grabbed me. That much I know. But who? Why?

Wrrrzzzzzzzz. Clank.

If that damned noise would just . . . stop. It comes in through a window I can't see. That . . . noise. That . . . grinding, scraping, scratching, humming, rumbling.

WrrrzzzzzzzClankWrrrzzzzzz.

NearFarAlwaysLouderSofter . . .

Wrrrzzzzzzzz. God! Numbing my brain.

Not just the noise the questions my own questions. I have never wondered so hard it's making me queasy all this not knowing my blood is screaming it's pounding in my temples I can taste my own bile I keep shaking and I want to peel my skin off—

And I want to kiss Gaia.

Did I? Once? I did, I think. She was soft. Her eyes took me. Took me right in. Nothing bluer, ever. Nothing so generous, or alone and . . .

Wrrrzzzzzzzzz clank wrrzz.

Shit, what the hell happened to my face? Oh Yeah, Guy With A Fist With A Ring. And the voice. Not the Fist's voice, somebody else's.

Pokey? Smokey? Low Key? Loki.

His voice, then the fist. Damnthathurt.

Then how come they haven't killed me yet? Or have they? Maybe I'm supposed to be headingforthelight already.

Jesus, I'm losing it. I'm not dead. Okay? *I'mnotdead.* Just . . . focus. Right, that's right. Focus.

I amSam MoonI am Sam . . . Sam I am.

Remember? Yes. I remember. I am sitting on my mother's lap yesterday last week now later. Athousand-yearsago. Letters are new, words are strange. I am small—

And safeAnd she is reading to me. Something about . . . what?

Eggs? Yes. And Ham. Green Eggs and Ham. Yes! And Sam I am.

I said,

Sam / am

and we laughed and laughed and laughed.

God I want to laugh again. Now. Right now.

Wrrrzzzzzzzz clank wrrrzzzzzzzz. Laugh!

Do I remember how? Try. You can't laugh if you're dead. Be alive. Laugh.

Try. I must be laughing, because look how they're looking at me.

Uhhg. Something burns my throat then my tongue then my lips. Laughing hurts.

And I'm vomiting. I'm puking.

That happens. Diabetic. Me.

It's warm on my chin slick smearing down onto my shirt. It reeks. Bad.

Someone comes, cleans me up. Not gentle. Not like Mom did.

Mom?

Wrrrzzzzzzzzzclankwrrrzzzzzzzz.

The noise, damn it! It's messing up the story. Inahouse-withamouseinaboxwithafox.

Wrrrzzzzzzzz. Clank. Wrrzz.

Focus. Remember . . . how did it start? Where was I before I was here? What was I thinking before I couldn't think? Focus . . .

Heat. And shoulders. And a silky throat.

Heather. Me. Together. So together. Mmmmmm . . . almost good. But I'm wishing beyond it. I'm wishing for Gaia.

Wrrrzzzzzzzz clank wrrzz.

And then . . . Gaia.

Gaia. Jesus. Gaia. No, don't go . . . I'm sorry. And then . . . running. Darkness and streetlights and . . . where? Where did she go? And then the arm across my chest, the hands around my throat.

And *wrrrzzzzzzzz* I'm here again, over the noise again. Still.

Oh, God. What the hell is happening? I don't know. I can't know. Knowing is somewhere else. And it all fades into the noise.

Wrrrzzzzzzzz clank.

Gaia?

Wrrrzzzzzzzz . . .

. . . zzzzzzzz . . .

DADDY'S HOME

HIS WEIRD TALENT HAD BEEN THE CAUSE OF
HIS WIFE'S DEATH. WOULD IT NOW TAKE HIS
DAUGHTER'S LIFE AS WELL?

FATHER KNOWS BEST

Tom Moore stared at his desk, which was piled high with top secret government files, profiles of the world's most threatening terrorist groups, and all other manner of classified information. At this moment, though, the most important document on it was the unfinished letter to his daughter.

> *Dearest Gaia,*
>
> *I was closer to you Saturday night than I've been in years. Close enough to be reminded that you have my eyes, your mother's nose, and our combined determination.*
>
> *Close enough to see you nearly shot.*
>
> *Close enough to save your life.*

The pen trembled in his hand. Thank God he'd been there. His bullet had only hit the punk's shoulder, but it had been enough. For the moment, at least Gaia had gotten away. Maybe the bullet had sent a message: Back off. Stand down. Give up. Tom could only hope. And anyway, there were other dangers stalking Gaia—ones far more grave, far less predictable.

One, he knew, was a sick son of a bitch with whom, forty-some-odd years ago, Tom had shared a womb.

The thought made him physically ill. His brother. His twin brother. A deadly psychopath with a vendetta against

Tom. Loki. Tom knew the name from the research his outfit provided. But he would have known it, anyway.

When they were children, his brother had fixated on the idea of Loki, the Norse god. A Satan-like hero, consumed by darkness and evil. It was no wonder that as an adult, he would adopt this moniker, under which to pursue his hateful purpose.

Tom said the word out loud. "Loki." It literally stung his vocal cords.

But what about his own name, his undercover name? Enigma, they called him. Definition: anything that arouses curiosity or perplexes because it is unexplained, inexplicable, or secret.

He gave a humorless laugh. Yes. That I am, he thought. I am a secret to my own child.

The name was dead-on. Tom Moore was an enigma, even to himself. He had been from childhood, when his remarkable talent had begun to make itself known. Why was he able to think the way he did? Why was he capable of solving the unsolvable? Why could his brain take in seemingly random patterns of words and numbers and make sense of them? He could decode, decipher, predict, and presume with terrifying accuracy.

In high school he'd discovered, much to his amusement, that he could open any combination lock in the building. Handy for dropping little love notes into the lockers of cute girls (his buddy Steve's idea, and favorite pastime). But even now, so many years later, he still wanted to know why he could work codes and riddles so easily. Not *how*. He didn't care how, but how *come*? Why should this responsibility have fallen to him?

And it was such an awesome responsibility. He had no formal, written job description. In fact, as far as he knew, there was not a shred of printed information on him anywhere. But in his own mind he'd boiled his job description down to one sentence: Save the world.

Perhaps it was better that this ability had wound itself into the double helix of his DNA instead of his twin brother's. At least, Tom told himself, he used his skill for good. If Loki had been born with such a knack . . . Tom shuddered to think about it. Genetic predisposition was a freaky thing.

Gaia, for example. Her body chemistry was a source of even greater astonishment. It was as if the gods had said, "Let's give her brains, and beauty, and charm, and grace, and physical strength, but hold the fear. No use mucking up the gene pool with that useful emotion."

Again, why?

Tom let out a long rush of breath, expelling the question with the air in his lungs. He'd wondered too hard, too long on that one. Ironic: The only other conundrum besides himself that he couldn't solve was his own daughter.

So instead, he hid from her. And hid her, too.

Apparently not so well.

Because now Loki had her in his sights. And that filthy little street punk, whose ignorance was surpassed only by his willingness to hate, was stalking her.

Tom looked down at the unfinished letter, ran his finger over the greeting.

Dearest Gaia,

His talent had been the cause of his wife's death. Would it now take his daughter's life as well?

Not while there was breath left in his body, he vowed to himself.

He picked up his pen, hesitated, then added another line to the letter.

Daddy's home.

Then, as he did with every other note, letter, and card he'd written to Gaia over the last five years, he stuffed it into a file drawer and locked it away.

Not sending it was hard.

But sending it would make things so much harder.

SLIPPING A DISK

Kudos on the successful completion of Test One. You are now to commit an act of theft—a very specific act. George Niven has a computer disk that is of interest to us. You will find this disk and drop it off in Washington Square Park. There will be a man there to receive it. He will be disguised as a homeless man and he will have a cart. Bring the disk to him, Gaia, and do it fast. Time, after all, stops for no man. Not even for Sam . . .

"They want me to steal from George," Gaia said, tearing her eyes from the note.

"Huh?" Ed blurted, following along as Gaia hurried down the hall, second period completely forgotten.

"What do they want one of George's disks for?" Gaia wondered aloud. She'd practically forgotten Ed was there. George used to be a Green Beret with her dad, and they'd been in the CIA together. Were the kidnappers somehow connected to the government?

Oh, shit. Maybe George still had connections. Maybe he had nude photos on someone in the Pentagon. Or maybe the disk simply contained his recipe for barbecue sauce, and this was just another sham test, to get her to prove she was in this 100 percent.

But what if it wasn't barbecue sauce? It was possible. After all, she'd sensed that George had always known where her father was. He never said anything; it was just this gut feeling she had. And now that her dad was back in town . . .

Could something terrorist-related be going down in Washington Square Park? Something involving CJ and the late Marco, and all those other small-time white-supremacist swine?

And what did any of this have to do with Sam? Why hadn't they just taken her?

If only they had just taken her.

"Gaia, have you heard a word I've said?" Ed's voice suddenly broke through her stream of consciousness.

"No," she answered, unfazed.

"Well, I was just wondering if we're forgetting about school for the day, since you seem to be heading for the exit," Ed said.

Gaia stopped as the automatic door swung open with a loud buzz. "I think you should stay here," she said, glancing briefly at Ed's wide brown eyes.

"No way," Ed said determinedly. "This is no time to become Independent Girl." He pushed his way through the door and out onto the street. Fortunately, the school administration was a tad lax about keeping an eye on the handicap exits.

"Ed, I'm not *becoming* anything," Gaia said, stomping

after him. A brisk October wind caught her hair and whipped it back from her face. "I just don't want you involved."

"I'm already involved," Ed said, staring straight ahead.

"Ed—"

"Gaia."

The tone of his voice made her pause. She might as well let him come home with her. She'd derail his efforts then. Somehow. She couldn't have him out on the street with her, where he was an easy target.

"Fine," she said, unwilling to let him get the last word. "But stay out of my way." She sidestepped past him and walked a few feet ahead, making sure to keep up a fast pace.

Gaia and Ed were halfway to George and Ella's house before either one of them spoke. Actually, she would have liked his advice, but how could she ask for it?

A) That would make her look needy, and she'd rather be dead than needy.

And

B) He didn't have all the facts.

As far as Ed could assume, George's computer files were most likely limited to bank statements and hints on preparing tangy marinades. He didn't know about George's past, which might in fact turn out to be continuing on into his present.

The question: Was Gaia willing to turn over one computer disk, which might, perhaps (and that was one gigantic perhaps there), contain a bunch of classified government crap that could help some terrorist destroy the world?

Or could she just let Sam die?

"So . . . does this disk or file or whatever have a name?" Ed asked finally. "Maybe it'll give you some clue about what it is."

Loyal *and* smart, that was Ed. Gaia scanned the remainder of the note and found the name.

And stopped in her tracks.

The file was called Scaredy Cat.

NO WARRANT

Ella had left a note. Obviously Gaia had overlooked it in the commotion of the morning.

She found it on the hall table when she barreled in.

> *Surprised George with a day trip to the country. We won't be home until late. Ella.*

"Finally." said Ed. "Something goes your way."

"Lucky me," Gaia responded, crumpling the note and tossing it over her shoulder as she tore through the house toward George's office. The stupid note reeked of Ella's perfume—some one-of-a-kind, New Age concoction she paid an arm and a leg for. Some freaky witchlike person in Soho produced it exclusively for her. It smelled like dead roses on fire and it made Gaia gag.

Gaia headed straight for the disk organizer on George's desk and quickly flipped through the contents. Nothing promising.

Like there was really going to be a disk marked Scaredy Cat in big red letters. Like anything could be that easy. Gaia pulled out a drawer and dumped the contents on the desk. Papers flew everywhere, and pencils, paper clips, and tacks scattered across the smooth wooden surface. A string of worry beads hit the floor and rolled noisily into the corner.

"George is gonna love that," Ed said, wheeling into the room.

"Somehow neatness isn't my number one priority at the moment," Gaia said, rooting around in the mess. Again, nothing. Gaia groaned in frustration and went for the file cabinet.

Ed hit a key on the computer keyboard, reviving the machine from sleep mode. "Listen," he said, not taking his eyes off the screen, "I've become pretty proficient on this little modern convenience lately. I mean, until Arthur Murray comes up with swing lessons for paraplegics, there aren't a whole hell of a lot of ways for me to kill time."

Gaia didn't want to laugh, but for his sake she forced a smile.

"So I'm gonna hack around for a while and see if I can figure out who sent that e-mail," Ed said as the computer whirred to life.

"That's great," Gaia said absently. Great was an overstatement, but Ed locked up in George's office was a lot safer than Ed out on the street with some psycho kidnapper running around.

Gaia quickly leafed through files with yuppie titles like "IRS Federal" and "Appliance Warranties." She slammed the drawer so hard a framed certificate fell off the wall and clattered to the floor.

"Gaia, you're scaring me," Ed said.

"This is taking too long," she said, bringing her hand to her forehead and scanning the room for possible hiding places.

How many tests had the kidnappers set up? What if she didn't have time to complete them all? That disk could be anywhere. His briefcase. His underwear drawer. A safe-deposit box at some random bank. It could be with George in the country, for all she knew.

She glanced at the captain's clock on the wall. There was no time.

Gaia slammed her fist into the file cabinet. It didn't hurt nearly enough. But it did knock down a picture of Ella.

The picture clattered facedown on the desk. Gaia studied it for a moment. Pay dirt.

The front part of the frame wasn't sitting flush against the backing. It was bulging slightly, and there was a gap between the two parts. Gaia turned it sideways, gave one good shake, and the next thing she knew, she was holding several disks, one of which was labeled Scaredy Cat. God, what a lucky break.

"I'm outta here," she said, grabbing her bag.

"Wait!"

But she couldn't wait. If she waited, she might have time to think about the fact that someone out there wanted information on her. Her. Not some secret government stash of anthrax or the plans to the Pentagon.

Her.

Gaia Moore.

And Sam might die because of it.

She wasn't waiting around to think about that.

NOT A
PERFECT
WORLD

YOU'VE GOT A NICE ASS, FOR AN ANGEL.

ONE DAYDREAM

CJ leaned against the outer wall of the arch that led into the park. He liked that arch. It was this big, beautiful thing—a knockoff of some bigger one from . . . where? France, maybe. He'd probably know if he hadn't quit going to school.

Who cared what it was called, anyway? He just liked it. He liked to look at beautiful things.

Like her.

Weird. He hated her. But man, he had some pretty crazy fantasies about her. She pulled him. All that strength and power wrapped up in all that soft sexiness. It gnawed at something in him.

Sometimes he thought about killing her.

Sometimes he just thought about her.

There was one daydream in particular he returned to over and over. In it, he'd be chasing her through the park, and she'd be totally freaked-out scared, and he'd grab her from behind—rough, but not enough to do any real damage. Maybe just a small bruise. A lasting ache.

And he'd spin her around and her hair would get all tangled up in his fingers.

Then she'd look up at him with those intense eyes, those sky-colored eyes, and she'd start begging. First just begging him not to kill her, but then it would change.

She'd be begging him to kiss her.

And damn, he'd kiss her right. And then . . . then she'd love him. And he'd have the power. All of it.

But CJ knew better. He knew to put hate in front of love every time. That was the way it was with him and his boys. Hate put you in control, but love controlled you. So he let his mind slither back to hating her.

And then, as if he'd conjured her, she was there.

Sun in her hair. And that body. Those lips . . . on his lips.

Shit! Enough of this bullshit. He had to breathe deep. Once. Twice. Steady. He had to remind himself that the one thing he wanted to do more than kiss her was kill her. He *needed* to kill her if he wanted to stay alive himself.

He adjusted the sling on his arm. The other asshole he wanted to kill was whoever the hell had shot at him Saturday night.

The bullet had punctured his biceps, and damn, it had hurt. Still hurt. One of his boys had cleaned it out and given CJ the sling. Can't go to the hospital with a gunshot wound. They report it to the cops.

But CJ was sure it had hurt even more when Tarick had twisted it that morning. That wasn't a pain CJ was going to forget anytime soon. And it was all because of the bitch.

CJ focused on Gaia.

She paused, tilting her chin in his direction, like maybe she could hear him thinking about her. His heart thunked in his chest. His hand clenched into a fist. But she didn't see him. She kept walking.

Why wasn't she in school? This chick was damned unpredictable.

He watched her walk for a moment, liking the way her hips moved, imagining kicking her hard in the stomach. In some remote recess of his mind, he knew this made him a damn sick dude. In the one remaining brain cell that could still tell good from bad, he understood his thinking was damaged.

But he'd turned on the world, and right now she was his closest target.

GUARDIAN ANGEL

Okay, now *this* was a problem. There were, on this crisp October morning, eight—count 'em eight—homeless people by the fountain in Washington Square Park. And five of them were the proud owners of shopping carts.

Why hadn't the kidnapper foreseen this possibility?

Maybe he had. Maybe he just needed a little comic relief, and watching Gaia try to find the correct one was it. Will the real undercover operative for Sam's crazed kidnapper please stand up?

Well, at least she was able to eliminate the three cartless ones right off the bat. That left only five derelicts from which to choose.

The note had said a homeless *man*, hadn't it? Yes, it had. So the two bag ladies were out of the running.

Three remaining contestants. Gaia would need a closer look.

She clutched the disk in her pocket. She should have copied it. But Ed was at the computer, and if the files really were about her, there was no way she could let him see the contents. It would have taken too long to get him out of there, get everything copied, and clear off the hard drive.

Too much time away from the task at hand. Saving Sam.

She approached the first homeless man—a guy who appeared disconcertingly young to her. Thirty-eight, thirty-nine years old at the most. In a perfect world, he'd be walking his kid to kindergarten right now, grabbing a cab to his corner office on Wall Street, making the upright decision not to sleep with his secretary.

But this was not a perfect world, this was New York. And the guy was rooting through a trash can in search of his breakfast.

"Excuse me . . ."

He kept digging.

Gaia stepped forward. She could smell him now, ripe with his own humanity.

"Excuse me."

The guy whirled. "Get the hell away from me, bitch."

Well, that was uncalled-for. So much for charity. She frowned at him. "I'm supposed to—"

"This is *my* trash can," he thundered, shaking a half-eaten apple at her. "Mine! So go 'way. Go on! Get out! Mine!" He bit the apple, then placed it inside a filthy old tennis shoe in his shopping cart (presumably to snack on later).

Yummy. Next?

Gaia made her way toward a slumped figure sitting on the ground. A crudely printed cardboard sign propped up in his lap read Iraq War Veteran.

Well, that didn't take long, Gaia mused grimly. The Iraq War began—what? Seven, eight years ago? She would have imagined it took at least a whole decade for one's life to fall apart so completely.

Gaia approached him, then bent forward and whispered, "Are you . . . looking for me?"

The guy looked up at her. "Yes," he said.

Thank God. Gaia reached into the pocket of her jacket for the disk. She drew it out, then hesitated. How could she be sure this was the guy?

"Yes" the man said again. "I am looking for you!" He reached out and grabbed Gaia's hand, wrenching the disk from her grasp with his grimy fingers.

Please tell me this is the right guy, she pleaded to herself silently. He grabbed the disk for a reason, right?

"I've been looking for you for a long time," the guy said. "You're the angel of the Lord, ain'tcha?"

And the reason was . . . he was totally insane.

Oh, shit.

"You've come to take me on to the Promised Land. I knew it the minute I saw that hair. That's the hair of an angel, all right. Only the Almighty Himself makes that color hair."

"Yeah. The Almighty and L'Oréal," Gaia snapped. She leaned down toward him. "Give me back the disk."

"No!" he shouted, clutching the disk. "You've come to save me!"

"No. I've come to save Sam."

"So call me Sam." He was full of logic. "Just bring me on to heaven. Lead me there, angel. Take me."

"Believe me, mister, if *I* brought you to heaven, we'd most likely get jumped on the way." Gaia made a grab for the disk, but the guy was quick. He stuffed it into his grubby shirt.

"Give it to me," she demanded evenly.

"No! Not until you bring me to meet my Maker."

Gaia was starting to see red. Oh, he was going to meet

his Maker, all right. He just wasn't going to like the method by which Gaia would send him.

She pressed her fingers to her temples in frustration, demanding some patience from herself. She didn't want to have to pound the guy. He was already so pathetic as it was. She glanced around the park, hoping for inspiration, and found it.

"Okay," she said at last. "I'll bring you to meet your Maker. But if I do, you have to give me back my disk. Deal?"

The man nodded.

Gaia helped him up and started walking. He followed.

"Hey. You've got a nice ass for an angel."

Gaia almost laughed in disbelief. How could she have come to this? If her situation hadn't been so totally dire, she would have allowed herself a long, cathartic laugh. "The Lord's a real stickler for fitness," she muttered.

Gaia led him straight to one of the homeless people she'd eliminated in the first round. He was taller than her Desert Storm vet, with long, flowing gray hair and mismatched sneakers. "There he is," she said, pointing.

"That guy? In the ripped-up overcoat? That's God?"

Gaia nodded, hating to lie even under these circumstances. Hadn't somebody once said there was a little bit of God in every one of us?

"He don't even have a cart!" Gaia's companion was incredulous.

"Go figure."

The man scowled at her. "Listen, angel, you better not be shittin' me."

"Angels don't shit people." That much had to be true.

"He's drinkin' whiskey."

"Yeah, well . . ." Gaia shrugged. "He's been under a lot of pressure lately."

The homeless man hesitated, then reached into his shirt and withdrew the disk. Gaia snatched it before he could change his mind. She was about to run, but he spoke, and the emotion in his voice pinned her to her place. "Thank you, angel."

Gaia swallowed hard. "No sweat."

She took off for the fountain, putting her conscience on ice.

Her real contact was seated on a bench near it. She was beyond irritated at herself for not noticing the obvious signs before. So much for maintaining her wits.

The guy was straight from central casting, with his dirt-streaked face half hidden beneath a tattered hat, the shabby clothes, the wire shopping cart filled with trash bags and empty cans. What differentiated him from the others was that, unlike "God" with his mismatched sneakers, this guy was wearing a brand-spanking-new pair of expensive lug-soled boots.

Gaia approached him, feeling hollow. This man was one of the kidnappers. This man was in some way responsible for what was happening to Sam. He or someone he knew had inflicted pain on the person she loved.

She could have killed him, but that might get Sam killed.

There was no choice. For now she would do as they said. She wouldn't ask questions.

She reached into her pocket and withdrew the disk, keeping her eyes firmly fixed on the visible lower half of the man's face. There was nothing recognizable. She memorized every detail in case she needed it later.

Cleft in the chin. Small scar on the jaw. Patchy stubble. Dark complexion.

Gaia moved closer, ready for even the slightest movement on his part. But he remained motionless, seemingly unaware of her.

She stepped up to the cart, dropped the disk into it, then turned to walk away.

"Tkduhplstkbg," the guy mumbled.

She stopped. "What?"

"Plastic bag. Take it."

Gaia squinted against the bright sunshine. On the handle of the shopping cart hung a small plastic bag from a Duane Reade drugstore. She reached for it cautiously. It was heavy.

She recognized the weight, and a surge of disgust filled her.

"No," she said.

The man lifted his eyes to her and glared. "Take it."

Gaia felt her free hand clench into a tight fist. One nice solid jab to the bridge of his nose and this guy would wake up in the next zip code.

But she couldn't. She had to think of Sam.

So she took the bag with the gun in it.

RENNY

STREET SONG
for Her

Sidewalk sweet, she stands alone
In night and streetlamp
While the world sweats summer and
sirens sing
And hate pours down from the city sky
like a wicked rain,
it wets us all
until we're soaked with anger.
and fear enough
to make friends of enemies

and choices that burn like the heat
like the blades, like the bullets
like the broken promise
that I make
Even as I watch her where she stands
two steps from evil
one step from me
But in this world
You walk with danger
or you walk
alone.

WHAT THE HELL IS THIS?

HE COULD SEE THE SLIM SILHOUETTE OF A
SWITCHBLADE IN THE PUNK'S BACK POCKET.

Gaia sat on the edge of the fountain and placed the bag between her knees. She stuck one hand in, letting her fingers brush the butt of the gun for a moment before fitting her palm around it. It felt dead and weighty.

And familiar.

Gaia hated guns. But she knew how to use them.

Her father had taught her marksmanship. While other daddies were taking their nine-year-old daughters to toy stores and ice cream parlors, Tom Moore was bringing Gaia to the firing range, or far into the woods with a rifle and a rusty tin can for a target.

And she'd been a natural. From the start, she'd rarely missed, and by the time her father had finished training her, she didn't miss at all. Even now, years away from the experience, she could still hear the report of her last shot in the forest behind their home. The deafening explosion of the shotgun, the distant screaming *ping* of the bullet hitting the can.

It blended in her memory with another explosion and another scream.

Instinctively she let go of the gun. She pressed her fingers against her eyes to make the memory go away.

Think of Sam. Think of him.

She fished around inside the bag, in case there was something else. There was.

A note.

"Of course." Gaia withdrew the note and read it.

Within the next twenty minutes, you will commit a crime. You may choose your victim, but you are to limit your territory to this park.

"My territory?" Gaia snarled.

You are not to go easy on this victim. The enclosed is to assist you in this task. You will also be required to enlist the assistance of a young man named . . .

Gaia felt the presence beside her at the exact second she read the name.

Renny.

She looked up and blinked. Renny was standing there, staring at her. This kidnapper had some major timing going on.

"Did I scare you?" he asked, taking a small step back.

"Not quite," she said.

He swallowed, gulped.

"Please tell me you're done with those skinhead assholes," Gaia said, looking Renny hard in the eyes, her mind leaping from one suspicion to the next.

"I am." Renny looked down at his sneakers. "But it's not

that easy," he murmured. "You try living on the streets with-out anybody to watch your back."

"You don't live on the streets." Gaia said.

He met her gaze, his eyes almost black. "I don't *sleep* on the streets, Gaia. But I live here."

She considered his reasoning. It was true. Renny had nowhere else to go. From the sorry state of his clothes and the random bruises he was always sporting, home seemed less than appealing. So he lived for this park, those chess tables. And in how many places would a thirteen-year-old Hispanic poet be accepted? She sighed, remembering some of the verses he'd recited to her. That edgy, soulful poetry of his made her feel as though he'd scraped the words up off the sidewalk and strung them together into something that sang.

He straightened his shirt with his still small, wiry hands. Sometimes his obvious frailty pained Gaia—especially when he was trying to act tough.

She put her thumb beneath his chin and nudged it upward, so that he was looking her in the eyes. "Who sent you here?"

He shrugged.

"Don't bullshit me, Renny. This is important. Whoever sent me this . . ." She held up the bag, noting the sincerely puzzled expression in his eyes. "You really don't know?"

He shook his head hard—a childlike gesture. It made her heart feel empty.

"Tell me what happened."

He sat down on the rim of the fountain and leaned forward to rest his elbows on his knees. "I got a phone call at home."

"What were you doing at home on a Monday morning?" Gaia asked, trying to sound stern. She could barely pull it off.

"I go home for lunch sometimes," he said, shrugging. She narrowed her eyes at him. "Hey, you're not in school either."

The boy had a point.

"Go on," Gaia said.

Renny took a deep breath. "Guy says, 'Go to the fountain in the park.' So I go."

"Did he threaten you?"

Renny gave her a lopsided grin. "Not really. 'Cept his voice sounded like he ate nails for breakfast, so I figure it's better if I do what he says."

Gaia was about to ask if the nail-eating voice had mentioned Sam, then thought better of it. The less Renny knew, the less danger he'd be in—relatively speaking, anyway. If the kidnapper knew his name, not to mention his phone number, he was already in this up to his eyeballs, based merely on the fact that he was associated with her.

"We have to pass a test," she said softly.

"A test?" He whistled low. "That doesn't sound good. That's what the guys told me just before they handed me that pistol to point in your face."

Gaia considered inquiring as to what sort of punishment Renny had faced in the wake of failing that test, but decided against it. She didn't think she could handle that at the moment.

"We have to, uh, commit a crime."

His big eyes got bigger. He said nothing.

"Something random. Something sort of rough." She held up the bag. "There's a gun in here."

"Damn."

"Yeah, damn," she said, staring across the park at a couple of fighting pigeons. "We've got to do it here. Now."

Renny mulled this over for a minute or so. "Why?"

"I don't want to tell you. Just trust me. If we don't . . ." She finished with a shrug.

"I'm in," he said.

Gaia nodded. She wasn't sure if that was good news or bad news. She had to think, to figure out the best way to go about this. Maybe there was a way to make the crime look real without actually harming anyone. She did know there was no way in hell she was going to fire that gun. She'd wield it, swing it around at whomever she ultimately chose to hassle, but she would not pull the trigger. The kidnapper would just have to settle for that.

Her eyes roamed the park, landing finally on the chess tables.

And there he was.

She recognized him immediately. The sleazebag. The well-dressed, self-important slimeball she'd played once—and only once, because he kept grabbing her thigh under the chess table. His name was Frank, she believed. He was about forty-seven, forty-eight years old but looked at least sixty with all his wrinkles. Tanning-salon regular, diamond pinky ring, woven loafers, even in October. Jerk.

Gaia despised him. He'd hustled Zolov once, taking advantage of one of the sweet old guy's less lucid moments. Gaia figured Frank had walked away with Zolov's entire Social Security check that day, then used it to pay Lianne.

Lianne. Another pathetic story. Lianne was fourteen and a prostitute. Gaia was repulsed by her, but somewhere in her heart she felt sorry for her, too. The girl must have had one horrifying life to resort to turning tricks. And Frank was her best customer. Illegal, and disgusting.

The more Gaia thought about it, the more she decided she wouldn't entirely loathe roughing up Frank.

All she could hope was that wherever the kidnapper was watching from was far away enough to make Frank look like an innocent citizen, undeserving of Gaia's attack.

Without a word, she stood and made her way toward the chess tables.

Without a word, Renny got up and followed her.

Tom wiped his glasses on the inside of his shirt, then replaced them on the bridge of his nose. He was dressed blandly, in khakis and a denim shirt. Over his reddish blond curls he wore a suede baseball cap in dusty blue. The brim was tugged low on his brow.

He was invisible, leaning there against the tree. Watching.

Watching as his daughter strode purposefully away from the fountain. There was a scrawny kid with dark hair and golden skin tagging along with her.

But what was in the bag?

He lifted the brim of his cap a fraction of an inch and squinted at the plastic bag she was clutching. His heart took a nosedive when he realized what was in it. The outline of the object bulged unmistakably against the black and purple of the pharmacy's logo.

Unmistakable to him, at least. Tom sent up a silent prayer thanking the gods for the indifference of New Yorkers. They would probably not even notice the girl, let alone the bag, let alone its contents.

She leaned down and whispered something to the kid. Pointed to the bushes. The kid nodded and they kept walking.

He kept his eyes trained on her as she crossed to the chess tables. A small, sad smile kicked up the edges of his mouth. Chess. His favorite game. And Gaia's. The first time she'd beaten him she'd been only eight.

Tom stepped away from the tree for a better view, looking utterly preoccupied with nothing in particular, but seeing, feeling, every step she took.

She was approaching a middle-aged guy in an ugly designer suit who was seated on the losing side of a chessboard.

The kid looked a little jumpy. This bothered Tom. Street kids didn't get jumpy without a good reason. And this kid looked downright nervous. Maybe even scared.

Gaia didn't look scared. Gaia never looked scared.

What she looked, lifting the bag and pressing it to the shoulder of the ugly suit, was determined. Tom moved away from the tree.

Why was she doing this? Had his leaving poisoned her so badly that she'd taken up petty crime? Or was there more to it?

Of course there was. He knew that whatever burden of the life he'd given her, for Gaia, nothing would ever be exactly as it appeared. Nothing would ever be simple. There would always be layers, dimensions, motives, and questions. And horrible choices.

But why was she choosing this? What had brought her here? Had her confusion and loneliness made her an easy mark for a gang? Had his absence led her to join one? Had she, in search of something resembling a "family," been sucked into their evil world?

No. Not Gaia. The girl was smart and, he knew, good. Good at her core, good in her very essence.

This was something bigger. More dangerous. Something enormous must have been at stake. And clearly her sense of urgency was overshadowing her good judgment.

This was not robbery for robbery's sake.

But it was still robbery.

Tom had to stop her, but how? Could he create some kind of distraction—knock over a homeless guy's cart, perhaps? Draw her attention away from what she was about to do, long enough to bring her back to her senses?

He took two long strides in her direction, then stopped cold.

The punk. The punk he'd shot at the other night. His arm was in a sling, and he was running toward Gaia.

Tom shuddered. He could see the slim silhouette of a switchblade in the punk's back pocket.

He meant business.

Tom should have rid the world of this menace Saturday night, when he'd had the chance. But Tom had let his emotions affect his accuracy. He'd missed his opportunity.

And now his hands were tied. This was a crowded park, in broad daylight. So for the moment, much to Tom's revulsion, CJ would have to be allowed to live.

Tom wondered what Gaia had done to piss CJ off. Maybe the kid had come on to Gaia once, and she'd blown him off. With a creep like CJ, a broken heart could easily become a fatal attraction.

There were only two things Tom knew for sure. One was that for the second time in less than forty-eight hours, he was going to have to put himself between Gaia and death. The other was that he was willing to do it.

YOUR MONEY OR YOUR LIFE

Frank looked up from his near-defeat on the chessboard and raised one bushy eyebrow at Gaia. "What the hell is this?"

Gaia, her hand on the gun inside the bag, pushed the barrel harder into his shoulder. "*This* is a gun." she told him in a matter of fact voice. "Let's go somewhere a little more private."

"Oh, for Christ's sake."

Renny took off for the bushes that lined the east side of

the park. "Follow the kid," Gaia said. Frank just stared at her, wide-eyed.

"Let's go," said Gaia, cocking the hammer.

"Jeez! Hey. Jeez!" Frank wriggled up from his seat and slowly followed Renny. His opponent, for obvious reasons, got up and fled. Two people at a table nearby scooted farther away. Gaia didn't have much time.

She shoved Frank in the back so he would hurry up, and he ducked behind the bushes. Gaia could only hope that the all-knowing kidnapper could see them back here and wouldn't miss her command performance.

Renny went to the edge of the bushes to keep watch, and Gaia grabbed Frank by the back of his collar, jerking him around to face her. He swore, swatting at her like a cartoon boxer, managing to clip her on the chin. She released him, used the hand that wasn't holding the gun to slap his face, then grabbed a handful of his greasy hair and pulled him to her.

"Didn't your mother ever teach you not to hit girls?" she asked, her nose practically touching his. He smelled like bourbon and chewing tobacco. Gaia had to struggle to keep from hurling.

Renny turned from his post. "Give us your wallet," he demanded in a forceful voice that sounded like it came from someone much bigger and older.

"You're supposed to be keeping watch," Gaia spat out. Renny turned around again.

"Give us your wallet," Gaia echoed.

"Yeah. Yeah, sure." Frank shoved a trembling hand into his breast pocket, withdrew a fat billfold, and slowly offered it to Gaia. For a moment it just sort of hung there between them, off the tips of his fingers.

It was almost too easy. Gaia had a feeling the kidnapper had been hoping for a bit more drama. The asshole had thought this out well. Do this too quickly and easily, and the kidnapper probably wouldn't be satisfied.

Take too long and she'd end up stuck in jail.

And Sam would die.

Gaia swallowed hard and narrowed her eyes at Frank. "Look petrified," she ordered. "Cry."

Sweat poured from his temples down his cheeks. "What, are you kiddin' me?"

"Does it look like I'm kidding?"

He gave a nervous laugh. "No, sweetheart. It don't."

His use of the word *sweetheart* nearly caused her to slap him again. "Cry," she repeated dryly, casually lifting her knee into his groin.

"Uhhnnfff!" Frank doubled over. "You little . . ."

"I don't see any tears." Gaia hissed, taking hold of his fleshy neck and applying a firm grip to the pressure point.

"Ahhh . . ." Frank's face contorted in pain, then he let out a satisfactory sob.

Gaia didn't let go. "No more sharking Zolov or anybody else," she commanded fiercely from above.

"Yeah," moaned Frank. "Yeah. Okay."

"Gaia?" Renny said tentatively. "I think we have to go."

She let go of Frank's neck and took a small step backward. He straightened up cautiously and handed over his wallet.

"This never happened," she hissed.

To her surprise, Frank gave her a cold smile. "Aye, yo. You think I'm gonna tell anybody I got held up by two little shits like youse? A freakin' Rican who ain't got hair on his chest, and his partner, the prom queen?"

At that Gaia shoved the bagged pistol right under his chin. "You *ever* insult me like that again, and I'll kill you!"

Then she grabbed Renny and ran.

Prom queen, my ass.

MEANWHILE, BACK AT THE ARCH . . .

CJ was heading toward her like a tiger running down a wounded gazelle.

Gaia had no idea, focused as she was on committing her felony. The guy in the ugly suit was doubled over.

But Tom's eyes were trained on the tiger. The tiger had his hand on the knife.

Tom sprang into action. He hurdled a park bench, dodged someone on skates, and connected with the tiger in a hit that would have done Lawrence Taylor more than proud.

CJ hit the pavement.

Tom kept running.

And Gaia was gone.

TWO BLOCKS LATER . . .

The cop skidded up to the curb and got out of the car as though he were auditioning for a walk-on in *NYPD Blue*.

"Hey! You two."

Damn.

Gaia could feel the change in Renny as he walked alongside her. He tensed and his body temperature climbed at a rate that was actually detectable.

Fear, she thought. So those are the symptoms, huh? Her own body was cool, heartbeat slow and steady. Even when faced with losing Sam, the guy who made the future seem worth living, still she didn't feel fear. She felt anger, determination, frustration. But no fear. If she couldn't feel fear for Sam, couldn't feel the heartrending, temperature-raising emotion that every other human being felt, could she really love him?

She was drifting. She had to focus. She had to make use of the capabilities she had, not mourn the one that was missing.

"Don't panic," she whispered to Renny. "They can smell it." Or so she'd heard.

"Young lady . . ."

Gaia turned and graced the cop with an innocent smile. "Were you talking to me, Officer?"

"Yes."

He was really young. It could have been his first day on the job. He had one of those square chins that was pretty much a prerequisite for joining the police force.

"Is something wrong?" Gaia asked. She made no attempt to hide the plastic bag. Both the gun and Frank's wallet were still in it.

"I've just come from the park."

She looked suitably blank, patient. Renny, however, was bouncing, shifting his weight, preparing to split. She wished he'd just stand still.

"There was a mugging," the cop continued.

Gaia gasped. Nice touch. "Oh my God."

"Nothing too serious. Guy's wallet was stolen. Couple of eyewitnesses said it was two kids. Boy and a girl." He cleared his throat, an unspoken apology.

He hated this. Gaia could tell. A serious young law enforcement officer like him should have better things to do than hassle a couple of kids. Gaia could actually see him thinking this. She wasn't sure whether to be thankful for or repulsed by his obvious attraction to her. It might just get them out of this.

"Well, we didn't see anything," she said with a dainty shrug. "We weren't even in the park."

The cop nodded. "Why aren't you two in school?" he asked, as if it had just occurred to him.

"We're home-schooled." Gaia fired this out so quickly that even she believed it. "My mom teaches us." She put an arm around Renny's shoulder, pressing down ever so slightly, to get him to quit fidgeting. "This is my stepbrother."

Another nod from Glamour Cop. He hesitated, as if he might ask for their names, but didn't. He turned to get back in the car, then turned back.

"By the way, what's in the bag?"

"The bag! What's in the bag?" Gaia knew she sounded like an idiot, but the question had caught her off guard. She'd thought they were home free.

"What's in the bag?"

Nothing. Just a gun and a stolen wallet.

Then she heard Renny say, "Tampons."

It was all Gaia could do to keep from laughing out loud.

"Tampons," Renny repeated, snatching the bag from Gaia. He held it out to the cop, but his eyes were on Gaia. "I hope I got the right kind," he said in the most disarmingly innocent tone Gaia had ever heard from him—maybe from anyone. "Superabsorbent, you said, right? The deodorant kind?"

He turned his doe eyes back to the cop. "She gets embarrassed, see, so I go into the pharmacy and get 'em for her." He gave the bag a little shake. "Wanna check?"

The cop, looking embarrassed himself, shook his head. "No," he said with a slight croak. "Not necessary."

He ducked back into his car and drove off.

Gaia was gaping at Renny in disbelief. "Where'd you learn to lie like that?"

"I dunno." He threw her a crooked grin. "Home school, maybe?"

Gaia wanted to hug him, but of course she didn't. Instead she pressed her index finger forcefully into his chest. "Lying. Bad. Stealing. Worse. I only did this because somebody's life is in danger, and I had no other choice."

Renny opened his mouth, probably to ask whose life, but Gaia barreled right along.

"From now on, I want you to stay the hell away from

that stupid gang. You don't need them to watch your back."
She paused, hoping she could pull off the next sentence without sounding like a total Hallmark card. "You've got me, all right? I'll . . . watch your back."

She didn't wait around to see the expression on his face.

GAIA

Media people who have a problem with rap music, contro-versial movies, or premarital sex like to throw around the term "family values."

I don't mind saying I don't even know what the hell they're talking about.

I mean, okay. I'm not an idiot. I *know* what they're talking about—two parents, with college degrees, kids in clean sneakers, mass or service or temple (whichever is applicable) every weekend, meat loaf on Monday night, freshly cut grass, and a minivan. Yeah, I know what they mean.

I just don't know it from firsthand, personal experience. Anymore.

Consider my family, for example. My current one, that is. Absentee (big time) father, well-meaning concerned guardian, bitchy wife of guardian, chess geeks whose last names I don't even know. That, at present, is as close as I come to having a family.

Can you imagine this crowd sitting down to meat loaf and mashed potatoes some evening?

And what about Renny? He's been so brain-poisoned he actually thought he could purchase himself a family (of violent, hate-obsessed misfits) with a bullet to my face. What makes me ill is wondering how majorly screwed up the kid's real family must be in order for violent misfits to constitute an upgrade.

But the only family I can seem to think about right now is Sam's.

They've got to be somewhere in the realm of decent, don't they? Or else how could they have produced such a perfect human being as Sam?

All right, so he's not *perfect*—there's that 108-pound wart on his ass (you know her as Heather), and the guy's a master of the mixed signal. But if he's not Mr. Perfect, he's certainly Mr. Pretty Damn Close.

The thing that's turning me inside out now is the fact that, for all I know, his parents are sending him a package of homemade peanut butter cookies baked by his little sister (for some reason, I imagine he has one), with a note

saying that Uncle Mort says hi and they'll see him on parents' weekend. Maybe they are at this very second dialing
his number, calling him up just to say hi, and since he's not
answering, they'll simply assume he's at the library, studying for some huge exam.

Maybe they're eating meat loaf and mashed potatoes,
and complaining that he only calls home when he needs
money.

But the point is, their son's life is in danger and they
have absolutely no idea.

That's killing me.

I mean, okay, *my* life is in danger and *my* father has
absolutely no idea. But somehow that doesn't bother me
as much as Sam's family not knowing.

I guess maybe because I'm figuring if they knew,
they'd actually care.

Whereas if my father knew, he'd have to stop and
think to remember who I was before he could go back
to whatever it is that he's been doing all these years and
continue to not give a shit.

SHE'S NO ANGEL

IT WASN'T THAT SHE DIDN'T WANT TO PRAY FOR
SAM. SHE JUST WASN'T SURE HOW.

It didn't make sense.

Ella had dragged him all the way up to Greenwich, cooing and purring about some private time together, enjoying the romance of the countryside on an autumn morning. So what did she do the moment they arrived?

She dropped herself into a chair at the most Manhattan-like cafe she could find and ordered a double martini. At ten forty-five in the morning.

George ordered coffee for himself, then reached across the table and took her hand.

"This was a great idea," he said. "You and me, the country . . ."

Ella nodded, glancing around the cafe, waiting for her martini.

"So what's on the agenda? Picnic on the Sound? A little sailing, perhaps?"

Ella sighed. "Oh, I don't know. Shopping, maybe."

"Shopping?" George raised an eyebrow. "Honey, you can shop anytime in New York. I thought the idea was to come up here and do something that involved grass and trees and quiet country lanes." He'd known when he married her that she wasn't exactly an outdoorswoman, but surely even the most pampered Manhattanite would be enchanted by the old-time New England charm of this town.

Ella wrinkled her nose. "Country lanes, George? Really."

"Sure. Me and you, the breeze, the sunshine. Some cozy little grotto somewhere . . ."

She looked as if she was considering it. "Well . . ." She sighed, lifting her dazzling eyes to his.

A wave of pure attraction washed over him. The truth of it was that he didn't really much care what they did, as long as they were together. He would try to talk her into doing something slightly more romantic than signing credit card receipts, but he wouldn't push. Whatever she wanted was, in all sincerity, fine with him.

So he was smitten with his own wife. So sue him.

The beverages came, and George let go of Ella's hand to allow the waiter to deliver her martini. When he reached for it again, she made a quick grab for the drink.

George sat back in his chair, telling himself she was just thirsty.

"What time is it?" she asked.

He checked his watch. "Close to eleven. Why?"

Ella lifted one shoulder in a shrug. "We'll take the two-thirty train back to Grand Central."

"Back?" George tore open a sugar packet and poured it into his coffee. "We just got here. Listen, there's supposed to be a beautiful little horse farm just a few towns away. I read about it in the travel section of the *Times*." He gave his wife what he hoped was an irresistible grin. "How about we shop this morning, then we can spend the afternoon cantering through some of those sprawling open fields we passed on the way into town?"

"Those weren't open fields. Those were people's yards."

He laughed. She didn't.

"C'mon. What do you say to a little horseback riding?"

She sighed again, causing her ample chest to swell against the satin of her blouse. "I'm not exactly dressed for riding," she said, then gently, seductively caught her lower lip between her teeth. "But if you really want to . . ."

She had him. And they both knew it.

"Shopping it is." George lifted the cup to his lips, tamping down the prickle of disappointment. A moment or two passed before he spoke again. "Have you noticed that Gaia's been acting a little distracted lately?"

"Distracted?" repeated Ella, as if she herself hadn't been paying attention. She looked over her husband's shoulder and out the window.

"I'm worried about her."

"Don't be." Ella traced the rim of her martini glass with one slender finger. "She's a teenager. They're a species unto themselves. What looks peculiar to us is perfectly normal for them."

"Normal, huh? Saturday night she came home sweating, panting, all out of breath—"

"Oh?" Ella pursed her lips in disdain. "Were you waiting up, George?"

"No. Well, not exactly, I just happened to be awake."

Ella laughed. "And did you go to her? Ask her if all was well? Tuck her in?"

George shook his head. "Maybe I should have."

"She's seventeen!" Ella exclaimed in a patronizing tone. "And as far as the sweating and panting goes, well, that's exactly the kind of reaction a teenage girl would experience after spending hours teasing some poor boy in the backseat of his car!"

"C'mon, Ella," said George, his face flushing at her inference. "I don't think Gaia—"

"Oh, please! She's no angel, George, as much as you'd like to believe she is." Was it his imagination, or was there bitterness behind her voice?

"She's been through a lot," George said, eyeing his wife warily.

Ella rolled her eyes. "So you've said—often."

"I still think I should have talked to her the other night," George said, turning his profile to her and staring out the window. "She's lost so much." George had no idea what it was like to be a teenage girl. He could barely recall what it was like to be a teenage boy. But he knew what it was like to have someone he loved snatched away. He remembered that vividly.

"We're all she has," George said, finally turning back to Ella. "Maybe she's lonely—"

"Fine, George," said Ella, sighing. "Gaia's lonely. Not horny—just lonely. The point is, she probably would have told you to mind your own business, anyway." She paused, then said pointedly, "She's not our child."

At this George felt a familiar jolt—a longing. *Our child.* His, theirs, hers. His eyes searched Ella's questioningly.

"Oh, no." She held up her hand like a traffic cop and laughed again. "Don't even go there, George Niven. We've discussed it." Her other hand went to her firm, flat tummy. "This figure is not to be tampered with." She cleared her throat, then added, "Yet."

It was the most unconvincing "yet" he'd ever heard in his life. The waiter returned with more coffee for him and a fresh martini for Ella. Three olives this time, instead of two. Clearly he hadn't heard her remark about flat-tummy maintenance. Or maybe he just liked her.

They sipped their drinks without further conversation until the silence was interrupted by the bleating of her cell phone.

She touched the screen. "Yes?"

George watched her near-expressionless face as she listened. After almost two full minutes, she said, "Fine." Then she hung up.

"Who was that?"

"No one important," she said, plucking a plump olive from the toothpick in her glass.

George smiled teasingly. "No one important who?"

She looked at him. "If you must know, it was Toshi. My feng shui appointment has been canceled for tonight."

"Oh." George lowered his gaze to the table.

Toshi, huh? He wanted to believe her, but at the same time he had a very strong hunch that the call had had nothing to do with feng shui.

If Ella had any hunches regarding his hunch, she didn't show it.

She went right on drinking her martini.

And, he imagined, waiting impatiently for two-thirty.

ANOTHER WEST SIDE STORY

Gaia stuffed Frank's tacky eel-skin wallet into the pocket of her faded sweatshirt jacket and shoved the gun into the bottom of the messenger bag. She took a deep breath and let it out slowly.

So she'd just conducted her first mugging.

It was not a good feeling. Gaia kicked at a crumpled-up McDonald's bag as she walked along the cracked sidewalk. She didn't like playing the part of a lowlife, even if the joke was on Frank.

But it was all about saving Sam. Gaia booted the bag into the sewer. The end justifying the means, and all that. Very Machiavellian.

So where was the next test? Once again she was left with downtime while Sam was sitting alone somewhere, suffering. Gaia felt her heart squeeze painfully as she remembered Sam's swollen face. She pressed her eyes closed, as if she could block out the image. Could she find fear—even a tiny shred of it—if she kept that image in her mind's eye?

This was torture. Maybe that was the point.

Trying to distract herself, she pulled out Frank's wallet again and flipped it open. There was a stack of bills inside, and Gaia pulled them out, counting quickly so that no street thugs would spot her and get any ideas. Three hundred and fifty bucks. Not bad. What the hell was she going to do with it?

When she looked up, Gaia noticed she had stopped right in front of St. Joseph's Church. That couldn't be a coincidence. She stuffed the money and wallet back into her pocket and ducked inside the church.

The place was perfectly quiet. There was no one in sight, and the sunlight streaming through the stained-glass windows revealed dancing particles of dust. Gaia found herself thinking how weird it was that all churches always smelled the same. Not that she'd been to very many—just enough to know they all had that same damp, smoky smell.

As Gaia wandered down the carpeted center aisle, she wondered how many times "Amen" and "Please, God" had been whispered in there. She got the feeling that if she listened carefully enough, she might hear the echoes.

It occurred to Gaia that if the kidnappers were still watching her closely, a deserted church would be the perfect place for them to attack. Gaia wished they would. It would be nice to get this over with. Kick some ass, find out where Sam was, get him, and then go the hell home. She was tired of this already.

There was an alcove toward the front of the church with a brass stand in it. On the stand were rows upon rows of stubby white candles in little glass holders, some red, some blue. Gaia smirked. Religious *and* patriotic.

Gaia knew what the candles were for. One night when she'd first moved in with George and Ella, she'd stayed up late, unable to sleep, and watched a rerun of *West Side Story* on TV. Natalie Wood, as Maria, had a little setup like this one with the candles and everything, right in her apartment. She was lighting candles and saying prayers.

Gaia went to the alcove and found what she was looking for—a worn wooden box with "Donations" painted painstakingly across the front. Gaia was pretty sure she was supposed to make a contribution before lighting a prayer candle. Someone had to pay for all that wax. Fine with her. She stuffed Frank's money into the box. She figured that $350 bought her the right to start a bonfire. But she wasn't exactly good with prayers. She wasn't even entirely sure of what religion she was supposed to practice. Her family was one big melting pot.

Next to the candles there were a bunch of skinny sticks, like extralong toothpicks, sticking out of a little pot of sand. The ends on some of them were charred.

Okay, I get it, she thought. You use a lit candle to light the stick, then use the stick to light your own candle.

She picked up one of the long, fragile sticks. Should she or shouldn't she?

Part of her felt like a serious hypocrite. But a bigger part of her felt she needed help from wherever she could get it.

She breathed in the church smell and thought about Sam. He didn't deserve this. No one deserved this. It was all her fault.

Then she poked the stick into the flame of one of the burning candles. What prayer went with that one? she wondered. Had it been bigger than hers? Had it been answered?

She held the stick over an unlit candle and for a moment just watched the flame dance. Then, in spite of her $350 donation, she slammed the burning end of the stick into the sand and got out of there.

It wasn't that she didn't want to pray for Sam. She just wasn't sure how.

A NEW DVD RELEASE

Gaia ran all the way home, hoping at every turn that she'd be stopped by another crazed fake homeless man with a note. No such luck.

She was ready to scream with frustration when she rounded the corner onto Perry Street and caught a glimpse of George and Ella's front stoop. There was a package. Time for a sprint. It seemed like forever before the box was in her hands, but the card had her name on it. And since she didn't belong to the Jam of the Month club or anything, she was pretty sure it was from her friendly neighborhood kidnapper.

She let herself inside (still no Ella, thank God) and took the stairs to her room in threes. After slamming her bedroom door and locking it behind her, Gaia pulled the Duane Reade bag out of her messenger bag and shoved it, gun and all, under her bed.

Then she tossed her messenger bag on her mattress, sat down at her desk, and opened the box. Wonderful. There was another DVD inside. And, of course, another note. This was getting old.

"Wonder what this movie's rated," Gaia muttered.

Gaia gathered up her stuff again and jogged back downstairs to the living room. She shoved the DVD into the DVD player and hit play.

Gaia's eyes narrowed as an image of her own face—so close up she could have counted the pores—flickered onto the screen. The camera panned back to reveal her and Renny sitting by the fountain. She felt the blood start to rush through her veins, bringing an angry flush to her face.

Whoever had filmed this had been so close. How could she have missed him? How stupid was she?

Lowering herself onto the plush couch, Gaia watched as she and Renny crossed the park. It was like some kind of morbid home movie.

Isn't Gaia adorable, sticking that pistol into Frankie's shoulder, stealing his wallet, kneeing him in the groin?

She hit the off button, pulled the DVD out of the slot, and proceeded to break the disk in half. After that, she did the same to the DVD of Sam and Heather, which was still in her messenger bag. Then she unfolded the note that had come with the new DVD, and read it.

Then she read it again.

Suddenly Gaia really wished she'd lit that candle.

You are doing surprisingly well. Your next test may not be so easy. Your friend in the wheelchair is to be your next victim. No violence is necessary. What we want is for you to HUMILIATE him. In public.

This humiliation, Gaia, is to be thorough. Uncompromised.

You will emotionally destroy this young man.

And if you are wondering why . . . don't. You need no reason other than that I require you to do it.

IF YOU FAIL, SAM MOON WILL DIE.

GAIA

TOP TEN WAYS TO EMBARRASS A KID IN A WHEELCHAIR

10. Buy him a pogo stick.

9. Ask him how often he has to have his tires rotated.

8. Tell him you'd like to borrow his chair to guarantee yourself a good seat for *Cats*.

7. Attach a bumper sticker that reads WARNING: I BREAK FOR ORTHOPEDIC SURGEONS.

6. Totally fawn over him, and tell him how sorry you feel for him.

5. Totally ignore him and pretend he doesn't exist, like everybody else does.

4. One good shove down the handicap ramp.

3. Invite him to visit the top of the Statue of Liberty.

2. Ask him, "You must really feel like a loser during the national anthem, huh?"

1. Say something—anything—of a sexual nature, implying that it's not just his legs that are permanently limp.

I can't believe I am even capable of coming up with these. It makes me sick. I make me sick. How am I going to do this?

Why are they making me do this?

LIKE LOX?

AND THEN THE WORLD WENT SURREAL ON HIM.

BECAUSE GAIA WAS NOT GAIA.

SEDUCTION 101

Ed rolled his chair out of his eighth-period class and into the crowded hallway. He'd made it back to school in time for the chem exam, which, unfortunately, had been even more difficult than he'd expected. With all of the insanity running through his head, he'd be lucky to pull a C plus. Of course, in light of what was happening to Gaia and Heather, not to mention Sam, a C plus didn't sound too terrible.

The good news was that the morning's searching had yielded major information.

It was the noise. A noise he knew. Or used to know.

He'd sat there in George's study for over an hour, viewing the video e-mail of Sam over and over. Just as he was about to pack it in Ed had noticed a noise in the background. It had been there all along. He couldn't imagine how he'd missed it, unless his eyesight was shutting down from all the staring and his ears were taking over. But as soon as he detected it, he recognized it.

Wrrrzzzzzzzz. Clank. Wrrzz.

It was a noise he himself had made for years. A noise he'd never make again.

And he knew there was only one place in New York City where that noise could occur precisely the way it sounded in the background of the e-mail.

Wrrzzzzzzzz. Clank. Wrrrzzzzzzzz.

"Ed, man! Totally nice ride. You got serious air on that one, dude. Is this the most bodacious ramp in the city or what? Let's see it again. Go for it!"

Wrrzzz. Clank.

Yeah, Ed knew the noise.

He pushed aside the memory and gritted his teeth at the way the crowd in the hallway parted for him.

At least it meant getting to a private place to use his phone faster, although the chances of Gaia being home were slim to none. If the girl was going to insist on being the reluctant superhero, the least she could do was invest in a cell phone.

Ed rounded a corner, and there she was. Right in the middle of the jostling, locker-slamming crowd. No dialing necessary.

His smile was automatic. (Not to mention the reaction from a more southern portion of his anatomy.) He waved, relishing the way he could see her eyes burning like blue flames, even from this distance.

"Good news," he began, but the rest of his greeting caught in his windpipe. She was striding—no, more like stomping—in his direction. Panic engulfed him. What had happened? Had Sam been hurt? Worse thought. Had she?

She stopped about a foot in front of him.

And then the world went surreal on him. Because Gaia

was not Gaia. Everything about her said hatred—the rigidity of her shoulders, the tightness of her face.

"Hey," she barked. Yes, barked. It was a horrible sound, one he couldn't reconcile with the sexy, slightly raspy voice he loved hearing over the phone every night. He stared at her, peripherally aware that people were slowing down, glancing their way. They were curious, but not committed just yet. School was over, after all. There were soccer balls to dribble, lattes to drink, boyfriends to kiss.

"Hey . . . freak."

Okay, now she had their attention. Ed opened his mouth to say something but hadn't the slightest idea what that something should be. His eyes slid over her carefully. Was she bruised? No. Drugged? Didn't seem to be. Brainwashed? Not likely.

What was going on?

She said it again. "Hey, freak."

Ed wished he could make himself meet her gaze. "Something I can do for you?"

A strangled sound came out of her mouth. It took him a second to understand it was supposed to be laughter.

"I doubt it," she said. "In fact . . ."

He noted that her fists were clenching and unclenching.

"In fact, I doubt there's anything you can do for any girl in this school."

This earned her an "ooh" from the onlookers, and she

let her eyes fall purposely to his midsection. Ed felt scalded by the heat of them. His heart hit the badly scuffed floor. She couldn't possibly have just said that.

"So am I right, Ed?" she prodded. "I mean, we all know you're paralyzed from the waist down, but I'm curious. Does *anything* still work?"

Horror filled him as she came closer. She placed one hand on each of his chair's armrests and smiled wickedly. "Aren't you going to tell me?" she asked in a seductive tone he might have liked under different circumstances. "Or am I going to have to find out for myself?"

This piece of cruelty was rewarded with another "ooh."

Ed's brain vaguely registered that not one single son of a bitch in the crowd was making an attempt to defend him. But he didn't actually care about them. He cared about her. Too much.

And she was destroying him. Why?

His voice decided to work without his permission, and he heard himself say, a bit pathetically, "You're enjoying this, aren't you?"

"Yes," she assured him, still smiling. "I like torturing you. About as much as I like lox."

Lox.

"Like lox."

"Hate it."

His heart surged. This wasn't real. She was faking. He

pulled his eyes to hers at last. And she answered him. It wasn't a word, or an action, or even an expression. It was something deeply unnameable in her eyes.

This was her next test. For some inexplicable purpose, the kidnapper wanted her to hurt him. So be it. He'd play along.

Unfortunately, one of the male spectators chose that moment to get righteous. He stepped forward and said, "Leave him alone."

Ed wouldn't have believed it, but in that second he could actually *see* her resolve falter. One word from a pseudo-Samaritan and she was ready to crumble—her belief in this heinous charade was that fragile.

He felt her begin to back away, and he knew he couldn't let her. Too much was riding on it. Sam's life. More important, possibly her safety.

So Ed lifted his chin. "You wanna know if it still works?"

She blinked, clearly taken aback by this reaction. He kept his eyes glued to hers. *Don't quit, Gaia. I understand. Don't back down.*

One corner of her mouth twitched.

"Yeah," she said, her reluctance audible only to him. "I wanna know if you're still man enough to do it."

"Well, that depends." Ed reached forward, catching her around the waist and pulling her onto his lap. "Are you woman enough to make me want it?"

The crowd's "oohs" rose to a crescendo now, and the applause that erupted froze her.

"Cmon, Gaia," he urged, knowing she had to bring this full circle to satisfy the kidnappers. "Make me."

"Fine, I will."

"Fine. So do it."

"Fine."

She leaned toward him—somehow the movement was at once gentle and violent—until her mouth was dangerously close to his.

"Principal!"

Suddenly the crowd scattered like rats, leaving Ed unkissed and alone in the hall with Gaia, who was sitting sidesaddle across his thighs. Now that they were alone, she made a move to exit his lap, but didn't get far.

"I think maybe you should get off me now," Ed suggested calmly.

"I'm trying!" Gaia snapped in reply. The zipper on the outer pocket of her cargo pants was caught on his sweater, and she was struggling to disengage herself. "I promise you this is not what I want to be doing right now."

He chuckled. "Yeah, you just keep telling yourself that, Gaia."

Ed could hear the principal's footsteps approaching the corner of the deserted hallway. Gaia let out a little yelp of frustration.

"Scared?" he baited.

"Annoyed," she said. She let go of the zipper and met his eyes for a second. "And very sorry," she added under her breath. "Not scared."

She tried jerking her leg sideways, and wound up straddling him.

"We might want to wait until *after* the principal's come and gone," he said.

The sound of the principal's whistling floated toward them. "I really think you should get off me, Gaia."

"Hey, nobody told you to put me on your lap," Gaia said calmly. She stopped struggling. Was she just going to let them get caught like this?

"Well, nobody told you to seduce me in the middle of the hall!" Ed said, trying to push her off him. She really was stuck.

"As a matter of fact," she hissed, lowering her face to his until their noses were touching, "you're wrong. Somebody did."

Then came the principal's booming voice. "Mr. Fargo! What is the meaning of this?"

Suddenly his head contained more than its allotted share of blood. Ed toyed with the idea of making a joke—something about extra credit for biology class—but decided against it.

"Miss Moore, kindly remove yourself from Mr. Fargo's . . . er . . . lap."

"If you get me some scissors, that just might be possible," Gaia said.

Sarcasm. Ed closed his eyes. Good strategy, Gaia.

Principal Reegan gave them his patented I've-seen-it-all-already-so-don't-even-bother stare. "I'll inform Ms. Strahan that she can expect you both in the detention hall," he said. He turned on his heel and walked off.

"Good one, Gaia," Ed said with a sigh.

Gaia stared after Reegan. "Do you think that means he's not going to get me some scissors?"

ARMOR

HEATHER GANNIS WAS NOTHING IF NOT BRAVE.
SHE PROVED THAT EVERY DAY, DIDN'T SHE?

DETENTION

By the time Gaia and Ed arrived at the detention hall, Ed had a hole in his sweater, and Gaia had a chunk of blue cotton sticking out of a zipper on her thigh. Apparently it was a slow day for the school rebels. The place was practically deserted. Of course, Robbie Canetti was there because Robbie Canetti was always there.

He looked up from his notebook when Ed and Gaia entered. "Hi," he said.

Ed said hi. Gaia didn't bother. Ms. Strahan glanced at them, then went back to correcting papers.

Ed wheeled himself to the back corner of the room, and Gaia flung herself into a chair, letting it scrape against the floor loudly. Her leg immediately started to bounce up and down. There was no way she was staying trapped in this box for the next hour.

She leaned forward, pressing her elbows into her knees to stop her legs from spasming. "I have two things to say," she said, looking Ed in the eye. "One, I didn't want to do what I did out there. I really am sorry."

"I know," Ed answered seriously. "What's the second thing?"

"The second thing is that I'm outta here." She stood up and started past him, but Ed grabbed her wrist.

"I know where Sam is," he said.

Gaia froze. Relief, confusion, and disbelief rushed through her, clouding her vision. She fell back into her chair. "What?"

Ed shot his eyes toward Ms. Strahan, then Robbie. When he was sure neither was listening, he whispered, "I know where they're holding him."

It was all Gaia could do to keep from screaming. She wasn't sure if she should hug him or kill him. "Why didn't you tell me this before?"

Ed actually blushed. "You didn't exactly give me a chance back there, G."

"Where is he?" Gaia demanded, feeling a strong urge to hold him upside down and shake the words right out of him.

Clearing his throat, Ed pushed his hands against his armrests and shifted in his chair. The gesture took forever. "He's in Tribeca. I actually pinpointed the street." Ed's expression was all self-satisfaction. Gaia was leaning away from hug and toward kill, but she kept her cool.

"How did you figure it out?" she asked in a whisper.

Ed leaned forward. "I just kept replaying the e-mail," he said excitedly. "By, like, the nine billionth time, I started to register this sound in the background. Over and over, this sound. And I recognized it. It's skateboarders."

"Skateboarders?" Gaia hissed, her shoulders so tense

they were practically touching her ears. "Ed, skateboarders can be anywhere."

"No." Ed shook his head. "This noise was distinct. It was boards on a ramp—an extreme ramp, with a major slope. And I know for a fact there's only one ramp like that in this whole city. I practically used to live there."

His eyes were glassy, and she could tell he really missed this home away from home.

Gaia would have loved to let him slip into a fit of nostalgia, but this wasn't the place, and it definitely wasn't the time.

"Ed."

He rubbed his hand over his face. "Anyway, I heard that sound in the background, and I realized that Sam's got to be somewhere in the vicinity of that ramp. He's gotta be in one of those buildings."

Gaia stood up. "So let's go."

"Go? Gaia, we can't go."

"Ms. Moore?" Ms. Strahan warned. Gaia didn't care.

"Why not?" she asked Ed. "Because we've got detention?" She looked around the room, holding her palms out like a balance, pretending to weigh the options. "Let's see. Sam's life, detention. Detention, Sam's life." She frowned at him. "I'm going."

She started for the door, but Ed reached out and grabbed her wrist.

"Ms. Moore," came another warning.

Ed actually yanked on her arm, tugging her backward and forcing her into her seat. She looked at him for a moment, stunned.

"No, Gaia. Not because we have detention," Ed hissed, his eyes flashing. "Think about it. You know the kidnapper's watching every move you make. You're at his mercy. If he figures out you're planning a search-and-rescue operation, he might just kill Sam on the spot."

"Yeah, but . . ."

"I know you want to swoop in there and rescue Sam," Ed said. "But you have to make sure you're thinking straight."

Gaia sighed in exasperation.

"Even if you could get to Sam without having the lunatic kidnapper catch on, how are you going to get him out?" Ed asked. "The guy's a mess, Gaia. He's weak, remember?"

Gaia felt as if her head were being pumped full of molten lava. She pressed the heels of her hands to her temples and squeezed her eyes shut.

"So why'd you even bother to tell me where he was?"

"Because I knew you'd want to know," Ed whispered, shaking his head. "Look, Gaia, I'm aware you're not going to let me tell you what to do. I'm just telling you what I think."

She gave the desktop a good slap. Everyone in the room jumped but her.

"Okay, I've had about enough of this, Ms. Moore,"

Ms. Strahan said in what Gaia assumed was supposed to be a threatening tone.

"You got something against hearing what I think?" Ed whispered with a grin.

"I've got something against being trapped in a classroom when I should be out doing something constructive," Gaia answered, standing again. "And don't ask me what, because I don't know, but I have to get the hell out of here!"

"Gaia—"

"That's it, Ms. Moore."

But Gaia barely registered the warnings. She was already halfway down the hall.

RENT-A-COP

Heather did not leave school immediately following first period.

That would have been the cowardly thing to do, and Heather Gannis was nothing if not brave. She proved that every day, didn't she? Swimming with the sharks (as she secretly referred to her friends) with only her Almay pressed powder for armor.

So she'd stayed at school and toughed it out. She'd handled all those pitiful looks they threw at her, the feigned sympathy, the understanding hand pats. It was so patronizing. Didn't they know she knew? Didn't they realize she could see through them like a Victoria's Secret peignoir? They loved that she'd been humiliated. They got off on it.

As soon as the final bell sounded, Heather escaped them all.

And now she was on her way to Sam's dorm.

She walked—all right, so it was more like a subdued run—toward Washington Square Park, taking the opportunity to think. There hadn't been a clear thought in her head all day. The rigors of maintaining a stiff upper lip, seeming to be grateful, and acting suitably flustered had taken all her energy. She had also been forced to accept hug after hug after hug from all those guys who said they only wanted to comfort her, but really just saw her grief as perhaps their only chance to press their deprived bodies against her legendary one.

Pigs. Idiot pigs. But, she reminded herself for the twelve zillionth time, she'd invited popularity, worked for it, and now had to live with the consequences. What was that old saying? Live by the sword die by the sword. Yep. Same went for popularity.

By the time she reached Fifth Avenue, Heather was convinced she had it all figured out. Sam had secretly filmed them, and then somehow had carelessly allowed the DVD to fall into the wrong hands. The hands of Gaia Moore.

Or maybe it hadn't been carelessness on Sam's part. Maybe it had been part of a horrific conspiracy. Maybe—for some reason she could not even begin to imagine—Sam had recorded their encounter, then *given* the DVD to Gaia to screen in econ.

That would explain why Gaia had shown up that night. That would explain why Sam had run after her. They were working together to ruin Heather's life.

Why? She had no idea. But she was definitely going to find out.

Heather reached Sam's dorm, stomped into the lobby, and was met by the security guard.

Right. She'd forgotten about that little roadblock.

"Can I help you?" he asked.

Heather smiled automatically. The guy was beefy, maybe in his late twenties. She could tell this rent-a-cop position was probably a dream job for him—second only to his lifelong fantasy of changing his name to the Raunchy Raider and becoming the darling of the professional wrestling circuit.

"Hi," she said. "I'm just going up to visit my boyfriend."

He drew himself up tall. He was obviously very important. "I'll need to see your university ID."

Lucky for Heather she could blush on command. "You think I'm in college?"

The guy smiled. "Aren't you?"

Heather shook her head coyly. "I'm only in high school. But he's expecting me. . . ."

"Sorry, sweetheart."

Don't *sweetheart* me, you pumped-up piece of shit. "Please?" She smiled and gave him her best little head tilt. "Look. He gave me a key."

She produced Sam's dorm key from the back pocket of her jeans. Okay, so he hadn't actually given it to her. She'd stolen his spare copy in a fit of immaturity back when they'd first started getting serious. It had made her feel special to have it—her boyfriend's college dorm room key. And her friends had thought she was beyond lucky. Now her petty crime was about to come in handy.

"Look, honey," meat-for-brains said, "I don't care if the guy gave you his key. I don't care if he gave you his tuition money, all right? The bottom line is, you're not getting in here without a valid New York Univeristy ID."

Heather ground her teeth. "Can't you call him? He'll come down and get me."

The guard's eyes slid over her body like maple syrup on a stack of pancakes. "I'm sure he will." He picked up the phone. "What's his number?"

She gave it to him. He dialed.

"Busy?"

"What?"

"The line's busy."

This threw her. Sam's line was never busy. A black hole formed in her stomach. Maybe he had it off the hook.

Maybe he was so desperate to avoid her that he'd instructed this steroid-shooting side of beef who used too much hair gel not to let anyone fitting her description anywhere near the elevator.

Disgusted, Heather turned on her heel and stalked out onto the cold street.

THE WORKS

"So now what?"

Gaia shrugged. "I don't know." Ed had followed her out of detention, and now she was following Ed down the handicap ramp. A late afternoon chill crept into the neck of her sweatshirt, causing goose bumps to break out on her skin. "Maybe they're gonna have me scale the Empire State Building in my underwear."

"I'd like to see that," Ed joked.

"Seriously. There's got to be another test, doesn't there?" Her eyes made a wide sweep of the area. "But what? When?"

Bring it on, she willed silently. Come on! It was like waiting to throw a punch, or waiting to have one thrown at you. Come and get me. Come and get me.

When they reached the sidewalk, Ed angled his chair to allow a food vendor to pass by with his stout, steaming cart.

"Y'know what's weird?" Ed asked. "The last tests came at you like rapid fire, so where the hell are they?"

"Maybe the guy's taking a coffee break," Gaia deadpanned. "Maybe he's a union kidnapper."

Ed's face became tentatively hopeful "Or maybe you're done."

"Done?"

"Yeah. Maybe they're satisfied," Ed said with a shrug. "Maybe the next message is gonna be, "You may reclaim your diabetic boyfriend at your earliest convenience."

"Don't call him my boyfriend," Gaia said.

"Yes, ma'am."

Absently Gaia watched the hot dog vendor drag his moving eatery to a halt. When he banged open a metal compartment, the uniquely New York aroma of frankfurters and sauerkraut reached her. Her stomach growled fiercely, and she realized she hadn't eaten a thing since the three bites of bagel she'd had at breakfast.

"Hungry?" she asked Ed.

"Sure."

Gaia approached the vendor. "Two. With the works."

"The works," the guy mumbled, grabbing two empty rolls and placing the hot dogs into them.

Gaia watched as he clumsily spooned relish and onions onto them. More of the condiments wound up in his hand than on the dogs. Well, maybe if the jerk took off those dark glasses and pulled his hat up from over his eyes he'd be able to see what he was doing and—

"Sam says hi."

Gaia's eyes snapped up to the vendor's face. He thrust the hot dogs into her hand. Her first instinct was to shove them both up his nose. The guy pulled off his sunglasses and gave her the hands-down wickedest stare she'd ever seen. Anyone else would have passed out from the ferocity of it, but Gaia met his gaze. And, since she *had* been born with whichever chemical component created hunger, she took a sloppy bite of the hot dog.

The sham vendor was obviously thrown by her calm.

"Sam says hi," he repeated, less icily. He reached into his apron, removed a piece of paper, and held it out to her.

"She glanced over her shoulder at Ed. "He's out of hot pretzels," she said sarcastically. "Will you settle for a ransom note?"

Ed was wide-eyed. "God. Are they everywhere?"

Gaia took the note, and seconds later the phony hot dog guy was gone.

She handed Ed his hot dog, which he just sort of stared at, as if he'd never seen one before. Gaia decided to read to herself and give Ed a couple of seconds to recover.

Clearly you did not understand what I meant by HUMILIATION, as you and your friend in the wheelchair are still on speaking terms. Momentary embarrassment in the school corridor was not what I had in mind, Gaia. I wanted him out of your life, but I see this has not happened. For this reason, you will perform another test, the most difficult thus far. Before I return Sam to you this evening, you will be required to . . .

Gaia looked up from the note and blinked at Ed.

"What? What does it say?"

"Uh . . . it says I'm doing really well. Listen." She skipped to the final paragraph, cleared her throat, and read aloud. "'Sam will be turned over to you this evening at ten p.m. in Washington Square Park. Choose any pathway. I will find you. FYI—Mr. Moon's health is failing, so I suggest you be prompt.'"

"Is that all it says?"

She swallowed hard and nodded. No reason to tell him

how personal the kidnapper was getting with his notes. No reason to tell him—

"Man. He must be pretty sick." Ed was looking pale.

"It says I have to get his insulin from his dorm room," Gaia murmured. His room. Like she wanted to revisit that memory anytime in the next century.

Ed nodded. "Hope we can get into his room."

"You'd be surprised how easy it can be," said Gaia, frowning.

"That's if it's unlocked," Ed reminded her.

"True." Her eyes dropped unwillingly to the note, that one sentence . . .

Ed lowered an eyebrow at her. "You okay?"

Gaia nodded.

"Well, you might not be after I make this next suggestion." He took a deep breath. "I think we're going to need Heather."

"Need Heather? For *what*?" Gaia asked. "Fashion advice on what to wear to a hostage rescue?"

Ed tossed his untouched hot dog into a nearby trash container. "For the key to Sam's room. I'm guessing she's the only person we know who might have one."

Gaia felt her muscles tighten with anger. He was probably right. And the last thing she needed was to get nabbed for breaking and entering. She wouldn't be helping anyone from jail. Having Sam's room key was crucial.

She ate the rest of her hot dog in two angry bites, then glared at him. "Heather it is," she said with her mouth full.

Ed watched her swallow with a look of near disgust. He'd never looked at her like that. But then, she figured she was doing a pretty good impression of a boa constrictor.

"Are you sure you're all right?"

"I'm fine," she lied, glancing at the note again—at another part she hadn't read out loud. At the part that said, *"Kill CJ."*

A LITTLE BUZZ

LOKI HOVERED THERE ANOTHER MOMENT,
ALLOWING HIS ICY LAUGHTER TO RAIN DOWN
ON SAM.

IT'S A DATE

"Hi."

CJ turned. The woman was talking to him. The beautiful woman in the tight blouse.

He did his little shoulder thing—loosened himself up. Slouched. "Wus'up?"

She smiled. "I've seen you around, you know."

"Yeah? Well, I ain't seen you." At least not in a while. She used to walk through the park every day, but not lately. It was hard to forget a body like that. She smelled great. Expensive. And her legs went on till Tuesday.

"What's your name?"

"CJ."

"Nice to meet you, CJ."

She reached for his hand and shook it. Talk about silky skin.

"Listen CJ, I don't usually do this sort of thing, but I was hoping you might like to go out with me. Tonight." The way she fixed her eyes on him made things inside his body stir. Things he didn't even know were there.

Brain cramp! This gorgeous, uptown piece of ass was asking him out? Sure as hell sounded like it. For a moment there was no Gaia.

"Uh . . . uh . . ." Damn, he had to get it together.

"Well?"

Shit, this one was friendly. She was pressing her palms against his chest now.

"You don't have plans, do you?" she asked in a husky voice.

Well, as a matter of feet, he did. He was going to kill Gaia tonight. But then again, maybe he could do both.

The woman was giving him this very seductive little pout. "Please say you'll meet me tonight. There's a band playing in the park. And I love to dance. . . ." She pushed her hips against his and swayed. "Do you like to dance?"

CJ nodded. He liked her perfume. It was giving him a little buzz. Smelled like burning flowers or something.

"Good. So it's a date, then?" She tossed her hair back and looked up at him through her thick lashes. "We'll meet tonight, in the park."

"Yeah. Yeah." He backed up from her slightly, trying to play off the fact that every inch of his body wanted to pounce on her right now. No use letting the lady know she had the power. "That'd be cool. In the park."

"I'll meet you at the fountain," she said, making even the word *fountain* sound dirty. "Say . . . nine-thirty?"

"Yeah, sounds good."

"Till then . . ."

"Yeah."

She turned to walk away, and he remembered that walk. He and Marco used to study it. When she'd gone half

a block, he called out to her. "Yo, girl. What's your name?"
She didn't bother to answer.

TO: L
FROM: E
RE: CJ

Arrived in NYC early and met with pawn. He'll meet
me in the park at nine-thirty.

If all goes as well as this, he should be dead before
the band plays its first set.

WHAT THE KIDNAPPER
SAID

Loki crumpled the memo and dropped it into the waste-
basket.

"Dead before the first set?" He smiled sardonically.
"That's what I like to hear." His laughter was an ugly, guttural rumble in his throat. He turned to Sam.

Poor, poor Sam.

Dying, really, right before his eyes. A shame.

Loki walked toward his hostage, who was huddled in a shivering heap on the floor, and studied him in silence for a long moment.

Well, he could understand what his niece saw in the boy. He was certainly nice-looking. At least, he had been, before that unfortunate incident in which his face collided with that fist. Tsk, tsk. And, of course, his medical condition was really taking its toll.

"Sam?" Again, louder. "Sam!"

The boy lifted his head slightly and let out a ragged breath.

"Sam Moon," said Loki thoughtfully, rolling the name over his taste buds as though it were a new wine he was tasting. "Tell me about yourself, Sam."

The only reply was the shuddering of Sam's body.

"Cat got your tongue, boy?" Loki sneered. "Ah, yes. Just as well. I generally prefer to do the talking in situations such as these. I do so enjoy being in control."

He was circling Sam now, like the predator he was. "You're aware, I imagine, that my niece is quite taken with you?" His eyes turned hard as he stared at the prone form before him.

Loki stopped walking, folded his arms across his chest, and glared down at Sam. "That, as you must understand, is not an easy thing for an uncle to accept. I wonder, would you be worthy of her? Because an uncle has certain expectations for his only niece, Sam. He wants the best for her, wants only her happiness. I know it may not feel that way, given current circumstances, but it is true. Gaia you might say, has become my whole world."

Loki lifted his foot and used the toe of one of his three-hundred-dollar wing tips to give Sam's languid body a hard nudge. "So tell me, Sam Moon," he demanded. "Are you the boy who might make Gaia's dreams come true?"

Loki hovered there another moment, allowing his icy laughter to rain down on Sam.

Then in a voice so slick and close to silence that Loki barely heard it himself, he asked Sam Moon one last question.

After that he walked away, the heels of his expensive shoes drumming the highly polished floor of the loft.

He didn't turn around.

He should have.

WHAT THE HOSTAGE HEARD

He felt the laughter before he heard it. An ugly rumble from across the room. Guttural, like an animal choking.

The first footsteps—approaching. A presence, near. Then, words:

Sam Moon.

I enjoy . . . control.

Gaia . . . taken with you . . . my whole world.

A kick to his rib cage. A shouted question:

. . . dreams come true?

And then, in the slightest whisper:

Do you love her, Sam?

Sam's bruised eye throbbed as he lifted his head. He had not attempted to use his voice in nineteen hours, but with what he sincerely believed might be the very last breath in his body, over the sound of fading footsteps, Sam answered.

"Yes."

ED

Gaia and Heather.

When you look at them and take them at face value, one might wonder how one person (namely, me . . . and possibly Sam) could love them both in one lifetime.

Gaia is tall, blond, powerful, and favors brown clothing.

Heather is shortish, brunette, a slave to the masses, and never wears brown unless a respected fashion writer tells her it's the "new black."

But Gaia and Heather are more alike than the general public might think.

The first similarity? They'd both kill me if they heard me say that.

The list goes on.

Neither one of them is as brave as she thinks she is. They both have a lot of secrets. (Heather's I pretty much know, Gaia's I'm not sure I want to know.) They both have trust issues. I've never known two people with such a gift for sarcasm. They are both extremely beautiful.

And they both have a thing for college guys.

So it's not hard to see why one guy could love them both in the same lifetime.

The real question is, why do I bother?

PHONE TAG

"HEATHER? IT'S JEFF LANDON. . . . SO, UH,
ARE YOU BUSY SATURDAY NIGHT?"

Rrring. Click. Beep.

"You've reached the Gannis residence. Please leave a message at the beep. Thank you."

"Heather! It's Megan. Oh my God! I am still so totally freaked out by what happened at school today! I can*not* believe Sam, like, actually recorded you guys doing it. And gave it to *Gaia*? That's like—ugh—*so* unbelievably tasteless. It's like, okay, why don't we all just go on *Jerry Springer*? I mean, like, what if you are wearing weird underwear or something, y'know? Okay, so, like, call me as soon as you get in. Bye."

Click. Beep.

What kind of idiot was Megan? She knew Heather didn't have her own phone line. She knew Heather's answering machine was in the family room, where anyone could overhear a message coming in. Heather's parents were actually really good about not snooping, and they would never purposely listen to an incoming call. But what if they happened to be passing through the family room while Megan was ranting about she and Sam "doing it"? Idiot.

Rrring. Click. Beep.

"Hi, it's Ashley. I skipped school today to get my hair highlighted, but I just heard the best dirt! This morning somebody actually showed a DVD of people having, like, *sex*—in school! Well, no, I mean, they weren't having sex in school. They showed the DVD in school. The sex was, like, someplace else. I don't know who was on the DVD, though 'cuz I heard it from Jen, who heard it from Mallory, who heard it from . . . I dunno, like, somebody. But now I'm, like, so bummed that I dropped AP econ! Oh! Hey! You're still in that class, aren't you? So *you* must have seen it. Cool. All right, so call me with the info!"

Click. Beep.

It had been going on all day. She'd already erased at least twenty messages on this very topic. But she refused to take the phone off the hook, in case Sam tried to call.

To explain himself.

To apologize.

To tell her he'd had nothing to do with that damn DVD.

She'd come home from the disaster at the dorm and spent the last hour lying on the family room sofa, screening calls.

Rrring. Click. Beep.

"Heather! It's Jeff Landon. Heard about your film debut. Whoa. Didn't know you were into that kind of thing. So, uh, are you busy Saturday night?"

Beep.

Heather chucked a throw pillow at the answering machine. It missed by about three feet and bounced off the top of the television. She sighed, then rolled over onto her stomach. Sam's dorm room key bit into her hip. It was still in the front pocket of her pants. She pulled it out and stared at it for a second before flinging it, too, across the room, where it knocked over a framed photo of her and Sam at a Yankees game.

Rrring. Click. Beep.

"Heather, it's Megan again! Are you there? Pick up! I just heard that band Fearless is playing in the park tonight. The drummer's a total hottie! Wanna go? Maybe it'll, you know, cheer you up or whatever. Call me."

That was it! Heather had officially had it. She was taking the phone off the hook, and for all she cared, Sam could go to hell. Let him call. Let him get a busy signal. Let him come over with a dozen long-stemmed roses and apologize in person, like a normal boyfriend!

She was just reaching for the handset when the phone rang again. She jerked her fingers away as though she'd been shocked, then listened.

Click. Beep.

"Hi, Heather. It's Ed. Fargo. Listen, I realize this call must come as a shock, but I have something really serious I need to talk to you about. It's important. It's . . . uh . . . about Sam. He's in trouble. Well, actually, not trouble. More like danger. There's something we have to get out of his room. We're talking life and death here. Sam's life and death. So we were thinking, since you probably have a key to his room, you would bring it to us. Heather, you've got to help us . . ."

Heather picked up the handset. The machine shut off, routing Ed's voice directly through the phone as she pressed it to her ear.

"Heather? Are you there?"

She had two words for him: "Who's us?"

THE KEY

"What do you mean, she doesn't want me involved?"

"I mean," said Ed, wheeling fast to keep up with Gaia's furious pace, "she's all for helping Sam, but she doesn't want you to be a part of it."

"*Part* of it? Part of *it*?" Gaia punched her right fist repeatedly against her thigh as she walked. "Doesn't the airhead realize that I *am* it? Didn't you explain that to her?" Gaia slammed directly into a man in a business suit, sending him sprawling. "Sorry" she mumbled over her shoulder. The guy swore after her but was too busy restuffing his briefcase to give chase.

"No, I didn't. I'm guessing it would have done more harm than good." Ed stopped at the corner, waiting for the light. He glanced warily over his shoulder. Gaia half hoped the suit would come yell at her. She needed a good excuse to hit something.

When Ed had explained that Gaia was involved, the news had, naturally, sent Her Royal Heatherness into convulsions. After some careful negotiations, Ed had managed to get her to agree to discuss it in person—without Gaia.

"So she's not expecting me?" Gaia asked, holding her hair back from her face to keep it from whipping into her eyes.

"No," Ed answered, staring at the rushing traffic.

"Great."

Gaia stopped fuming long enough to check out the neighborhood. It was a little to the east of the area that was really upscale. It wasn't bad. But there was nothing much to recommend it, either. The streets were lined with smallish apartment buildings that were falling into disrepair—chipping paint, cracked moldings, windows scratched with graffiti. Plus it seemed like the garbage hadn't been hauled off in weeks.

"Where are we going?" Gaia asked.

"Heather's."

Gaia lifted an eyebrow in the direction of the nearest worse-for-wear apartment building. "You mean she doesn't live in some yuppie co-op somewhere in the eighties?"

"Not anymore," Ed said flatly.

They continued in silence for two blocks, then turned a corner and found Heather waiting for them on the sidewalk in front of a nondescript, graying apartment building.

Ed waved. Heather fired Gaia a hateful look from thirty paces off.

"I told you not to bring her," Heather said, crossing her arms over the front of her suede jacket.

"This is important," Ed told her. "Gaia's involved whether you like it or not."

Heather looked like a rabid alley cat. She ignored Ed, focusing all her attention on glaring at Gaia. "Are you sleeping with Sam?"

Gaia rolled her eyes. "Oh, give me a break—"

"Are you?" Heather's mouth contorted with fury.

"Heather!" Ed blurted. He wheeled his chair between the two girls. "This isn't about you," he said firmly, leveling her with a stare. "This is about Sam."

Heather glanced at him, a flicker of interest in her eyes. "Right, so what's going on? How do you even know him?"

Gaia let out an exasperated sigh. The girl had a talent for pointless questions.

"It doesn't matter how I know him," Ed said. "What matters is he's been kidnapped."

"Kidnapped?"

The color drained from Heather's face, and Gaia felt her stomach flop.

That was what fear looked like. Gaia found herself fighting back a wave of what could only be called jealousy. She cared for Sam more than anyone would ever know. Yet again she felt deep discomfort at the knowledge that when his life was threatened, she couldn't feel this most basic emotion. But a conscience-free zone like Heather Gannis could. Heather could have natural feelings when the guy they both loved was in danger.

Gaia felt like a voyeur as she watched the tears forming in Heather's eyes. She made herself look away.

"By who? Why?" Heather asked.

"We're not sure," Ed said. "Somebody's holding him hostage."

"Oh my God!"

"We think we can rescue him, but we're running out of time."

"Rescue him? When?"

Probably needs to check her Week-at-a-Glance, Gaia thought cynically. *"Sure, I can pencil in Sam's rescue for tonight—unless there's a sale at Abercrombie."*

"Tonight," said Ed.

Morbidly curious, Gaia watched Heather closely, feeling an inexplicable loneliness. Heather's eyes were so huge, so filled with terror, they threatened to overtake her whole face. She was actually quaking. Gaia couldn't pull her eyes away. She knew what fear looked like. But what did it *feel* like? *What?* And would she ever know the extent of what she was missing?

"Oh my God." Heather said, her voice quivering. "Oh my God, oh my God!"

"Calm down," said Gaia. "Freaking out isn't going to help anything."

"Shut up!" Heather glared at her. "Just shut up and go away."

"She's not going anywhere," said Ed.

"I don't even want to look at her!" Heather sputtered.

"Then don't," snapped Gaia. "Just give us the key so we can—"

"You're not going without me!" Heather exploded. "Sam is still *my* boyfriend. And besides, it's not the key that's the problem. It's the pit bull of a security guard."

Gaia remembered the guard. She'd slipped by him without much trouble on her own, but all three of them? A towhead, a homecoming queen, and a Boy Scout on wheels. They weren't exactly an inconspicuous bunch.

Heather turned to Ed, and her voice ironed itself into a reasonable tone. "I have to do *something*. I want to help him."

"You'll be helping him by giving us the key," said Ed. "That way, we can get his insulin and bring it to him tonight when they release him in the park—"

Gaia brought her hand down hard on Ed's shoulder,

effectively shutting him up, but not soon enough. She watched Heather's face as the information was sent to her mental mainframe.

Damn.

"I'm coming with you. I have to be the one to bring it to him." Suddenly she was overcome with either real emotion or really good acting technique. Her eyes filled with tears again, and her breathing was fast and shallow. "He'll need me," she cried. "He'll need me to take care of him. I'm going with you."

"Oh, no!" Gaia exploded. "No way."

"Heather," Ed said calmly, "It's too dangerous."

She glared in Gaia's direction. "Why is it too dangerous for me and not her?"

Gaia wouldn't have minded showing her. Instead she said, "It's dangerous for everyone. Especially Sam. But I'm going because the kidnapper contacted me in the first place."

Something shifted in Heather's eyes as she digested this information. She seemed to suddenly grow smaller. "Why you?"

"I don't know," Gaia said honestly.

"Heather crossed her arms over her chest. "Who do you think you—"

"Yo! Enough!" They both snapped their heads around to face Ed. "This isn't helping Sam."

Gaia swore under her breath. Sam's life was in jeopardy,

and here she was arguing with Bad-Attitude Barbie. She had to let Ed work on Heather alone for a minute. She turned and headed back toward a small convenience store she'd noticed near the corner.

If all else failed, she could knock Heather's lights out and just take the key.

But something told her that wasn't going to be necessary. Ed would be able to convince her. Maybe it was the residual tenderness she heard in his voice every time he talked to her or about her. Maybe it was the way Heather changed— almost indiscernibly, but still, *changed*—when Ed looked at her, as though something were happening inside her that she didn't want or expect. It was as if Heather were locked out of her own soul and somehow Ed still had the key.

For the life of her, Gaia could not figure put why that annoyed her so much.

But it did.

THE RIPPLE EFFECT

Gaia was coming out of the store, finishing up her Mars bar, when Ed appeared.

"I've got good news and bad news," he said.

"Is the bad news that you couldn't think of anything more original to say than that?" Gaia asked through a mouthful of nuts and chocolate. She crumpled the wrapper and shoved it into her sweatshirt pocket with the two other chocolate bars she'd bought. Gaia didn't know much about diabetes, but she thought Sam might need them.

"So where is she?" Gaia asked, glancing past Ed.

"She'll meet us here in a few minutes," Ed said, studiously avoiding eye contact. "She went inside to get the key."

Gaia's body rippled with relief. "She's going to give it up?"

"More or less," Ed answered, picking at the hole in his sweater.

"I'm not sure that's possible, Ed," Gaia said impatiently.

"She's coming with us to the dorm," Ed said, pushing his shoulders back, trying to look defiant. "There's no way around it."

Gaia tilted her head back, staring up at the rapidly darkening sky. "Do you think she's gonna be able to keep her head when she sees Sam in the park, all beaten and bloody, being shoved around by some guy in commando gear who's holding a sawed-off shotgun to his head, and who knows what else?"

Ed looked a little white. "She'll be long gone before we get to the park."

Gaia had to bite her lip to keep herself from commenting on his use of the word *we*. He didn't know it yet, but *he* was going to be long gone, too. There was no way she was going to drag Ed into that little scenario. But perhaps it was best not to mention that just yet.

"What makes you so sure she'll be gone?" Gaia asked, leaning back against the brick wall of the convenience store.

Ed smiled and his eyes filled with mischief. Gaia knew what was coming before he said it.

"Because I have a plan."

BRAINLESS

HE DIDN'T THINK HE COULD HANDLE THE
HUMILIATION IF HIS FIRST-EVER COVERT-ACTION
PLAN CRASHED AND BURNED.

MISSION:
NOT-SO-IMPOSSIBLE

Ed wheeled his way into the dorm and took a look around. The lobby smelled of beer-dampened carpet and the bottle's worth of Tom Ford with which the guard had obviously drenched himself.

Hmm. Ed would have pegged this one for a Paul Smith type. Go figure.

"Hi."

Behind his desk, the guard averted his eyes and gave him a nod.

Typical. Can't look the cripple in the eye.

Ed aimed for the elevator.

Waiting . . . waiting . . .

Okay, so gimme the ID speech already. He checked his watch. Seven twenty-eight. C'mon, buddy. Ask for the card.

Nothing.

Ed hit the elevator button hard. The Neanderthal glanced in his direction and dredged up an awkward grin.

Damn! Don't tell me the quasi-cop is too softhearted to hassle a guy in a wheelchair.

Above the elevator, the number 3 lit up. It would reach ground level any second, and Ed would be able to roll right on. No distraction, no clear avenue for Gaia and Heather.

Over his head, the number 2 blinked orange.

"Excuse me," he said. "I'm heading up to see a friend, but I'm not sure I'll be able to find his room. Those letters and numbers are kinda confusing. Can ya help me out?"

Not until you see my ID, right? Go ahead, say it!

"The letter stands for the wing," the guard explained. "A is to the right, B to the left. There are four rooms to a suite and they're all clearly marked."

"Thanks," Ed muttered. He was starting to sweat. He didn't think he could handle the humiliation if his first-ever covert-action plan crashed and burned.

For a second the guy just looked at Ed and seemed to be trying to decide what to do.

C'mon, brainless. Card me, already. Then the elevator announced itself with a loud *ding*, and the door opened.

"I've never been in any of these dorms before," Ed said. He raised his voice a few decibels louder than necessary. "I don't go here."

There! Now he's got no choice.

The Neanderthal cleared his throat. "Listen, pal," he said in a regretful tone. "I really can't let you up if you don't have an ID."

Finally! Ed narrowed his eyes as the elevator door slid closed. "What do you mean?"

"University policy. Sorry." The guard shoved his beefy hands into his pockets. Damn, he was uncomfortable. "Non-students can't—"

"Nonstudents?" Ed challenged, spinning his chair toward the guard. "You sure you don't mean people in wheelchairs?"

The guy looked at him, waylaid. "Huh?"

"C'mon, man. You know the real reason you're not letting me get on this elevator is because I can't walk into it on my own two feet," Ed said, his face growing red. He should get an Oscar for this one.

"No. That ain't it." Now the Neanderthal was sweating, too. "It's just—"

"Yeah, right! I've seen this crap before," Ed shouted, gripping the armrests on his chair. "It's always the chair. It's discrimination."

Now the guy was getting pissed. "It has nothin' to do with the chair. It's the rule. No ID, no admittance."

Ed gave him a disgusted look, then turned his chair again and reached for the elevator button.

"Hey!" barked the guard, hurrying out from behind the desk. "I told you—"

"What are ya gonna do?" Ed chuckled wickedly. "Hit me?"

With that, they began to argue in earnest.

"All right, we're going in," Gaia said from her position outside Sam's dorm.

Heather rolled her eyes, but when Gaia pushed through the lobby door, Heather followed. Ed had managed to lure the guard out from behind his station, so Gaia and Heather tiptoed behind the guard's back and slipped into the stairwell.

All politeness, Gaia held the door open, allowing Heather to go through first. No idiot, Heather shot Gaia a suspicious look, but Gaia could practically see her train of thought. Heather didn't want Gaia behind her, but the thought of getting to Sam's room first was tempting.

Heather sneered at Gaia and brushed past her. "You're welcome," Gaia snapped in a whisper.

Heather started to jog, and Gaia followed close behind. It was torture having Heather's scrawny ass in her face, but it was going to be worth the sacrifice in about five seconds. Gaia let Heather get up three half flights of stairs before she made her move.

Gaia reached up and grabbed Heather's ankle, sending the girl sprawling on the concrete landing between the first and second floors.

"Get off me!" Heather yelled.

Holding Heather down with one hand, Gaia seized the

key from Heather's grasp with a mercury-fast action that would have done even the most seasoned New York purse snatcher proud.

Gaia pulled Heather to her feet. "Sorry, but it was necessary," Gaia muttered.

"I-I'm going to-to *kill* you," Heather shrieked, struggling to no avail.

"Me first," Gaia said, trying not to enjoy the terror in Heather's eyes. She wasn't going to kill her, of course, though it was tempting. She did, however, need to shove Heather down a few steps, both so she could get to Sam's room without further interference, and so the overweight guard could catch Heather.

Gaia gave Heather one hard push, and Heather yelped. She stumbled down the half flight and landed at the bottom with a thud. It looked like it hurt at least a little.

At that moment Gaia heard Ed yelling at the guard. Right on cue.

"Some chick just snuck into the stairs! Yeah! Yes! I swear! Brown hair! Pink shirt!"

Heather was struggling to her feet as Gaia heard the sound of the lobby door to the stairs banging open.

It was time to get out of there.

"Later, Heather!"

Gaia took off up the stairs. She heard Heather start after her, but the guard had already caught up.

"Where do you think you're going?" he asked, panting.

"Get *off* me!" Heather screamed, "Gaia! *Gaia!*"

Gaia smiled as she sprinted down the fourth-floor hallway.

DORM ROOM REVISITED

Gaia stood outside the door of room B4 and held her breath. The last time she'd been here Sam had been making love to Heather.

How could she bring herself to go in there?

"Don't be such a sentimental idiot," Gaia told herself, shaking off the self-inflicted melodrama. "This is a college dorm room, I should have a nickel for every sexual encounter that's taken place in here."

She slid the key into the lock.

The doorknob fell off in her hand.

For a moment she just stared at it.

Son of a bitch!

The damn thing had been broken all along! Not even lockable. So they hadn't needed the key after all. And, by association they hadn't needed Heather. What a waste of time!

Then again, it had provided the opportunity for Gaia to give Heather a good hard shove. Truth be told, that had actually been kind of cathartic.

She opened the door. And there it was. Sam's bed.

Gaia stepped into the room, keeping her mind on her task. Insulin. Must find insulin. Don't even look at that framed photograph of Heather over there on the dresser. Could she possibly be wearing any more lip gloss?

Insulin, damn it! What was the matter with her?

Gaia seemed to remember the stuff had to be refrigerated. Her eyes swept the room and found a minifridge in the corner. She opened the door. Two bottles of mineral water, a small mountain of those plastic packets of duck sauce that come with Chinese takeout, and a small zippered nylon case.

She opened the case. Pamphlet of instructions. Vials. Syringe.

A wave of emotion washed over her. It was like holding the definition of *vulnerable* in her hands. Sam—perfect, brilliant, gorgeous Sam—had this to contend with. This frailty. This tiny physiological flaw, this infinitesimal defect in body chemistry. This burden. This disadvantage.

Tell me about it.

She stuffed the case into the oversized pocket of her cargo pants, then got up to leave. But there was that damn bed again.

Gaia hesitated perhaps a fraction of a millisecond. Then she threw herself onto the bed. Don't think about the fact that the last time you saw it, Heather was between the sheets. Think about Sam.

Sam's bed.

Sam's sheets. Sam's pillow. Gaia buried her face in it, breathing deeply. Maybe there was something of him still clinging to the pillowcase—an eyelash, maybe, or an echo of a dream.

"Oh, God, Sam . . . I'm so sorry."

She clutched the pillow to her body.

I don't want to kill anybody, her brain said for the hundredth time since she'd read the last directive. *I don't want to kill. I don't want to kill.*

Images flooded her mind, drowning her brain. Sam at the chessboard. Sam coming to see her in the hospital. Sam on the park bench.

And then it was CJ. CJ chasing her down Broome Street. CJ in the police lineup. CJ holding a gun to her head. And firing. And . . .

Gaia sat bolt upright.

She knew what to do.

SAM

Rook to knight four.

Queen's knight. Castle. Pawn.

Wrrrzzzzzzzz. Clank.

I see Gaia's fingers on a chess piece. She pushes the smooth, angular knight with her index finger. And Zolov clicks his false teeth in appreciation of her genius.

The sound bullies me.

Wrrrzzzzzzzzz, clank, wrrzz. I only want to sleep. Sleep. But my levels are off, and my own blood poisons me.

Time is running—check.

Checkmate.

Blackness surrounds me, cold, flat, then it erupts into a pattern of squares. Clean, sharp-cornered red bruises interrupt my blackout. The board spins in its own dimension until I am above it, leaning, knowing, playing. I hear the sound of the plastic piece scraping the cardboard squares.

Wrrrzzzzzzzz.

The hunger is huge. The blackness quivers. I place my hand around Gaia's on her knight.

And sleep.

BRING IT ON

OH, GOD. IS THIS WHAT FORGIVENESS FEELS LIKE?

Gaia found Ed waiting at the Southwest corner of Fifth Avenue and Tenth Street—the designated meeting spot. It was dark out, and he sat in a square of light pouring out of the lobby of the building behind him.

"Get it?" he asked.

"Got it." She nodded, patting the nylon case inside her pocket. "C'mon, let's go. There's somewhere I have to be."

Gaia started walking toward the park, and Ed quickly caught up with her.

"How'd it work out with Heather and the guard?" Gaia asked, hoping to keep him from asking where exactly she had to be.

A shadow of guilt crossed his face. "It got pretty hairy. She was ballistic when they tossed her out."

"Tossed her out, huh?" asked Gaia, savoring the image. "You mean that literally, right?"

"Pretty much," Ed said. "From what I overheard, it seems our little Heather tried to get in to Sam's room earlier today. The guard recognized her and thought she was some crazed stalker, so he totally ignored her when she was shouting about you getting away. They took her to the main security office. She fought him like you wouldn't even believe, kicking, swearing, snorting. . . ."

"So she didn't get around to implicating you?" Gaia asked, glancing up at the arch at the north end of Washington Square Park. It was illuminated at night, and Gaia couldn't help thinking it was beautiful. It was kind of like a beacon.

"I'm sure she tried," Ed said, following her gaze. "But no way were they gonna believe her." He shook his head. "Man, I feel sorry for the guy who had to interrogate her."

"What time is it?" Gaia asked. If he noticed she wasn't really paying attention to the conversation, he didn't say anything.

He checked his watch. "Only eight ten. We've got plenty of time before we have to go to the park."

"Excuse me?" Gaia said. *"We've* got plenty of time?"

"What is it with you women and pronouns today, huh?" Ed asked.

Gaia shoved her hands into her pockets. Her fingers automatically closed around the candy bars. "I'm serious, Ed. I'm going to do this alone."

Ed scoffed. "No, you're not."

"Yes, I am."

"No, you're not."

"Yes, I . . ." Gaia threw up her hands. "Ed, this isn't open to debate. You said it yourself to Heather—it'll be dangerous."

He had no idea how dangerous, of course, because he was unaware of the last note's final directive. But she wasn't about to tell him she'd be murdering a gang member in cold blood this evening, which wasn't exactly the sort of thing that required an escort. He stopped wheeling. "And you think just because I'm in this chair . . ."

"Oh, please! Save the politically correct guilt trip for somebody who gives a shit, okay?" Gaia spat out. "Yes, you're in a wheelchair. Yes, in this case it's a liability. It makes you slow, and obvious, and a real easy target."

Ed looked at her a moment, then turned away.

Damn. She hadn't meant that the way it sounded. Well, no, actually she'd meant it exactly the way it sounded. It was the truth, for God's sake. Of course, she'd neglected to mention her most important reason for not wanting him there.

"Listen," she said, not quite gently, but as close to it as she could stand to get. "I'm not saying this stuff to hurt your feelings—if I wanted to do that, I'd tell you what I really think of your taste in clothes." He didn't face her, but she could feel him smiling. "I've got to do this myself, Ed. Because . . ."

At last he turned. "Because?"

"Because if anything happened to you . . ." Gaia pulled her jacket close to her as the wind picked up, and sighed. "If anything happened to you, the world would be a much sadder place," she finished so quietly she wasn't certain the breeze had left any of her words for Ed to hear.

A few hundred years went by before Ed finally spoke. "Thanks, Gaia."

"Yeah, whatever." Gaia picked at a hangnail. "Let's not make this a mush fest, okay? You know you're, like, my only friend on the planet. So what good would it do me to let you take a bullet to the skull?"

She handed him Heather's key, careful not to let her hand touch his.

"Get this back to her," she said.

"Don't you want to keep it?"

Gaia shook her head. "He gave it to her, not to me."

"Yeah," Ed replied softly, lowering his eyes. "I know exactly what you mean."

She figured he was thinking back on his bygone relationship with Heather, because his tone was tender in the extreme. She sighed again.

"I gotta go," she said, looking off toward the center of the park.

He raised his eyes, surprised. "Now?"

"Yeah, well . . . I have to stop back at my place. I've gotta get something." Something she really didn't want to get. Something that should just have been left in its uninspred hiding place forever.

Gaia hesitated, waiting for an appropriate lie to shove its way to the front of her brain. Then her mind zoomed back to the Duane Reade bag, the cop, Renny.

"Tampons."

"Oh." Ed's face flushed faster than Gaia had ever thought possible. "Well, uh . . . be careful."

She grinned. "With the tampons?"

"Gaia!"

"I'll be okay." Her brows knitted together, and she stared at Ed seriously. "I'll be okay as long as you stay far, far away from the park tonight."

Ed sighed and shook his head. "Fine."

She was three steps away when she turned around again. "Promise me, Ed. Promise me you will *not* come to the park."

He nodded. "I promise."

If she hadn't been thinking so hard about killing CJ, she might have recognized that Ed was as good a liar as she was.

SEDUCTION 201(AP)

Ella would never get tired of doing Loki's dirty work.

Especially when it involved her running her hands over the bare chests of well-built young men like CJ. Okay, so they were rolling in the dirt behind a bush off some pathway in the park—not exactly a classy setting. But she knew how to make the best of any situation.

This one was as sexy as he was mean. She'd always liked that combination.

Marco was good. CJ was much, much better.

And he was amazed by her. Well, of course. He was probably used to teenage sluts with grungy hair and too much black eyeliner. He'd never seen actual silk this close before, let alone touched it.

Now, here's where I sigh for him, nice and deep—make him think I've never had anything this good before.

CJ smiled hungrily.

He's so proud of himself. Look at him showing off! It was almost cute.

That's right. One more button.

He breathed her name. Or what he thought was her name. So amazed. So grateful. He had no idea there was a blond assassin on her way there to murder him.

Well . . . if you've gotta go, this is definitely the way to spend your final hour.

He asked why she was laughing.

"I always laugh when I'm ready," she said seductively. "Are you ready?"

Over his shoulder, she checked her watch. Ten till ten. There was a sound from a nearby tree. It was a miracle she even heard it over CJ's moaning and heavy breathing. It was a signal: *She's here.*

Okay, you darling, dangerous boy . . . Let's make this quick.

"Yes, CJ! Yes . . . *Yes!*" Perfect timing! And then . . .

"CJ, I hear someone. . . ."

He rose to his knees with a nice lazy smile, tugged up his jeans, and peered through the leaves.

"Shit!"

"What is it?" He was looking for his shirt. No luck.

"Shit. It's her. I gotta go. Sorry."

The "sorry" threw her a bit. *I suppose I have to act like I care.* "Don't go, CJ! Wait!"

He didn't even realize she'd taken his gun.

He leaned down and gave her a hard kiss on her mouth and told her he'd see her again; he *promised*—in this rough, almost heartbreaking voice—that he'd see her again. Then he took off. She sat up, buttoning her blouse, surveying the damage to her skirt.

Gaia, he's all yours.

Gaia entered Washington Square Park.

It was nine forty.

The concert was supposed to start at ten. The band was already doing sound checks. The squeal of feedback from the microphones echoed above the gathering crowd. Gaia watched the arriving fans with a combination of interest and longing.

What must it be like, she wondered, to have nothing else to do on a Monday night besides go to a concert in the park? No gangbangers to ice, no hostages to free . . .

What's it like just to be normal?

Well, she decided, looking around at the crowd, *normal* was a relative term—this was the West Village, after all. Tattoos and navel rings required.

So where the hell was CJ?

It was almost funny that she was looking for him for a change. The problem was, she hadn't expected to actually have to look. He'd been like clockwork in the past, always just sort of there—lurking, looming, stalking. Tonight, though, when it was absolutely imperative that their paths cross, he was a no-show.

How nauseatingly ironic was that?

Reasoning that even a brainless wonder like CJ might

find the band concert too public a place to hunt his prey, Gaia plunged into the semidarkness of the pathway that led to Washington Square West.

She'd noticed that morning that a few leaves had begun to change. Change. Die. It was all in how you looked at it, but where just weeks ago there had been nothing but thriving greenery, there were now little glimpses of color. Throughout the expanse of billowing green, the brown-red leaves clung like scabs. They drew the eye automatically, as though to remind you that death refused to go unnoticed.

The shadows engulfed her, and the trees muffled the sound of the band and the band watchers. It was odd—even after all the horrific stuff that had happened to her in this park, she still liked it, liked the way it smelled, liked the way it rustled. She marveled at the weird, restless peacefulness of the place.

Even tonight. Even with a .38 in her waistband and CJ on the prowl.

And Sam . . .

Was he here somewhere? What if the kidnapper wasn't really going to release him? What if . . .

No. She couldn't dwell on that possibility. Sam was here. He had to be.

Did the kidnapper have him in a half nelson behind some tree, a rag stuffed in his mouth to keep him quiet? Then again, if Sam was in as bad shape as the last note had indicated, none of that would be necessary, would it?

So maybe he was writhing in the dirt in unbearable agony, clinging to his gorgeous existence by a mere thread, closer—like the drying leaves—to death than to life.

Gaia's skin prickled; her heart was practically doing the lambada in her chest. She wouldn't have Sam back until she dealt with CJ. So where was he?

"C'mon, you dirtbag. Show your ugly face."

Even as she whispered it she heard him. He was maybe fifteen feet behind her but approaching fast. And then he was on her, his hand slamming down on her shoulder, jerking her around to face him.

She reached out with both hands, grabbed him around the neck, and yanked his face down to connect with her head.

Nose—busted. No question. Good. It would go nicely with the sling on his arm. He staggered backward, groaning. "You bitch!"

"Whatever." Gaia nailed him with a series of front kicks to his gut, then spun around, swinging her left leg in a high arc that landed like a wrecking ball against the side of his jaw.

He fell sideways, hitting the pavement with a rib-bashing *thud*. Gaia pressed her foot between his shoulder blades, pinning him to the ground while she reached into the waist of her pants for the gun.

"You know," she said through clenched teeth, pressing the gun into the flesh behind his right ear, "as much as you really do deserve to die a very painful death . . ."

He flinched as the sole of her sneaker dug deeper into his back.

"As much as you deserve it . . ."

She sighed and lifted her foot. It took him a second to recognize he was free. As soon as he did, he leaped to his feet, and Gaia found herself making the very incongruous observation that this idiot was running around the park at night in October without a shirt on.

He stood very still, staring at her. She held the gun about an inch from his chest.

She had to make it look real without actually killing him. Had to make it look as though she'd tried and failed.

She cocked the hammer. "Hit me," she said, slicing her voice down to a whisper."

"Huh?" He was looking at her as though she were nuts. Maybe she was.

"Hit me," she snarled again, waving the gun.

CJ, obviously, was not very good at following directions.

She leaned closer to him. And wanted to gag. *Smoked rose petals*. Another divergent thought: The freaky witch in Soho is scamming Ella good. Unless . . .

Gaia ducked. CJ's heavy fist caught her in the cheekbone,

throwing her slightly off balance. Good enough. She aimed the gun into a tree and fired.

Apparently CJ was only just realizing he'd left his own firearm elsewhere. He froze.

Gaia stumbled a little for dramatic effect, then pointed the gun at him. "Look out, asshole. This one's gonna be closer."

She aimed and fired. The bullet passed so close to CJ's face he could have kissed it.

"That's two," she whispered, watching as CJ fell to his knees and covered his head with his arms. He was begging her not to shoot.

Again she pulled the trigger.

CJ winced.

And Gaia whispered, "Bang!"

She had to. Because the bullet that should have been loaded in the third chamber of the gun's barrel was safety hidden in a Duane Reade bag under Gaia's bed.

It was as if eternity made itself visible, swelling around her, slowing the spin of the earth. Gaia swore she saw leaves changing in the chasm of time that elapsed between the steely click of the trigger and CJ's moment of recognition.

No bullet.

She gave him a wicked smile. "Déjà vu, huh?"

That's when he ran.

Gaia let out a huge rush of breath, then swung her gaze

across the shadows that shrouded the path. She knew the kidnapper was out there somewhere, watching. "Hope you fellas got all that," she muttered. "Hope you bought it."

Her answer was two heavy hands coming down on her shoulders. Hard.

Evidently they hadn't bought it at all.

EYES LIKE HERS

SHE COULD FIGHT LIKE A MACHINE, FULL FORCE,
PUMPED ON FURY AND DESIRE.

911

Okay, so maybe lying right to her face wasn't exactly the best way to make her fall in love with him. But what choice did he have?

"Promise me you will *not* come to the park tonight."

Yeah. Right.

Sure, she was gutsy. Sure, she was powerful, and capable, and—all right, he'd even give her deadly. But she was his. At least in his heart she was his, and even a—what was it she'd called him? A liability? Yeah. Even a liability like him knew that you absolutely, positively did not let the love of your life do something like this alone.

So he followed her.

The band crowd was a good cover. He had to keep his distance on the path, though.

She still hadn't spotted him. He was at least twenty yards behind and to her left, in the shadow of a rest room building. He didn't have a weapon; he didn't even have the use of his legs. He did, however, have a cell phone, which he would use to dial 911 the minute it looked like Gaia was in trouble.

What was he thinking? It always looked like Gaia was in trouble. What he meant was, the minute it looked like Gaia was out of her league. That's when he'd call for help.

Ed watched as a figure emerged from the bushes, and

when he recognized it, he felt fear more intense than he could ever have imagined. It was that gang punk CJ. The one who'd tried to kill her.

Shit! Keeping his eyes glued to Gaia, he flipped the phone open. *(9 . . . 1 . . .)* "Whoa! Nice head butt!" *(End)* Man, could she kick! Bam, bam, bam!

She had the looks of a supermodel and the speed of Jean Claude Van Damme. Ooh! Right in the jaw. Nice. CJ went down.

Another cramp of fear gripped Ed when he saw Gaia reach into the waistband of her pants. What the hell was she doing with a gun? And what the hell was she standing there *talking* to CJ for?

Ed's heart jerked in his chest, and then he was watching CJ hit her! The bastard!

(9 . . . 1 . . .)

Holy shit! She fired, missed, but ha! The sound had sent CJ to his knees. Okay, she was back in control. *(End)*

The next shot was close! And then she was pulling the trigger again. And . . .

No bullet?

(9 . . . 1 . . . 1 . . . Send)

"Ed?"

He looked up. "Heather?"

Gaia's arms were pinned behind her back when the man appeared from out of the bushes. He was dressed—appropriately enough, Gaia supposed—in black. Black slacks, very expensive black sweater, and black shoes, also pricey. She immediately discarded any assumptions that the kidnapper was somehow connected with CJ's scrubby little street gang. These guys were big-time crime. Money. Maybe even brains.

"You failed!" growled Mr. Monochromatic.

Gaia shrugged as best she could with the compromised use of her arms. "I tried."

"Not good enough!"

"It's not my fault you boneheads loaded the gun wrong!" Gaia reasoned.

"Shut up!"

She rolled her eyes. "Fine, I will."

Gaia struck like lightning. She shoved her elbow upward, a nice crack to the underside of her captor's chin, freeing her arms. Before the man in black even had time to advance, she'd delivered one powerful jab to the back of guy number one's neck, knocking him out. He hit the ground like a rag doll.

Then, in one graceful sweep, Gaia turned and wrapped the man in black up in a headlock, pressing the gun—the fourth chamber of which did contain a bullet—to his temple. "I'd prefer to let this do my talking for me anyway."

The guy grunted.

"I want Sam!" she called to the darkness. "Now. Or this guy's dry cleaner is gonna be looking for a way to get brains out of cashmere!"

Somehow, impossibly, this little corner of the park seemed to be deserted. Had they cleared the area or something?

The guy laughed.

Gaia made herself ignore it. "A trade!" She shouted. "Sam for this guy. Right now. Or I blow his freakin' head off."

The guy laughed again. Gaia arched an eyebrow. He wasn't supposed to be laughing. He should have been begging his buddies to make the trade, save his life.

"What's so funny?" she demanded.

"Shoot me," the guy said. "He won't care."

"What's that supposed to mean?" Gaia asked. "Who won't care?"

"I mean," gurgled the man in black (because Gaia's forearm was still crushing his esophagus), "my employer won't give a damn." The mirth had vanished from his voice now. "He'll probably kill me himself for this."

Damn it! Gaia loosened her grip but didn't release him. She had to think. She had to . . .

Sam!

He was there. Being pushed out from behind a stand of broad oaks by another black-clad villain.

Gaia's heart lurched. Oh, God, Sam! He looked half dead. Gaia had never seen skin so pale before in her life.

His face was covered with a sheen of sweat that matted his dirty, greasy brown hair to his forehead. One of his eyes was swollen shut, and the other twitched like a dying bee's wing. There was a spot of blood beneath his right nostril. The jerk in the suit was dragging him like a sack of flour.

Gaia was so overwhelmed with grief that she almost let go of her own charge. She caught herself in time, though, gave him a nice whack with the butt of the gun, then let him crumple to the ground, unconscious.

"Sam!" she screamed.

Did he flinch? Had he heard? Hard to tell. She made a move to go to him, but his captor had suddenly produced an automatic weapon.

And he was aiming it directly at her heart.

HYSTERIA

"Jesus!" If Ed weren't already sitting down, he might have passed out. "Heather!"

She was standing there, holding the cell phone she'd just

snatched out of his hand. He could hear the operator's voice coming through the mouthpiece.

"Hello? Nine-one-one emergency? Hello?"

Apparently Heather was oblivious. She punched the end button.

"How dare you feed me to the wolves like that!" Heather fumed, hands on hips.

He quite seriously wished he could strangle her. "Heather, listen. I'm not kidding around. You have got to get out of here!"

"You can't tell me what to do, Ed," she spat out, her eyes wild. "It's not like we're going out anymore."

Like he'd ever told her what to do when they were together. He decided to chalk that inane remark up to hysteria, which she was clearly on the verge of.

"Heather . . ."

"Where the hell is that little bitch?" she demanded. "And where is Sam? He'd better be all right, or I swear I'm holding you and Gaia responsible. Now, where are they?"

Ed clenched his teeth and jabbed his finger in the direction of a spot on the pathway, roughly twenty yards ahead. "There they are."

Heather looked.

Fortunately, he was able to reach up and flatten his hand over her mouth in time, or her shriek would have certainly given them away.

He slammed the silencer onto his .44, then stepped out onto the path in front of CJ, who skidded to a flailing halt. The kid had his gun now. He must have found it and grabbed it so that he could go back and finish Gaia off.

That wasn't going to happen.

Blood still gushed from his nose, and his bare chest was scraped raw. When he saw the gun, his dark eyes got huge. He lifted his hand and aimed at the gunman's chest. That was all that was needed.

Perhaps the last thought ever to register in CJ's brain was something along the lines of *He's got eyes like her.*

The bullet hit him just above the bridge of his ruined nose, right in the place where all thoughts began.

And ended.

He remained on his feet a good five seconds, a tiny rivulet of crimson trickling from the corner of his mouth, his eyes bulging with what looked more like surprise than anything else.

Then his knees buckled.

And he began to fall.

And with the soundless echo of the boy's last, unspoken plea raging in his mind, Tom Moore disappeared into the darkness before CJ even hit the ground.

BOOGIE KNIGHTS

Gaia heard it, like something out of a dream.

A song. What was it? She knew it. An oldie. The lead singer's intro over the sound system came floating through the cool night to reach Gaia.

"A classic from the seventies . . . 'Rescue Me' by Aretha Franklin . . . so let's boogie!"

Boogie? Oh, please.

And then the bouncy time, and in the singer's gravelly West Village voice, the lyrics: "Rescue me, I want your tender charms, 'cause I'm lonely, and I'm blue. I need you, and your love, too. . . ."

Great. So now the hostage rescue had a sound track.

A surge of memory nearly blinded Gaia as the familiar song wrapped itself around her. Her mother and father, one night in the cozy family room of their house. The radio blaring. It was a classic even then. "Rescue Me." She was six. Laughing. So were they. Dancing. All of them. They were dancing.

Rescue me. Rescue me.

The scream ripped itself from her throat, drowning out the distant melody. Gaia threw herself at the man with the gun, slapping his arm out of the way, sending the gun spiraling into the night sky. He lunged for her, and Sam, unsupported, slipped to the ground.

Her fist plowed into the guy's abdomen, lifting him off his feet. Her foot slammed into his rib cage. She heard him grunt. "Ugh!"

Ugh. We have an ugh. Do I hear an ummphff? She grabbed a handful of his hair and shoved his face down hard against her knee.

"Ummphff!"

We have an ummphff, ladies and gentlemen!

The guy dropped forward, landing on his hands.

Gaia closed by giving him a good old-fashioned kick in the ass. His chin hit the pavement with a sound like breaking glass.

And then her own breaking began—the breaking down, the shutting off, the surrender of all strength. She was familiar with the experience; it happened every time. She could fight like a machine, full force, pumped on fury and desire. Her might was boundless, but only as long as that fuel was in supply. This fight had sucked up every ounce of energy she possessed.

And now she was spent. Her knees softened. Her limbs tingled. Breathing took on an entirely new caliber of effort.

And the lead singer of the band sang, "Rescue me."

It wasn't just in her head, as it seemed. It was blasting through most of the park. She staggered toward Sam, fumbling in her pocket for his insulin, and went down on her knees beside him.

"Hang on," she whispered. At least she thought she whispered it. Maybe she just thought it. He opened his good eye—just a slit, but still, it opened. "Hang on."

She prepared the syringe according to the directions she'd forced herself to memorize on her way from her house to the park. In her weakened state, the needle seemed to weigh a thousand pounds, and then it was entering Sam's flesh. Swift, smooth. Strangely intimate. She was injecting life back into him.

She withdrew the needle. The night spun in slow circles. The singer sang, "Rescue me." Gaia told herself to get up. Stand. Run. For help. But she couldn't seem to lift herself from the pavement.

As it turned out, she didn't have to. The guy in the black sweater was on his feet again. He grabbed Gaia and hauled her up. Her legs buckled. He was crushing her against him, her back to his chest.

Oh. A knife. At her throat. How inconvenient.

And Sam. On the ground, stirring now.

The shot came from behind her. An excellent shot, piercing her captor's shoulder but leaving her untouched. He went down, screaming.

She staggered forward a few steps and landed in the grass.

A man—a golden-haired man—thundered onto the scene. A police officer? No. The Incredible Hulk?

A knight. Yes. A valiant knight.

To rescue me.

Gaia wanted to smile but couldn't seem to send the message to her face.

The knight was standing over her now. His face was

so concerned, so familiar. *Dancing in the living room, and laughing with Mom. Rescue me.*

The knight was her father.

He crouched beside her, lifted her head, stroked her hair. Oh, God. Is this what forgiveness feels like?

"Gaia?" he whispered. "Gaia, I don't want you to misunderstand. I'm not who you think I am."

She squeezed her eyes shut. *Please don't say that.*

"I'm not Tom. But I'm your family. I'm . . . your father's brother. His twin."

She finally made her mouth work. "His . . . brother?"

The knight nodded. "I've wanted to find you, and take care of you. But I wasn't sure how you'd react. So I waited. Tonight I had no choice but to show myself. I'm sorry if this is painful, Gaia. I'm so sorry. But I'm here now. I'm with you. You're my brother's child. And I love you."

Gaia drank in his words. An elixir. A potion.

She had a family. She could feel the strength returning to her body, with the hope. With the love.

"There's a lot to explain," he whispered, "but I can't now. I have to go. As long as you're safe . . ."

Gaia opened her eyes and looked at him. "No . . ."

He nodded, stroking her hair. "It's all right. You'll understand soon. I promise, I won't be far. I'll come back for you. I swear it."

Gaia struggled to sit up. It was as though her nerves had turned into live electrical wires.

Then her uncle placed one gentle kiss on her forehead, and he was gone.

Don't cry, she told herself, greedily pulling air into her lungs in quick, sharp breaths. Don't.

Her uncle had saved her. Her family.

"Gaia!"

She turned. "Ed?" But before she could ream him for following her, she spotted a figure flinging itself toward Sam.

Her eyes widened. "Don't . . . even . . . tell me."

"She saw the whole thing," Ed said.

Gaia watched Heather pick up the nylon case from where it lay on the ground beside Sam. She watched her place her perfectly manicured hand on his forehead, her perfectly glossed lips on his cheek.

And she watched Sam open his eyes.

She was a good twenty feet away, but even from that distance, Gaia heard his whisper. It seemed to explode the deepness of the night. "Heather?"

"Yes," sobbed Heather. "I'm here Sam. I'm here."

Gaia saw him try to smile and she saw his grateful eyes move from Heather's face to the nylon bag and then back to her face. His voice was trembling with exhaustion and emotion when he asked, "Did you . . . save me?"

Gaia closed her eyes. This wasn't happening.

To her credit, Heather didn't say yes. But she didn't say no, either.

GAIA

Sam is okay.

He thinks Heather saved him, but he's okay.

CJ's dead.

I didn't kill him, but I saw them zipping up the body bag and hoisting him into the ambulance, so he's dead.

I have an uncle.

I'd never heard of him before today and he's been absent for my entire life—even longer than my dad—but I have an uncle.

Before today I hadn't thought it was possible for life to get any more surreal.

Today proved me very, very wrong.

TWISTED

BY FRANCINE PASCAL

JERKUS
HIGHSCHOOLENSIS

Pretty people do ugly things. It was one of those laws of nature that Gaia had understood for years. If she ever started to forget that rule for a second, there always seemed to be some good-looking asshole ready to remind her.

She stumbled up the steps and pushed her way inside The Village School with five minutes to spare before her first class. Actually early. Of course, her hair was still wet from the shower and her homework wasn't done, but being there—actually physically inside the building before the bell rang—was a new experience. For twelve whole seconds after that, she thought she might have an all right day.

Then she caught a glimpse of one of those things that absolutely defines the high school circle of hell.

Down at the end of the row of lockers, a tall, broad-shouldered guy was smiling a very confident smile, wearing very popular-crowd clothes, and using a very big hand to pin a very much smaller girl up against the wall. There was an amused expression on Mr. Handsome's face.

Only the girl who was stuck between his hand and fifty years' worth of ugly green paint didn't look like she thought it was funny.

Gaia had noticed the big boy in a couple of her classes but hadn't bothered to file away his name. Tad, she thought, or maybe it was Chip. She knew it was something like that.

From the way girls in class talked, he was supposed to be cute. Gaia could sort of see it. Big blue eyes. Good skin. Six-five even without the air soles in his two-hundred-dollar sneakers. His lips were a little puffy, but then, some people liked that. It was the hair that really eliminated him from Gaia's list of guys worth looking at.

He wore that stuff in his hair. The stuff that looked like a combination of motor oil and maple syrup. The stuff that made it look like he hadn't washed his hair this side of tenth grade. "What's the rush, Darla?" the Chipster said. "I just want to know what he said to you."

The girl, Darla, shook her head. "He didn't . . ."

Her big pal gave her a little love pat—enough to bounce her from the wall and back to his beefy hand.

"Don't give me that," he said, still all smiles. "I saw you two together."

Gaia did a quick survey of the hall. There was a trio of khaki-crowd girls fifty yards down and two leather dudes hanging near the front door. A skinny guy stuck his head out of a classroom, saw who was doing the shoving, and quickly ducked back in. Gaia had to give him some credit. At least he looked. Everybody else in the hallway was Not Noticing so hard, it hurt.

Gaia really didn't need this. She didn't know the girl against the wall. Sure, the guy with the big hands was a prime example of *Jerkus highschoolensis*, but it was absolutely none of Gaia's business. She turned away and headed for class, wondering if she might avoid a tardy slip for the first time in a week.

"Just let me . . . ," the girl begged from behind her.

"In a minute, babe," replied the guy with the hands. "I just need to talk to you a little." There was a thump and a short whimper from the girl.

Gaia stopped. She really, *really* didn't need this.

She took a deep breath, turned, and headed back toward the couple.

The easiest thing would be to grab the guy by the face and teach him how soft a skull was compared to a concrete wall. But then, smashing someone's head would probably not help Gaia's reputation.

Words were an option. She hadn't used that method much, but there was a first time for everything, right?

She could try talking to the guy or even threatening to tell a teacher. Gaia didn't care if anyone at the school thought she was a wimp or a narc, or whatever they called it in New York City. That was the least of her problems. Besides, they already thought she was a bitch for not warning Heather about the park slasher.

Before long, Gaia was so close that both partners in the ugly little dance turned to look at her. Tough Guy's smile didn't budge an inch.

"What?" he said.

Gaia struggled for something to say. Something smooth. Something that would defuse this whole thing. She paused for a second, cleared her throat, and said . . .

"Is there . . . uh, some kind of problem?"

Brilliant.

The guy who might be named Chip took a two-second look at her face, then spent twice as long trying to size up the breasts under Gaia's rumpled football shirt.

"Nothing you gotta worry about," he said, still staring at her chest. He waved the hand that wasn't busy holding a person. "This is a private conversation."

The girl against the wall looked at Gaia with a big-eyed, round-mouthed expression that could have been fear or hope or stupidity. Gaia's instant impression was that it was a little bit of all three. The girl had straight black hair that was turned up in a little flip, tanned-to-a-golden-brown skin, an excess of eye shadow, and a cheerleading uniform. She didn't exactly strike Gaia as a brain trust.

Not that being a cheerleader automatically made somebody stupid. Gaia was certain there were smart cheerleaders. Somewhere there had to be cheerleaders who were working on physics theories every time they put down their pompoms. She hadn't met any, but they were out there. Probably living in the same city with all the nice guys who don't mind if a girl has thunder thighs and doesn't know how to dress.

"Well?" demanded Puffy Lips. "What's wrong with you? Are you deaf or just stupid?"

Gaia tensed. Anger left an acid taste in her throat. Suddenly her fist was crying out for his face. She opened her mouth to say something just as the bell for first period rang. So much for being on time.

She took a step closer to the pair. "Why don't you let her go?"

Chip made a little grunting laugh and shook his head. "Look, babe. Get out of here," he said to Gaia.

Babe. It wasn't necessarily an insult—unless the person saying it added that *perfect* tone of voice. The tone that says being a babe is on the same evolutionary rung as being a brain-damaged hamster.

Gaia glanced up the hallway. Only a few students were still in the hall, and none were close. If she planned to do anything without everyone in school seeing it, this was the time.

She leaned toward him. "Maybe *you'd* better get out of here," she said in a low voice. She could feel the cheerleader's short breaths on the back of her neck. "You don't want to be late for class."

The sunny smile slipped from Chip's face, replaced by a go-away-you're-bothering-me frown. "Did you hear me tell you to go?"

Gaia shrugged. It was coming. That weird rush she sometimes felt.

"I heard you. I just didn't listen."

Now the expression on Chip's face was more like an I-guess-I'm-going-to-have-to-teach-you-how-the-world-works sneer. "Get the hell out of my way," he snapped.

"Make me."

He took his hand off Darla and grabbed Gaia by the arm.

Gaia was glad. If she touched him first, there was always the chance he would actually admit he got beat up by a girl and charge her with assault. But since Chip made the first move, all bets were off. Everything that happened from that first touch was self-defense.

Gaia was an expert in just about every martial art with a name. Jujitsu. Tai kwon do. Judo. Kung fu. If it involved hitting, kicking, or tossing people through the air, Gaia knew it. Standing six inches from Mr. Good Skin Bad Attitude, she could have managed a kick that would have taken his oily head right off his thick neck. She could have put a stiff hand through his rib cage or delivered a punch that drove his heart up against his spine.

But she didn't do any of that. She wanted to, but she didn't.

Moving quickly, she turned her arms and twisted out of his grip. Before Chip could react, she reached across with her left hand, took hold of the guy's right thumb, and gave it just a little . . . push.

For a moment Puffy Lips Chip looked surprised. Then Gaia pushed a little harder on his captive digit, and the look of surprise instantly turned to pain.

He tried to pull away, but Gaia held tight. She was working hard to keep from actually breaking his thumb. She could have broken his whole oversized hand like a bundle of big dry sticks. The real trick was hurting someone without really hurting someone. Don't break any bones. Don't leave any scars. Don't do anything permanent. Leave a memory.

"What do you think, Chip?" Gaia asked, still pushing his thumb toward the back of his hand. "Should you be shoving girls around?"

"Let go of me, you little—" He reached for her with his free hand. Gaia leaned back out of his range and gave an extra shove. Chip wailed.

"Here's the deal," Gaia said quietly. "You keep your hands to yourself, I let you keep your hands. What do you think?"

Chip's knees were starting to shake, and there were beads of sweat breaking out on his forehead. "Who are—"

"Like I really want you to know my name." She pushed harder, and now Gaia could feel the bones in his thumb pulling loose from his hand. Another few seconds and one was sure to snap. "Do we have a deal?"

"Okay," he squeaked in a voice two octaves higher than it had been a few seconds before. "Sure."

Gaia let go. "That's good, Chip." The moment the physical conflict ended, Gaia felt all her uncertainty come rushing back. She glanced up the hallway and was relieved to see that there was no crowd of gawkers. That didn't stop her from feeling dizzy. She was acting like muscle-bound freak girl right in the main hallway at school. This was definitely not the way to remain invisible.

Puffy Lips stepped back and gripped his bruised thumb in his left hand. "Brad."

"What?"

"Brad," he said. "My name isn't Chip. It's Brad."

Gaia rolled her eyes. "Whatever." She lowered her head and shoved past him just as the late bell rang.

Another day, another fight, another tardy.

THINGS GAIA KNOWS:

School sucks.

Ella sucks.

Her father sucks.

Heather Gannis sucks *big time*.

THINGS GAIA WANTS TO KNOW:

Who kidnapped Sam?

Why did they contact her?

What was with all those stupid tests?

How could she have let the kidnappers get away after everything they'd done to her and Sam?

Why did Mr. Rupert use the words "all right" more often than most people used the word "the"?

Who killed CJ?

Why did she never know she had an uncle who looked exactly like her father?

Was said uncle going to contact her again?

Did she even want him to after he'd been nonexistent for her entire life?

Why did anyone in their right mind *choose* to drink skim milk?

Was she really expected to pay attention in class when there were things going on that actually mattered?

THE DECISION

Even back when his legs worked, Ed had never been fearless.

He sat in his first-period class and stared at the door. Any moment, the bell would ring. Then he would go out into the hallway and Gaia would appear. Any moment, he would have his chance. In the meantime, he was terrified.

People who had seen him on a skateboard or a pair of in-lines might have been surprised to hear it. There had been no stairs too steep to slalom, no handrail Ed wasn't willing to challenge, no traffic too thick to dare. Anyone would tell you, Ed Fargo was a wild man. He took more risks, and took them faster, than any other boarder in the city.

The dark secret was that all through those days, almost every second, Ed had been terrified. Every time his wheels had sent sparks lancing from a metal rail, every time he had gone over a jump and felt gravity tugging down at his stomach, Ed had been sure he was about to die.

And when it didn't happen, when he landed, and lived, and rolled on to skate another day, it had been a thousand times sweeter just because he had been so scared. It seemed to Ed that there was nothing better than that moment after the terror had passed.

Then he lost the use of his legs and grew a wheelchair on his butt, and everything changed. A wheelchair didn't give the sort of thrills you got from a skateboard. There were a few times, especially right after he realized he was never, ever going to get out of the chair, that Ed thought about taking the contraption out into traffic—just to see how well it played with the taxis and delivery vans. That kind of thinking was scary in a whole different, definitely less fun way.

Legs or no legs, Ed wasn't sure that any stunt he had pulled in the past had terrified him as much as the one he was about to attempt.

He stared at the classroom door, and the blood rushing through his brain sounded as loud as a subway train pulling up to the platform.

He was going to tell Gaia Moore that he loved her.

He was really going to do it. If he didn't faint first.

Ed had been infatuated with Gaia since he first saw her in the school hallway. He was half smitten as soon as they spoke and all the way gone within a couple of days.

Since then, Ed and Gaia had become friends—or at least they had come as close to being friends as Gaia's don't-get-close-to-me forcefield would allow. To tell Gaia how he really felt would mean risking the relationship they already shared. Ed was horrified by the thought of losing contact with Gaia, but he was determined to take that chance.

For once, he was going to see what it was like to be fearless.

SOUR SEVENTEEN

One idiot an hour. Gaia figured that if they would let her beat up one butthead per class, it would make the day go oh-so-smoothly. She would get the nervous energy out of her system, add a few high points to her dull-as-a-bowling-ball day, and by the time the final bell rang, the world would have eight fewer losers. All good things.

It might also help her keep her mind off Sam Moon. Sam, whose life she had saved more than once. Sam, who was oblivious to her existence. Sam, who had the biggest bitch this side of Fifth Avenue for a girlfriend but didn't seem to notice.

And still Gaia couldn't stop thinking about him. Daydreaming her way through each and every class. If her teachers had tested her on self-torture, she would have gotten an A.

Gaia trudged out of her third-period classroom and shouldered her way through the clogged hallway, her cruise control engaged. Every conscious brain cell was dedicated to the ongoing problem of what to do about her irritating and somewhat embarrassing Sam problem.

It was like a drug problem, only slightly less messy.

It was bad enough that Sam was with Heather. Even worse was Heather getting credit for everything Gaia did. Gaia had nearly lost her life saving Sam from a kidnapper.

She had gone crazy looking for him. And then Heather had stepped in at the last second and looked like the big hero when her total expended effort was equal to drying her fingernails.

Not to mention the fact that the kidnappers had gotten away after they spent an entire day ordering her around as if she were a toy poodle.

Gaia suddenly realized she was biting her lip so badly that it was about to bleed. Whenever she thought about how the nameless, faceless men in black had used her, she got the uncontrollable urge to do serious violence to something. Then, of course, her thoughts turned directly to Heather.

And the fact that Heather had sex with Sam. And the fact that Heather had taken credit for saving Sam. And the fact that Heather got to hold hands with Sam and kiss Sam and talk to Sam and—

Gaia came to a stop in front of her locker and kicked it hard, denting the bottom of the door. A couple of Gap girls turned to stare, so Gaia kicked it again. The Gap girls scurried away.

She snarled at her vague reflection in the battered door. In the dull metal she was only an outline. That's all she was to Sam, too. A vague shadow of nothing much.

For a few delusional days Gaia had thought Sam might be the one. The one to break her embarrassing record as the only unkissed seventeen-year-old on planet Earth. Maybe even the one to turn sex from hypothesis into reality. But it wasn't going to happen.

There wasn't going to be any sex. There was never going to be any kissing. Not with Sam. Not ever.

Gaia yanked open the door of her locker, tossed in the book she was carrying, and randomly took out another without bothering to look at it. Then she slammed the door just as hard as she had kicked it.

She squeezed her eyes shut for a moment, squeezed hard, as if she could squeeze out her unwanted thoughts.

Even though Gaia knew zilch about love, knew less about relationships, and knew even less about psychology, she knew exactly what her girlfriends, if she had any, would tell her.

Find a new guy. Someone to distract you. Someone who cares about you.

Right. No problem.

Unfortunately, it had only taken her seventeen years to find a guy who *didn't* care about her.

ABOUT THE AUTHOR

New York Times bestselling author Francine Pascal is one of the most popular fiction writers for teenagers today and the creator of numerous bestselling series, including Fearless and Sweet Valley High, which was also made into a television series. She has written several YA novels, including *My First Love and Other Disasters, My Mother Was Never a Kid,* and *Love & Betrayal & Hold the Mayo.* Her latest novel is *Sweet Valley Confidential: Ten Years Later.* She lives in New York City and France.